WRAITH

WRAITH

JUDITH AND GARFIELD REEVES-STEVENS

THOMAS DUNNE BOOKS
ST. MARTIN'S PRESS
NEW YORK

THOMAS DUNNE BOOKS.
An imprint of St. Martin's Press.

WRAITH. Copyright © 2016 Softwind Productions, Inc. All rights reserved. Printed in the United States of America. For information, address St. Martin's Press, 175 Fifth Avenue, New York, N.Y. 10010.

www.thomasdunnebooks.com
www.stmartins.com

Designed by Omar Chapa

Library of Congress Cataloging-in-Publication Data

Names: Reeves-Stevens, Judith, author. | Reeves-Stevens, Garfield, 1953– author.
Title: Wraith / Judith & Garfield Reeves-Stevens.
Description: First edition. | New York : Thomas Dunne Books, 2016.
Identifiers: LCCN 2015046108| ISBN 978-0-312-65907-3 (hardcover) |
    ISBN 978-1-250-02257-8 (e-book)
Subjects: LCSH: Terrorism—Prevention—Fiction. | Future life—Fiction. |
    BISAC: FICTION / Suspense. | FICTION / Horror. | GSAFD: Suspense fiction. |
    Occult fiction. | Ghost stories.
Classification: LCC PR9199.3.R428 W73 2016 | DDC 813/.54—dc23
LC record available at http://lccn.loc.gov/2015046108

Our books may be purchased in bulk for promotional, educational, or business use. Please contact your local bookseller or the Macmillan Corporate and Premium Sales Department at 1-800-221-7945, extension 5442, or by e-mail at MacmillanSpecial-Markets@macmillan.com.

First Edition: April 2016

10 9 8 7 6 5 4 3 2 1

For Amber and Denise and Mike and Scooter,
stellar hosts in our alternate dimension

We are no monsters, we're moral people
And yet we have the strength to do this
This is the splendor of our achievement
Call in the airstrike with a poison kiss

Priests and cannibals, prehistoric animals
Everybody happy as the dead come home
Big black nemesis, parthenogenesis
No one move a muscle as the dead come home

——SHRIEKBACK

WRAITH

SEPTEMBER 15, 1940

"It's a chorus of the damned," von Varendorff shouted.

Kapitänleutnant Gunther Prien gave his second watch officer a sharp look of disapproval, though privately he understood the young man's unspoken fear. The roar of the storm did sound as if the gates of hell had opened deep within the sea-worn rocks of the dark shore ahead. The wild strength of it could be felt as much as heard, the rising wind and crashing waves drowning out even the frantic snapping of the flag flying proudly from the U-47's conning tower. Its bold swastika was a defiant challenge here in the midst of enemy territory.

Unlike Oberleutnant von Varendorff, Prien was not an overly religious man. He couldn't afford to be. He was the Fatherland's most highly decorated U-boat commander. Though he had, in the war's early stages, taken efforts to ensure enemy crews had time to reach their lifeboats before sinking their ships, he'd also sent thousands of the enemy to their deaths, more than eight hundred in just the sinking of the HMS *Royal Oak* at Scapa Flow. He would not allow himself to imagine he heard their cries, as he was certain his junior officer did. He would not dwell on his enemies' fate. Odds were good it would be his fate as well someday, and soon. About Germany's survival, though, there was no need to calculate the odds.

Expeditions such as this—so bold, so unorthodox, so brilliant—assured nothing less than victory. Just as the National Socialist Party drew its inner strength from the unquestioned supremacy of the Aryan race, now the Wehrmacht would draw its military strength from the ancient knowledge of the greatest of the Aryans: the Nordics.

His submarine pitched in the rough Atlantic sea, but Prien kept his binoculars fixed on the barren coast of Britain's vassal state, the so-called Dominion of Newfoundland. The seven-man archaeological team from the Ahnenerbe Institute had been gone almost an hour, their third landing in as many days. With each landing, Prien's crew grew more concerned that their luck couldn't hold, that it was inevitable a local fishing boat would just by chance catch sight of them on the surface. Then the bombers would come, and the warships.

But Prien had no such worries. This was no ordinary patrol. It was destiny.

An hour from sunset beneath darkening clouds, he saw what he waited for.

Flashes of light from a signal lantern on the shore spelled out the message that could end the war and ensure the birth of the Thousand-Year Reich.

Wir haben es gefunden, the coded message read.

We have found it.

The cave was where the ancient map had placed it, in a stark cliff twenty meters from a distinctive outcropping called the Raven's Beak.

In the nine centuries since the cave had been mapped, the sea and ice had eroded its entrance. What had once been an opening large enough for a dragonship to enter for safe harbor was now an erratic mound of fractured boulders and fallen rocks. They obscured the passage beyond for all but those who knew what to look for.

Where Prien's inflatable dinghy had landed, the researchers from the Institute had fixed a rope ladder to the slick, wave-smoothed rocks leading up the small mouth of the cave. Beyond, more lanterns had been lit, glowing in the mist of the cold damp air, marking a path down the far side of the rocky barricade.

Prien held the guide rope tightly as he climbed down. It had been almost three weeks since the U-47 had left port. He could feel the solid ground heave beneath him as if he were still at sea. Behind him, he heard von Varendorff slip and fall, but the junior officer needed no help to get up and keep going. Who would want to miss history being made?

Fifty meters into the cave, sheltered from the ferocious wind and crashing waves of the storm, the scent of the sea became stronger, concentrated by the now-still air. The effects of erosion diminished and the piles of fallen rocks ended. Lanterns revealed what the cave must have been almost a thousand years ago: a calm inner pool of seawater, a wide band of moss and kelp ringing the dark basaltic walls, showing the high-water mark. But on this day, Prien had no interest in marine biology or geology. He reached level ground and picked up his pace, eyes fixed on the prize at the cave's end. The dragonship.

The huge vessel had settled over the centuries, some timbers disintegrating, but most preserved where they had listed onto dry rocks. The single mast had fallen, but the intricately carved dragon head atop the ship's prow remained upright, guardian of the treasure it had borne here for safekeeping.

The archaeologists had positioned a camera tripod near an almost-complete section of decking. The photographer was mounting on it his Arriflex 35 camera. The footage he shot would likely not appear in a public newsreel until long after the war, but Prien knew Commissar Himmler would view it within days of the U-47's return. The Institute and its mission to collect objects of the occult were of Himmler's own creation.

"Have you opened it?" Prien asked as he set foot on the deck.

"*Nein.*" Dr. Achterberg clicked his heels in salute, his voice trembling with devotion. "Not without you, Kapitänleutnant." The short and portly researcher was the Institute's civilian specialist for this expedition, an expert in the runes and symbols of their shared Aryan heritage. He had personally traveled to Oslo to assist the Reichskommissariat Norwegen in the search for the map that had led them here.

Prien gave a quick nod, acknowledging the man's gesture. He had taken part in enough propaganda outings for the war effort that he had become used to such reverence from civilians, though it still made him uncomfortable. He was a soldier doing his duty, and for that no special consideration was necessary.

"Shall we proceed, sir?"

The man who approached him now was anything but a sycophant, and treated Prien as an equal.

Unteroffizier Martz was the expedition's military commander, late of the Ehrhardt Brigade, now an NCO in the Ahnenerbe Institute's military special unit Sonderverband Z. The Z was for *Zauber.* Magic. So far in their worldwide quest for artifacts of the occult, Martz and his men had seen action against bandits in Egypt and Morocco. Here, though, if Dr. Achterberg's translations were accurate, they would encounter no resistance.

"Please do," Prien said.

The photographer angled his camera to take in the small, once-leatherbound chest held in place on the decking by rusted iron brackets. It was no larger than an ordinary train case for overnight travel, but what it contained defied all reason.

The chest's leather covering had rotted to reveal metal walls beneath. Embossed on the side was a runic symbol of three interlocked triangles that Prien recognized from the photographic copies of Achterberg's map. Such scholarship. Such precision. He felt pride for his race.

As the camera whirred, Martz used a hammer and chisel to break the corroded clasp that secured the lid. Then, with a glance at Prien, who nodded his assent, he opened the chest. One of Martz's soldiers quickly leaned forward, held a lantern above it, angling it to fill the chest with light.

Three stones within glittered, two the size of small eggs, one a thin disk no larger than a playing card.

"No," Prien said. "Take that away."

The soldier instantly swung the lantern aside.

In the shadows of the chest, one stone still shone with a pale blue glow.

"*Mein Gott,*" Achterberg whispered.

The chest was the treasure of a great, though nameless, Viking warrior. Someone who had not only commanded this ship, but a fleet of them. So Prien knew perfectly well what two of the stones were, for they were common enough to find in the possession of lesser men who sailed uncharted oceans a thousand years ago.

The polished black lodestone was used to magnetize slivers of iron that would serve as a compass.

The semitransparent sunstone was a thin pane of a mineral held by a thin gold frame. Held up to an overcast sky, its natural polarizing effect would create a dark cross that pointed to the unseen sun's position.

Both those stones revealed hidden aspects of the physical world.

The third stone, the einstone, revealed aspects of the world beyond.

"Kapitänleutnant?" Achterberg nodded to Prien again, gestured to the chest.

Prien hesitated. He knew the legends. "Is it safe to handle?"

Achterberg smiled as if suppressing laughter. "Of course. There are no dead men here. We're all alive."

The doctor's two civilian associates quietly held their own amused laughter. Martz and his two soldiers didn't change their stern expressions.

The photographer made a signal to indicate he was running out of film.

Oberleutnant von Varendorff made a move forward, as if to take the einstone from the chest, to spare his commander the risk of any danger.

Prien waved him back, irritated, stepped to the chest, reached in without hesitation.

The einstone felt cold. Its ice blue glow vanished in the sputtering light of the lanterns. He could see the same triangle symbol had been carefully inscribed on the stone's rough surface.

Prien turned to the camera, held up the stone, smiling, and gestured for the other members of the expedition to step into frame with him, to share this great moment for generations to come.

Three of the seven men survived.

One was the photographer, quick-witted enough to grab his camera with the film that showed exactly what had happened in those final seconds.

Prien and von Varendorff also lived, because of the sacrifice of Martz and his soldiers.

Dr. Achterberg died first.

When finally developed and studied in Berlin, the film showed the shape that formed behind the doomed scholar, blurred and indistinct though Achterberg himself was in focus.

Prien thought that in the archaeologist's last moments of life, he must have realized his mistake.

Vikings buried their dead on ships. Which meant there *was* a dead man here.

The great warrior whose tomb this was had risen, proving the legend of the einstone was true even as he destroyed the genius who had deciphered the runes that told its story.

Prien had seen the warrior's massive arm reach *through* the doctor's chest from behind, then twist as if wielding an invisible sword, tearing the frail archaeologist in half.

After that, Prien had seen only the wet and slippery rocks beneath his boots as he and von Varendorff heeded Martz's warning and ran.

Gunfire echoed in the cave. Bullets ricocheted. Muzzle flashes strobed.

Men screamed.

No one else escaped.

Prien returned to his U-boat and made for port at full speed, not daring to cause any additional deaths anywhere near the einstone's power, now locked in the safe in his quarters.

Eight days later, within minutes of coming ashore, he passed it over to another unsmiling officer from the Institute's military branch.

Only then did Prien feel relief. Not because he was no longer in the presence of the stone, but because, based on what he had seen, he knew that the war would be over within a year. How could it not be?

An army of soldiers who could never die could never be defeated.

Even a facile amateur like Hitler couldn't squander an advantage like that.

Ten months later as the U-47 filled with icy water to take him to his own ocean grave, in his last moments of his life, Prien thought of his wife and his daughters, and then realized with a shock that he had been just as blind as Achterberg.

If the einstone could create an invincible army, then how had the Vikings failed to conquer Britain a thousand years ago?

What other powers did the stone possess?

And what price did it exact from those who tried to wield it?

PRESENT DAY

1

Only forty feet away.

It was late at night, and the two *sicarios* were bored. They saw and heard nothing of the soldier's advance on them. They were gunmen for the Sinaloa Cartel, assigned this night as sentries. Here in the lifeless moonscape of the Sonoran desert, they had no reason to think anyone would be insane enough to confront them and risk the wrath of the powerful men they served. They were invincible.

That attitude made them an easy target.

One gunman sat slouched in a black Range Rover. He and his partner had parked it across the narrow dirt road, though any intruder could easily drive around. The desert's sparse brush and dry rocky soil was no barrier to vehicles.

The second gunman maintained a watch beside the Rover, his AK-47 rifle carelessly hanging on its strap from his shoulder.

In still air, crickets sang. There was a breeze, but only just. If the moon had been full, instead of a new thin crescent, they might have seen a dry branch move or a dead leaf stir. Or the slow wave of shifting leaves among the scattered clumps of jojoba and brittlebush: the only sign of the soldier's presence as he closed in on them.

Thirty feet.

The sentry in the Rover lit a cigarette, and two hundred feet away, General Stasik Borodin blinked as the small yellow star of a lighter's flame flared against the speckled blue wash on the screen of his thermal imager. The appropriateness of the moment appealed to him. A last cigarette for the condemned.

The general changed the aim of his viewer, training it on his soldier. ODIN.

Twenty feet.

On-screen, ODIN's heat signature was barely discernable, a cloud of pixels, the palest of blue against darker blue, shifting continuously from what might be the shape of a man to something more ephemeral, as if imaging only an illusion of reality.

Ten feet.

Inside the Rover, the glow of the first sentry's cigarette tip brightened, dimmed. Outside, the second sentry rested his rifle on the Rover's hood, stepped away, unzipped his pants. At the side of the road, a pool of heat grew as he relieved himself.

Closer now, another unseen dry branch moved. Another unseen dead leaf stirred.

On-screen, the general watched a pale cloud coalesce, a shadow taking form behind the sentry on the roadside, directly in view of his partner, if he'd paid attention.

A sudden scream cut off a second after it began, but was loud enough and long enough to alert the sentry in the Rover.

On-screen, the yellow shape that was the second sentry moved abruptly, a cigarette's tip flickering as it spun away, tossed through the vehicle's window. The door burst open and the sentry leapt out.

On-screen, a cool blue cloud swept over the sentry's yellow form. This time the scream was a strangled gasp followed only by sudden heat blossoms—blood against a windshield—glowing brightly for an instant before darkening as they cooled.

The general lowered his viewer, nodded to Captain Konstantin Korolev, crouched beside him.

In Russian, Korolev spoke softly into a small radio. The mission continued, on schedule. The van could proceed.

Six minutes later, the tires of the Russians' dust-streaked panel van crunched over gravel as it drove into a floodlit courtyard. The structure beyond, stucco with a red-tile roof, was modest, at odds with the expensive cars parked outside. The cartel had intended the house to be little more than window dressing—

nothing that would call attention to itself or what lay beneath it. But the Mercedes and Bentleys were the giveaway, incompatible with such impoverished surroundings, and thus easy to identify.

ODIN had arrived at the nondescript building first. The bodies of two more gunmen, backup to the pair of sentries on the road, lay sprawled on the ground, chests flayed open, shards of broken ribs startlingly white in the floodlights' glare.

The small hacienda's windows shone with light. No sign of awareness of what had happened just outside.

The general looked past the hacienda, to the scattering of pinpoint lights a mile or so distant, rippling in the desert air: a small community of homes across the border. Arizona.

Soon.

In the courtyard, the general's five-man squad opened the back of the van, hefted out the six VEKTOR containment units.

Each of the prototype devices could have been mistaken for a metal footlocker: scuffed drab green paint, three feet long, two feet wide and high. Unlike a simple locker, each unit also had a small control panel with a number pad and screen display. To one side of the panels, eight-digit tracking codes, each different, were stenciled beneath the same figure: the three interlocked triangles of the *valknut*. It was an ancient Norse symbol found on the graves of warriors, also known as the knot of the slain. It had been etched onto the original einstone, though not by its unfortunate most recent owners. Knowing that the history of the remarkable object reached back far beyond the madness of the past century, the general had selected it as a fitting insignia for the *tenevyye voiny*, his shadow warriors.

Five of the units were sealed, and all status lights on their panels glowed steady green. The sixth, ODIN's, was open. Only one of its six lights was green; the other five pulsed red. The unit's charge was fading.

"Sir, we're ready."

Beneath Korolev's military precision, General Borodin sensed unease. This man was loyal to him, as was the squad he led. But none of them were used to this technology. Borodin was. He had had no choice.

"Have them assemble."

Captain Korolev joined his four-man squad as they took up their positions: each man standing beside an individual unit. Though they were dressed as civilians in jeans and denim jackets, that they were soldiers was obvious. Each with broad shoulders, powerful chest and arms, lean face. But not just soldiers: *Spetznas*. Special forces.

Korolev alone stood out because of the long scar that ran across the side of his head, a slash of white flesh startling against his close-cropped, black hair, fading into his cheek. Scars were to be expected; he was a decade older than the other four and had seen the most action. At fifty-five, Borodin was the oldest, and his own scars were of a different nature: those of the heart that had turned his short hair, and his annoying three days of stubble, death white. Combined with his lean frame and deeply lined features, he looked older than his actual age. His blue eyes still burned with the drive and purpose of youth, though these days that purpose was personal. The stirring patriotism and love of Motherland that in earlier years had inspired him had died long ago.

At Captain Korolev's signal, all five squad members entered security codes on the sealed units' panels, then stood well back as the safety locks disengaged.

The five units hissed open.

As always, there was nothing to see, until there was.

Five young soldiers, in black battle dress without insignia, stood at attention where none had been a heartbeat before. Expressionless, blank eyes stared straight ahead. The general didn't know what they saw. Nor did he want to.

He steeled himself to speak without emotion. "ODIN . . ."

A heartbeat later, a sixth soldier stood before him.

Borodin pointed to the hacienda. "Kill them all."

Six young faces changed. Eyes grew larger, darker, drawn back into the shadow of thickening brows as six mouths began to twist in soundless snarls and twelve hands became twelve clawed fists.

Borodin knew that, somehow, he wasn't seeing changes in what they looked like; he was seeing changes in how they *felt*. Whatever the truth of his perception, it didn't matter. What they could accomplish did. Those few who had seen the shadow warriors take action had another name for them, as old as their fabled insignia: *Berserkers.*

As one, the six turned to face their objective. As one, they took their first step, then the next, and then they were moving so swiftly it was as if their limbs blurred into smoke as they flowed across the courtyard, smearing like a torrent of black water to sweep up the hacienda's walls and doors and windows and—

—*pass* unobstructed through them.

Five seconds, then the first cries inside. Five seconds more, and the thunderous stitching of automatic rifle fire ratcheted, muffled only by the massive doors.

More shouts. More sounds of violation—falling, crashing. Bright flashes of weapons fire lighting up the windows.

Then the double front doors burst open and a man in a dark suit charged out, whirled around to raise an Uzi submachine gun to stop what melted through the wall to chase him.

A black-clad soldier. ODIN.

The man in the suit opened fire, no possibility of missing.

ODIN rushed forward, untouched, unharmed.

The man swung his weapon like a club, and it slipped through his attacker just as the bullets had. Shouting disbelief, the man swung again to no effect.

ODIN's face contorted, filled with rage as if he'd felt each bullet, each blow. His arms swung up, then down, and they passed—

—*into* the man's chest.

The man's expression of shock changed to one of searing pain and terror.

In the courtyard's floodlights, ODIN grinned, exultant, as his arms gained substance, no longer smoke but solid, as deep *within* the victim's chest spear-like fingers ravaged bone and organs.

The ghastly shrieking ended only when the soldier ripped the man's lungs out through his shattered ribs.

The lifeless body dropped to the ground and ODIN stared down at it, his features as inhuman as his actions, blood and gore clinging to him like savage war paint.

The hacienda was silent. The objective had been achieved. The cartel and its gunmen might have been prepared to face down the *federales* or even a Mexican Army unit at this location, as unlikely as that possibility might have been. But nothing could have prepared them for what they had faced.

General Borodin checked to be sure his men were ready by the units. Only then did he address the soldier, still focused on his kill.

"ODIN. To me. Stand down."

The soldier slowly raised his head, regarding him with deep-set eyes, defiant.

The general recognized the madness in them, the fury unleashed, unwilling to be contained again.

He spoke again, decisively, using the voice of command. "All of you. Stand down."

The remaining five silent soldiers re-formed beside their comrade, so quickly it was as if they had always been there. All with the same crazed eyes, blood-splashed bodies. Coiled potential trembling in uncertain balance.

"The mission is accomplished."

All too slowly, Borodin saw the change pass through them. Their faces lost the shadows and angles of bloodlust, became blank again. For a moment, they seemed to blur out of focus; then the blood spatter and bits of broken flesh that had clung to them fell free, fluttering to the gravel.

Borodin was in control again. He suppressed relief. There could be no sign of weakness before these soldiers. "Captain, call them back."

Korolev entered a code on the number pad of the unit beside him, and ODIN twisted into a thread of what might have been black mist, then was gone. In rapid sequence, the squad activated a second unit, then a third, fourth, and fifth, as one after the other, all but one of the silent soldiers vanished.

"General! At the window!"

Borodin reacted swiftly to Korolev's shout, at once seeing the spectral face of a young woman pressed against the glass of the hacienda's largest window. Her eyes were wide, her mouth gaped open, her features frozen in shock by what she'd witnessed.

She stared at him as if she somehow knew him.

Impossible.

Borodin turned to the last remaining soldier.

"TYR. New mission. Kill her."

Blurring with motion, TYR transformed, sped forward.

The woman in the window fell back from sight, swallowed by shadows.

A dark formless shape reached the window, passed through it.

Borodin waited for the scream.

The victims always screamed.

Tonight was different.

2

Since the separation, Molly's was the closest thing to home Matt Caidin had, so he didn't think it odd or even pathetic how much he looked forward to it at the end of his shift.

After midnight, he could always find a booth in the front window. Only a handful of other customers were scattered through the place, and none of them were other cops, so that was good. Arlington, Virginia, was small enough as it was.

Kris, or Jan, or whoever else was on shift, would bring him his coffee, ask if he needed a menu. He never did. A few minutes later, a Molly's Special Breakfast Scramble with toasted bagel and extra hot sauce would appear.

A few years back when he'd been in uniform, he'd check the newspapers while he ate, starting with sports. Now, he scanned the scores on his phone, but only by habit. He never remembered them. Never remembered the headlines, either. Most news was bad. He had enough of that in his own life right now.

"Need a top-up, hon?"

It was Jan. Matt looked up, remembering just in time to smile. However battered he felt these days, the gray-haired waitress had seen worse. It showed in her too-thin frame, too-bright makeup, and tired eyes that looked as haunted as his likely were. He guessed that's why she always kept his coffee mug full, and why he always tipped a bit more than he should, when he could. Mutual survivors, going through the motions, barely holding on.

"Sure thing." He slid the heavy mug across the scarred tabletop. "Slow night?"

Jan thumbed the lid of her coffee carafe, started to pour. One of her long fake nails had broken off, revealing the yellowed one underneath, rough with cement. "Too slow. Busy's better."

"Always." Distraction was always better, Matt knew. That was the secret he and Jan shared: The more distraction, the less time to think.

"Whoa!" The mug of coffee overflowed, hot liquid spilling onto the table. Matt reached to the carafe to change its angle, looked up at Jan's stricken face at the same time he heard the crash outside. Jan's vivid orange lipstick grew even brighter, as if lit by flame.

She stared out the window. "Ohmygod ohmygod."

Then everything happened at once, as bad things usually do.

Headlights. That was the light shining on Jan's face.

Matt shifted in the booth to look out in time to see a car flying through the air, a traffic light pole collapsing behind it.

In the flash of a streetlight through the windshield as the car flipped over, Matt saw the driver's face white with horror. The passenger beside her was only a shadow in free fall, arms reaching for her.

Sparks then, a huge spray of them as the car spectacularly landed on its side, skipped along the road past Molly's Café, and rose again, flipping over, sliding on its roof to hit a parked taxi. The noise of grinding, grating metal was hellish.

Matt was already up, passing Jan his phone. "Nine-one-one!" He shoved through the door, raced to the car. No other vehicles on the street this late on a Sunday night, early Monday morning. He heard electrical crackling coming from the totaled traffic light.

The silver car was midsize, two-door, something Korean. Its roof was flattened, its pillars twisted, crystals from the missing windshield flung about like scattered diamonds. If the driver and her passenger weren't wearing seatbelts . . .

Matt crouched by the driver's-side window, peered inside. Now he became aware of the hissing and creaking of fractured metal. White vapor streaming from the direction of the engine. The smell of gasoline.

The driver was upside down, wedged tightly in her seat's warped frame, everything dusted in powder from the slowly deflating airbag. Her eyes were open, their whites stark within the face-obscuring sea of red pulsing from her blood-soaked hair and the deep gash in her cheek.

He heard her wheeze. *Alive.*

"Can you hear me?" Matt called in to her.

The bloody face turned his way. Her eyes blinked, struggled to focus. "Daniel . . . ?"

The smell of gasoline was getting stronger. Matt grabbed at the door handle, pulled. The door was battered and bent, wouldn't budge. He registered the howl of approaching sirens as he turned to see other people on the sidewalk. Saw the stunned taxi driver, hands clasped atop his head as he stared at his ruined cab.

"Get over here! Check the passenger!" Matt yelled to him.

He changed position so his shoulder holster wouldn't dig into his side as he tried to see if there was any way he could free the driver. He reached in through the broken window, urged the taxi driver to action. "C'mon, buddy. Other side!"

The taxi driver remained locked in disbelief. Someone else shouted that the police were here. More sirens and squealing tires converging on the street.

"You can help me . . . ," the driver whispered.

Matt's fingers found her blood-slicked hand. Squeezed hard. Felt her squeeze back. Good sign. "Police are here. Ambulance coming." The driver's hand was cold. Not so good. "What's your name?! What's your name?!"

A moment passed, then clarity came to the woman's eyes, as if she suddenly realized where she was, and what had happened.

"You're not Daniel. . . ."

"Clear the area!"

Matt felt a strong hand on his shoulder, pulling him away. "Clear the area!"

Matt was pushed to the side, the woman's hand sliding from his as he heard the whoosh of spraying foam, saw the flash of blue and white and red emergency lights, and two firefighters attacked the car with the Jaws of Life to pry open the door.

Back on the sidewalk, Jan pushed beside him in the gathering crowd, thin arms wrapped around herself. "They going to make it?"

Matt had been a cop for twelve years. He'd seen enough accidents to know. He shook his head.

"God, life sucks," Jan said. "And then you die."

It took half an hour for the firefighters to extract the driver from the wreckage. Head and neck immobilized by a board and brace, her blood-smeared face blotched yellow from the coagulant powder they'd poured on her torn scalp, now covered in seeping bandages.

The paramedics quickly hoisted her onto a rolling gurney. Their faces were grim. Matt winced as he heard her sob with each slight movement.

"Daniel!" she cried, and Matt knew that whoever Daniel was, she'd never see him again.

As much as Jan was right—life did suck—and as awful as this moment was, Matt couldn't take the easy way out, going back into Molly's, to his coffee and his own life. He was a cop, and whatever had drawn him to that vocation—that need to help others, to make things right even as a child—it was still in him now, however crushed and useless he had allowed it to become.

He pushed past the paramedics, took the woman's hand, lightly squeezing it. "Daniel!"

"Shh," Matt lied. "I'm here. You're going to be okay." He squeezed her hand again. This time her response felt weaker, life ebbing.

She looked up at him through blood-matted lashes, her face a frightening mask of drying red and yellow. Matt could only hope she was looking at the one person she needed to see. Daniel.

"You can help me . . . ," she whispered.

"Sir, you'll have to follow the ambulance."

The paramedics were rolling her toward their vehicle. Matt kept up, hand gripping hers.

"Daniel . . . please . . . ," she said, softer than a whisper now.

The gurney hit the back of the ambulance with a clang. The front wheels folded up.

"Sir, stand back."

For a shocking instant the woman's fingers suddenly tightened on his, so hard Matt could not let go. She raised her head, eyes boring into his.

"Help me!" Her voice rang out, startling in its desperation.

Then her head fell back as her hand slipped from his, her eyes staring up at nothing, and the ambulance doors slammed shut on the gurney.

Matt was left standing on the street, the blood on his hands the only physical evidence remaining of his contact with her. Emotionally, he felt the sting of failure, loss, and—

The ambulance pulled away, moving slowly toward two police cars that blocked the road, their blue and red flashing lights reflecting in lazy circles in the dark windows of shuttered storefronts. Matt recognized two of the cops on duty: Hickman and Bailey. They were from his division. Bailey caught him looking, turned away with a scowl, as if he'd seen something contemptible.

Matt was getting used to that reaction. His attention was on someone he didn't recognize. A tall man in a dark suit standing by the police cars, waiting.

The police cars didn't shift position. The ambulance had to stop. The man in the suit held up a badge case for the driver.

A moment later, the vehicle's rear doors opened and the man jumped in. Only then did one of the police cars back up to let the ambulance proceed.

Matt watched as the ambulance disappeared from view. Something was different. What? Then he had it. No flashing lights or siren.

He sighed. He knew what that meant. No need to rush. No reason not to go back to his coffee and his own sorry existence, such as it was.

At least half of the café's staff was out ferrying coffee, tea, and muffins to the remaining cops and emergency workers. Jan had a coffee waiting for him in a paper take-out cup, and gave him back his phone. Matt was surprised how much his hand shook as she gave it to him.

"You want to get yourself to home and wash up," she said.

"Right." Matt felt sluggish. The adrenaline of the night was beginning to leave him, but too slowly.

Only then did it dawn on him that there had been only one ambulance. He asked Jan about the other person in the car. Daniel, he supposed. "Was the passenger okay?"

Jan shrugged. "Wasn't none. Driver was alone."

Matt took a careful sip of coffee. His hands still shook. In the flash of light through the windshield, he was certain there'd been someone else beside the driver.

Jan cupped her hands around his and the coffee cup to steady them. "Hon, you really want to get yourself to home."

"Yeah," Matt said. But he didn't move. His eyes tracked a driver from one of two tow trucks as she attached hooks to the pancaked car.

Jan understood what was stopping him. One survivor to another. "You can't save them all." Matt frowned, and Jan's hand went to her mouth. "Oh, hon, I'm so so sorry. I didn't mean—"

"Understood." How could she know the truth? He gave her the best smile he could muster. "See you tomorrow."

Most of the bystanders had departed now. The cops on duty stayed down the street by their cars, drinking free coffee, diverting what little traffic there was away from the scene until the tow trucks could clear the wreckage.

Matt waited until the silver car was dragged from the deep dent it had made in the taxi, sheet metal harshly scraping pavement. Then, on impulse, following the cop's instincts that usually served him so well, he circled the wreck to the passenger side.

He saw what he expected.

The passenger airbag had deployed.

Someone *had* been with the driver. Someone lucky enough to walk away from an accident no one could possibly walk away from.

Matt wondered what it would be like to be that lucky.

DAY TWO

3

Of the five members of the squad, Piotr Janyk spoke the best English, so the general selected him to handle the transaction. If the seller had any concerns about possible irregularities, the bundles of cash the redheaded young man passed to him would keep his questions to a minimum.

Unfortunately, it also prompted the seller to be too helpful.

"You boys driving outta state?" The seller was Honest Jim Johnson, an obnoxious parody of an American cowboy, Borodin thought. Johnson's once-white Stetson was sweat-stained. His cowboy boots worn, the silver toe tip missing from the left foot, his jeans tightly belted beneath an enormous gut. To the Russian general, this man was the embodiment of everything that was wrong with this country. Not that he cared. America was in its last days, rotting from within. It was no longer his enemy.

"We don't know yet." Janyk properly showed no impatience as Honest Jim laboriously filled in a bill of sale. The transaction was taking place in the motor home Borodin's squad was buying. An old Winnebago Vista Cruiser. The cheap laminate trim was peeling from the fold-down table and cupboard doors. The narrow shower stall in the back was edged with mildew. Captain Korolev, however, had examined the engine, a Mercedes diesel, and said it would make the journey to the objective. For his part, the general appreciated the collection of twenty or so souvenir stickers plastered across the vehicle's tailgate. Good protective color.

Borodin, whose own English he knew was passable, though more accented than Janyk's, sensed there was a point to Johnson's question. "Why do you ask?"

Honest Jim grinned. His teeth were cigarette stained. One was silver. "Could save you some money. See, you got fifteen days to register the sale with the MVD. You stay local, it'll cost you fifteen bucks for thirty days. You say you're nonresidents, you get ninety days, same price." He slid the bill of sale to Janyk.

Janyk looked to Borodin for his cue. "That's good to know. Are we done?"

The general frowned. There was $38,000 in cash on the fold-down table. Was this cowboy really talking about saving fifteen dollars?

Honest Jim looked anything but honest as he glanced from Janyk to Borodin. "Well, now. This being a cash transaction greater than ten grand, I do hafta fill out a bank declaration. Guess I'll need some kinda ID. Passport numbers, maybe. And you gotta tell me the, uh, source of your funds."

"Is that necessary?" Janyk asked.

Honest Jim's face gleamed with sweat. It was 10:00 a.m., the temperature was already in the eighties, and barely a breeze through the open windows. Outside, a handful of used cars and pickup trucks baked in the Arizona heat under a sun-faded sign showing a thinner, younger version of Honest Jim promising to SAVE YOU MONEY. "Well, now, there are ways to expedite the, uh, paperwork. But it does entail additional expenses."

Janyk glanced at Borodin, the question unspoken.

Honest Jim tried to close the deal. "If you're in a hurry to get started on your vacation, I could save you a whole lot of time and trouble."

Borodin agreed with the sentiment. Best to keep this simple.

Janyk reached into his faded denim jacket. Honest Jim tensed, then relaxed as Janyk withdrew another roll of bills and placed them on the table. "Two thousand?"

"Just what I was gonna say." Beaming with relief, Honest Jim made a show of tearing up another sheet of paper. "And that is that." He squeezed himself out from the narrow bench seat beside the table, handed Janyk a key. "She's all yours. Half a tank of diesel already in her, no extra charge."

Janyk walked forward to slide down into the driver's seat.

Borodin waited as Honest Jim shoved the bundled bills into a large brown envelope. "Can I help you fellows out with any maps? Directions? There's a fine barbecue shack 'bout five miles toward the highway." He jammed his copy of the bill of sale in with the money. Borodin knew it would be torn up later. As planned, there would be no record of the transaction. For a certain type of man, greed was something that could always be depended upon.

Honest Jim suddenly slapped a meaty hand against his back pocket. "Wup. Phone's a buzzin'. Better get that." He pulled out a phone, tapped the screen.

The camper van's engine started. Borodin saw Janyk looking back at him from the driver's seat. The general held up his hand, telling Janyk to wait.

Honest Jim peered at his phone's display, gave another of his teeth-baring grins. "Ah, that's okay. Just the little woman. She can leave a message." He went to slip the phone back into his pocket.

Borodin's hand shot out, twisted the cowboy's hand around.

On the phone's display, he saw his own face. Borodin spun Honest Jim around and locked his arm around the man's fat neck.

Honest Jim gasped a quick, desperate explanation. "S'only a pitcher for my wall of happy customers. No names if that's what—"

He said nothing else as the general sharply angled his head forward, cutting off the blood flow to the brain in seconds.

As Borodin waited for the struggling Honest Jim to sag in his grip, he looked out the window. The used car lot remained deserted. Only plastic pennants moved, stirred by the morning breeze.

Janyk returned as Borodin laid out the unconscious man on the floor.

"We could leave him in his office, set fire to it," he suggested.

The general stood up, stretched. It had been a long time since he'd engaged in hand-to-hand combat. He was pleased his reflexes and his instincts weren't diminished. It made him even more confident of achieving the mission's objective.

"No. We'll take him back to the house, dispose of him there. The authorities will think he's involved with the smuggling operation."

"To buy us extra time."

"We don't need extra time," Borodin said. But the mission he was on was his and his alone, so he added what he knew his men needed to hear, to have them continue to believe the lies he had told them. "Six days more, and then the world will know exactly what we've done to bring down this country, and honor us for it."

And I will have my revenge.

4

At 4:00 p.m. sharp, Matt Caidin arrived to take over the Special Services desk of District Two. He was a police lieutenant, twelve years on the job, with multiple commendations from tours in Major Crimes and Vice. But for the past nine weeks, he'd been assigned to after-hours phone duty in a cramped and windowless office behind the customer-service desk at District Headquarters. So far, he'd been using his hard-earned skills and experience as a detective to answer questions about bicycle registration, burial permits, and the location of impounded cars.

"Caidin." Even though the day-shift officer, a civilian employee, didn't wear a uniform or carry a shield, her tone told Matt she had the same disdain for him as the rest of the Arlington County Police Department.

"Ms. Barry." Matt had given up trying to change her opinion of him. He waited for her to gather her coat and retrieve her purse from a locked lower drawer. She kept to the side as she walked out through the doorway. "See you tomorrow," he said to resounding silence.

The Special Services after-hours phone rang seven times between four and six. That gave Matt opportunity to complete his daily ritual: using the desk screen to access the department's internal website for updates to the status of the Lowney case.

It hadn't changed, still on hold pending a final report from Internal Affairs. Though the site didn't say so, the IA investigation remained in administrative limbo until Matt's former partner, Sergeant of Detectives Jack Lowney, regained consciousness. Or died. Until then, the nature of Matt's involvement in that case remained subject to rumors and innuendo, because the truth of it was that the case to uncover corruption in the force was still ongoing.

Next, Matt checked the status of the Lowney fund. Jack had an ex-wife, a new wife, and three kids. Though the family knew his disability payments would continue while he was in the hospital, the criminal case hanging over him left them worried about the loss of his pension or, in the event he died, survivors' benefits. Still, three weeks after Lowney's failed suicide attempt, Matt's check had been returned. The unsigned note had called the scorned donation blood money. Even when the truth came out, he doubted the Lowney family would ever forgive him. His partner's death had never been part of the plan.

Between seven and eight, Matt took more than thirty calls about the department's initiative to loan engraving pens so people could mark their possessions and make them easier to trace if stolen. Local news had carried a story about the program. Matt dutifully added names and numbers to a waiting list for Ms. Barry to process when she came in tomorrow.

He ate a sandwich at the desk, drank coffee from a Thermos. Through the open door came the sounds of activity from the main hallway, a constant flow of officers and suspects. Socializing, but not with him.

Call volume diminished as *Monday Night Football* began; televised football being one of the best crime deterrents in Matt's experience, with basketball a close second.

He leaned back in the old wooden, unpadded office chair, waiting for the phone to ring again. Then his own phone buzzed. Caller ID said it was Helena. He knew what she wanted: How were they going to handle this month's bills? He ignored the call, stared instead at the cluttered bulletin board by the open door. Suspect photos. Union notices. Sublets and goods for sale, including cars.

He thought about the crash. The driver's icy hand, her insistent, dying plea for help. Calling for—

Matt leaned forward, accessed the department's internal site again, clicked through the accident reports from early morning. Then from the afternoon. Then from last night. Then through all three shifts again, to be certain.

There was no report of a single-car accident in the vicinity of Molly's Café in the past twenty-four hours.

Still, paperwork sometimes could be slow to reach the site, so he called the hospitals next. Georgetown University. Virginia Center. Arlington. No female accident victims—none serious, at least. He tried hospitals farther away. Nothing.

Incoming calls picked up again around eleven. Irate drivers looking for their towed cars for the most part, too many of them sounding over the legal blood-alcohol limit. Matt handled all the queries while he continued searching local news sites, then state, then nationwide. More nothing.

It wasn't right. He knew what he had seen, and in this era of tightening caution, or expanding paranoia, something else would have seen it, as well.

Matt logged back in to the department's internal site to access traffic control. In less than a minute, he was watching a video feed from the previous evening, as recorded by an overhead surveillance camera. The camera was mounted on the rooftop of a small office building across the street and a half block down from Molly's.

At time code 00:23:15, the accident happened. What had seemed to take minutes when witnessed through the front window of the café now unfolded in seconds. By 00:23:22, the silver car had come to a rest against the parked cab. Less than ten seconds later, Matt watched himself race for the driver's door. He leaned forward, his attention shifting to the passenger's side.

On the video feed, the startled taxi driver didn't follow through on Matt's order to check the passenger. The emergency workers came. They pulled Matt aside, and on-screen he stepped back out of sight of the camera with the other unseen gawkers gathered outside Molly's.

Thirty minutes elapsed. The driver of the car was cautiously, carefully extracted from the wreckage, stabilized, treated, placed on the gurney.

Matt kept watching. On-screen, he saw himself step back into frame, walk with the dying driver, hold her hand, then move with her out of camera range again to the unseen, lone ambulance.

By the explosively fused car and taxi, emergency workers packed up their gear. Matt saw Jan appear with a cardboard tray of take-out coffee cups, pass them out to all takers.

Then everyone was out of frame, leaving only the two ruined vehicles. The only on-screen movement came from the haphazard mound of fire-suppressant foam gradually settling over the silver car's front end.

One of the tow truck operators attached a chain to the car, and it slowly pulled free of the taxi.

Then Matt saw himself reenter the scene, become the first person that night to go to the passenger side of the silver car, peer in, see no one, even though the video feed confirmed that the passenger door had never opened and no one but the driver had emerged from the car.

He looked away from his computer screen, weighing his personal, conflicting observations. He was a trained observer. His eyewitness testimony was trusted in court. He *knew* he hadn't imagined the shape of a passenger, unless it had been something else? A bulky coat? A package? Some other object flying free in the car?

He closed his eyes, briefly relived the scene, but he remembered nothing new to challenge what he was certain he'd seen.

He returned to the main page for Arlington traffic control, called up new recordings from surveillance and traffic cameras along the road on which the car had approached, traced its route back from every intersection, looking for a camera installed with a low angle in a brightly lit location.

He found an ideal location five blocks away from Molly's, entered a time code ten minutes earlier than the crash, waited . . . waited . . . and then freeze-framed the silver car as it sped by.

The image was blurred by motion, but clear enough. Matt could see the driver at the wheel, and the passenger behind her, in the back seat.

For an instant, he felt relief, but it was that short-lived.

If the passenger was in the back seat, why did the *front* seat airbag deploy?

He checked other camera views between the well-lit intersection and Molly's, but all were from high angles and the car's interior was always in shadow.

Matt felt a familiar frustration. He knew the pieces needed to solve this particular mystery were out there and that when he had assembled them, the solution would look simple. But finding those pieces, that was the hard part of any detective investigation. At least this time he knew where to look.

He began backtracking the car again. Six blocks away. Seven. Then eight. And then, in the silence of his windowless Special Services office, he swore.

The video record of traffic at the ninth intersection was unavailable. As was the tenth. It made no sense. Video storage cost Arlington nothing: The Department of Homeland Security covered the bill for dozens of municipalities close to DC and other high-value cities across the country. In the event of disaster, it was considered prudent to have records that could be searched in order to track those who might have been responsible. Matt had been to briefings on the so-called "SPARROW" network of surveillance. Those video records would *never* be erased.

So it was a glitch. The recordings would be back in an hour, or tomorrow night. He returned to the video record from five blocks away, to confirm the passenger's position in the back seat.

Now that video was gone.

Matt blinked in surprise, sat back in his chair, contemplated returning to the original recording of the crash scene, but for no logical reason knew exactly what he'd find.

Nothing.

Apparently, he wasn't the only one interested in the crash, the passenger, and the driver.

He logged out of the site, general interest now full-blown suspicion.

At midnight exactly, Matt switched the Special Services phones over to the automated system, logged out, and twenty minutes later was sitting in his customary window booth at Molly's with five newspapers. The printed word was more difficult to erase than electronic. There was a chance, admittedly small, that some mention of the crash had been physically published before any electronic versions of the story had been purged.

Jan poured his coffee. "Looking for a new place or a new job?"

"I wish. Trying to find something about the accident last night."

"Is that even news these days?"

"Sunday night in Arlington. Not a lot else going on." Matt didn't bother sharing his suspicions.

"Huh. Need a menu, hon?"

"Nope. Special's fine."

"Coming right out." Jan headed off for the kitchen, writing on her order pad.

Matt started with the *Washington Times*. Then the *Post*. Front pages were all the same: gas prices down, dollar up, preparations for an international terrorism summit causing traffic delays in West Virginia. As he was flipping to the local news pages, he realized Jan was back, and he pushed the papers to the side. But no plate took their place.

It wasn't Jan.

"You can help me."

Matt looked up at a pretty young woman, maybe twenty-six, twenty-eight. Her new jeans and hooded pullover pegged her as a student at Georgetown, likely with parents who could pay the full tuition. From her hesitant expression, she was in unfamiliar territory. Out of her comfort zone.

"What's the problem?" Matt didn't bother wondering why she had stopped at his table. Everyone told him he looked like a cop. The cropped black hair was part of it. But he knew he also had the attitude, no question.

"I need to get to 610 E Street, southwest."

Matt raised an eyebrow. "In DC?"

Her sudden smile transformed her face. She was more than pretty.

"Yes." She beamed as if he'd just come up with something brilliant. "Washington DC. I have to get to DC."

Matt checked his watch. "You've missed the last Metro. So you'll need a cab."

She looked at him, expectant.

Matt found himself pulling out his phone in response to that look. "I can call one for you."

She cocked her head, as if trying to make a decision. Then, "No. No, it's all right. There's a cab on the street. I saw one parked."

"You sure?" Matt didn't recall seeing any when he'd arrived.

She nodded. "Yes. I saw a cab." She smiled again. "Thank you." She turned and walked toward the door just as Jan arrived.

"Special, bagel, extra hot sauce." The plates and bottle clattered on the table. "Was she selling something?"

Through the window, Matt watched the girl walk out onto the street, thinking that he'd liked her smile, wondering what or who was so important in DC. Then he realized Jan had asked him a question.

"What? Oh, her. No. Lost. Needs to get somewhere in DC, if you can believe it."

"From here? This time of night? Some people just ask for it, don't they?"

Matt looked at his Special Breakfast Scramble. "You're right." He slid out of the booth. "I'll be back."

"You're one of the good ones, hon."

Wishing that were true, Matt went out after his lost lamb. She wasn't on the street, either direction, but he did see a cab just making the turn on Clarendon, heading for the river.

Luck of the innocent. Or just plain dumb luck.

Reprieved but, surprisingly, also somewhat disappointed, Matt went back to his congealed special and his newspapers and again found nothing.

An hour later, he was back at his apartment, not his house. He didn't have one of those anymore. Helena did. His lawyer told him he'd made a big mistake. She'd likely end up keeping it after the divorce. But Matt didn't care. His wife's eyes told him he'd already lost everything anyway. What did a house matter after that?

So now he was bunking in a one-bedroom cell in a building mostly full of guys living solo. In transition, they called it. Some new, would-be politicos on their way up, eager to make their way inside the Beltway, and others like him, on their way out of a marriage, or on their way down, or both.

But none of them would be just like him in one regard: He doubted any of the other tenants were under a death threat. The Mauricio brothers ran a criminal organization that stayed in business thanks to their deep connection to local law enforcement, and by sheer brutality. Matt, by virtue of being untouched by corruption, had been selected by the police department's Internal Affairs Division to be IA's envoy to the dark side, to offer himself up, take the Mauricios' dirty money, and report back the name of every other cop who was doing the same.

Inevitably, word had gotten out about the covert investigation. Just as inevitably, the first reports had been garbled and incomplete. His partner, Jack Lowney, as untainted as Matt, had been identified as the snitch. Matt had wanted to end the investigation that same day, but his IA handlers said no. The misidentification of Lowney as their spy was a positive development because of the increased protection it provided Matt.

To maintain secrecy, IA hadn't informed Lowney of his role in the deception. They'd simply treated him like any other cop suspected of corruption: announcing his suspension while investigation into his alleged misdeeds was ongoing.

No one had suspected how devastating those accusations would be for Lowney. Matt knew he should have known. He had wanted to reach out to his partner, to whisper the truth, but he hadn't. That was a regret that would haunt him forever.

With Lowney's suicide attempt attributable to an IA investigation gone wrong, a course change had happened overnight. As if Lowney had indeed been the source of undercover information, arrests were made, among cops as well as members of the Mauricios' organization.

Ostensibly to protect his own involvement, Matt himself was treated as a possibly guilty participant, and while he wasn't arrested, he was put on desk duty.

His IA handlers maintained that by treating him as a dirty cop, the Mauricios would be less inclined to think that *Matt* had been the spy in their midst. Another few weeks for all the charges to be finalized and all the arrests made, and the truth would come out and Matt and his partner would be fully exonerated.

But Matt knew that since word of the investigation had leaked, IA was likely just as compromised as the rest of the force. Which meant that sometime in the next few weeks, it was just as likely that his name would be passed on to the criminals as the real police mole. Combined with the fact that his fellow officers were convinced he was on the take, Matt knew that no one on his own force would be there to help him. Not when the Mauricios decided to send a message to everyone else who might decide to act against them. So looking over his shoulder in the parking garage, pausing before entering the elevator, checking his apartment door for the tiny sliver of paper he had placed in the jam to see if his door had been opened in his absence—all that had become the new normal for Matt, and for no one else in his building.

Tonight, the sliver of paper was still in place. He opened the door, locked and chained it behind him. But he could still feel the target on his back. He knew he shouldn't, not behind the locked door, protected for another night. But he had long ago learned to trust his instincts, his feelings, whatever explanation there was for that sense that told him when something was coming, something that wasn't right. It worked well enough times he had learned to trust it.

He paused a moment by the locked door, waiting, but for what he didn't know.

Finally, though, he was certain. The apartment was empty. Whatever he felt, some dark shadow cresting over him like a wave about to break, it could only be the residue of the day, of the past nine weeks. He set the feeling aside, cracked open a window in the living room. The last tenant had been a smoker, and that mustiness had taken up permanent residence in the dingy carpet, walls, and furniture. He could hear the sounds of late-night traffic drifting up from the nearby parkway. A far-off siren.

Matt slipped off his shoulder holster and safed his revolver, got a Bud from the noisily complaining fridge, sat on a barstool at the kitchen counter passthrough, debated turning on ESPN or his laptop. He took a long draw from the bottle. Laptop. There had to be something about the crash he'd overlooked, or that someone else had. There had to be a reason for the traffic videos being selectively erased.

A sharp knock interrupted that thought.

Bottle in hand, Matt stared over at his door, running the odds.

His entry-phone hadn't buzzed, so whoever it was could have come from inside the building. But given the situation with Lowney, it could be some muscle from the Mauricio organization, finally come to deliver their message.

The knock repeated. Louder. Matt reached for his gun.

Then a man's voice: "Matthew Caidin. FBI. Open the door."

Matt heard the implicit threat and responded quickly, though he kept his gun at his side. Once at the door, he squinted through its peephole. *Okay...* What appeared to be a legitimate FBI badge case was in plain view. He slipped the gun into the waistband at the small of his back, opened the door, one foot in place to prevent it from being kicked open, one hand in place ready to slam it shut again.

"Detective Caidin, I'm Special Agent Caparelli."

The man was his age, taller, better dressed, longer hair. If the badge hadn't been legit, Matt wouldn't have IDed him as someone on an FBI salary.

"What's this about?"

The agent held up a photo. "Do you recognize this woman?"

Matt opened the door wide. "C'mon in."

The woman in the agent's photo wasn't smiling—it looked to be an employee identification photo. But it was her.

"Yeah, I talked to her tonight. At Molly's Café. What's this about?"

Caparelli's tone sharpened. "You spoke to her."

"I just said I did." Matt was worried now. And puzzled. The FBI must have known where he'd met her. How else had they tracked him here? He felt a flash of guilt. What if she hadn't been in the cab he'd seen? What if she'd walked to the wrong street and he hadn't looked hard enough for her?

"Tell me what she said."

"She was lost. She had to get someplace in DC."

"Did she give you an address?"

"Yeah," Matt said thinking aloud. "E Street, southwest. Six hundred block ... 610."

Caparelli's face tightened. He slipped the photo back into his jacket, and with that gesture, Matt suddenly knew where he'd seen this man before.

"Hold it," he said. "You were there, too. Sunday night at the crash. I saw you stop the ambulance. You got in the back. Is this girl somehow connected to that?"

It took a moment for the agent to reply, as if caught in some internal debate. "She is. Her name's Laura Hart, and she's a federal agent. You made contact with her at the crash scene Sunday night."

"That girl's FBI?" Matt shook his head. "Believe me, if I had met her at the crash scene, I'd remember and I don't."

"She was the driver of the car."

Matt grimaced as the pictures of destruction flooded back to him. "Not possible. That woman was . . . well . . . I didn't think she'd make it."

"She didn't," Caparelli said. "By the time I reached her in the ambulance, she was dead."

"Well, then, that's obviously not your girl. Look, it's late. I've told you what I know. If you check that address, you'll probably find her. I hope she got there okay."

"Mr. Caidin," Caparelli said, "you're going to come with me."

It wasn't a request.

5

CROSSWIND's most secure conference room exceeded the NSA's Tempest-class Level A standards. It was a room within a room—an acoustically dampened box mounted on thick rubber pads, webbed by copper mesh that functioned like a Faraday cage, blocking any electronic signals generated inside from being detected outside, even at a distance of less than a yard.

In that room, Sam Arlo handed Caparelli a tablet, already switched on. "Photos from a crime scene in Sonora, Mexico."

Caparelli swiped through the images: stark, graphic, shadowless in the dead-on brightness of a crime-scene photographer's flash.

"Twelve victims," Arlo said. "They think."

Caparelli understood the uncertainty. Limbs and other unidentifiable body pieces were strewn about as if by explosives, but no other blast damage was evident. No scorch marks. One photo showed small lamps, bottles, and glasses untouched on a small table that was still standing. Bullet holes in abundance, though. The walls were pocked with them. Hundreds. "This happened last night? You're certain?"

"*Federales* found them this morning." Caparelli's young manager of research removed his wire-frame glasses, rubbed his eyes, his dark olive complexion accented by the sparse black stubble dotting his usually clean-shaven head.

The overhead fluorescents were harsh. The effect wasn't helped by the conference room's unrelieved white walls. The project had been moved here before Caparelli became its head. He assumed the previous director, the legendary Dr. Nourem, had chosen the color or lack thereof to remind staff that despite being an operational arm of the intelligence community, the facility also functioned as a lab.

"This is what Laura saw, right?"

Caparelli corrected Arlo's terminology. "This is what she perceived."

"Saw" referred to visible light sensed by eyes and optic nerves. Since Laura had not been physically present in Sonora, sight had had nothing to do with what she had witnessed in that distant location.

Caparelli had listened to the voice mail Laura left for him the night of the accident. He had no need to torture himself by hearing it again. Her last words were burned into his memory, forever linked to the unanswerable question: Would she have died if he had answered her call?

Whatever had happened in these images, Laura had been a witness. She'd described it in her message. The tile roof and stucco walls of the structure. The gunfire. The bodies torn apart as she watched.

"But what's the tie to Borodin?" Caparelli asked.

Arlo seemed surprised by his question. "Obviously, if Laura was there as a perceiver, the general was there in the flesh. He's her target." He added, almost apologetically, "That's how it works."

Caparelli swiped through more of the images. Close-ups of disembodied heads. Number cards identifying severed arms and legs, bullet casings, sprays of blood on walls and ceilings. "So we accept that Borodin was in a compound in the middle of nowhere. In Mexico. Why?"

"Compound's less than two miles from the US border."

That got Caparelli's interest. "Did they find a tunnel?"

"Comes up in Nogales. Small house at the end of a residential street, at the edge of the desert. Border Patrol found another body there. But not like those. Shot, twice in the head. Some local used car dealer. They're saying it's a drug war. Rival gangs."

Caparelli knew that wasn't it at all. The nightmare scenario was real. "Borodin's in the country."

Arlo looked down at the image on the tablet in Caparelli's hands. Body parts. Bullet holes. The victims had firepower, put up a fight, and it had done them no good. "Seems like he's brought VEKTOR's latest technology, whatever the hell it is. But why?"

Caparelli didn't have an answer, but knew nothing else would matter until he did. "Whatever the reason, it has to be sanctioned."

Arlo seemed puzzled. "The Russians do shit all over the world. Same as us. But it's balanced, isn't it? We keep each other in check. Do what we can to be sure no one gets a real advantage."

Caparelli stared at the carnage on the tablet's screen. "Look at what that technology accomplished." He glanced at Arlo. "Maybe they think that now they do have a real advantage. Maybe they mean to use it."

Arlo wasn't inclined to argue. "Whatever it is, it's effective."

Caparelli glanced back at the door to the corridor. At the end of it, Detective Matthew Caidin waited in another secure, white-walled room. "The cop I brought in, the one who was at the scene of the crash, Laura contacted him. Tonight."

"No shit! Uh, sorry . . .'"

Caparelli shared Arlo's conflicting emotions, an unsettling mix of elation and despair.

"Did she . . . What did she say?"

"That she had to get here."

"She tell him about us, the project?"

"Just the address."

Arlo was excited, couldn't help himself. "She must have seen more than she put in her message. Felt she had to come in personally to report when . . . well, you know."

Caparelli agreed. That was his conclusion as well.

"Unfinished business," the young man said. "It's . . . classic, isn't it? Right out of the folklore."

Caparelli handed the tablet back to Arlo. "We'll finish it tonight."

"So she can . . . go."

Caparelli wouldn't allow himself to think that. The only way he could keep going was to do his job. "She's already gone. But she can still help us stop the general. Whatever he's here for."

In the disturbingly white and windowless conference room, the mysterious Agent Caparelli sat across from Matt. He had nothing in his hands and had placed no file folder, computer, or recorder on the narrow metal table between them. That told Matt that everything said here would be captured on video by unseen cameras.

He still didn't know what this place was, only its location. Caparelli, refusing any conversation in what he called an unsecure location, had driven them to DC, to E Street SW's 600 block, a huge recently constructed building that appeared to span the entire block as far as Matt could tell. What it wasn't was the FBI building.

In the underground parking lot, he'd seen no identifying signage, nor was there any in the elevator that had brought them to this floor. But while he'd no way of knowing what actual address he had arrived at, Matt felt certain he was where the girl had said she needed to go.

The dead girl from the car crash, according to Agent Caparelli.

Which was impossible.

Still, Matt reasoned, something had triggered the agent's late-night visit. Something that linked an FBI operative to a car-crash victim, and now to him. The fact that ordinary traffic surveillance video of the crash had been wiped from the system while Matt watched told him to brace for the unexpected. Even so, Caparelli's opening surprised him.

"A team of terrorists has entered the country with the intention of causing significant destruction and death. Do I have your attention, Detective Caidin?"

Matt groaned inwardly at his bad luck. Obviously, and inadvertently, he'd become mixed up in some undercover operation. *Had the girl in the photo been impersonating the driver of the car as part of an investigation, until the accident claimed that woman's life?*

"Absolutely. I'll do whatever it is you require of me."

"Laura Hart has vital information about the terrorists' plans and capabilities, and she needs to get that information to us."

Matt held up a hand. "Hold it. Which woman are we talking about? The one in the car or the one in the restaurant?"

"Both. They're the same."

Matt flashed through outrageous scenarios of twins, spies, doubles, couldn't find a match. "How could they be?"

Caparelli ignored his confusion. "We need you to make contact with Laura Hart again."

Matt felt as if he had missed part of the conversation. "Why? The girl I saw in Molly's, she only talked to me because she wanted to come here. What do you need me for? She knows where you are."

"Do you?"

Matt thought that an odd question. "I don't know for a fact, but I assume this is the address that she gave me at the diner. I mean, we're in the 600 block of E Street, right?"

"Any other assumptions?"

Matt had been part of a few similar conversations in the past, where the other side had been vague and evasive. The last time was two years ago, when a homicide investigation was quietly handed over to another investigatory agency. Eventually, the various parties decided to share the real story off the record. The victim had turned out to be a foreign national with an assumed identity, and he'd been executed by his own people. Pure spy stuff.

"I'm guessing you're not FBI," Matt said.

"Correct."

"CIA?"

"No, but from time to time we work with them."

" 'We'?"

Caparelli paused. Matt could sense that whatever it was the man was going to say next, it was a struggle. "What I'm about to tell you is so far beyond 'top secret' that if you even think of repeating it to anyone, your life as you know it will be over."

Five different smart-ass replies flashed through Matt's mind in an instant. But the look on Caparelli's face told him this wasn't the time for any of them.

"I understand," Matt said.

Caparelli's expression didn't change. "Two nights ago, Laura Hart died from injuries she sustained in the car accident that you witnessed. Last night, you spoke to her ghost."

"Is this is some sort of psychological test?" Caidin asked.

Caparelli counseled himself to remain patient. As director of Project CROSSWIND, he had lived with its reality for so long that he sometimes found himself forgetting how incomprehensible it all was, how bizarre it seemed to outsiders. But there was no time to ease this particular outsider into the situation.

"Under standard conditions, before I could tell you any of this, you'd have had to undergo a stringent security clearance investigation. Then I'd have everything: your bank records; tax returns; medical files; criminal record; affidavits from employers, friends, enemies, family members—anything I wanted.

"What I have learned about you is that despite an extraordinary arrest record, you're on desk duty with the Arlington County Police. Your partner's on life support from an apparently self-inflicted gunshot wound and not expected to regain consciousness. Preliminary evidence indicates he was being paid off by a local dealer and that you're somehow connected to it."

Caidin's face shut down, unreadable. "It's an ongoing investigation. I can't discuss it."

"I don't care one way or the other," Caparelli said. "Whatever shitstorm you think you could face because of those accusations, it is nothing compared to what will happen to you if you divulge *any* of what I'm about to say."

"Then don't tell me."

"Not your decision, it's mine. So I'll cut to the chase: The facility you're in is part of a classified intelligence program called CROSSWIND. Have you ever heard of remote viewing?"

Caidin mimed pressing a button on a television remote. "Like when I change channels?"

Caparelli ignored the sarcasm. "I'll make the explanation simple. We have perceivers—remote viewers—with the ability to separate their consciousness from their physical body and, for want of a better term, project it to another location. Laura Hart was one of our most gifted perceivers. Without any form of technological support, Laura could, in a sense, see and hear events thousands of miles away."

For just a moment, a look played over Caidin's face. It was one Caparelli had seen many time. Absolute disbelief.

"I'm not a science guy but . . . how could anything like that even be possible?" Caidin asked.

"For you, right now, it's enough to know that it is. Details aren't important."

Caidin's next words were those of one professional to another. "One thing I do know: If you can't back it up, then everything you say is crap. You've got to give me something."

"Fair enough," Caparelli said. "For decades, it's been widely accepted that consciousness arises from electrochemical activity in the brain. You'd agree?"

Caidin reluctantly nodded, as if expecting a trap.

"Except there's no experimental proof that confirms that concept. At best, researchers have been able to show that there's an *association* between consciousness and physical processes within the brain, but no evidence that conclusively establishes causation."

Caidin appeared to think that over. "So, it's chicken or egg: Does that electrochemical activity produce consciousness, or does consciousness produce the activity?"

"Close enough. To the outside world, at least, that's the extent of what's understood. But our researchers have taken a significant step past that: Human consciousness exists as a nonphysical field, and it's entangled at a quantum level with the physical structure of the brain. They're connected in the same way that a moving magnetic field produces an electric current, and an electric current can produce magnetism. Two different phenomena arising from one underlying cause, but—and this is the important part—under certain specific conditions each can exist on its own.

"It's the same for the brain's electrochemical processes and consciousness. In most cases, both exist at the same place and same time within us. In quantum physics, the principle is called superposition. Something like a photon, say, exists tangled up in all its possible configurations at the same time, as both a particle and a wave. But then, when that photon's measured or observed, the act of observation reveals that it's one or the other, never both.

"That's essentially what people like Laura can do. Somehow, they're able to 'untangle' their consciousness from their bodies while still keeping both connected, no matter how far apart the two components are. It's what Einstein called 'spooky action at a distance.' I doubt even he knew how appropriate the term is."

"You're serious about all this," Caidin said. Not a question.

"I have no time to be anything but. This facility's been in and out of operation in one form or another since the seventies. Twenty years ago, we had a breakthrough that led us to consistent, reliable results. We've been active ever since."

Caidin still looked skeptical. "But if that's true, if we can see and hear anything, anywhere . . . how can we ever be taken by surprise? How can there ever be terrorists here we don't know about?"

It was a question Caparelli had encountered many times before. His answer was well-practiced. "First of all, we have to know where and when to look, and that requires more traditional intelligence-gathering techniques for us to choose our targets. Second, there are technical limitations: The quantum fields that support nonphysical awareness are extraordinarily sensitive to certain electromagnetic disturbances. Remote viewing is almost impossible during daylight at any given target area because of interference from the sun. And those potential targets who are aware of our technology can also take steps to electromagnetically shield facilities from remote observation. But, as I said, these are details you don't need to know."

"So what do I need to know?"

"That under certain conditions, which I admit we do not yet fully understand, a person's separated consciousness can survive the body's death."

"Are you talking about . . . a person's soul?"

"That's a religious concept I have no authority to speak on. This facility deals only in science. What we've learned empirically is that the quantum field from which consciousness arises can, under certain conditions, be self-sustaining, be seen—perceived—by others, and persist after physical death."

"As . . . a ghost."

"That's as good a word as any. When we talk about the experiences perceivers have had, we use the term 'wraith.' A ghost can be many different things, take different forms, even appear as a dog or horse or other animal. But a wraith is an apparition of a person."

"What experiences?"

"We know that sometimes our perceivers can be seen or sensed or otherwise identified by their targets. Especially if their targets have perceiver-like abilities, or if there's been a long term association between the perceiver and target. Some sort of emotional connection.

"But all these technicalities aside, whether we say 'ghost' or 'wraith,' or 'manifestation,' we're confident that we've identified the natural phenomenon responsible for all the myths and legends of apparitions of the dead, in every culture, and in every time."

Caidin studied him. "So the woman in the car, Laura Hart, the woman I met in Molly's, she was one of your 'perceivers,' someone who could . . . send her consciousness away from her body, and she died in the crash, and then her wraith appeared to me."

Caparelli nodded.

"Why? I mean, why'd she choose me?"

It was the same question tormenting Caparelli. "Had you met Laura before? Maybe encountered her in your police work?"

"No. I'd remember."

Caparelli had feared that answer. If there had been no earlier connection between Caidin and Laura, then that left only one other answer. "Just as perceivers and their targets can build a form of emotional connection over time, it's possible there's also an emotional component involved in the creation—the manifestation—of a wraith. Your being there with her when she was close to death, physically sharing that emotionally intense, end-of-life experience with her, might have bonded her to you."

"You're saying what? Our fields 'entangled'?"

"Perhaps, but we're as much in the dark as you are. We've not studied the manifestation process in detail."

Caidin looked overwhelmed. "So . . . Laura Hart worked here, for you, and while she was 'out' remote viewing, she discovered something about the terrorists. And she was coming back here to report it, but before she could, she died in a car crash and . . ." Caidin shook his head. "And now her ghost, her wraith, is still trying to report—through me—to you."

"Because Laura has unfinished business," Caparelli said. "That also seems to be part of the traditional ghost phenomenon: The survival of the consciousness when there's a purpose unfulfilled."

"Okay, but why do you need me here? All I did was hold her hand, let her think I was someone else . . . Daniel. She kept calling out for Daniel. "

With an effort, Caparelli hid the wave of anguish that swept through him. "You're here now because if Laura linked to you when she died, that means there's a chance she can appear to you again. And we want you to let that happen."

"And then what?"

"She needs to tell you what she knows."

"Tell me again why she can't tell you."

"Because . . ." Caparelli stopped, then began again. "Because I wasn't there when she died. You were."

"And there's absolutely no other means to contact her?"

"There is not. This facility's present mission is remote viewing, and that's all our technology's designed for. In the future, we might find a way to apply it to the ghost phenomenon, but we have no means of doing that now." Caparelli paused. "Six days, Detective. That's the outside limit that a quantum field originating in the human body can remain self-sustaining on its own. Like a battery slowly running down. Since our perceivers' wraiths are connected to a living body, they can persist indefinitely. But once the body has died, that's how long a wraith persists. And Laura's already been disassociated for two of them. That means she has only four more days to deliver her last report to us. Through you."

Caidin took a deep breath. "What do you need me to do?"

Caparelli wasted no more time. "We'll provide the script for what you say to her. Questions to ask, names to mention, everything you need to have her recall whatever it was she was coming here to say."

"Recall? She doesn't know?"

"It's another part of the phenomenon. We believe Laura doesn't know she's dead."

"She doesn't know . . ."

"If you tell her," Caparelli warned. "If you lead her in any way to make that realization, you'll lose her. Along with everything she knows about the terrorists . . ." Sudden grief abruptly roughened his voice. "Along with everything she was . . . Gone forever."

DAY THREE

6

Evgeny Semyonovich Gorokhov was a rarity in Russia, almost a freak. He was seventy-eight-years old in a country where the average life expectancy for men had been, until recently, less than fifty-six. Unbowed by age, he was tall, his shoulders broad, his chest still massive, as if he had already been cast in bronze as a memorial statue in a hall of heroes, all features aggrandized to proportions larger than life. In the rarefied circles of his nation's spymasters and scientific elite, Gorokhov was exactly that: a legend.

He dressed the part, as well. His suits—always dark, somber, perfectly fitted—were Savile Row. The British tailors came to him, as they should. The heavy, gleaming watch he wore today, one of dozens in his collection, was by A. Lange & Söhne, a thrillingly exact instrument of platinum, gold, and sapphire. Gorokhov appreciated precision, and predictability. The timepiece's price was astronomical, though like most things he possessed, Gorokhov had not had to purchase it. Instead, it was a personal gift from the president of Russia, in recognition of a lifetime of service to the ideals the president was at last bringing back to their troubled nation.

The one characteristic that marked Gorokhov as a mere mortal was the ridged and mottled skin that rose along his neck, forming fingers of pale flesh that clawed across his face, the ravages of the third-degree burns that had kept him, as a teenager, socially isolated from his peers, an unsightly outsider. His father had paid the price for the drunken outburst that had set fire to his home, ruined his son's features, taken his wife's life. Gorokhov had seen to that punishment personally, and no one in his village had spoken against him when the authorities investigated his father's savagely beaten body, half buried in bloodstained snow. The people who knew him then understood his need for justice, and their need to fear the boy whose heart was as scarred as his skin.

But the isolation those scars had brought, and the seething resentment they had fueled, had helped forge his will, his ability to continue to do whatever must be done, without remorse, to ensure Mother Russia would not only survive, but prosper. It also accounted for the manner in which he was so revered and honored throughout his career. These days, those who did not consider him a legend tended to have their careers sidelined. In earlier days, those people had had their reputations ruined, or had simply disappeared.

Today, though, Evgeny Gorokhov was among those to whom his every word was a holy pronouncement. He was chief administrator of the Byuro Spetsial'nykh Issledovaniy. By itself, the name meant nothing. As a line item on the Kremlin's public spending reports, Gorokhov's Bureau of Special Studies amounted to nothing more than what the Americans would call "budget dust"— thirty million rubles, not even a million dollars.

But the five additional men and women in this cramped, hot, and electro-magnetically shielded monitoring room knew that the other, classified name for the BSI was VEKTOR. They also knew that its true funding was measured in the billions of dollars, as befitting an organization that, more than any other, ensured the nation's security from all attempts to weaken it, without and within.

For now, the chief administrator sat motionless in his chair, staring ahead at the dark glass wall, well aware that the others in the room, all standing, were terrified to speak to him. For now, the computer monitors were blank, and with nothing to do but wait, he glanced at his watch, just to observe and appreciate the orderly, measured sweep of its second hand, the unruly universe tamed.

But one of the technicians, Irina Roslyakova, a nervous young woman in a crisp white lab worker's coat, apparently misunderstood his action.

She blurted, "Three more minutes, Chief Administrator."

He gave her a slow, sidelong glance, gestured with a massive hand to the digital time display above the blank screens on the far wall. "As I can read for myself."

He saw Roslyakova flinch, bow her head, step back out of his sight line. She was twenty-eight, and two weeks earlier had been promoted three levels to become head of VEKTOR's mapping division, because the three technicians above her in rank had been arrested. Two had already been shot.

Point made, Gorokhov turned his attention back to the dark glass wall.

The glass itself was ordinary, fully transparent. It was the coarse metal mesh embedded in it that cut the transmission of light. But it wasn't so dark as to completely block the view of the projection room on the other side. In it, three perceivers waited as well, impatient in their reclining encounter beds.

The perceivers were three of VEKTOR's best. Number One, a tall man, soft and pasty in appearance, was renowned for capturing the coordinates of an American drone so precisely that the Iranians had been able to intercept and bring it down with minimal damage. Though, of course, the insufferable Iranians explained their feat as a triumph of their technological skills.

Number Two and Number Three, both women, were equally unimpressive in appearance, one young, the other older. But in addition to the innate talent to perceive, both women had impressive visual memory. Most importantly, none of the three operatives had any connection to what had happened three weeks ago.

Number One nervously scratched at his nose, taking care not to disturb the web of interconnected EEG electrodes attached to his forehead, temples, and shaved scalp. On the far wall of the monitoring room, the blank screen waiting to display his output flickered briefly as nerve cells fired randomly in response to the stimulus.

Behind Gorokhov, a senior technician, Igor Byko, also recently promoted, barked into his headset's microphone, "Number One, refrain from motion. Acquiring location in twenty seconds."

Gorokhov kept his full attention on the three perceivers. They were all motionless now, lying back, eyes closed, breathing slowly as they entered their sensitive, meditative state. Their shaved scalps glistened with sweat in the gaps between the electrodes.

"Ten," Byko intoned, and continued counting down until he reached "Three." Two seconds later, above the time display, the small panel displaying the installation's security status switched from all green to all amber. The electromagnetic shielding protecting the projection room had been disabled.

Though it was late afternoon at VEKTOR's underground facility, it was now midnight in New Mexico. There the sun's electromagnetic interference with the perceivers' efforts would be at its least disruptive. At the same time, while the monitoring room Gorokhov and his technicians were in remained shielded, the projection room in which the perceivers prepared to become operational was now unprotected, allowing each perceiver's consciousness to be sent forth. Studies, and exceptional espionage, had led VEKTOR to conclude it would take at least eleven minutes for America's NSA satellites to alert CROSSWIND personnel to the change of status in VEKTOR's shielding. They would then try to exploit the opportunity by having their own perceivers attempt to see what was happening here. Therefore, VEKTOR's perceivers now had just under eleven minutes to accomplish their mission.

The time display began to count down.

"One, Two, and Three in theta," the senior technician said.

Gorokhov checked the EEG displays himself, saw that the brainwave tracings of all three perceivers had fallen into the distinctive pattern of lessening frequency and greater amplitude than the alpha and beta waves of consciousness. At theta stage, each perceiver was now in what appeared to be light sleep. But Gorokhov knew they were searching.

Two minutes passed. The room grew hotter, filled with the clinical scent of warm plastic and electronics. Then one of the output screens flickered again with what appeared to be another random display of dark and light shadows.

"Number One now in gamma," Byko reported.

Gorokhov leaned forward. His chair creaked. Gamma waves indicated that though the subject was asleep, there was a form of conscious effort arising most significantly from the visual cortex. It was a brainwave pattern observed most strongly in Buddhist monks with extensive experience in meditation techniques, as well as being a hallmark of the most talented perceivers.

Whatever Number One perceived, this change in his brainwave pattern indicated his resting mind was attempting to find order in the sensations he was experiencing. The chief administrator had long since given up trying to comprehend how a projected mind could be aware of anything without sense organs. It was enough that it could.

"I think it's a road," Dr. Jelavich said. He was an older man, trained in the army, short white hair, a constant look of amusement.

The shadow patchwork on Number One's screen began to coalesce. From an engineering perspective, Gorokhov knew he was looking at a computer-generated image constructed from the neurons now firing in the man's visual cortex. All of VEKTOR's perceivers had spent thousands of hours in MRI scanners capable of resolving individual neurons. While the perceivers viewed carefully calibrated collections of films and photographs, the firing patterns of those neurons were precisely recorded. Now each individual perceiver had a database of millions of different readings from which a VEKTOR algorithm could match a particular pattern of signals from the perceiver's visual cortex to an approximation of the visual scene that could account for it. The technology had arisen from the increasingly successful attempts to provide artificial sight for the blind.

Although the images created by this technique, for now, were low resolution and rarely included color, they did allow specialists who lacked the talent to project their own minds to, in effect, see through the perceivers' disembodied eyes. This exponentially increased VEKTOR's ability to identify key mission targets.

Engineering aside, from a purely observational perspective, Gorokhov likened the experience to that of watching an old-fashioned photograph come to clarity in the red light of a darkroom, the image slowly emerging from a blank sheet of paper within a chemical bath.

By 00:06:00, as the output screens for Number Two and Number Three also began to resolve into visual images, Number One's output was now clearly that of a road, two-lane, lit by headlights of a moving vehicle and observed from within the vehicle's cabin. From time to time, at a frame rate of about one new image every four seconds, a bright smear indicated other vehicles passing in the opposite direction. The mission's targets were traveling.

With six minutes left in the safe window, all three perceivers had linked with the targets and were now traveling with them. Knowing the approximate location of the targets accounted for the swift success of tonight's attempt. In previous attempts over the past three weeks, targets had to be searched for almost randomly across multiple time zones, and there had been only two successful contacts. Since the night the chase teams had been slaughtered outside the Mexican city of Tampico, there had been no contact at all.

But now the details came quickly. Number Two concentrated on the immediate surroundings. Her output captured images of the vehicle's dashboard. The instrument configuration would allow VEKTOR experts to determine the most likely make and model of whatever was being driven.

Number Three now tried to capture nearby landmarks, difficult at night and in motion. Her efforts yielded only a series of road signs, most of whose lettering in the reconstructed images was too indistinct to be read, though Gorokhov knew she would retain the visual information with enough clarity to later transcribe what she was seeing.

With one minute left in the window, Gorokhov growled, angered that insufficient information had been collected to determine the current location of the vehicle. It would be twenty-four hours until another attempt could be safely made. Someone in this room would have to pay for that, be made an example—and from the tension he felt rising around him, they all knew it.

Then the unruly universe delivered an unexpected prize.

On Number One's screen, the road changed. The vehicle had turned, and come to a stop. Within seconds, on all three perceivers' screens, from three slightly different perspectives, a brightly lit building came into view, detail growing with each passing moment.

"Thirty seconds," Byko said.

Gorokhov raised a hand. "I want more detail. What kind of building is that?"

"A warehouse, I believe," Dr. Jelavich said.

Gorokhov gave a grunt of agreement. He could see the resemblance. There was a large sign as well, unreadable for now, but possibly captured in the three perceivers' memories.

"Twenty seconds." There was the metallic snap of safety covers being opened over the rocker switchers that would reestablish the projection room's shielding. "Standing by to recall."

"No." Gorokhov stood, knowing the risk he was taking. "Wait for the details to fill in. We need to know what that sign says."

Byko blurted out his apprehension. "Chief Administrator, by now the Americans will know that the facility's exposed. If CROSSWIND has perceivers already deployed, they—"

"You're excused." Gorokhov didn't bother looking at the nervous man. He kept his attention on the output screens, heard the door to the corridor click open, hiss shut as Byko left. No one dared argue with the chief administrator.

"There's a new light source," Jelavich said.

On Number Two's screen, a dramatic change in contrast. Now the woman was perceiving the interior of the vehicle in bright light. At once, Gorokhov understood that the vehicle's door had been opened; its dome light had come on. As the details filled in, there in the rearview mirror was a pattern he recognized. It was a face so familiar to Number Two's visual cortex that VEKTOR's algorithm was instantly able to match it. The final prize.

The driver of the vehicle was General Stasik Sergeyevich Borodin. Betrayer of the Motherland.

For five years, Borodin had served as VEKTOR's chief military liaison. He had personally developed the training and tactics employed by the pinnacle of VEKTOR's achievements: *tenevyye voiny*, the shadow warriors.

He also had been instrumental in crafting the overall strategy and operational tactics of Operatsiya Kosa—Operation Scythe—the masterstroke that would one day unleash the shadow warriors and in hours eliminate America's influence over Europe. In the days that would follow, the NATO Alliance would collapse as its nations at last understood that true strength and security could only be achieved by coming to terms with Russia, and not some powerless and degenerate upstart across the Atlantic. The younger leaders had embraced the general's plan as one that would lead their country to the greatness that was its destiny. But Gorokhov and the others of his generation, who had come of age under Stalin and seen their country rise to become a superpower under Khrushchev, understood Scythe for what it truly was: the final battle of the Cold War, the conflict that in their hearts had never ended, and now, at last, would be won.

Then, three weeks ago, the colonel who was to have led Scythe was found dead in his quarters. A heart attack. Unsuspected, but in Russia, not unusual.

With a year still to go until all preparations for Scythe were complete, General Borodin had valiantly stepped forward to take command of the operation himself, until a permanent replacement for the colonel could be found.

Forty-eight hours after Borodin had been given the command codes for accessing and deploying the prototype shadow warriors, he had disappeared with them. Two days after that, the colonel's autopsy results indicated the heart attack wasn't from natural causes. It had been induced by a *skorpion*, a radio-frequency device created by the KGB, no larger than a packet of cigarettes. When placed in contact with the victim's chest, even through clothes it was capable of sending the healthiest heart into uncontrolled arrhythmia from a single high-frequency electromagnetic pulse, leaving not a mark.

One of the devices was missing from the quartermaster's armory. The technicians responsible for stealing it were identified, interrogated, and the final truth was revealed.

The colonel's killer was Borodin.

Operation Scythe had been completely disrupted, the carefully constructed timetable in ruins, and whatever Borodin planned to do with the shadow warriors, it was unknown.

"We have him," the psychologist said.

"Recall and reestablish shields," Gorokhov ordered. In less than ten seconds, the three perceivers were stirring and the entire facility was shielded once again.

VEKTOR's chief administrator allowed himself a rare smile, and let the others see it to know they had done well. He turned to the young head of the mapping division. "The instant you've confirmed coordinates, inform the major."

And with that simple order, Gorokhov knew that Borodin was already dead, and the nightmare finally over.

7

"What is that stink?" New Mexico State Police Officer Ronnie Best waved his uniform hat in front of his face. The dank, closed-in warehouse storage unit reeked.

"Stiffs, what else?" Officer Jace Cruickshank had ten years on his partner in the NMSP, plus another six as a patrolman in Albuquerque. He pushed past Ronnie in the narrow doorway. "It's what they do."

"Not like this." The cavernous space looked to Ronnie as if a bomb had gone off. In an area dead center, about fifty feet by eighty, the cracked concrete floor was slick with a glistening stew of blood, thickened with ragged chunks of what Ronnie took to be human flesh, some pieces more recognizable than others. He was grateful the crime scene was so dark. Only a few thin shafts of sunlight penetrated the sealed, dirt-caked windows that ran along the top of the far wall.

Ronnie ran a finger under his collar to loosen it. The room's air was close, claustrophobia-making. It had to be at least thirty degrees hotter inside than out. He and Jace would have to take care that the sweat dripping off them didn't fall near the evidence. Flies buzzed everywhere.

"Don't think it was a bomb," his partner said. Jace was taking slow, deliberate steps around the worst of the mess, heading for the long workbench in the center of the open area. The workbench was constructed of two-by-fours and thick plywood, something someone had nailed together on the cheap. Its top surface held stacks of electronic black boxes with colored wires, tape decks, DVD players, and a few old television monitors, the fat ones with picture tubes. "Can't smell explosives. Nothing burnt."

"Something hacked these folks to pieces." Ronnie tried breathing through his mouth, but that only made the stench worse: He could taste it. He took a look around with his long, eight-battery flashlight, half expecting to see reflective eyes glowing back at him from the shadows. "Think maybe coyotes?"

"All this blood, then where're the tracks?" Jace bent down behind the workbench. A moment later, he stood up, hat in hand, bare forearm wiping his brow. "Two more under here. What's left of them."

Ronnie grimaced, played his flashlight over the floor along the other side, searching for a clean path to the workbench. A Crime Scene Unit team was on its way from Santa Fe. All he and Jace had to do was guard the place. Not that that would stop his partner from trying to find some vital clue before the CSU specialists did. He was always scrounging for a commendation and had scored a few of them.

Ronnie stopped near the workbench, at least five feet from the closest smear of blood and tissue. He aimed his flashlight down at the same slick pile Jace did, at what looked like a collection of splintered bones embedded in . . . things red and gelatinous. He recognized part of a jaw, complete with teeth, and what had once been a shoulder. Thin strands of what was probably clothing twisted through everything, its original colors and details obliterated by the amount of blood that had turned the fibers black.

Even with the stomach-churning smell, Ronnie was surprised he wasn't more upset. But this type of mutilation . . . it was so unreal, it was difficult to believe he was looking at the remains of people. Real ones.

"So, Sherlock. If this wasn't a bomb or an animal attack, what could chew people up like this? Meth head with a machete?"

Jace shrugged. "I wanna know what the vics were doing in here. That might tell us who snuffed them, and how."

"Illegal dirty movie stuff?"

"You wish." Jace's flashlight beam went to a far corner, settled on a desk with a closed laptop. He started for it.

"Don't touch anything. Feds won't like it."

"Yeah, yeah. Been there, done that."

Ronnie checked his watch. Shouldn't be more than half an hour more before CSU turned up. He glanced to the side of the bench. Saw a dark stain on the concrete that didn't look like blood. "Hey, Jace. You see this?"

His partner didn't turn around, kept going toward the desk. "What?"

Ronnie crouched down, carefully dabbed a finger in the stain. He didn't have to try to smell the liquid to know what it was. "Motor oil." He aimed his flashlight against the old wood wall, saw a mechanic's dolly, two tires, heavy duty judging from the thick tread, a box of Amsoil cans. "Someone parked a vehicle here. Small truck, maybe? Mighta been jacked. Could be the motive."

Jace had reached the desk and was examining it. "If this was a robbery, why leave the good stuff? Check this laptop."

Ronnie joined him at the desk. They both stood their distance, knowing the professionalism expected of them. "And look at that." Jace shone his light on a coffee mug by the laptop, open on the desk. Ronnie recognized the mug's logo: KOB 4, Eyewitness News. Out of Albuquerque. He watched it from time to time. "That's a long way from home."

A jarring metallic racket shook the warehouse.

They both reflexively spun, hands going to their holstered sidearms. The sudden glare of daylight from the rolling garage-type door was blinding, though Ronnie caught the silhouettes of three people standing there. Relieved, he saw no weapons, motioned to Jace to ease off.

The three walked forward. Two men, one woman between them. They held up badges.

"You are the officers who called this in?" the man on the left said. He had some kind of accent, but then who didn't these days? He also looked out of place here to Ronnie. Fair-haired, fair-skinned, too pale to have spent much time in New Mexico. He was in a suit, too, a dark one, with a tie. Crazy loco in this heat.

Jace, quick off the mark for any credit, answered at once. "Yes sir. Officer Cruickshank. This is Officer Best."

"Anyone else here?" the man asked.

"No sir."

Ronnie tried unsuccessfully to make out the man's badge, but the woman moved in front of him as if to block a closer view. Her hair was white blond, not much longer than the men's. Her dark suit, though, was definitely cut for a woman, and a good-looking one at that. Ronnie glanced down. No heels, though she was on the short side. Hiking boots. Unusual.

"Is there problem?"

She spoke with the same accent. *Slavic?* "No, ma'am," Ronnie said, "I just don't recognize your ID." Something wasn't right here. These people weren't with the Crime Scene Unit, and their badge cases didn't have FBI cards.

"That's understandable. It's NSA."

Ronnie looked at Jace. "National Security Agency."

His partner's eyes widened. "This is big."

"Is anyone else here?" the blond man asked again.

The other guy, same suit, same pale skin, hadn't been heard from yet, but Ronnie had already noticed that the man's eyes hadn't stopped moving over the warehouse since he and his pals had entered it.

"Ah, Jace . . . ," Ronnie began, but his overeager partner took the lead again.

"Officer Best and me, we got the call to check out the scene. Neighbors renting the other side of the warehouse called in about a ruckus last night."

"Anyone else coming?" the man asked.

"CSU's on their way," Ronnie said quickly. He saw the woman was checking out the workbench with a surprising lack of concern about disturbing it. Maybe NSA agents didn't often investigate crime scenes.

"Be careful, ma'am." Ronnie shone his flashlight at the floor where she'd stepped. There was a bloody boot print. "Evidence."

"Do you know what they were after?" the woman asked.

" 'They,' ma'am?"

"Criminals who did this."

"To be honest, ma'am, we don't know what happened here. Let alone who might've done it."

The woman half acknowledged his polite reprimand, went back to examining the components on the bench. She looked at Ronnie's partner. "What is this place?" Her tone definitely suggested she expected to be answered promptly.

"Not certain, ma'am." Jace sounded apologetic, though Ronnie didn't know why. Working out what had happened here was the job of the CSU and the detectives. "Maybe something to do with TV news?"

The woman seemed to find that interesting. She spoke in . . . Russian, maybe . . . to the man who'd stayed silent until now. Ronnie couldn't be sure. The conversation ended when she gave a nod, like a signal, and the two men split up, heading to opposite sides of the open space. They walked as if searching for something, but not really.

"Crime Scene Unit," the woman said. "When will they be here? For evidence."

From the hesitant way his partner answered her, Ronnie sensed Jace was finally clueing in to a possible problem. "Any second now, ma'am. We can confirm that with the two other officers checking the other warehouse unit right next door. They'll know."

The woman looked off at something in the shadows. "No. That won't be necessary." She reached inside her jacket, pulled out what must have been a gun because she shot Jace then. Once in the head.

Watching his partner's body crumple was for Ronnie like watching a slow-motion Red Zone playback. By the time it dawned on him that he should be drawing his own weapon, he heard a noise behind and turned. Saw the blond man with a gun.

And that was it.

Major Sofia Ilinichna Kalnikova looked down at the body of the American who had foolishly tried to outwit her. The state officer stared up, sightless, at the ceiling, his mouth opening and closing like a dying fish, a froth of blood bubbling on his slack lips. Aiming lower to be sure she destroyed the brain stem, the major directed another silenced round into his head. The unpleasant sound of labored breathing stopped.

A second silenced shot hissed in the warehouse as Captain Gregor Malkov delivered the coup de grace to the other officer.

The major turned her attention to the carnage littering the concrete floor. There was no question what happened here, or how.

"Berserkers." Kalnikova spoke in Russian, though the term in English sounded little different. It was the name she and her fellow soldiers had given to what the VEKTOR bureaucrats called shadow warriors. It more accurately described them and their capabilities. "But why? What did he want here?" The major's questions, in Russian, were for herself as much as her two agents. There'd be no doubt whom she meant. Thirteen days earlier, three teams had set out from Moscow in pursuit of rogue general Stasik Sergeyevich Borodin. Kalnikova's team had been sent directly to America, to remain in position as last-ditch backup in the event the general evaded the other two teams.

Those teams, aided by VEKTOR perceivers who had made sporadic contact with Borodin, had succeeded in tracing him, his squad, and the prototypes on the general's evasive hopscotch from Mumbai to São Paulo to Havana. The teams had finally made contact outside a dusty village north of the Mexican city of Tampico. The major measured her team's success by the fact that it had not been the first to face what the general had unleashed.

Those teams had died horribly, as had the victims here.

"Could he be after video equipment?" Colonel Vasilyev asked.

The team's FSB liaison had an easy command of English, but obviously needed better knowledge of what passed for suitable clothing in this region. The major's team had entered America virtually unnoticed, with identities, passports, and business visas to match their cover story. Here in America's desert states, though, the dark suits and business attire that had been unremarkable in New York stood out unacceptably. Kalnikova filed judgment for later action.

She and Malkov were the active members of the three-member team. Both soldiers. Both prepared to do whatever was required to keep General Borodin from selling VEKTOR's prize research to the Americans. The major, though, had begun to wonder: If that's what Borodin's intentions were, why hadn't the general simply turned himself over to the authorities once he entered the country?

"Why would he need video equipment?" Malkov asked. "Any phone can be a camera."

Kalnikova looked around the warehouse now turned slaughterhouse. The flies, the scattered body parts, reminded her of her time in Chechnya, though the smell was different, this flesh uncooked. Also like a strategic strike in a war zone, there was a purpose in this destruction. The general wouldn't unleash VEKTOR's ultimate creations on a whim. He'd wanted something here. What?

A radio clipped to one of the dead officers sputtered to life. American voices requesting specific directions for the compound, asking which gate they should use. The crime scene specialists were arriving.

Vasilyev looked to Kalnikova. At her signal, her two men immediately checked their weapons, snapped in fresh magazines, then took up position on either side of the open garage door.

Garage door. Kalnikova realized what she'd missed. "There was a vehicle here. That's what he took."

Vasilyev agreed. "Either the vehicle, or what it contained."

That made sense, too. VEKTOR's remote viewers had passed word that when General Borodin arrived at this warehouse last night, he appeared to be traveling in a motor caravan large enough to hold both his squad and all six prototype containment units. It wasn't likely he'd need a second vehicle for transportation. Whatever had been stored in here had been something special. Something else he needed for his plan. Whatever that turned out to be.

Kalnikova saw a laptop computer on the desk. She smiled. It was as good as a filing cabinet full of documents. She was folding down its screen as a white SUV with an official emblem pulled up and stopped outside the open garage door.

Three men got out, each in a blue nylon windbreaker. Two of them carried large metal cases. The crime scene specialists.

The major slipped the laptop under one arm. With her free hand, she held up her identification as she walked briskly toward the three men, announced herself: "Gentlemen, Maria Bennetov, National Security Agency."

Their momentary surprise lasted just long enough for Vasilyev and Malkov to pick them off.

Kalnikova helped drag the three bodies into the warehouse.

"Anything else?" Vasilyev asked.

The major took a last look around. If there were any further answers here, they'd be in the computer. "Burn them."

She glanced at the bodies of the crime scene specialists, noting their worn jeans, cowboy boots, casual shirts. That was the protective coloration her team needed, and which Vasilyev had failed to provide. "Then we go shopping," she said.

8

"Hey, hon, you're in early."

It was eight o'clock at night. Molly's Café was packed, alive with the hum of conversation and laughter and clatter of dishes. Most of the diners were couples, not the midnight stragglers and night-shift workers Matt was more accustomed to.

Jan scanned the crowded room. All the window booths were taken. The couple sitting in Matt's usual had just started to dig into their thick sandwiches and a plate of deep-fried onion rings.

"I can put you at the counter."

Chrome-trimmed barstools with cracked red-vinyl seatbacks ran along an old deli counter. Five stools were vacant.

"Sit exactly where you were last night." It was Caparelli's voice in his earbud.

"I'll wait."

"Could be a while."

"No hurry." Matt didn't know if that was true or not, but Caparelli had stressed consistency—maintaining the pattern—was important. He found a place to stand between the door and a glassed-in cooler where trays of thickly frosted multilayer cakes and deep-crust pies turned slowly. There were some well-thumbed newspaper sections hung on a rack, and Matt took one, running his eyes down an article about hot local real estate, the stream of words unable to dislodge his only thought.

Who was he actually waiting for? Or should it be, for what?

Thirty minutes later, Matt was in his regular booth by the window. He wasn't hungry, but ordered what he always did, same as he had when . . .

Jan poured coffee from her battered metal carafe. "Night off, or a new shift?"

"Got the week off." Caparelli had arranged it, though Matt didn't think the Arlington County Police Department had put up much of a fight to hold onto a publicly tainted officer condemned to desk duty. His IA handlers hadn't even contacted him to ask what was going on.

Jan gave him a look.

"Nothing bad," he said. "I'll be . . . working for a different department for a few days."

Jan was smart enough to know he wasn't telling her the truth, and kind enough to accept the lie. "A change is as good as a rest." She gave him a consoling pat on the shoulder, then threaded her way through the crowded tables, back through the swinging door to the noisy kitchen.

Matt looked out the window. Saw a small silver car flying through the air. Blinked and it was gone. Memory playing tricks.

He heard someone stop by his table, turned abruptly to see—

Jan. She put his Breakfast Scramble on the fake wood laminate, gave him another of her looks. "Expecting someone else?"

"No. Yes." He glanced down at the plate. "Looks good."

"Bagel's coming." She was gone again.

Matt ate without tasting, and Jan kept his coffee topped up, asking no more questions.

Finally, he pushed his empty plate away, wondering what to do next, then remembered something else he usually did. He pulled out his phone to check the day's scores and who was playing.

"You can help me."

Matt almost dropped his phone. Looked up.

She stood before him, softly backlit by the café's hanging globe lights. No model or movie star, but the energy that seemed to emanate from Laura Hart was, to Matt, the energy life gives, plain and simple. And real. It was Caparelli's crazy story that was unreal. A ghost? A wraith? No such thing.

"What's . . ." He coughed, his throat unexpectedly dry. "Excuse me.

What's the problem?" That's how he had answered before, without the interruption.

Laura didn't seem to notice, merely repeated what she'd said, telling him she had to get to 610 E Street, southwest.

"Is she there?" Caparelli's voice echoed in his ear.

Laura's clear green eyes clouded briefly. "In DC," she added.

That was new. Matt was sure she'd not said that before. He had.

"It's okay. We've got her on the scope now. Didn't see her enter. Keep talking."

Matt continued with the script he'd rehearsed with Caparelli. "You've missed the last Metro." Even though, this early in the evening, that wasn't true, Caparelli had said the key was to make everything familiar, let Laura take the lead.

He waited then as he'd been instructed, making no offer to call a cab, as he had before.

She blinked. "You can help me."

It was like a recording being run back, reset, replayed. A new thought struck Matt, disturbing in its simplicity. *If Caparelli's on the level, I'm actually talking with a corpse. . . .*

Then, another, more rational part of his brain kicked in, the part that had saved the human species from the madness of existence: the part responsible for denial.

Whatever Caparelli's outfit was up to, none of it jibed with the world Matt lived in. This *had* to be some kind of test, he reasoned. Maybe even of this girl. For all he knew, Laura Hart could be a turncoat operative.

Nothing had really changed. All he had to do was play his part, get the information Caparelli was after, then he'd be off the hook and the CROSSWIND boys and girls could go back to playing their top-secret games without him.

"I can help you," Matt said, then continued as instructed. He gestured to the empty seat across from him. "You'll be more comfortable if you sit down."

Laura looked at the other side of the booth, almost as if she'd never seen one before. Then slid into it, slowly.

"Coffee?" Jan gave Matt a wink as she arrived with the bagel.

"She drinks tea," Caparelli's voice interrupted. *"With lemon."*

"You want tea, right?" Matt said. "With lemon."

For a moment, Laura looked bewildered, staring first at him, then at Jan, before turning to her reflection in the window. She brought her hand to her face.

Jan looked at Matt, her eyebrows raised. "Tea, please, Jan," Matt said. "And a menu."

"Sure thing, hon." She left.

"Talk to her about the address. Get her to make the connection to work, to making her report."

Matt cleared his throat and Laura turned back to him.

"Six-ten E Street, southwest," he said.

"I need to go there."

"You've missed the Metro."

She looked thoughtfully at her hands resting on the tabletop. "I saw a cab." She looked out the window again. "On the street." She turned her attention back to Matt. "I've been here before. With you."

That was when Matt finally understood what was really going on. *This is what Caparelli wasn't man enough to tell me.* Whatever this girl's job had been, she'd been exposed to something disturbing enough to unhinge her, make her *think* she was the ghost of her coworker, the driver who'd died two nights ago. That's why all this effort to support her delusion, pull her in for treatment.

"Yeah," Matt said. His irritation grew as he replayed in his mind Caparelli's convoluted cover story, how the agent had manipulated him into this. Not that he could have prevented it, Matt knew. There was no recourse against covert ops. Better just to fade away without drawing any more attention to himself. He continued with his script. "You were here with me, last night."

Laura bit her lip. "No . . . not last night. I was with the general. I'm not sure where . . ."

"Get her focused," Caparelli's voice hissed. *"Say the address again. Get her thinking of her job."*

Matt repeated the address. "That's where you work, right?"

"Yes." Laura's face brightened. "I work for Vanguard Research Associates. We prepare background reports on potential new hires for the personnel departments of *Fortune* 500 companies. I'm a research associate."

"That was her cover. Give her the sign."

Caparelli had taken Matt through a standard recognition code used by his project's field personnel. At the time, Matt had felt ridiculous, as if he'd stepped into a James Bond movie. Now feeling even more the fool, he said, "I was in your office and saw three pictures on the wall. The one in the middle has a blue frame."

Laura stared at him, and as Matt waited for the countersign he became intensely aware of how the overhead lights were reflecting as golden highlights in her flecked green-brown eyes, and the way wisps of chestnut-colored hair escaped the loose mass she'd tied back. The bustle and din of the café faded into the background. It was as if he and she were the only ones in Molly's.

"I like the one on the right," she finally said. "It has a red frame."

Matt blinked, and the rush of reality, the noise of life, came back to him. "It's closest to the window," he completed.

Laura leaned closer. "What department are you in?"

"Tell her you work for Daniel."

"I work for Daniel," Matt said.

"I have to tell him something."

So I guessed right, Matt thought. *This girl* is *delusional. She does think she's the woman from the car crash. Caparelli had better be—*

"Lemon's coming." Jan plunked down a mug and a metal pot on the table. A tea bag floated in the mug.

Laura's gaze fixed on the steam rising from the mug.

This poor kid needed professional help. What the hell was he doing here? "Tell me," Matt said.

She looked up, as if confused. "I told you. Didn't I?"

"Don't contradict her. Keep her talking."

"You told me a lot," Matt said, improvising on the spot. "But I don't know what part to tell Daniel. Is it something about . . . about the general?" Caparelli hadn't said anything about a military connection, but it was one way to prompt her. One way to push this charade to a quicker resolution.

"Careful!" Caparelli's voice snapped. *"Lead her—but don't feed her information."*

Matt's patience with the agent was almost at an end. Whatever the purpose of this conversation was, Laura Hart was suffering from some sort of emotional break, and Caparelli, who was probably responsible for her condition, was playing her with his coerced support, and without regard for consequences.

"The general?" Laura asked. "Borodin?" Her breathing quickened, in and out.

Matt hesitated, unsure.

"Caidin! Agree with her!"

"Yes. Borodin."

Laura stared at him, as if she were listening to a different controller speaking to her through a separate earpiece.

He was losing her attention. He cast Caparelli's script aside. "Was General Borodin the man in the car beside you?" Maybe this woman's coworker, the driver of the car, had had some highly placed military in the passenger seat with her? That could explain why the mystery passenger—or his or her body—had been spirited away discreetly. Because there *had* been a passenger—Matt knew that for a certainty. That airbag had deployed. The traffic tapes had been wiped.

"What are you doing? Don't add details!"

But the damage was done. Laura was agitated now. "In the car," she said. "The car. He was just there. Not the general."

"Stop her!"

"One of the others. One of . . . ODIN? No . . . not that one . . ."

"Stop her now!" Caparelli shouted so loudly that Matt was surprised Laura didn't hear him. But she was staring down at her mug of tea again as if mesmerized by it, talking softer, faster.

"It was TYR he sent. . . . All those people who died in the house . . . They never saw them coming. . . ."

"Say the address, Caidin! Get her off this! Restore the pattern! You have to—"

Caparelli's voice was drowning Laura out. Matt yanked out the earbud.

"Six-ten E Street," Matt said. "I can help you." He reached to touch her hand, just as he had the dying driver's.

Immediately Laura shuddered, almost convulsed, gripped his hand so hard a shock of pain shot through him.

Startled, Matt looked down. Their joined hands dripped blood.

"You!" she said. "You were there! I saw the taxi, and he was beside me, and you were there—here—in the window when—"

"Everything okay, hon?"

Laura whirled, startled, and pushed up from the booth, pulling Matt's hand with hers, hitting the mug of brewing tea and sending it flying toward Jan and—

Matt's outstretched hand was suddenly, achingly, impossibly, empty.

Laura Hart had *vanished.*

9

Before this mission, Stasik Borodin had visited the United States only twice. Once to New York City. Once to Washington DC. Both times, he'd traveled under false names, part of an official military delegation whose every moment was precisely scheduled. All "free time" activities, from museum visits to a Broadway performance of *The Lion King*, had been carefully managed, supervised. Neither trip, intentionally, had allowed any experience of the real America.

But now, in the early evening, here he was in this foolish country's heartland, outside a Walmart Supercenter in Colorado Springs, just off the highway.

"It could be a camp of Roma." Like him, Captain Korolev was fascinated by the scene before them. The enormous parking lot was home to seven motor homes larger than Moscow city buses, four smaller RVs the equal in size of their own Vista Cruiser, six pickup trucks with assorted camper roofs, cars with trailers, and cars with no attachments—all of them lined up where electrical and water hookups were made available.

The general gazed out at the small windows of the vehicles lit by amber light, heard the hum of generators, muffled television, and warring music creating a dense aural backdrop like the rush of ocean waves on beaches.

"But instead of traveling from village to village, I understand they go from store to store." Korolev drew in a deep inhalation of smoke from an insipid domestic cigarette, then flicked it away on the pavement.

"Pick that up," Borodin said. "We must be . . ." He searched for the words in English. "Politically correct."

Korolev laughed at that notion, but he retrieved the still-glowing butt, then settled back against the Winnebago to wait for Piotr Janyk, their comrade with the best command of English.

Another ten minutes and another cigarette, and Janyk wheeled a large shopping cart out of the Walmart's brightly lit main entrance. Its wire basket was filled with purchases.

Janyk handed the sales receipt to Borodin.

"You found everything?" the general asked.

"Even the automotive paint."

Borodin hadn't expected any difficulties. This morning, he had consulted the Walmart website. Each item on the supply list was ordinary, innocuous, and in stock.

"Good," Korolev said. "We'll make over the van tomorrow. Give it twenty-four hours to cure, then continue."

The general was pleased. All was on schedule, exactly as he had planned, exactly as he had led his men to believe. "Janyk, give me cash."

Janyk handed over a roll of bills. "McDonald's?"

Borodin allowed himself a smile. "An army travels on its stomach." He turned to Korolev. "Have the others help you unload into the van."

Korolev slammed his heavy fist against the side of the Winnebago, shouting at the others to fall in as Janyk rolled the shopping cart to the rear of the motor home. That was where they'd parked the van they'd acquired—stolen—from the warehouse on the outskirts of Santa Fe. Now it was on a car trailer, covered by a blue plastic tarp. To be safe from inspection, the squad had already exchanged the van's license plates twice with plates from similar models. Tomorrow, though, thanks to Janyk's shopping venture, it would be dark blue instead of white. With its aerial mast disassembled and stowed inside until it became necessary, the former television news van would continue to be invisible when it came time to drive it openly to the target site.

Such an easy country, the general thought. Such a wonder America hadn't come under attack from within more often.

It was a ten-minute walk to the McDonald's on the other side of the highway. Borodin set out across the brightly lit lot, enjoying the chance to move after driving all day.

As he passed the last filled row of cars parked near the entrance to the lot, he became aware of someone keeping pace with him. Not breaking stride, he pulled his mirrored sunglasses from a jacket pocket, holding them up as if to clean them, angling the lenses to reflect the view behind.

Female. Short. Pale blond hair cut short. In jeans and jacket, cowboy boots. Casual dress, but her bearing was not.

Borodin knew Colorado Springs was a major center for the American Air Force, and he'd seen many personnel on its streets, in and out of uniform. It could be nothing. But if not . . .

He had no need to check the Beretta secured in the holster under his arm—its safety was already off. He replaced his sunglasses in his jacket, then turned around as if he had forgotten something, making the first movement in reaching for his gun. If the woman was a harmless civilian and did not react, he'd simply rub his shoulder and walk past her. If not, he'd ensure she couldn't radio any colleagues.

But when he turned, her own gun was already aimed at him, half concealed by her jacket.

"Don't." She spoke in Russian.

Borodin slowly eased his hand away from his holster. He didn't recognize her, but even in that one word her accent told him she came from Moscow, or had been educated there. Most likely from the FSB, Russia's Federal Security Service. It was the latest incarnation of the KGB, though little different. But who she served wasn't important. There was only one way she could have found him with such precision. She had been sent by VEKTOR.

"I'm not alone," she added.

"I have no doubt." The general scanned the closest cars to see if he could spot her backup. She could be bluffing, though her steady gaze suggested otherwise. "What now?"

"I would like to talk first." She moved closer to him, though she was careful to keep out of reach.

"What happens second?'

"You and your men return with me. With the prototypes. You're all pensioned off as honorable men. There are no reprisals."

"No written reports."

"If you've done nothing wrong, why would there be a need?"

The general felt the day's heat still radiating from the black asphalt in surprisingly strong contrast to the cool evening breeze. Headlights still continued to rush by on the busy highway. Two people talking in a Walmart parking lot would attract no attention, unless . . .

He made his counter offer. "In six days. I'll go home with you then. With the prototypes."

"You're negotiating with me?"

Borodin shrugged with Russian fatalism. "You haven't killed me yet."

"General Borodin, I've come to you out of respect. The respect I have for you. The respect your countrymen have for you. I've made you a generous offer because it's what you deserve."

She respects me? Borodin read between the lines. "You're not FSB?"

She stood at attention, shoulders squared. "Major Sofia Ilinichna Kalnikova, Seventy-sixth Airborne."

Borodin felt himself slip into the measured calm of battle. His country hadn't sent a civil service thug to stop him—instead, he faced a combat-seasoned paratrooper. There were few women in the 76th, but those who had graduated from the Ryazan Academy were superachievers, easily the equal of the top male graduates, if not in strength, then in deadly skill.

"I am honored," he said.

"So I ask you again. Will you return home. As ordered?"

"In six days."

"Not acceptable."

Borodin swiftly reviewed the possible scenarios. He couldn't draw his Beretta in time. He couldn't reach her to physically attack before she shot him. He wouldn't surrender to her. Only one way out.

"Major Kalnikova, do you like Big Macs?"

She stared at him, uncomprehending.

"I'm going to McDonald's. Come with me." Without waiting for a response, Borodin turned and began walking away from her.

"I'll shoot."

"You won't."

A silenced round pinged off the asphalt beside him, close enough that the general felt its impact through his boot.

He halted, but did not turn around. He knew what VEKTOR wanted: an answer for the unanswerable. "You've been ordered not to kill me because those who sent you wish to know why I'm here."

"They do. But I don't."

Borodin changed tactics. He'd go back with her, as far as the Winnebago. It would be his squad of five against however many she'd brought with her, though the number of her forces was irrelevant. Nothing could withstand what he had brought with him. The inevitable consequences might well attract attention, but in the end, there was no way she could win or he could lose.

He turned back to her. "Very well. Then we shall—" Borodin stopped talking as behind the major a coil of black smoke resolved from the night.

Major Kalnikova still held her small gun in the open, close to her side where a distant observer might not notice it. "What happens next, you were going to ask?"

But the general already had his answer.

Sofia Kalnikova gasped as she felt the sudden chill against her unprotected neck, a touch that made her skin crawl. Knew exactly what it meant.

Berserker.

She threw herself forward, twisting to land on her shoulder and roll as strictly by reflex she emptied her gun uselessly into the apparition, knowing each bullet would pass through without effect.

Before her, the coil of black smoke took on its embodied state, no different in appearance from a real soldier, a living man. But it was no such thing.

It reached out toward her, long arms dissolving into jagged claws. Its angry mouth opening wider than any human mouth could stretch. Its eerie wail that of a raging wind.

She knew she was already dead, but again her reflexes refused to admit defeat.

As if a flesh-and-blood attacker were about to leap onto her, her hand sought and found within her jacket the device she had been prepared to use on Borodin if all else failed. The same device Borodin had used to put himself into a position of authority.

The berserker raced at her.

She swept out the *skorpion.*

The small, handheld unit, little larger than a phone, was set to discharge.

On a human attacker, positioned on or near the chest, it would induce a heart attack.

But berserkers were no longer human, and Kalnikova knew it was a useless attempt, driven by instinct, not reason.

She tensed, waiting for death to claim her.

The berserker *flowed* over her upraised hand.

The *skorpion* discharged with a muffled thump of its capacitor.

And the berserker *screeched* as in a blossom of electric sparks its once-human shape now billowed like a dissipating storm cloud, roiling into graying mist, then—

Nothing.

Kalnikova was on her feet in an instant, facing Borodin. His expression revealed his shock at what she'd done—as great as her own.

He reached for his gun.

In the same moment, Kalnikova ducked to the side, bracing for the impact of his bullet, only to see from the edge of her vision the general suddenly crumple as a puff of something dark burst from his arm. Then she saw something else that made her scramble to her feet.

Two more black coils forming.

"Major! Run!" Vasilyev and Malkov burst from their protective cover among the rows of parked cars, guns out, but not shooting. Her team had seen what she had done. Both men were fumbling in their own jackets, replacing their guns with *skorpions.*

Kalnikova ran for the general. He was kneeling on the ground, hugging his blood-soaked arm to his chest.

She kicked his gunshot wound before he could dodge her attack, then scooped up his Beretta as she heard Malkov scream.

Kalnikova wheeled to see a black-clad soldier pass his hand *into* Malkov's temple, then twist. His skull cracked like an eggshell. Fragments of white brain matter spewed forth in a gush of blood. His *skorpion* dropped, unused, to the ground.

Vasilyev charged at the berserker next to Malkov's body, his own *skorpion* raised, but the dark shape vanished the instant before the device discharged into empty air. He turned to Kalnikova in fear.

The major shuddered. She knew what to do with that emotion: use it, channel it, direct it toward victory. But what she felt now was not fear. It was repulsion, primal.

Her hand shook as she jammed the Beretta against the general's temple. "Call them off! Do it now!"

He stiffened in refusal.

Kalnikova began to squeeze the trigger.

And in the time it took her to draw a breath, a dark hand formed around hers, sank through her skin, her flesh, her bones, and then did something impossible that left her gaping at her hand now pulped and fused into the metal of the general's gun.

The sudden assault drained Kalnikova's body of all its strength and she fell back, helpless. Through her veil of shock, she looked up to . . . Vasilyev? No.

It was Borodin and two of his berserkers. His lips moved as if he spoke to her, but she couldn't hear, couldn't focus through the flash and pulse of sudden light. Red then blue, red then blue. The colors getting stronger, brighter. The general turning to look into them . . .

Kalnikova blinked.

Red and blue. She understood. The spinning lights of a police car.

She turned her head to see one skid to a stop as both its doors sprang open and two officers jumped out, a man with a hand weapon, a woman with a shotgun.

She saw the berserkers charge the officers. As if from a distance, heard the blast of the shotgun as it fired directly into the chest of a berserker. The cries of disbelief, then pain, soon followed by the silence of death, as the unharmed dark shape reached through the female officer's ballistic armor, penetrating deep into her chest, then slashed upward through her shoulders and dismembered her.

The other officer emptied his gun into his attacker. Then he, too, had his arms ripped off, his gut burst open.

Kalnikova felt her own crushed hand on fire. The searing heat that shot up her arm to her chest caused her pulse to pound with the thunder of her heart, turning her view of the parking lot to red.

She shook her head to clear her vision. The fiery heat was real. The berserkers had passed *through* the police car like a deadly black wave, and its gas tank had exploded.

The spreading fire was hotter than the asphalt she lay on, but not as hot as the burning pain in her hand.

All thoughts of her mission, success or failure, receded. She was simply a creature in distress needing shelter. So she began to crawl, and by the time police backup was on the scene with firefighters and an ambulance, only the truly dead were there to greet them.

10

On the evening of June 26, 2004, a dirty bomb detonated outside the Capitol Building, spreading two kilos of radioactive cesium-137 dust across Washington DC.

The president and his wife were rushed from their residence to the third sub-basement level of the White House and driven by electric cart to a classified evacuation transport hub under Union Station. There, they boarded an underground maglev train and within thirty minutes had arrived beneath Blue Ridge Summit, Pennsylvania. Their final destination was the Continuity of Government facility code-named Raven Rock. Less than sixty minutes after the initial explosion the president prepared to address the nation from the television studio in the Army's Emergency Operations Center.

That was the 2004 scenario for TRAIL RIDER, a yearly exercise run by the Secret Service and multiple other government agencies to test disaster preparedness. Since the president was in Ireland that day, his role and his wife's were taken by two Secret Service Agents. They were among the twenty-six victims who had died in the EOC studio that night. Investigating those deaths had been Daniel Caparelli's first encounter with CROSSWIND.

At the time, he had been Master Sergeant Caparelli, a Special Agent in the Army's Criminal Investigation Division. He had investigated murders before, but nothing like the scene that awaited him in that studio: twenty-six bodies battered so badly that none had an unbroken bone. Yet the skin of each victim was intact and there was no blood anywhere.

The lone survivor, found unconscious beneath other bodies, described a cloud that had moved through the studio like a miniature storm, sweeping up individuals, spinning them, throwing them against each other and against the walls, floor, and ceiling.

The story was, of course, unbelievable. It was also exactly what had happened.

After the first day of the investigation, the small team of Army CID investigators and Secret Service agents had been joined by CROSSWIND personnel. Two months later, when the investigation was closed, and after Caparelli had survived an attack by the phenomenon that had killed the others, he was released from the CID to join the other organization. More than a decade later, he was running it.

But even after all that time, Caparelli remembered very clearly his initial surprise and confusion upon learning the secret of CROSSWIND's operational capabilities. However, he had not experienced what Detective Caidin had upon learning the same: disbelief.

Caparelli had grown up in a family in which tales of second sight and the paranormal were accepted as fact. Why wouldn't they be? His grandmother had predictive dreams more often than chance could explain. His aunt was banned from playing cards in casinos across the country, though she'd never been caught cheating—because she had no need. And his sister's only child, in his charge since her mother's untimely death, had always had an uncanny ability to find lost objects.

For that reason, and others, including the thought that he could more easily protect her and care for her, Caparelli had personally recruited his niece into CROSSWIND. Laura Hart.

He might as well have been driving the car Laura died in himself.

No matter what else he and CROSSWIND found out about the circumstances of Laura's death, there was no escaping the terrible knowledge that his niece's death was his fault, and that whatever echo remained of her was inextricably bound to a stranger.

All because late one Sunday night, he had seen her name come up on his caller ID, and thinking that there would always be time enough tomorrow, he hadn't taken her call.

No matter what else, there was no coming back from that.

⚊

Forty-two of the 183 personnel assigned to CROSSWIND knew exactly what its purpose was. Three of them, with Caparelli, met in the facility's image analysis lab to review surveillance video from Molly's Café. For the video, the cameras had been positioned in an unmarked surveillance van parked across the street. The café was brightly lit, so the incident had been recorded at optical wavelengths suitable for imaging manifestations.

Simultaneously, in an assessment lab on the same floor, two other technicians and a psychologist ran Matt Caidin through what was, to CROSSWIND, a standard battery of tests to identify any latent sensitivity the detective might have in regard to remote viewing perception. In lay terms, they were testing him for psychic powers.

Previous studies by many researchers had established that a measurable electromagnetic field was generated by the electrochemical activity within the brain. CROSSWIND researchers had taken that work further and determined that the brain's EM field was not just a side effect of the brain's biochemistry, but an actual component of the universally experienced but so-far impossible-to-define phenomenon of self-awareness.

In research terms, that phenomenon was classified as "the hard problem of consciousness": Was there a nonphysical component to human consciousness?

Clearly, humans exhibited self-awareness, and considered from a strictly physical perspective, that self-awareness must arise from the particular arrangement of the molecules making up the brain and the way they interacted. The evolutionary chain that led to such complexity could be traced back to primordial forms of life and the way in which the simplest cells respond to their environment in the most basic way, blindly avoiding bad conditions and seeking good ones—all behaviors governed by electrical signals generated within and between cells.

The more different types of sensory input a life-form was capable of receiving, and the complex behaviors the life-form could undertake in response to those inputs, had led eventually to a consciousness of self. Responses to certain complex conditions were no longer blind, but involved a semblance of analysis and choice. Where simple life-forms would always avoid bad conditions, humans might willingly endure those conditions, knowing, for example, that the exertion of planting crops under a blazing sun would result in food, not immediately, but months in the future. Consciousness, having arisen from basic biological processes, thus became something more than just blind reaction, while still believed to be anchored in the complex chemical interactions of the brain.

Intriguingly, though, if those interactions were interrupted by means of an anesthetic, or by a jarring physical blow, or by delivering a small electric current to a thin, irregularly shaped section of the brain called the claustrum, consciousness vanished, even though other sections of the brain continued to function. That implied consciousness didn't arise from the brain's *overall* activity, but from a specific subset of activities. However, when consciousness vanished, so too did the distinctive EM field associated with it.

Detailed measurements of that field in conjunction with monitoring brain activity had led CROSSWIND researchers to conclude that the field carried a neural imprint of the originating brain's structure, a finding that answered another great mystery about the nature of consciousness: so-called "brain-dead" patients with no measurable brain activity who nonetheless could recall in detail events that took place around them in their hospital room or operating theater prior to their resuscitation.

For CROSSWIND researchers, then, the hard problem of consciousness was one on the brink of being answered. Human consciousness did have a non-physical component: the EM field imprinted with the brain's neural structure.

Observing the video playback of the event with Caparelli were Sam Arlo as well as the project's senior interface technician, Dr. Norma Chu. The third was one of the project's eight remaining perceivers, Leo Kushner, a tall, rawboned man who affected an untrimmed beard that gave him the look of a wild academic. Kushner had been with the project for more than a decade, frustrated by his awareness that his ability to perceive was only a fraction of that of the others.

Like Caparelli, none of the three others in the lab had had direct experience with a postmortem manifestation of a perceiver's consciousness—what the public would call a ghost. In the more than forty years the US military and intelligence communities had been utilizing remote viewing at an operational level, the official records described only a handful of similar incidents. None with a good outcome.

The café manifestation appeared to be another example.

In addition to being capable of perceiving sensory inputs while existing only as a disembodied field, other capabilities of the brain were also imprinted. One mirrored the section of the cerebellum responsible for what the experts called proprioception, the sense informing the brain of the body's physical shape and position of its limbs.

For CROSSWIND's perceivers, like Laura, who could separate their consciousness from their body, the brain's proprioceptive feedback somehow created a macroscopic interface, similar in theory to the atmospheric temperature inversions that gave rise to mirages. In this case, the interface formed between the EM field and the air projected the perceiver's body not only visually, but with a simulated—manifested—physicality.

Whatever mechanism was responsible for the manifestation's ability to also become solid, with simulated mass *and* temperature, the source of it was an even harder problem, the solution still unknown and a matter of intense research. A perceiver with the ability to project his or her mass, and thus take action at a remote site, could change the world's balance of power overnight. Ongoing research into discovering if such an ability was possible remained one of CROSSWIND's highest R&D priorities.

What was known was that, however projected physicality was accomplished, the phenomenon involved an energy-intensive process. The leading theory was that the field extracted so-called vacuum energy from the manifestation's immediate environment. CROSSWIND researchers considered this a possible link to the anecdotal reports of a sudden drop in temperature associated with apparitions commonly called ghosts. Sam Arlo's researchers were already refining equations that suggested this theory might soon become fact, and that whatever ghosts might be, they were nothing supernatural. Even in the nonphysical realm beyond death, science ruled.

On a large, wall-mounted video display in the darkened lab, Laura Hart's manifestation approached Matt Caidin's window booth and said, *"You can help me."* Voiceprint analysis had confirmed the voice was Laura's. The source of the video's soundtrack was the microphone Caidin had worn.

Arlo tapped a control on the arm of his chair to freeze the image. "Exactly when did she manifest?"

"We don't know," Caparelli said. "We had a second camera on the front door, but Laura didn't come through it. I'd guess she took form near the door, but already inside the café. Well within range of Caidin."

Range was an important consideration. Early on in the analysis of remote viewing, CROSSWIND's researchers had realized that a disassociated consciousness could not usually appear at any given coordinates. In most cases, there had to be a receptive mind nearby, someone with whom the remote perceiver could achieve rapport. Subsequent CROSSWIND experiments had worked out the approximate effective range: twenty meters, little more than sixty feet.

"So she manifested in a crowded restaurant," Chu said. The slight, almost fragile, gray-haired psychologist had been with the various incarnations of the project since it had been code-named STAR GATE, more than twenty years earlier. She'd been Laura's personal interface technician. "And no one noticed?"

Though Chu spoke about her charge with professional detachment, Caparelli knew her level of concern was as high as his. The connection between a perceiver and his or her interface technician was hyperfocused. Had to be. For reasons still to be determined, intense emotions were key to the experience.

"No reaction from customers on the video." To Caparelli, this was easily explained. "Busy place. People coming and going. Even if someone did see Laura materialize directly in front of them, their first choice would be to think they hadn't noticed her before."

"As in, 'I don't believe in no ghosts.'" Arlo made a note on his tablet computer, restarted the playback. All watched in silence until Caidin's recorded voice asked: *"Was General Borodin the man in the car beside you?"*

"Pause," Chu said. The video froze. "That's new information. Borodin in the *car*? Where did that come from?"

"I'm not sure yet," Caparelli said. "Keep listening."

Arlo restarted the video.

"In the car. The car. He was just there. Not the general. One of the others—"

"Others? What others?" Kushner asked.

On the screen, Laura continued. *"—One of . . . ODIN? No . . . not that one . . . it was TYR he sent . . . all those people who died in the house . . . they never saw them coming . . ."*

This time, Caparelli had Arlo stop the playback. "ODIN and TYR. Nordic gods. Obviously code designations. Question is, where'd Laura get them?"

Chu looked perplexed. "They're not from any of her mission logs."

Kushner agreed. "I've never encountered them, either."

There was no easy explanation for what Caparelli proposed next, but it was the only possibility that made sense to him. A disturbing one. "There is one obvious answer," he said, "When Laura made contact with Borodin, wherever he was, there was a VEKTOR perceiver with him."

Chu understood Caparelli's reasoning. "VEKTOR back-traced Laura's projection, and one of their perceivers manifested in her car."

"Exactly," Caparelli said. If a perceiver's consciousness reached out to a location where another perceiver was present, in a matter of moments the second perceiver could identify and connect to the first, then project itself back to the first perceiver's location, like radar automatically locking onto the launch site of a missile and instantly firing back. The phenomenon was called back-tracing, and was the key reason why both CROSSWIND and VEKTOR shielded their facilities. Neither side in their ongoing psychic war wanted one of their perceivers to come back from a mission with an uninvited passenger.

In the beginning of that war, the CIA had called their project SCANATE. It wasn't a secret code name, but a confidential acronym for the project's ultimate goal: to assess the ability of some people to *scan* for military targets simply by concentrating on map coordinates. By any other name, it was clairvoyance.

The time was 1970, and the much more public Cold War openly raged between the United States and the Soviet Union. America had just beaten the Soviets to the moon, and so the Soviets turned their attention to other arenas where they felt confident they maintained the lead.

One of those arenas was the investigation and exploitation of what were known as psychic powers, or as the Russians called them, bioenergetics.

The initial Soviet program was designated DIAMOND FIRE.

Fifty years later, its code name was VEKTOR.

"Why would the Russians do that?" Arlo asked. "All the intel Laura witnessed in the past month points to General Borodin's planning to do something *off* the reservation, *without* official sanction."

"Perhaps because VEKTOR's in on it," Chu said. "Which means Borodin's *not* acting on his own."

Caparelli had reached the same conclusion. "I agree. The general's presence on our soil suggests a sanctioned operation."

"For what possible purpose?" Kushner asked.

Caparelli had another thought to run by them. "To field-test their new technology."

Chu frowned. "And we still have no idea what that is."

"We know it's deadly," Caparelli said, "and it works well. My guess is that the Russians have somehow weaponized the quantum-field generator they've been using to enhance their perceivers' abilities."

Arlo looked thoughtful. "That could make sense—we've been working on the same for a while now. If they've come up with a device that generates a directed energy pulse to disrupt matter at the quantum level, they'd essentially be switching off the nuclear binding forces that keep molecules locked together. The target would fly apart. A pretty brutal weapon. Definitely matches the damage Laura reported in Mexico. Something there literally transformed the victims' flesh into an explosive."

"But why bring new technology here where we can see it?" Kushner asked. "Why not keep it inside VEKTOR's protected labs? They've got safeguards there to block our perceivers, same as we have safeguards here to block theirs."

"Because those safeguards aren't infallible," Caparelli said. "They can be compromised if the strength of the projections is sufficient."

"Shall we get back to it?" Chu said. "I want to see what happened next."

Arlo restarted the video.

On the screen, Jan, the waitress who had required extensive debriefing after the event, walked toward Matt Caidin's booth with a small white plate of lemon slices. Later that night, it had taken Caparelli considerable time to convince Jan that Laura's disappearance had been unusual, but not impossible. Jan had finally accepted that Laura had run out of the restaurant very quickly while she was distracted by having been shoved into another table. It was easier to believe something that made sense.

On the screen, Caidin reached for Laura's hand, and Laura's body arched in spasm.

"You! You were there!" she said. *"I saw the taxi, and he was beside me, and you were there—here—in the window when—"*

"Everything okay, hon?" the waitress asked.

As if startled by the question, Laura rose, whirled around—and vanished.

Chu leaned forward, intent. "Run that again for me. Slow motion."

Arlo ran the recording back, then stepped it forward, one frame at a time.

In one frame, Laura was there, blurred by motion. In the next frame, nothing, not even a blur. The video had been shot at thirty frames per second. Laura disappeared in less time than that. Jan the waitress stared blankly at the empty space, her shock so apparent that it was understandable she had clung to Caparelli's explanation that she hadn't seen what was so clearly impossible.

Chu sat back with a sigh. "So that's it."

Kushner looked more morose than usual. "She realized what she was, and she's gone."

"Maybe not." All eyes turned to Caparelli. "The video shows Laura hearing new information from Caidin. It's not the wisest thing to give a consciousness fixed in one specific time. But there's no indication on that video that shows that Laura actually understands her situation."

"So she still doesn't know she's dead?" Kushner asked.

"If she doesn't, it means there's a chance she isn't lost to us," Caparelli said. "Not yet. Everything points to these manifestations being able to persist for six days before their energy dissipates entirely. That gives us three more days to attempt contact again."

Hope flickered in Chu's eyes. "For Detective Caidin to make contact, you mean."

Caparelli nodded.

"What makes you think that'll work?" Kushner asked.

Caparelli hadn't achieved his position by shying from the truth. "We know emotion is at the heart of this phenomenon. Intense, primal emotion. Laura was in a horrific car accident, her body shattered, in unspeakable pain . . ." He hesitated, fighting down his own emotions, his own pain. "In that state, in those last moments of her life, Laura forged a psychic bond with Caidin, a link just like a back-trace. That connection's strong, and it's the only one we've got."

Arlo and Kushner were careful not to look at Caparelli, but Chu's sympathy was instant. "Daniel, what are you going to do?"

There was only one thing he could do. "Bring Caidin into CROSSWIND. All the way."

11

It was mid-September, but already winter in Magadan, and Evgeny Gorokhov didn't mind in the least. Winter was the heart and soul of his beloved country. The cold and snow had defeated Napoleon and Hitler, but to Russians, always contrarians, the cold was a nurturing fire: one that forged strength through adversity.

With that thought in mind, VEKTOR's chief administrator leapt from the stone dock and plunged into the frigid water of the small quarry lake. The shock of his sudden immersion set off every nerve receptor in his skin with such intensity, the cold became a sensory experience without comparison. It wasn't a temperature. It wasn't anything physical. It was the taste of captured lightning. The sound of the full moon sparkling on ice. It was Mother Russia, and she gave him life.

He floated to the surface, exhaled a cloud of vapor, and laughed at the two bulky soldiers bundled up in their cold-weather gear, watching him warily.

Gorokhov waved a massive pale arm at them, shouted, "Come in, come in! Like a summer's day in Sochi!"

They both gave him wry grins and remained where they were. While he was on station at VEKTOR's main facility, they were part of his security contingent, and they knew him and his habits well enough. Why he needed security protection in what was essentially the middle of nowhere remained obscure to Gorokhov, representing nothing more than a bureaucrat's paranoia. The city of Magadan was a desolate port at the top of the Sea of Okhotsk, a lone industrial outpost in Russia's far eastern northlands, on almost the same latitude as the tip of Greenland, halfway around the world.

As a port in the Old Times, Magadan had been the destination for uncounted boatloads of prisoners bound for the gulags. Their labor had built the town, the roads and railroads, and most importantly, worked the region's mines, including the officially closed complex that now served as VEKTOR's home.

Certainly the Americans could attempt to send their perceivers here, and had, though the well-shielded underground facility had never been breached in that manner. But how any security planner could think that there was a real risk of American spies turning up here in person was beyond Gorokhov's understanding.

So as chief administrator, he ignored the rules set down for him, and swam in the small quarry lake whenever he needed to clear his mind—as long as he did so during daylight, when CROSSWIND perceivers would be challenged to see past the electromagnetic interference caused by the sun.

Gorokhov splashed back to the dock, striking past chunks of floating ice. As he climbed the badly rusted metal ladder to the stone dock, his soldiers hurried to him with a thick bathrobe, towels, and heavy, fur-collared coat. His vehicle, a Land Rover Challenger, was parked, engine running and heater on, thirty meters up the path leading to the abandoned quarry's main gravel road.

He toweled his bare scalp and fringe of stark white hair, grunting with pleasure, invigorated by his swim and by the soldiers' ongoing bafflement. As he slipped on his coat, one of the soldiers opened a vacuum flask of tea, poured the steaming liquid into a glass.

Gorokhov expected the man to bring it to him, was puzzled when, instead, the soldier put the flask and the glass back on a large rock, then turned to the road, one hand shifting his slung rifle forward.

The soldiers exchanged a look, and the second man stepped in front of Gorokhov.

The chief administrator frowned, annoyed. "You think I have enemies *here?*"

Then he realized what had put the soldiers on alert: a car engine, diesel, approaching quickly. He pushed past the soldier supposedly protecting him and went to get his own damn tea.

A car door slammed somewhere up the path. Running feet on gravel. "Put down your rifles," Gorokhov said. "When they come, it will be by helicopter, or drones." He sipped the tea, felt completely vindicated when a labored voice cried out, "Chief Administrator!"

"It's only Popovich," Gorokhov said.

The soldiers relaxed.

Gherman Popovich was VEKTOR's deputy administrator. He was a slight man, prone to quick movement, nervous tics. Gorokhov thought of him as a bird. But for all his peculiarities, he was a brilliant logistician and ensured the facility ran with the precision Gorokhov demanded, and rewarded.

Right now, the deputy administrator was also winded, merely from running the thirty meters from his vehicle to the quarry dock. His face was pale, his cheeks bright red like an Englishman's.

"Have you come to join me for a swim?" Gorokhov asked.

Popovich looked horrified at the thought, and Gorokhov laughed. He motioned to the soldiers to step away so he could talk in private.

"Obviously, something is wrong." For the moment, Gorokhov wasn't overly concerned. Popovich saw the world and his work in terms of problems. Gorokhov saw only solutions.

"It is." The deputy administrator coughed in the cold air.

"Catch your breath." The chief administrator ran through a mental checklist of what could possibly have prompted his deputy to rush to the quarry rather than wait another thirty minutes for his return. One reason made more sense than any other. "The major has reported?"

Popovich shook his head. "That's what's wrong. She missed the communication window."

"Nothing from the others?"

"No, sir."

Gorokhov poured the tea from his glass, watched it steam, then freeze to slush on the stone dock. This *was* a serious issue, after all.

Popovich was recovering his breath, but his aura of panic remained. "If we've lost a third team of operatives . . ."

Gorokhov tried to calm him. "A single missed window doesn't signify loss of mission."

The deputy stepped closer. "In her last contact, she had located the general. She was going to confront him."

"In Colorado Springs."

Popovich nodded, a man stricken.

Gorokhov looked out across the quarry lake, at the rough stone walls shaped by the picks and shovels of thousands of nameless workers paying their debt to the Motherland. The fact that General Borodin had gone rogue on American

soil with operational shadow warriors was not only a massive failure of VEK-
TOR's internal security apparatus, it threatened to become a destabilizing incident. It could destroy Russia's international standing, just as Operation Scythe
was designed to obliterate America's. Gorokhov knew what the equivalent of the
old gulags was in today's Russia, and was determined they would not be his fate,
no matter what steps he had to take.

"There are two backup windows, correct?"

The deputy administrator gave a short, swift nod. "Over the next twelve
hours."

Gorokhov knew there were no VEKTOR perceivers who had been specifically trained to target Major Kalnikova. The army was very strict about
protecting their officers from that level of possible surveillance. But if she had
failed, then she was likely already dead. General Borodin was a different matter.
He had been one of VEKTOR's own. He could be tracked more easily.

"Prepare the prime team to locate the general at every opportunity."

Popovich widened his eyes. "So often, sir? Borodin's a sensitive. He'll become aware."

Gorokhov dismissed that concern. "He already knows that's what we'll do.
It's the only way we have to discover what he thinks he's trying to accomplish in
America. The presence of our perceivers won't be a surprise. And it might reveal
the major's fate. With certainty."

Popovich accepted his superior's logic. "And . . . if she has failed?"

"Then we must hope that whatever the general is planning, he fails as well."

Worry returned to Popovich's eyes. "If he does, and CROSSWIND recov-
ers even a shard of einstone from one of our prototypes . . ."

Gorokhov help up a hand to silence his deputy, signaled to his soldiers it
was time to go. "One problem at a time. First, we stop the general. If we cannot,
then the only way to be certain the prototypes don't fall into enemy hands is to
destroy the enemy."

"But how . . . ?"

To Gorokhov the solution was obvious. But he had no need to share it
until necessary.

Unexpectedly, he shivered, pulled his fur coat tight, surprised to realize
his feet were numb with cold. The water soaking his wading shoes had frozen.
He put an arm around Popovich's shoulders, started up the path with the soldiers.
"We'll get back where it's warm, have some proper tea."

Popovich said nothing, merely trudged on beside him.

Gorokhov trained his gaze on the rough stone blocks he passed, thinking of the prisoners who had died for their country. And he thought of the thousands more, so recently arrived, waiting for their turn to make the same glorious sacrifice.

It would be a difficult decision to take VEKTOR into the next phase of operations so soon. But if that was what was required, then so be it. From such terrible adversity would come unconquerable strength, and the Russia of old, the world's one true hope and superpower, would at last be restored.

12

To Matt Caidin, Laura Hart had seemed anything but dead. Her eyes had possessed the spark of life. Her smooth, soft hand had felt warm in his. Her living presence had been palpable. Then, in a heartbeat, she had vanished into nowhere.

Matt had no idea what he was in for next, but whatever it would be involved a medical lab filled with humming equipment deep inside CROSS-WIND's DC facility. While Caparelli and his colleagues were reviewing their surveillance video down the hall, Matt was going through a series of tests, the exact purpose of which was not disclosed to him. *Were there side effects of ghost exposure?* he wondered.

The CROSSWIND lab was harshly lit and blinding white, and Matt found himself the center of focus of four intent young technicians in pristine lab coats who moved quickly and efficiently as whatever they were assessing was fed into machines with complex screens and flashing lights. It should have been reassuring that there were no shadows here where unknown terrors could lurk, but as far as Matt was concerned, reality's old rules were undergoing alteration, and the deeper implications of what he was seeing, doing, learning were fanning a small flame of supernatural unease at the very edges of his thoughts.

The metal examination table was even colder than the cool air in the lab. Matt's only covering was a thin paper gown and the socks they'd let him keep. He shivered as a briskly cheerful and dreadlocked young technician attached EKG leads to his chest and his ankle. She also placed a band of EEG contacts around his head.

Next, a densely freckled technician—did this one even shave?—expertly and painlessly drew three vials of his blood, one large, two small. Then a tall and heavyset technician with the pockmarked skin of youth hit him with a steady barrage of questions, some of them standard: Did he smoke? Drink? Do drugs? Exercise? Take supplements? Suffer from insomnia? More particular were the subsequent questions asked by a fourth technician, also young, petite, with multiple piercings and cropped white-blond hair with jet-black roots: Did he gamble, and did he win a lot? Had he ever narrowly avoided an accident or dangerous situation because he'd had a lucky hunch?

Matt tried questioning them in turn: Where did the blood that had dripped from his hand and Laura come from? Why, after her ghost dematerialized, had that blood still remained on him? And what had happened to the still-tacky residue that someone had swabbed from his hand and then sealed in an evidence bag? The swab was taken just after they'd hustled him into Caparelli's car.

But all Matt got for this effort was a correction to his terminology. The freckled tech helpfully told him he hadn't seen a ghost. He'd perceived a manifested wraith. Any other answers would have to come from Director Caparelli.

The four technicians then disconnected his leads, drew a fourth vial of blood, offered him juice, and returned his clothes to him. The blond with the piercings drew a screen around him for privacy.

"How long do I have to wait?" Matt asked.

"No idea," she said. "We only work here."

A long hour later, Caparelli walked into the lab.

Matt leaned back against the wall on a nondescript vinyl chair. He drained his paper cup of bad vending machine coffee, stood up.

"How're you feeling?"

"You've got my test results. You tell me."

"You screwed up royally tonight."

"I was supposed to know what I was doing?" Matt crumpled his empty cup and tossed it into the open trash can.

"The wraith's frame of reference is a very specific point in time."

"Her name is Laura."

"That person's dead." Caparelli's tone betrayed no emotion. "We're dealing with an echo—an energy field that has information stored in it. What we need to do is extract that information before the energy dissipates and the information becomes irretrievable."

Matt looked beyond Caparelli to the lab's blank screens and computers. The comforting light of science no longer shone in this room. By the time he'd dressed and pulled back the screen, the four young technicians were long gone. The medical equipment was switched off, all screens dark.

"Well, I held your echo's hand," he said. "And that hand felt . . . strong. And it bled."

"All explainable. If not now, then it will be, eventually. There've been tales of fiery rocks falling from the sky for thousands of years. But science didn't accept the reality of meteorites until the turn of the nineteenth century. Not until enough legitimate astronomers had seen rocks fall from the sky firsthand and enough legitimate chemists and geologists had analyzed them."

"And the connection between this and my experience is . . . ?"

"Wraiths—quantum-field manifestations—are today's meteorites. A natural phenomenon that someday will be described—and explained—by science."

"Huh," Matt said. "Except back at the turn of the nineteenth century, the US government didn't decide to make knowledge of meteorites top secret."

"Trust me. If meteorites had a strategic value, that decision would have been made."

It had to be one, maybe two o'clock by now, and Matt guessed he wasn't being sent home soon. So he sat down again, too tired to argue further. "Okay, so now ghosts have strategic value, and that's why all of this is classified."

"CROSSWIND has nothing to do with ghosts," Caparelli said. "Our work, for now, is remote viewing, what perceivers do—what Laura did." He pulled a stool in front of Matt's chair, sat on it like a doctor talking to his patient. "And the strategic value of what we're doing has required the US government to step up three times to date, to publicly denounce research into ESP and psychic abilities.

"More than fifty years ago, the CIA got into the remote-viewing business with Project ULTRA. Ten years later, that became Project SCANATE. None of this was publicly acknowledged. Every time word started to leak about the results we were getting—the intelligence we were collecting from supposedly secure Soviet sites—the project would shut down in one department and re-open in another with a change of name. But the whole time, civilians were working for the CIA at Stanford, and the Army had its Project GONDOLA WISH, and the NSA had Project GRILL FLAME—they ran it out of Fort Meade before they handed it back to the Army as CENTER LANE."

Matt's weariness was giving way to suspicion. He sure as hell didn't have the clearance for this kind of background. What was Caparelli up to?

The director continued. "Back then, perceivers were tracking Soviet subs invisible to satellites. They were stopping North Korea from undertaking an invasion of the South—because we were able to map hidden rail lines and tunnels, and our diplomats were able to show those maps to the Chinese.

"But with successes as notable as that, there's talk. Mid eighties, a news columnist blew the whistle on the whole effort. So the Army responded to the leaks by commissioning a study that *proved* the whole field was bogus and publicly shut it down. Nothing to see here, move along. What no one stopped to ask was: If remote viewing was bogus, then why had it been funded by the CIA, the NSA, and the Pentagon for more than twenty years? The answer? Because it works.

"So . . . the Army shut down CENTER LANE, and the very next day, SUN STREAK started up at the Defense Intelligence Agency, to eventually become STAR GATE. The intelligence those perceivers obtained helped trigger the collapse of the Soviet Union. Naturally, that success prompted more talk, and resulted in another public exposé.

"So the CIA responded by doing what it always did. It issued a three-hundred-page independent report proving that remote viewing did *not* work and, moreover, that it had *never* worked. And they held back the more than 80,000 pages of operations reports proving that it did.

"November 28, 1991: STAR GATE shut down and all research into remote viewing ended. American taxpayers could rest easy knowing their tax dollars weren't being wasted on pseudoscience. More importantly, the Russians could be reassured that we weren't at all close to replicating their success in the field. November 29, 1991: CROSSWIND began operations, and here we are."

"Excuse me," Matt said. "The Russians can do this, too?"

"No question. The fact of it is, they've been doing it longer and better than we have. They're why we got into the field in the first place: To find out why Russian scientists were pouring the equivalent of hundreds of millions of dollars into what our scientists initially considered fantasy."

Matt heard a familiar low buzzing sound, and Caparelli pulled a small phone from his jacket, read its screen.

"You do know how this sounds," Matt said.

Caparelli tapped the screen. "You're just not used to it yet."

"I don't plan to be."

"No choice." He put the phone away, got to his feet.

"She's coming back?" Matt was startled by the quick pleasure that thought brought him.

"Over the next three days, there's a chance."

"What happens to keeping this all a secret if she shows up and disappears again in front of a restaurant full of customers?"

"We're trying a different approach this time," Caparelli said.

"How different?"

Caparelli got to his feet and pushed the stool aside. "Someone else will brief you. I have to go."

Matt's detective instincts kicked in again. "What was that message?"

Matt could almost hear the debate the man was having with himself about how much more he could or should reveal. He made a decision.

"The terrorists have struck again. On home soil."

Matt felt sick. "Casualties?"

"From the condition of the bodies, hard to tell."

"Laura's information . . . her report . . ."

Caparelli nodded. "In the next three days, there's a chance we can find out why the terrorists are here, and what their final target is."

"And Laura's the only one who can tell you."

"She can't tell *me* anything, Detective. This all depends on you."

Then he left, and Matt was on his own again.

Caparelli shut the door connecting the lab to the situation room. Computer displays, video screens, maps, and whiteboards ringed the area, but it was the three main screens on the far wall that held the interest of the six CROSSWIND personnel already present. The screens showed images that at first impression were of the massacre in the Sonoran desert. Aside from the body parts in pools of blood, though, the other details were inconsistent. This crime scene appeared to be an oversize garage or warehouse, not a hacienda.

"Where and when?" Caparelli asked.

Arlo was at a computer built in to the center table. On its screen, a live video feed from the same site showed investigators at work, most outfitted in white jumpsuits with helmets. A few others keeping well away from the gore sported blue FBI windbreakers.

"Storage facility about an hour out from Santa Fe. Discovered yesterday, late afternoon."

Caparelli stiffened. "How close to Los Alamos? White Sands?"

Burton Hirst, the project's lead analyst, changed the map display to show that section of New Mexico. "Other way, sir. Southeast." Hirst sounded disappointed, as he did about most things. He was a heavy man with a perpetual scowl, who insisted on wearing a suit to work, yet was always rumpled. And always insightful.

Caparelli saw a workbench in the photos, stacked with electronic gear. "Another drug operation? Stolen goods?"

A technician with a wireless headset answered. "No, sir. State police say it was rented to a video company. Three owners, all presumed to be among the dead. They shot commercials for local business, tourist clips, picked up local news stories on assignment."

"Why were they targeted?"

"Don't know yet. But get this..." Arlo entered commands on his keyboard, and new images on the right-hand screen showed the bodies of two men in state police uniforms, both shot in the head at least twice. Other images added three more to the count, all male, plainclothes, with head wounds.

"Two state police and who else?" Caparelli asked.

"State crime scene investigators."

Caparelli tried to connect the dots, couldn't. "They're intact."

"Correct," Hirst said. "Agents on site think we're looking at two separate incidents in the same location, about six to eight hours apart."

That gave Caparelli his framework for creating a scenario. "So, VEKTOR targets the video company for whatever reason. Six to eight hours later, state police respond to...?"

"Noise complaint from another tenant at the storage facility," Hirst said.

"Police arrive, see the mess, call for forensics... and a second party takes them out."

Arlo turned away from his computer. "Hold it. Why a second party?"

To Caparelli, it was obvious. "Second round of victims were shot, not mutilated. And why would Borodin wait around for hours? He's got to know that we know he's here and we're after him."

Arlo looked back at the large screens. "I guess it depends on why he was there in the first place."

"What's missing?" Caparelli asked.

The technician with the headset took over, cupping her hand over her earpiece. "Sir, the agents haven't been able to locate an inventory list on site, so they can't be certain what was there. But they have found two high-end video cameras, lights, sound-recording gear. Right now, it looks like the only thing they can be sure was taken is a 2010 Ford E-Series van, white. It's described on the parking records of the facility."

Caparelli walked closer to the screens, focusing on details to try to understand the pattern. "Why would Borodin kill three people to steal something so basic? To get that far from the border, so quickly, he's got to have transportation already."

Arlo made a correction. "There're eight people dead."

"But Borodin's only responsible for three we can be sure of," Caparelli said.

"Then who killed the police and forensics team?"

Caparelli saw only two possibilities. "Either there was something in the storage unit so valuable that by coincidence someone else tried to steal it after Borodin did and surprised the police. And you know what I think about coincidences.

"Or, there's someone else out there having better luck tracking General Borodin. Someone who's only six to eight hours behind, and they're the ones the police surprised."

Arlo frowned. "Who else would be after him—*and* willing to kill police?"

"Someone who knows what VEKTOR technology is and wants it for themselves."

Arlo's face cleared. "Which means we have two terrorist groups duking it out for whatever the general's brought into the country?"

Caparelli agreed. "And apparently each group wants to use that technology against different targets; otherwise they'd be cooperating."

Arlo ran a hand over his shaved scalp. "So when do we take this to Homeland?"

"We don't," Caparelli said. He had no desire to raise CROSSWIND's profile at the Department of Homeland Security. There was enough tension already between the two agencies that he preferred operating out of sight, and out of mind of Homeland's voracious bureaucracy.

Caparelli could see his manager of research didn't think keeping the situation in house was the best decision.

"Then all this leaves us in exactly the same situation we were before," Arlo said. "Putting everything we've got on Caidin, hoping he can contact Laura again. Shit."

"Or," Caparelli said, "we find out who this other group is that's after Borodin, and join forces."

Arlo took off his glasses to see Caparelli more clearly across the table. "Join forces with someone who's killed five cops?"

Caparelli knew the equations of battle, understood the concept and the price of the term "acceptable loss." "To protect this country from further attacks," he said, "it won't be the worst thing we've done."

DAY FOUR

13

Borodin's gunshot wound was not the problem: The temporary incapacity of his right arm, bound with dressings and held in a sling, would not affect the outcome of his mission. Losing two of his six shadow warriors so early did.

TYR had not returned from its pursuit of the mysterious woman Borodin had glimpsed at the Sonoran desert target site. It was possible the warrior had simply destabilized, permanently, as had occasionally happened in field trials, even though the containment units' batteries had been adequately charged.

HOD's fate, though, was unexpected.

Borodin had been startled to see Major Kalnikova use a *skorpion* to forcibly destabilize HOD. In hindsight, the concept of a focused electromagnetic pulse being capable of destroying a shadow warrior made sense. Borodin had no doubt that modifications to the containment units could be designed to increase a warrior's field strength, so it was possible a defense could be found. But for now, the *skorpion*'s unexpected effectiveness added new urgency to his timetable—he had to strike his target before the Americans understood the nature of the threat they faced and realized the CIA's own version of the *skorpion* could be an effective countermeasure. That his warriors could be destroyed by physical weaponry was a disturbing revelation, but not, in the end, surprising. No military plan ever unfolded precisely as predicted. War was always a race between the sword and the shield, and the sword always won.

For his mission, Borodin had estimated casualties among his shadow warriors of 33 percent during the final assault on the primary target, most probably from mechanical failures of the containment units. But even that failure rate would leave the mission equipped with one more warrior than the minimum of three required to achieve success. With the loss of both TYR and HOD, he no longer had that safety margin.

Which meant he would have to resupply as best he could.

Fortunately, a candidate was at hand.

Colonel Yuri Vasilyev, FSB. Wounded, captured, and still alive.

But not for long.

In those critical minutes following the major's attack and the explosion of the police car, Borodin's team's had made a successful withdrawal from the Walmart parking lot.

The second responders included firefighters, whose efforts were directed at extinguishing the flames and recovering the bodies of their police comrades. Before a cordon could be established, several of the cars and other vehicles from the makeshift camp at the edge of the parking lot slipped away.

Among them had been the general's Winnebago, with Colonel Vasilyev bound and gagged in the back, and its trailer with the covered-up van.

Now, near dawn, the Winnebago and its trailer were parked out of sight of Highway 25 in a dusty gully off an unpaved road that was little more than a trail flanked by rock walls and trees.

Borodin was chewing aspirins from one of the first-aid kits Janyk had purchased with the other supplies. The kit's only painkillers were nonprescription, but any pain beyond the reach of aspirins would serve to focus him on what had to be done next.

While Captain Korolev and the squad prepared the equipment outside, Borodin remained inside the Winnebago. He took the gag from Vasilyev, and the FSB officer spewed filthy words of hate. But words had long since lost their ability to inflame the general. He replied by offering his prisoner water.

Vasilyev gulped mouthfuls from the plastic bottle Borodin held for him. Then he asked for something stronger.

"No, it will dull your senses."

"That's the point." The FSB officer was pale, drenched in sweat. In the Walmart parking lot, LOKI had grabbed the colonel by the left shoulder, solidified a fist, and Vasilyev had collapsed screaming before passing out.

Now the shoulder was a scabbed mass of flesh, bone, and fabric, indented as if a large predator had torn a chunk from it. The blood supply to the colonel's left arm was blocked. The skin visible on his hand was mottled, blue-black. Borodin could smell decay beginning.

He held up the water bottle again, but Vasilyev angrily shook his head. The movement made him wince. He strained to look at the ruin of his shoulder. "What did you do to me?"

Borodin felt no responsibility for this man. "VEKTOR did not send you after me without telling you what you'd face."

Vasilyev glared at him, defiant. "What happens now?"

Borodin regarded him with pity. *He ought to know,* he thought. "Are you married?"

"Why should I tell you that?"

Borodin suddenly brought the water bottle down hard on the colonel's shoulder, and the man flinched and swore viciously at him.

"Are you married?"

Tears glistened in Vasilyev's bloodshot eyes. "Yes . . ."

"Her name."

"Natalya . . ."

"Children."

"A son."

"Ah. I too had a son." *Misha.*

"We know. . . . We all know."

"What is your son's name?"

"You will never get to my family."

"I have no need to. I want only the names of those close to you. Those you care for."

Borodin saw the flash of terror in his prisoner's eyes. Now the colonel understood what was to happen. Intense emotion was the key to establishing the self-sustaining energy field that could enable a personality to survive physical death. And there was no emotion more powerful than fear fueled by pain.

"Give me your son's name," Borodin said.

"No . . . no . . . anything else. . . . I'll tell you everything. . . . There were three teams dispatched. . . . You stopped two in—"

This time Borodin brought his left fist down on the colonel's shoulder.

"Aleksandr! His name is Aleksandr. Don't please don't . . ." Vasilyev began to weep.

Korolev opened the door, looked in. "General?"

Everything was ready. Borodin gave the order. "Prepare him."

Not even Borodin was certain that what he and his squad were about to attempt would work in rough conditions in the field. Outside, in the glare from the Winnebago's headlights, concealed from anyone who might get past the two lookouts posted closer to the dirt road, TYR's containment unit, its battery fully charged, yawned open, waiting to be filled again. Adjacent to the containment unit, the squad had spread a rubber sheet on the ground, nailed it into place with four plastic tent pegs, one to each corner.

Vasilyev screamed and struggled as Korolev and two other members of the squad wrestled him onto the sheet. With nylon rope, they bound the colonel's legs to a sturdy plank of wood, then tied the plank to two of the pegs. They did the same with his arms, spread-eagling him faceup, all four limbs pulled taut.

Korolev then picked up a length of common copper household wire, bought like the other materials at the Walmart supercenter. About four meters of it was already stripped of insulation, and he wrapped the bare wire tightly around Vasilyev's head, threading a few loops under his chin to hold it fast. He then ran the insulated portion of the wire to a connector secured in the copper mesh of TYR's containment unit and twisted the exposed copper at its end into position. This connection to the unit's nanoscale Faraday cage was simple enough. What made the process possible was the connector's thin wafer of einstone: the miraculous mineral that resonated at the same frequencies as the electromagnetic field from which human consciousness arose.

Working methodically, the three men next doused Vasilyev with water, soaking him to increase the conductivity of the wire. The colonel moaned.

Borodin knelt beside him and with his left hand grabbed the man's jaw to turn his head. "Look at me! Look at me."

The FSB officer shuddered, but did as he was ordered.

Borodin locked his eyes on Vasilyev's. For just a moment, *Misha's* eyes stared back at him, with the same look of fear, betrayal.

Borodin blinked, escaped back to the empty present. "Colonel Vasilyev, your body will die today. But I can save you. Look at me and say you understand."

The responding strangled whisper was almost unintelligible. But the general saw more than despair in those horror-glazed eyes. Hope.

"Again. Say you understand that I can save you. Keep saying it."

Vasilyev sobbed as he complied, as if repeating an urgent prayer, over and over.

Borodin glanced up at Korolev. The captain brought down the sledgehammer on Vasilyev's right knee, and the snap of cracking bones was instantly joined by a keening wail of agony. In the cool dawn air, the colonel's breath was a cloud of vapor caught in the headlights.

"Think of Natalya," Borodin shouted over Vasilyev's cries. "Think of Aleksandr."

The other kneecap splintered.

"Know that I can save you and look at me! Look at me!"

The general's grip tightened on Vasilyev's jaw then as Korolev put the sledgehammer aside and picked up the knife to begin the more precise work.

Together, Borodin and Korolev kept the colonel conscious for two hours into the day, on the very edge of death and life, until the moment of transfer when the wafer of einstone glowed bright blue and TYR's containment unit could be closed with all status lights green.

The general had his new soldier. He left the burial of that soldier's body to his squad.

14

Major Kalnikova was no longer in Colorado Springs to repatriate a rogue army general. She was a wounded soldier out of uniform behind enemy lines: justification for any action she might take to stay free, save her life, and complete her mission.

Her chosen target was female, perhaps fifty, thin, weak. She'd just emerged from the hospital's employee entrance into the floodlit parking structure and was walking quickly in the direction of an area marked DOCTORS ONLY. Her long knit jacket floated like a cape over green surgical scrubs. A canvas handbag swung from one shoulder.

The woman stopped beside the driver's door of a large, black SUV. Kalnikova recognized its Cadillac emblem. The woman dug into her bag, searching through its contents. Kalnikova stepped out from behind a concrete pillar and strode purposefully toward her. She saw the woman react to her firm footsteps, the loud clicking of her cowboy boot heels. "Doctor," Kalnikova called out. "You forgot something."

The woman looked up, puzzled.

In that moment of hesitation, the major was beside her, KA-BAR folding knife snapped open, the blade small but the meaning clear.

"Do as I say and I won't hurt you."

The woman instantly looked down, deliberately avoiding further eye contact, held out her bag. "Money, cards, keys . . . Here . . . Take it."

"I don't need money. I need doctor."

The woman shook her head. "I'm sorry. I don't have access to drugs."

Kalnikova thrust out her right hand. It was wrapped in blood-soaked bandages she'd fashioned from strips torn from her plaid shirt. She wore her denim jacket closed.

The woman looked up, assessing Kalnikova's wound with professional detachment. "Gunshot?"

"Car accident."

"The hospital doesn't have to report that. The ER can look after you. I won't say anything about the knife."

"You will look after me." Kalnikova raised the knife just enough to make her point. "Or I kill you and find another who will."

The doctor drove. Kalnikova sat beside her, the canvas shoulder bag at her feet, the doctor's phone switched off and its SIM card removed.

The driver was Roberta Long, an orthopedic surgeon. Kalnikova confirmed the name on the doctor's driver's license, credit cards, hospital ID, and on a prescription bottle of Percocet.

"Sample?" Kalnikova held up the bottle.

"I have a ruptured disk."

Kalnikova studied the doctor as streetlights flashed over her. Now that she knew the symptoms to look for, she saw them. The doctor must have taken some of her own medication just as her shift ended. She was not as frightened as she should be.

According to the navigation screen on the dash, Long's HOME location was thirty minutes from the hospital. Kalnikova checked all the street signs as they crossed intersections, made certain the marker for the car on the screen didn't deviate from the route map. She also kept checking the speed limit to be sure the doctor attracted no attention by driving too fast, or too slowly. The doctor did as she was told.

Kalnikova was not surprised. She'd chosen well.

Home was a small tract house on a suburban cul-de-sac. All the houses had driveway carports, but Long's was different. It was empty. The rest of the houses were similar in design, but most of their driveways had two or three cars. Additional vehicles were parked on the street. Pickups and SUVs for the most part; at the house next door to the doctor's a new Mercedes was as out of place as the rusted brown van four houses down. Other than that, there was nothing remarkable. Except for outside-entrance and walkway lights, all the windows of the houses were dark at this late hour. A neighborhood asleep.

Long drove her SUV into the carport, and motion-sensor lights winked on. Before they'd left the hospital, Kalnikova had asked who else would be at the doctor's house, and the woman had told her no one.

The night air was cool, and Kalnikova's mutilated hand burned. She was tempted by the doctor's Percocet, but that would come later, when her injury had been treated. She needed to remain alert until she could return to the motel room she had rented, retrieve the laptop she had taken from the warehouse, and report to VEKTOR, explaining why she had missed three scheduled communication windows. Only then, with her ability to track Borodin restored and her superiors developing a new plan, would she allow herself to rest.

Long's front door was secured by two deadbolts and a door-handle lock. The reinforcement was a sign of local crime, no matter how peaceful this street looked. Just like Mother Russia. The whole world was in decline.

Once inside, Kalnikova watched Long enter a code into a beeping number pad to switch off the security alarm. There was a chance the doctor had input a panic code, but even if she had, Kalnikova had warned her that help wouldn't arrive in time to save her.

The major had Long take her on a tour of the house. All windows were barred. Kalnikova hadn't noticed bars on the other houses. Something didn't feel right. "What are you protecting?"

"People target doctors. They think we're all rich."

Kalnikova recognized a lie when she heard it. "Or maybe, they know that you have drugs."

Long's involuntary step back confirmed this.

"Where are they?"

"I don't know what you're talking about."

Kalnikova struck her with the back of her left hand, the knife she held adding weight to the blow. "I am not playing game."

The stash was hidden in a bathroom, behind panels at the back of open shelves holding folded towels. Kalnikova was impressed. There were hundreds of bottles of prescription medication. Painkillers, mostly. More than half OxyContin, but antibiotics as well, all from the doctor's hospital. Seeing the collection, Kalnikova knew for certain the doctor had not entered a panic alarm. Long didn't want the authorities here any more than she did.

"Back to kitchen," the major said. It was time Long saw what her task was.

"My God, a car did this?" The doctor's mouth fell open in shock as she gingerly peeled back the last blood-sodden strip of cloth from the ruin of Kalnikova's right hand.

"Heavy car."

The doctor inspected the damage more closely. "While you were holding a gun?"

"I need you to remove it."

The insubstantial hand of the berserker had grabbed the major's hand and gun and then solidified *inside* them. Now it looked as if the Beretta and her hand were one. The tips of her swollen fingers jutted out of puddled metal.

"I . . . I'm not sure I can. Was there a fire, too?"

"I need gun cut out. I don't care how. Then clean, give me stitches, cast, whatever . . . and antibiotics. Then I go."

With Kalnikova following her, the doctor gathered her supplies, efficiently readying the kitchen to be an operating theater. She brought a table lamp from the living room to add bright light to the island counter. She laid out sterile gauze, surgical tweezers and clamps, even scalpels that she took from her collection of stolen drugs.

"You've done this before, yes?"

The doctor took another look at the fused hand and gun. "Not this."

"But like it. Gunshot wounds. Knifings. For people who don't want to go to hospital. The people you sell your drugs to."

"A lot of people don't have insurance."

Another lie. Kalnikova smiled. "Ah, so you are humanitarian."

The doctor led Kalnikova to the sink, had her hold her injured hand steady, doused it with a dark purple antiseptic liquid from a plastic squeeze bottle. The major bit her lip as the liquid stung an area where the nerves were still intact.

"You should let me give you an anesthetic. At least a local. You'll still be conscious."

"No. I won't know what you inject me with."

The doctor gave up and arranged towels under her patient's arm and hand, positioning them on the island counter, under the table lamp. Next, she filled a second squeeze bottle with sterile water and handed it to Kalnikova.

"Squirt this where I tell you."

The major was ready, and Long donned a paper surgical mask. She made

Kalnikova wear one as well, then leaned over the ruined hand. She used tweezers to pick at small shreds of flesh and splinters of bones, freed others with her scalpel, while the major directed a stream of sterile water to each site the doctor worked on.

After half an hour, Long straightened up with a weary sigh, pulled down her mask. "This isn't going to work. I need X-rays, a microsurgery suite . . . and even then . . ." The doctor put her scalpel down.

Kalnikova ran the odds. She was days, if not weeks away from the actual medical treatment she required. Until then, she still had her orders, but completing them meant she couldn't risk capture by either Borodin's team of traitors or the American authorities. Only one option.

"You will cut off hand."

Wisely, Long didn't argue.

The tourniquet was tight.

Kalnikova refused the offered IV drip, but did accept the proffered water. She also drank a great deal of it as suggested.

She did not look away as Long sterilized a stolen bone saw.

An hour later, when Kalnikova finally closed her eyes, she could still feel her right hand burning. But it was just a phantom memory.

To seal the newly exposed cut, the doctor had stitched together flaps of skin over the stump of Kalnikova's right forearm, except for two corners where plastic tubing allowed the wound to drain. Clean white bandages wound up to her elbow.

The doctor was as pale as her patient. "You need someone to check that in twenty-four hours, change the dressing." She gave Kalnikova sealed blister cards with antibiotic pills, and a new digital thermometer still in its packaging. "Take your temperature every two hours. Any increase, you *have* to get to a doctor. This was not exactly a sterile environment."

Kalnikova's head pounded. She knew she had to sleep soon. She asked for a bottle of Percocet.

Long stared at the pills she'd handed over.

"If you take them now, will you still be able to drive?" Kalnikova asked. Victims always made it easy if they were handled properly.

The doctor's gaze shifted from the pills to her. "Where?"

"Bus depot. I go on with my life; you go on with yours."

Kalnikova saw the expected relief that flooded through the doctor. "No problem. I can drive you there. It's only twenty minutes."

Kalnikova returned the bottle. "Then go ahead."

Hands trembling, the doctor shook out four yellow lozenges into her hand, then swallowed them in one gulp. "You should take something, too."

"Soon," Kalnikova said. "Drink something. To get those down."

The doctor relaxed, her ordeal at an end. She went to the sink, ran the water. Kalnikova was right behind her.

In a single swift motion, the major hooked her left arm around the doctor's neck, pressed her head forward with her thickly bandaged right forearm, felt the woman's body tense for only a few seconds, then go limp.

Kalnikova maintained her stranglehold for another thirty seconds, to ensure consciousness would never return. Then she dropped the body to the floor and at last screamed to release all the pain of this night, and of the violent action she'd just taken.

She took another few moments to settle, then went to the front hall closet, where she'd seen a collection of plastic shopping bags. She chose a suitable one and returned to the kitchen, where she pulled it over the unconscious doctor's head. She never woke up.

Only then did Kalnikova allow herself two Percocets. She emptied the doctor's canvas shoulder bag, retaining only the cash, about eighty dollars, and the key fob for the black SUV. To these, she added extra medication and bandages, small plastic tubs of yogurt and a waxed carton of orange juice from the refrigerator, and a box of crackers from a pantry cupboard.

She found fresh clothing in the doctor's bedroom, then headed into the bathroom for more towels. They'd be useful for the seepage from the drainage shunts in her forearm. One pale pink towel high on the top shelf caught on something. Kalnikova gave it a hard tug, and it came loose, dragging a small black object behind it.

Kalnikova's chest tightened.

It was a radio microphone, small, sophisticated, and clearly not part of the doctor's home security system.

There was only one explanation: The doctor was a thief and the authorities knew. She was under surveillance. Most probably, the authorities had heard everything that had happened here, or would play back the recordings soon.

The major dropped the towels and ran for the kitchen, where she scooped up the canvas bag of supplies.

She opened the front door.

Four men and one woman. Bulletproof vests. Guns drawn.

Each vest read POLICE. Four houses down the street, the back door of the out-of-place rusted van was open, lights from electronics bright inside.

Of course. Kalnikova accepted that she'd missed the obvious. There was no excuse for failure.

"Drop the bag," the biggest man shouted. "Hands on your head."

Kalnikova let the canvas bag slip from her left shoulder, held up her left hand and her bandaged right stump.

"Hands," she said, and then, because she was Russian, she threw her head back and laughed.

15

Sam Arlo briefed Matt on the new plan, then drove him home.

It was coming up on 4:30 a.m., Wednesday morning. It was still dark, the night air humid after a light misting of rain.

Matt was feeling shell-shocked. In the past forty-eight hours, almost everything he knew about life had changed, including that life didn't necessarily end at death.

Once, long ago, he had wholeheartedly accepted that there was an afterlife. His parents had raised him to believe in it as a reward in heaven, or punishment in hell. Like most children, he had absorbed his parents' views without question.

Later, like most teenagers, there came a time for questioning everything. In the midst of those roiling years of youthful revolt, his grandfather had died.

The elderly man had been frail, but mentally sharp, and had his family's love and their company at the end. Matt had felt the ache of his granddad's loss, but then had been puzzled by how emotionally devastated his parents were. What had happened to their faith in his grandfather's continued existence? Their belief that they would be reunited with him in time?

Matt had been troubled by the possibility that his own parents didn't truly accept what they had tried so hard to have him believe. His need to question those beliefs grew. Then, two days after his funeral, Matt's grandfather had come to him.

The memory of his grandfather's visit was perfectly clear—no sense of a dream, no half-remembered fog. Matt had awakened in his room just after 3:00 a.m.

according to his alarm clock. He had switched on his bedside lamp for no particular reason. His grandfather was standing at the foot of his bed, casting a shadow on the wall behind him.

He was younger, no longer frail. He wore the leather flight jacket that still hung in his closet at the home—the one he had let young Matt try on so many times, the one he had worn in the Army Air Corps, a pilot from the Greatest Generation fighting the Last Good War. Matt remembered thinking how new the jacket looked, its lifetime of wear and scuffs and scrapes erased as if they had never happened.

"It's okay, Matty," granddad had told him.

Matt remembered that he wasn't startled or frightened. He remembered sitting up in bed and thinking that he should get his mother and father because they'd like to see granddad, too.

"Let them sleep," granddad said. "I just wanted you to know that it's okay."

At the time, those words had made sense to Matt, as if they were part of a much longer conversation. After hearing them, he had simply gone back to sleep, untroubled.

In the morning, he woke at dawn as the sun shone through his window, and the only indication of his grandfather's visit was that the bedside lamp was still switched on.

It was years before he had talked to anyone about that night. When he did, it had been at a dinner party with a few friends and Helena, before they were married. The conversation fueled by wine had swung round to ghost stories. Matt hadn't called his grandfather's presence a "visit." He called it a dream. Vivid and memorable, but nothing more than a troubled brain offering solace to a saddened teenager. Certainly that was the proper explanation for all the other so-called ghost stories recounted that night: mere wishful thinking.

But the odd thing was, since he had had that dream of his grandfather, he was no longer troubled by the thought of his own death. Whenever the inevitability of his end crossed his mind, almost instantly he would hear his granddad's voice, passing on that same message from so long ago.

"It's okay."

△△

Streetlights strobed by on the rain-slicked road.

Arlo looked to be in his late twenties, but drove as if he were in his teens, with an almost childlike enthusiasm for his red Corvette. Amber lights were merely a signal to jump to light speed. The few other cars on the road were simply stationary obstacles to swerve around and leave behind.

Matt reflexively pushed his brake foot hard against the floorboard after one of Arlo's sudden lane changes caused them to swing out beyond a slow-moving street sweeper and into the path of an oncoming bus. Just because he wasn't troubled by the thought of his own death didn't mean he was in a rush to face it. "Uh, you said we didn't have to hurry?"

At the CROSSWIND facility, Arlo had explained that Laura's ghost—her quantum-field manifestation—could only be counted on to appear at night. That's when potentially disruptive interference from the sun's radiation would be at its weakest. So the new plan wouldn't begin until after sunset tonight, when Matt would be stationed in an apartment in Merrifield. A place Laura knew well. Her home.

"We don't *have* to hurry, but the streets are never this clear." Arlo gave Matt a quick grin, then downshifted as a traffic light changed to amber, too far away to challenge.

The lights ran long this early in the morning, and Arlo impatiently revved the 'Vette's engine at the intersection.

"Does it happen to everyone?" Matt asked. "Ghosts, I mean."

The light turned green, and Arlo slammed the car forward. "Course not. Otherwise, they'd be everywhere and everyone would know about them."

"So what about survival?" Matt asked. "For everyone. Even if we don't all become . . . manifestations. Does our consciousness continue?"

"Everyone at the project asks the same question. We don't have the answer. Not yet." The Corvette slowed almost to the speed limit. "On the one hand, we've all got brains and consciousness, so it stands to reason we can all generate the quantum field that's at the root of the phenomenon. On the other hand, almost none of us can separate our consciousness from our body."

"Like Laura."

"Yeah, so maybe only perceivers have the special brain chemistry that produces a self-sustaining consciousness after physical death." Arlo gave a half-grin to Matt. "Screwed up, isn't it? Turns out there might an afterlife, but it has nothing to do with religion. It's only for a chosen few who won some kind of genetic lottery. High Church of the Holy Rollers of the Dice." The Corvette unexpectedly came to a complete stop before making a right turn on a red light. Arlo looked deep in thought. "Not like we're missing much, though. Even if a perceiver's consciousness survives death, it can only last for six days."

"But all the stories . . . Aren't some places supposed to be haunted for years? How does that fit in?"

"Yeah, well, we go back and forth on that. When we measure the quantum field strength in lab experiments, we can calculate the energy requirements to maintain it. The math comes out of a theory called spontaneous symmetry breaking. Applies to all sorts of freaky quantum effects. Works out that the strength of the field produced by the human brain has a self-sustaining persistence of about a hundred and forty hours, plus or minus five. After that, well, the field essentially hits a tipping point and winks out."

"So castles haunted for years . . . ?"

The Corvette's engine roared as Arlo took a corner hard and Matt's seat belt automatically tightened. "Those stories could just be an extension of the folklore. Or maybe there's something in the construction of supposedly haunted places that helps maintain the field. Maybe ore-bearing rocks or exotic minerals or metal beams or some kind of architectural alignment of walls create a natural resonating chamber that keeps the field from losing energy. We've kicked around the idea of creating a magnetic bottle to keep a field energized, maintain it for an indefinite time. But there's really no need for it."

"Wouldn't it help your perceivers to stay separated longer?"

Arlo shook his head. "Rules of the game. They're never gone for more than a few hours. We even have to time their sessions according to the influence of the sun at their target site, because they usually can only function reliably from about an hour past sunset to an hour before dawn. Then we have to adjust for local magnetic conditions. Including sunspots and solar flares. It's a complicated business. And then, the most promising targets, say the Chinese premier's office? Those, believe me, are safeguarded like you'd not believe."

"How?"

They were on Matt's street now, and Arlo turned off his navigation. "Same techniques used to screw with radio communication. You know: jamming signals, conductive mesh, the usual stuff."

Matt held back his desire to laugh—Arlo had a knack for making the profound concept of disembodied consciousness surviving death nothing more than a matter of nuts and bolts.

"Don't get me wrong," the young man continued. "Remote viewing is a powerful technique, but it's got limited application. Still, we've stopped a lot of bad things happening because of it, and the longer we keep it secret, the less chance there is that someone of interest will take measures to block us."

Arlo turned back just as the Corvette hummed to a smooth stop in front of Matt's building. "And here we are. A driver's going to pick you up at noon and take you to Laura's apartment. We'll have it fully wired for sound and video, so Caparelli can talk you through the whole encounter."

"If there's an encounter," Matt said.

"Like I told you, manifestations have a better chance of happening some-place with significant emotional meaning to the individual who died—kind of like lightning drawn to a lightning rod. If you think of the legends, then the place of death is almost always a place where sightings happen, especially if it's a result of an extreme or violent event.

"We figure that's why Laura showed up in that café, just a few yards from where she died. Too many people there, though, to try that again. So, according to her psychological profile, her apartment is a refuge for her, emotionally speak-ing. With you there, that link you have with her, the odds are way better than good that that's where she'll turn up."

Matt put his hand under the door latch, but wasn't ready to go. He still had so many questions. "Tell me something. If Laura wants to report to you guys so badly, why doesn't she just show up at CROSSWIND?"

Arlo gave a little shrug. "Far as we know, the disassociated consciousness exists in a frozen moment of time. Legends also speak to that. You know, people seeing ghosts repeating actions, over and over, never completing them? Right now, our working theory is that Laura died *wanting* to *go* to CROSSWIND. So when she manifests, that's the desire driving her. *Going* there. Not *being* there."

Matt knew his expression was the reason for Arlo's grin. "Yeah. It is kind of crazy-making at first. But after you've studied it for a while, you realize it's all part of nature. Bottom line is when we measure it in the lab, every aspect of the phenomenon obeys all the laws of physics, just in new ways that no one's used to yet. But you'll get there."

Matt wasn't so sure, but he said good night and heaved himself out of the low car. He heard the Corvette speed away on the deserted street.

The lobby of his building was small, brightly lit, and empty. An elevator opened as soon as he touched the call button.

By newly formed habit, Matt half-stepped out on his floor, to check both directions in the corridor. The Mauricio organization was patient.

The corridor was clear.

He checked his apartment door. The small sliver of paper was in place, undisturbed. The door hadn't been opened since he'd left.

He pushed the door open.

No one burst out to pistol-whip him.

Matt relaxed. He stretched and yawned. A shower. A beer. Then bed. He could think again later in the morning.

He turned and locked the door behind him. The security chain slid home with a satisfying clunk.

"You can help me."

Matt wheeled around.

Laura . . .

She stood inches from him.

Waiting.

16

Matt felt time slow, as if caught in a sudden gunfight, a skidding car, the deadly charge of a knife-wielding criminal.

His senses heightened on full alert, every detail of this frozen moment set out in exquisite detail.

He wasn't afraid—by instinct and by training he was *ready*. But for what, his conscious mind had no concept.

The temperature in his apartment dropped suddenly, as if a cold wind had gusted through the walls.

Her eyes were bright. Her breath warm. He felt the heat of her presence, standing so close, now masking the cold.

"You can help me," she said again. He heard her through the drumming of his heartbeat. He remembered what he'd been told to do.

"What's the problem?" he asked. The words came out dry, raspy.

She didn't seem to notice. "I need to get to 610 E Street, southwest."

"You've missed the last Metro." Too late, Matt realized he'd not said all he should. "If you mean in DC." The words felt awkward. He half expected her to vanish again.

She only blinked.

"I'm driving," she said. "I think I'm lost."

Matt stared at her, unsure. *That's all new. . . .* He had to get her back on script. Caparelli had said that was important.

"I can help you," he told her.

She waited.

He remembered what else Caparelli had had him say in Molly's. "You'll be more comfortable if you sit down."

Her smile was sudden, brilliant. Matt was surprised again by how much it affected him, warmed him. He relaxed. How could this girl be a ghost? How could *she* be part of something frightening?

Then he remembered the slip of paper. How she had vanished from the restaurant. However she had come here, she hadn't used the door.

"Thank you," Laura said. She looked around, went to the couch. Sat down. The cushions sank beneath her, and he finally noticed what else was different about this appearance, this manifestation.

Her clothing.

In the café, she'd been wearing jeans, a hooded pullover—student clothing, he had thought. But now, she was in a tailored pantsuit—gray, white blouse, corporate office wear. Her hair had also changed. It was still pulled back, but this time, tight. Formal. *How can ghosts even* have *clothes?*

She tilted her head at him, as if curious about something, about to ask a question.

He tried to stay on Caparelli's script. "Would you like some tea?" he asked.

She smiled again, pleased. "I like tea."

"With lemon, right?"

Her mood changed, became uncertain. "Do we ... Have we ... ?" Once again, she looked around his apartment, frowning. She put her hand on the arm of the couch, as if about to get up. Matt saw the gleam of clear lacquer on her manicured nails. How could that be?

"We met at work." It was all he could think to say.

She locked eyes with him, wary. "You mean ... Vanguard Research Associates?"

Matt reacted blindly, gave the recognition code. "I was in your office and saw three pictures on the wall. The one in the middle has a blue frame."

She relaxed, sat back on the couch, bestowing on him a knowing look now. She gave the countersign. "I like the one on the right. It has a red frame."

"It's closest to the window."

"I understand," she said.

Matt stared at her, waiting.

"What department are you in?" she asked.

"I, uh ... work for Daniel."

She frowned. "Everyone does. But which department are you in?"

It's like disarming a bomb, Matt thought. *One step at a time.* "I thought . . . you had something to tell him."

"Possibly. I suppose it depends on how I do in the interview."

"Interview?"

She leaned forward, conspiratorial. "At Vanguard . . . You work there. . . . You know." A whisper. "The Project."

Insight blossomed in Matt. *She has to get to CROSSWIND to report.* That's the purpose driving her. But now, for whatever reason, she no longer remembered *why.* So she'd found another reason, another memory of another time she had to go there: the day of her first interview.

But that was the extent of Matt's understanding. He had nothing left to go on. Nothing more to say. Caparelli had been insistent that he not lead her in conversation and that he not add new information to the situation she was reliving.

As the silence between them stretched out, Laura began to look concerned.

"Is something wrong?" she asked.

In that moment, Matt felt the burden of responsibility dissolve. Without Caparelli to whisper instructions in his ear, there was no way he could ensure that this particular encounter would be successful. He could only do his best to get her to tell him what she knew, any way he could.

"I'm sure you'll do well," he assured her. "You'll get the job."

She almost laughed. "I've had my share of luck, I know. But this time, honestly, I'm not even sure what the job is."

Matt wondered if he should make tea, but was loath to leave her sight. What if she disappeared for no reason other than his inattention?

"What did they tell you it would be?"

"Important. Psychology. That's my major. Working with government agents. Which I think means spies. Is that what you do?"

Matt didn't want to get into any discussion that might require him to know the same details she did. It would be too easy to reveal he really wasn't part of CROSSWIND. "I handle security for the Project," he said. "Not really involved in the day-to-day operations."

"So that's why you're part of this test?"

"Test?"

"You know. Recognition code. Sign. Countersign." She gestured to the apartment. "This is part of the interview, isn't it? I mean, it looks like an apartment at night. But my interview's for ten a.m. So . . ." That troubled expression came to her again. "I don't remember how I got here."

Matt spoke quickly. "Everything's all right," he said. "You're correct. It's part of the test. The Project's highly classified. And . . ." He didn't know what he was going to say until he said it. ". . . so we're testing you on how well you can keep secrets."

"I don't know any secrets." She suddenly stood up. "How long have I been here?"

"It's been a lengthy process." Matt did his best to sound reassuring. "But it's almost over. And you're doing very well."

"Where's my bag?"

"Your bag . . . ?"

"My purse. It has . . . my car keys . . ." She held a hand to her head. Closed her eyes. "How did I get here?"

"You drove," Matt said. "Your car's downstairs in the garage."

She walked away from him, to the sliding glass door that led onto the balcony.

Matt's apartment was on the fifth floor. Outside, a few trees on the street stood out, their dark leaves outlined in silver by the streetlights shining up through them. In the apartment building across the street, only three windows were lit from within. Just past it, off to the right, appeared dark clouds of trees lining another street, and beyond that, distant office towers, every window glowing. The night sky was already brightening with approaching dawn.

But none of those details registered on Matt as he stepped up behind Laura at the balcony door. He saw only her reflection in it—perfect.

She put her hand on the glass. "That's real out there, isn't it?"

He stood beside her, wishing he knew what she was thinking, what she knew—if she knew—about what she had become.

"You're in Arlington," he said.

She turned to him, her eyes searching. "I know you."

"That's right."

She touched his face, her fingers trailing down his cheek.

Matt felt the hair on his neck bristle, his arms prickle with gooseflesh, as if somewhere deep inside, some primitive part of his brain recognized just what it was he faced.

But Laura's hand was warm.

She suddenly stretched up to kiss him, her soft lips lightly brushing his.

Matt jerked back, startled, and her face flushed.

"I'm sorry," she said. "You must think..."

Acting on instinct, not thought, Matt reached for her hand. "No, no, it's all right."

"The dog..." She peered out through the window. "You know the one. You've seen it. It's barking again. I'm frightened."

"You don't have to be." Matt heard nothing.

He could see her struggle to remember him.

"You can help me." Her eyes looked anxious. "My bag...My car keys. Where did I put them? I know I drove here."

She stared at their joined hands as if surprised. "You were there..." Her hand slipped from his.

Matt took a deep breath. "Where?"

"Driving..." She moved away from him, back toward his living room as if looking for something. "I was driving here...no...to Vanguard...the Project..."

"CROSSWIND," Matt said.

"But the interview was a long time ago." She turned, troubled. "Is this part of the test?"

"It's not a test."

Her restlessness escalated sharply, and Matt went for broke before she could flee. "You needed to report to Caparelli. You needed to tell him something about General Borodin."

The air felt electric. Matt half expected to see lightning strike.

Laura brought her hand to her mouth. "I saw the general. Saw his..." She blinked, overcome by some sudden memory. "I was at home. I connected in delta sleep...a spontaneous link...It was so strong. I heard everything. Saw everything."

She looked at him imploringly. "I called Daniel! That was protocol. He wasn't...wasn't there...but...I had to report. Had to go in. Record it. I..."

She stopped. Swallowed hard. "I was in my car. I was driving."

Her breathing became shallow, rapid. "He sent one after me..."

"Who did?" Matt asked. "Sent what?"

"In my car!" she cried. She wrapped her arms around herself, eyes wild, remembering. "It back-traced me! *Manifested!* I lost control! I swerved! And... and..."

She stared at Matt with eyes wide with sudden recognition. She turned toward the glass door. To the lights beyond, the reflections, the—

She turned back. "In the window—*you were there! You were there when I . . . when I . . .*"

Tears welled in her eyes and she was—

Gone.

DAY FIVE

17

If there was any other solution to this newest development, Gorokhov couldn't see it. For one of the rare times in his sixty years of service to his country, that made the big man hesitant. He always preferred to have options to compare. But in this case, there were none. Not that he could let his concern show in front of the others at the table. Apparently, though, he had stayed silent too long.

"Chief Administrator . . . ?" Popovich was tentative, but clearly some response was needed.

Gorokhov looked up from the set of glossy prints that had been made of the perceivers' output screens from their most recent session. He nodded sagely, projecting an aura of calm. "All very interesting," he said. "But given the possible repercussions if our analysis is in error, we must be more than certain. We must be convinced."

He glanced around the makeshift conference room. Two walls were bare rock, from the days this facility had been a mine. The other two walls were constructed of unpainted drywall, one with several video screens mounted on it, the other with a locked wooden door leading to a rock-walled tunnel. A space heater hummed in a corner, though it failed to bring the room to a comfortable temperature. His staff, seated around the plain wooden conference table, wore jackets and sweaters. None tried to hide his or her own uncertainty.

Gorokhov addressed his new head of mapping. "Do you have absolute confidence in the location of this incident?" If there was enough margin of error in the calculations that had determined where this perceived event had taken place, then that could also affect the time it was believed to have occurred. Despite the assurances of his experts, the projection of a disembodied consciousness was still more art than science.

Irina Roslyakova nodded, grim. "It corresponds to the direction the general was known to be traveling, and with the distance he could have been expected to cover in the time since the major's . . . disappearance."

Gorokhov understood her reluctance to use the word "death." Major Kalnikova was missing, as were the two officers accompanying her. But until the major's fate was confirmed, the chief administrator felt justified in continuing to expect that eventually she would make contact again. She was driven. She was expert. She was Russian. Defeat would not come easily to her.

"And these images . . ." Gorokhov turned next to VEKTOR's senior technician. "Would they benefit from further rendering?"

Igor Byko looked back at his own set of images. They showed a blocky reconstruction of the Winnebago caravan the general was known to be driving. The vehicle was parked, headlights glaring, illuminating a group of men kneeling around a figure spread-eagled on the ground. The visual reconstruction algorithms had recognized one of the men, and his features had been filled in from the database of previously identified individuals: General Borodin. The algorithms had also recognized and filled in the details of the object on the ground beside the prone figure: a VEKTOR containment unit.

"It *might* be possible to identify the other members of the general's squad."

Gorokhov wasn't interested, took on a sharp tone. "We know who the traitors are. What we don't know is, who they have captured." His thick finger tapped his own copy of the image. "Is this the major? Has Borodin actually transformed her into one of his shadow warriors?"

A long silence followed, broken finally by the psychologist, Dr. Jelavich. "It would explain why the perceivers couldn't link with her."

Gorokhov didn't accept that. "Even if she were dead, the perceivers should be able to make contact with some essence of her, for six days at least." Spontaneous post mortem contact had happened before, Gorokhov knew, even without the einstone.

"Of course, of course." The psychologist made every effort not to appear to be in disagreement with his superior. "I simply meant, if what remained of her after death was captured in a containment unit, then she would be effectively shielded from contact." He gestured to indicate the room around them. "As if she were protected within our own electromagnetic shields."

Whatever phenomenon was at the root cause of remote viewing and the creation of what the world would call a ghost, it wasn't something that disappeared at the moment of physical death. Instead, it faded over the course of days, a dying fire. If that fire could be captured in one of VEKTOR's containment units, channeled by an einstone resonator, and held secure in a magnetic field powered by external batteries, then it could persist much longer, perhaps forever. Whenever it was released from the containment unit, it definitely could be sensed by a perceiver.

Gorokhov accepted the psychologist's unspoken apology, then looked across the table at his deputy. "What about you? Nothing to add?"

Popovich had meekly folded his thin hands on the table, didn't look up from his set of the prints. "I think, perhaps, the situation is moving out of control."

To Gorokhov, it seemed as if all others in the room held their breath. He kept his own flash of anger subdued. "Would you care to explain, Deputy Chief Administrator?"

His deputy reluctantly made eye contact. "Out of . . . out of our control, sir. We are a highly specialized organization. But we don't have the experience or personnel to run actual operations on the ground in a foreign land."

If it had just been the two of them, Gorokhov would have encouraged him to continue in detail. While his deputy was not astute about matters of interpersonal politics, he understood operations and the need to plan for the worst possible outcome. But with the others present, Gorokhov could not allow his leadership to be questioned.

"Are you suggesting that Major Kalnikova was not sufficiently experienced to take on Borodin? As I recall, you selected her." He made it easy for the others to hear the disdain in his tone.

Popovich's face drained of color.

"I *recommended* her, and the others on all three teams, from the security personnel already seconded to us. I believe . . ." He swallowed hard, as if understanding how close to the precipice his words were taking him. "I believe we should expand our choices."

"Go directly to the army. For assistance."

Popovich nodded, nervous, voice cracking. "Yes, Chief Administrator."

"Let me tell you what I believe." Gorokhov spread his hands over the prints in front of him. "VEKTOR has the resources to deal with this, on our own."

Popovich couldn't seem to stop himself. "But . . . using those resources will bring the same risk Borodin has created for us—complete exposure." He looked back at the tabletop. From the corner of his eyes, Gorokhov could see the others do the same.

"Is that all?" Gorokhov asked.

Another short, swift nod.

"Then we're done. Imaging will continue to render the output screens to reconstruct additional details. Mapping will recheck the location from the beginning. Operations will prepare two sets of perceivers. One to stay with Borodin . . ." Gorokhov saw that his senior technician was about to protest, cut him off. "And I don't care if the general becomes sensitive to the point where he can begin to *see* the perceivers. You will stay with him."

The technician acquiesced without a word.

Gorokhov continued. "The second team will continue to attempt a link with the major." He smiled. "Perhaps our friends at CROSSWIND captured her and she is safely shielded within their facility as she steals all their secrets for us."

Everyone but Popovich smiled in reply, as expected.

Gorokhov stood and the meeting was over. Popovich hung back until he was the last to leave, remained in the doorway.

Gorokhov knew this was his opportunity to bring his deputy back into the fold, to remind him that questioning his chief administrator in front of the others was never acceptable. "Did you have something more you wished to say to me?"

"I apologize for speaking out of turn."

Gorokhov studied his deputy closely, saw the uncharacteristic iron resolve hidden in his eyes, heard the lie in his tone.

He's hiding something from me? Gorokhov thought. "I appreciate your counsel," he said. "But in private, next time. Yes?"

"Of course, yes. Thank you, Chief Administrator." He nodded as if grateful, then hurried away.

Gorokhov was puzzled by his deputy's reaction, resolved to pay closer attention to his activities and his communications in the coming days.

It was one thing for VEKTOR to have been potentially compromised by the great general, Borodin. The man was legend, and there had been no indication of his treachery until after the fact. But if there were those in Moscow who thought Gorokhov must be held responsible for that failure, the chief administrator abruptly realized that Popovich would be the first person they would reach out to, to 'correct' the situation.

Here, alone, Gorokhov allowed himself a smile, a gentle laugh. As valuable as his deputy was to him, if Popovich had indeed made the fatal decision to ally himself with those in Moscow who harbored doubts about VEKTOR's current leadership and the impending Operation Scythe, then one night not too far off, the thin man would finally get his chance to swim in the quarry lake.

Because Popovich and Moscow weren't the only ones who could plan for the worst possible outcome. If, indeed, Kalnikova had failed and Borodin either sold his shadow warriors to the Americans, or unleashed them for some unknown purpose for all the world to see, Gorokhov didn't see that as a problem. He already knew what the solution would be, the only solution that there could be.

Initiate Operation Scythe. Not next year when all the tests and plans were complete, but immediately.

True, that eventuality would remake the world in ways that couldn't be completely foreseen, and Moscow might be taken by surprise by the chaos that would follow. But in the end, Gorokhov had no doubt that it would be he, and Mother Russia, who would be left standing as America was reduced to rubble and the rest of the world cowered in fear.

As it should.

18

"You show me yours, I'll show you mine," Owen Lomax said. He was an assistant director in the Department of Homeland Security's Office of Operations Coordination and Planning, and he smiled with benign curiosity as if he couldn't think of a single reason why the director of CROSSWIND sat across from his desk this morning.

Caparelli returned the director's friendly smile, hiding his own true intent as thoroughly as he knew Lomax did. That was part of the role he had to play today, because of Detective Matt Caidin.

At five this morning, Caparelli had received a call from Caidin and everything had changed. The echo of Laura, all that she had been, had finally remembered what had happened to her, and that was the end of it. Manifestations never recurred after realizing what they were. The legends all said so; empirical evidence confirmed it.

With no possibility of obtaining further information from Laura about Borodin or his plans here, Caparelli had no choice but to do what he had told Sam Arlo he wouldn't: play a more dangerous game by reaching out to the Department of Homeland Security and requesting its assistance, without revealing any of CROSSWIND's secrets. Remote viewing would remain an effective weapon in the arsenal of intelligence gathering only as long as potential enemies refused to believe it existed.

As a matter of policy, CROSSWIND was an SCI compartment within the National Security Agency. The initials stood for Sensitive Compartmentalized

Intelligence—information that not only required a recipient to have the proper security clearance, but also a justified and adjudicated need to know. More than that, CROSSWIND's "product" was further classified as not just SCI, but ECI: Exceptionally Controlled Information. Even CROSSWIND's budget was "waived," which meant no mention of it appeared in the "black budgets" prepared for congressional committees, where all secret programs that didn't appear in the public record were required by law to be listed for the purposes of oversight.

All this contributed to the reality that CROSSWIND was, to all intents and purposes, a wholly independent agency, invisible to Congress, and answerable only to the president.

In situations where intelligence gathered by remote viewing was to be used strictly within the National Security Agency, CROSSWIND's reports were classified internally as "human intelligence," called HUMINT, and presumed to have been obtained by traditional spycraft. No further explanation of how the intelligence had been gathered was required.

In other situations, when CROSSWIND intelligence needed to be passed on to another government intelligence agency, Caparelli reported it to the director of the NSA. Alone among the 30,000 employees of the agency, the director was fully briefed on CROSSWIND's methods. When the director in turn passed that intelligence on to the directors of other agencies, including the Department of Homeland Security, it was at such a high level that in most cases no attribution was required.

Occasionally, though, there were times when CROSSWIND intelligence needed to be acted on so quickly there was no opportunity for going through the protective but lengthy official channels. In those situations, Caparelli was authorized to take direct action, provided CROSSWIND's methods remained undisclosed.

That much was known to Homeland, which made the department eager to absorb the apparently independent agency into itself, just as it had so many others.

Caparelli was determined to never let that happen. His concern was that if CROSSWIND ever came under Homeland's control, then within weeks, if not days, the reality of remote viewing would become known to tens of thousands of government agents and analysts. At that point, keeping that truth from spreading beyond them to the nation's enemies would become impossible.

Just as those enemies today knew enough from other intelligence leaks to avoid unencrypted satellite phones and timed their movements to the passage of spy satellites, inevitably they would establish electromagnetic safeguards to protect themselves from perceivers. CROSSWIND would become a curious footnote in history, its technology and techniques relegated to the National Cryptologic Museum, its perceivers reduced to experimental subjects at best, sideshow freaks at worst.

As a professional, and a patriot, Caparelli had made the survival of CROSSWIND as a fully independent agency his priority. He owed it to the people who had dedicated their careers and their lives to CROSSWIND's mission. He owed it to his niece. He owed it to the country. He knew that simply by walking through Owen Lomax's door, he was putting all that at risk.

This wasn't the first time Caparelli had taken the Homeland tiger by the tail. A year ago, when official channels would have been too slow, CROSSWIND needed to disguise the source of vital intelligence its perceivers had obtained through remote viewing. To accomplish that, they had used Homeland Security to unknowingly participate in what the NSA innocuously termed the "parallel construction" of evidence.

CROSSWIND perceivers had, through remote viewing, discovered details of a domestic terrorist plot to attack a liquid natural gas production plant near Dallas. It was vital for that intelligence to be given to the FBI, but equally as important to hide the details of how the information was obtained.

Caparelli had contacted Lomax, asked for his department's assistance in correlating surveillance satellite imagery with ground-truth photography of the same sites, taken at the same time. It was a standard method of measuring the effectiveness of various types of camouflage. Caparelli had led Lomax to believe that the exercise might result in obtaining new observation techniques from the mysterious CROSSWIND.

As orchestrated by Caparelli, the area his agents staked out while CROSSWIND satellites supposedly observed from orbit just happened to include the remote ranch house where the plotters were assembling their explosive-packed vehicles.

The Department of Homeland Security, whose agents had therefore accidently but honestly stumbled upon the plot, took full credit for preventing the attack. But though he couldn't prove it, Owen Lomax knew he and his department had been expertly used.

Over the next few days, his request to be told the source of the original intelligence had moved up the chain of command to the Oval Office, where it had been rebuffed. Ever since the Dallas operation, he had set his sights on CROSSWIND and, so far, Caparelli had been able to resist Lomax's methodical plan to bring all government intelligence resources under DHS guidance. Lomax maintained it was a logical, efficient, and cost-effective way to ensure all vital intelligence could be shared quickly, without facing the roadblocks of petty rivalries, and without costly duplication of resources.

Caparelli understood the ideals that drove Lomax, but in no way believed they could withstand the reality of having a specialized, independent operation like CROSSWIND controlled by a bloated bureaucracy with more than 200,000 employees. As far as Caparelli was concerned, it was an arrangement that could only make sense to an organization that had failed to see the irony in choosing as its new headquarters what used to be the country's largest psychiatric hospital.

Now, in a small, windowless office in the newly renovated St. Elizabeths Hospital compound housing the DHS, Caparelli put a thick, red-covered file on Lomax's desk. "We're both on the same side, Director. Everything my people have is in the file. Nothing held back."

Across the desk, Lomax gave Caparelli a measuring look; he knew a lie when he heard one. But this wasn't the time for confrontation. Not yet.

Caparelli waited patiently as Lomax initialed the file, broke the seals. His actions were precise, almost delicate for such a large man, all muscle as far as Caparelli could tell, too large for the confines of his generic civil service office. The desk was an inexpensive black plastic slab with chromed metal legs. The carpet squares were thin, with a mottled gray pattern designed to hide soil and wear. The walls were an off-white textured panel of some kind, held in place by glossy plastic strips. The room felt as if it might have been constructed specifically for this meeting, and perhaps it had. As much as the DHS wanted access to the secrets of everyone else, it revealed as few of its own as possible.

Among the limited amount of nongeneric content in the office was what Caparelli took to be Lomax's personal photographs, hung beside the standard-issue portraits of the president, vice-president, and secretary of the department. The other photos in thin black frames were of Marines in desert camouflage, in country, by a burned-out tank, on a Humvee, in a mess tent. Lomax was in each picture, big grin, cold eyes. His head was shaved back then as it was now, black scalp glistening in the desert heat, but the thick mustache he had today was new.

On a bookcase filled with cryptically titled binders was a last personal item: a folded burial flag in a triangular presentation case. Caparelli didn't ask.

Lomax flipped through the file until he came to the photographs from the warehouse outside Santa Fe. Caparelli watched carefully, didn't detect any reaction to the carnage.

"Interesting blast damage." Lomax might have been talking about the weather.

"Not an explosion."

"That's what I mean. Bodies torn up. Nothing else is." Lomax picked up one of the glossy prints to examine it more closely. "Hmm. The intact bodies here were shot."

"Two state police officers and three forensic specialists. A few hours after the initial killings. Nine-millimeter rounds."

Lomax put the pictures down, laid a large hand over the file. "You have a theory?"

"Details are in the file. Bottom line, we believe two teams of terrorists are on US soil. Came in through a drug tunnel from Mexico, heading northeast."

"Target?"

"That's why I've come to you."

"Their affiliation?"

"Russian."

That got a reaction: puzzled surprise. "Russian what? Gangsters? Involved with the Mexican cartels?"

"We believe they're former or current military."

Lomax sat back in his government-issue swivel chair, making it squeak in protest. "Russians aren't above aiding terrorist organizations with intel, matériel, instructors . . . But active agents here? Seems too provocative, even for their president."

"Might help if we knew what they were after."

Lomax flashed him a tight smile, as cold as they were in the photos on the wall. His war hadn't ended. "Correct me if I'm wrong, but isn't your organization the one with magical intel-gathering expertise?"

"We don't conduct domestic operations," Caparelli lied.

Lomax didn't challenge him. "So if I understand you"—he patted the thick file—"instead of roping us into a fake 'assessment' operation like last year in Dallas, now you're just magnanimously passing on to DHS news of terrorist cells operating on home soil, without providing any source or verification. And in return you want us to tell you their target."

"We share the same mission."

Lomax gave him a thoughtful look, and Caparelli could tell their match was about to begin in earnest. "I need something else, Agent. How many are there? What weapons? What the hell tore up those people if not an explosive? And, well, how the hell do you know what you know?"

Caparelli was prepared. Philosophical differences aside, Lomax was a reasonable man. "What I can say is, we believe there are fewer than ten people involved. Weaponry could be whatever they could hand-carry through a drug tunnel. What killed those people . . . Something chemical? Something mechanical? We've never seen anything like it before. Don't even have a hypothesis."

The two men stared at each other for long moments. It was obvious Lomax wasn't convinced.

"You asked," Caparelli said finally. "I answered. Is there a target of opportunity in the direction they're heading?"

"America is a target-rich environment. Shopping malls. Passenger trains. Office buildings. You have to give me more to go on."

"If they planned on striking soft civilian targets, they would've acted by now. So we believe they have a specific target. They're heading northeast. To DC? Manhattan? Is there anything that speaks to a terrorist opportunity at this particular time, instead of last week or next month?"

"Maybe they're going to go to ground. Hide out for a year."

"Then they wouldn't have left the bodies to be discovered and draw our attention. They're planning something soon. Not worried about being tracked, just keeping a few steps ahead of us. What about the Joint Anti-terrorism Conference? Starts in four days."

Lomax rolled his head side to side, to crack his neck. "Well, now, that is an obvious target. The elected leaders of fifteen nations coming together to form a new coalition to fight terrorism around the globe, complete with their senior military and intelligence personnel." Lomax shook his head. "But when you think of the repercussions of attacking that gathering, where's the upside in sending the world's economy crashing into a black hole when all fingers are going to be pointed at the one country not invited? Russia.

"Besides, the site's the Greenbrier, in the middle of wide-open country. Terrorists would need an armored division to get anywhere near it. And we'd still stop them with Hellfire drones before they reached the first perimeter."

"What else?"

Lomax glanced over at his trophy photos. "The conference is bringing a boatload of foreign leaders and dignitaries over here. The British prime minister's addressing a joint session of the House and Senate the day before the summit starts. That puts almost every elected official we have in the same place at the same time. That'd be bad for us, for Britain, not so much for the rest of the world.

"Then, the president's speaking to the United Nations General Assembly the day after the summit ends, and the Russians will be there. But again, no upside to an attack on the *entire* UN. Terrorists would be killing friends as well as enemies.

"Anyway, DC and Manhattan will be locked down as tight as the Greenbrier. Nothing will drive in and out. Nothing will fly anywhere near any of those three sites."

"Then there has to be something else. A not-so-obvious target."

Lomax didn't bother to hide his skepticism. "A target that the *Russians* would want to take out even at the risk of starting a war with every other country in the world."

"Read the file," Caparelli said. "You'll know everything we know."

Lomax smiled. "Oh, I doubt that. But I'll read it. And I'll send a watch alert for ten Russian terrorists to our teams. Best I can do for now. Until I know more." Lomax stood. The meeting was over. "Any idea when that will be?"

"Our source on this has dried up."

Caparelli could see Lomax didn't believe that, either. But then, he wouldn't have believed what Caparelli's source had been. So that didn't matter.

What did matter was that as much as Lomax wanted to take the reins of CROSSWIND, Caparelli had successfully maneuvered the DHS into providing on-the-ground resources as CROSSWIND's perceivers redoubled their efforts to locate Borodin by other means.

To Caparelli, that meant Homeland and CROSSWIND were doing what Lomax wanted them to do: working together. In a perfect world, Lomax would take that as a win. But as he left the director's office, Caparelli knew their game wouldn't end that easily.

The moment the door closed behind Caparelli, Lomax jabbed the white button on his desk phone. "You heard all that?"

Over the intercom, the response was immediate. "Lima Charlie." The phrase meant loud and clear. Agent Rick Ames and Lomax had served together, still used Marine jargon.

A moment later, the side door opened and Ames entered. He was Secret Service liaison to Operations Coordination, the Secret Service having been swept up by DHS on Day One. He was a smaller man than Lomax, but not by much. Despite their positions in two different civilian organizations, they were still Marines, always would be.

"So what's your theory?" Lomax asked.

Ames leaned against the wall, arms folded. "I think he told us what he knows, but he don't know squat. Sure doesn't know about our prisoner, that's for certain."

Lomax agreed. He checked his watch. Less than an hour ago, a Russian female had landed at Andrews Air Force Base aboard a DHS Gulfstream V, in chains. Last night outside Colorado Springs, she had murdered a physician who had been under surveillance in a prescription drug investigation. Such a happy accident.

Under normal procedures, it might have taken days for the Russian female to be identified and come to the attention of the DHS through Immigration and Customs Enforcement, another of its subsumed agencies. But in this case, local police had discovered her amputated right hand, wounded in a manner local medical authorities couldn't classify. That triggered a Chemical-Biological-Nuclear Threat Alert that had flashed through the chain of command in minutes. Less than an hour later, the woman's photograph and fingerprints had been processed by the department's Automated Biometric Identification System, which noted her most recent entry into the country four days ago at JFK International Airport. The system also called up a prior entry, two years earlier, with the same biometric signature, but a different name. That had triggered another automated threat alert.

Again without human intervention, the woman's biometrics had been flashed to four other specialized databases, including ones at the Department of Justice, FBI, and CIA. But her positive ID had come through within minutes from the fourth database: the Defense Intelligence Agency's Biometric Processing Unit at Fort Meade. The end result was that within eighty-seven minutes of the CBN Threat Alert, Owen Lomax had a new operation to coordinate at the

DHS: find out why a Russian army major was in the US with false documents and a bizarrely mangled and amputated right hand.

Caparelli's phone call a few hours later had been like a gift from heaven, as were the photographs he'd provided of the mutilated bodies at the warehouse crime scene.

That was the power of coordination, Lomax knew. With one central source to which all data flowed, the ability to assemble those pieces into a coherent whole was greatly enhanced. Before consolidation, too many uncommunicative intelligence agencies had been the proverbial blind men clutching their own particular piece of the elephant, no one possessing a clear grasp of the nature of the beast.

Lomax knew that Caparelli didn't share his vision for the unification of the nation's intelligence operations. What the source of that resistance was, Lomax didn't know, though he accepted that Caparelli was sincere in somehow thinking it was for the best. That would make the coming confrontation between them more difficult, Lomax knew. But that confrontation was inevitable, and after today, it was imminent. Whatever else was going on here, once the Russian terrorists were dealt with and the security of the country was assured, Lomax considered CROSSWIND and its secrets to be his primary target.

Not every part of the old St. Elizabeths Hospital campus had been repurposed into offices. A small section of one historic building maintained the facility's original legacy and had been renovated to become a state-of-the-art infirmary and extended-care facility. The infirmary was for the treatment of department personnel with work-related wounds and injuries, as well as for the rehabilitation of interrogated prisoners. The extended-care facility, similar to those maintained by the other intelligence agencies, was for the safe confinement of former employees who both knew too much and suffered from dementia. Here, all the caregivers had security clearances, so it was no longer necessary to drug or isolate those who had secrets yet were no longer capable of honoring their secrecy oaths.

For now, the Kalnikova woman was being held in a secure infirmary suite as a medical patient. Whether she would later need treatment as an interrogated prisoner would depend on the outcome of her first meeting with Lomax and Ames.

The infirmary's senior physician was Darryl Mars. He waited for the DHS director and Secret Service agent outside Kalnikova's suite. Mars was a former Air Force flight surgeon, tall, imposing, and always gave the impression there was someplace else he'd rather be.

"Have you determined the cause of her injury?" Lomax asked. The three men knew each other. There was no need for pleasantries or small talk on their particular battlefield.

Mars used a tablet to show Lomax and Ames X-ray images of the prisoner's amputated hand and severed wrist. "It's nothing chemical, biological, or nuclear," the doctor said. "So, nothing contagious or dangerous for you to be around."

Lomax couldn't make sense of the images. He could see the ulna and radius bones of the woman's forearm were intact to the wrist. But in the images of the hand, it was difficult to identify any specific bone, other than a few phalanges that were recognizable, though not in the normal positions of fingers and thumb. The X-ray images were further confused by solid white splinters—metal of some kind, but not typical shrapnel.

"Was the hand crushed?" Ames seemed to be having the same trouble reading the images as Lomax.

"The bones and tissue show signs of a similar type of compression trauma," Mars said. "But in that case, we'd expect the hand to be flattened, as if it had been, I don't know, placed in a vise. That's not the case here. Plus the condition of the embedded metal and plastic fragments is totally baffling." He tapped the screen to display a straightforward photograph of a Beretta semiautomatic pistol. Lomax IDed it as a Px4 Storm. An effective personal weapon, though he preferred his Sig. Both used 9 mm ammunition. The same used to kill the police and forensics technicians outside of Santa Fe.

"You're looking at pieces of this model of handgun," Mars said. "It's the sort of trauma we might see if she had been in close contact with an explosive device while holding the gun, and the blast shattered it and drove the fragments into the hand but . . ." Mars hesitated, as if knowing how foolish he was about to appear.

But Lomax already knew what the doctor was about to say, spared him the necessity. "She sustained no blast damage."

Mars narrowed his pale eyes at Lomax. "You know what caused this?"

"No. But I've seen it before." Lomax nodded to Ames. "Let's do this."

Mars refrained from asking any more questions. In this profession, everyone had secrets.

Kalnikova was floating peacefully, her burning hand a bad dream she had had once, and could barely remember.

It was the pain medication, she knew. She suspected the dose she'd been given was far more than medically necessary. Questions were coming, and she knew they'd be serious, because no one had asked her any yet.

"Sofia Kalnikova?"

The name sounded familiar, then she realized two men were standing by her bed. The room was so unremittingly bright, they were little more than black shadows. But she blinked her dry eyes a few more times, and slowly they came into focus.

She wanted to laugh when she saw how typical they looked: soldiers pretending to be in business suits. CIA, she guessed. Or some other kind of spy. But her throat was as dry as her eyes.

"Where is this?" Her voice was raspy. She had been given her first shot of a painkiller just before getting into an ambulance for a ride to an air station. She had a vague recollection of being helped onto a small jet, and then only flashes of a short flight, another ambulance, and then waking in this hospital.

"You're in the United States." The shadow that spoke to her was the larger of the two men, the black one with the mustache. *Very Stalin*, she thought, then tried to laugh again. "Illegally," he added.

Kalnikova concentrated. "I would like to contact Russian embassy."

"That's not going to happen."

She coughed to clear her throat, and the other shadow did something at the side of her bed, held a small cup of ice to her lips. She reached to hold the cup herself, then was startled to realize she was in restraints. Her left hand, and the thickly wrapped stump of her right wrist, both.

"This is necessary?" she asked.

"For who you are, for what you've done, this is like a luxury vacation," the mustache man said. "It can get a lot worse. And it will."

She knew what was coming. Drew in a deep breath, tried to fight back the cobwebs of whatever they had pumped into her. "Unless . . . ?"

"Full cooperation."

The vagueness of that statement told her the Americans were fishing. That gave her some leverage. She needed to know how much.

"In what matter?" she asked.

"Why'd you kill Dr. Roberta Long?"

More fishing, she thought. If this were a murder investigation, she'd still be in Colorado Springs, being questioned by local police.

"Was accident." She slurred her speech, as if the medication had more of an effect than it did. She tried moving any part of her missing right hand and succeeded in making her wrist throb with dull pain. She needed her edge back.

"Audio recording doesn't support that."

"I'm very tired."

She saw the two men exchange a look, but her vision was blurred and she couldn't see what passed between them.

"What happened to your hand?"

Interesting. Could that be the reason she was being questioned by these men? They recognized the type of wound it was? Or, perhaps, they couldn't.

"Is not obvious?" Kalnikova asked. She would not be the first to give up information.

The big man loomed over her, but she wouldn't meet his gaze. She closed her eyes, instead, as if drifting off in a drug haze. But she focused her thoughts on picturing and naming all the pieces of an AK-47 as she stripped it and reassembled it in her mind's eye.

"This is what's obvious," he said. "Nine people are dead. The doctor you suffocated. Two police officers and three technicians shot with the same bullets used by the gun that came apart in your hand. And a three-person video crew with the same type of wounds you have.

"So," the man concluded, "what I need to know is, am I going to charge you as a Russian national who accidently killed a drug dealer, which means you'd be sent back to Russia to serve your sentence, or am I going to charge you as a terrorist who's slaughtered nine innocent Americans, which means life in an isolation cell in a supermax prison? You see my dilemma?"

Kalnikova opened her eyes, felt clarity return to her. Not the clarity of her military training, but of a chess game: pure strategy.

"You are offering me deal," she said.

"I said what I said. It's your turn to talk."

She ignored him. "You are offering this deal so early for one of two reasons.

The first, you are desperate. The second, you have no intention keeping deal. You do not look desperate."

Kalnikova saw the men exchange another look, and the smaller one, who had given her the ice, started for the door.

"We'll figure out what happened to your hand without your help," the man with the mustache said.

"No doubt you will," she agreed.

The smaller man left, shut the door behind him.

The big man who remained stepped closer to her bed, put his hands on the safety railing, as if she could go anywhere while restrained.

"You're tough, Major. I get that."

There was something about the way he said her rank, the first time it had been mentioned. "You are soldier," she said.

"Marine."

Kalnikova nodded. "Officer?"

"Major."

She smiled. "We are equal then. You say, 'Brothers in arms.' Lucky happenstance, yes?"

"Not quite equal. You're my prisoner."

Kalnikova blinked again, and her vision cleared finally, to show her the steady gaze of the man by her bed.

She stared at him, judging him. "Not prisoner," she said. "Partner."

His expression didn't change, and he didn't look away. "How so?"

"We have same mission."

"That would be?"

"The man responsible for . . . hurting those people. For what happened to my hand . . . I was sent to stop him."

It was nothing she saw, but she felt the connection that suddenly sprang up between them. Warhounds catching the scent of prey. The promise of action. *What is a man like this doing in a business suit?* she asked herself.

"Who is he? Why is he here?"

"Why? I don't know. The people who sent me, they don't know. Who he is, that I do know."

"The condition of the bodies, your wound . . . Does the person you're after have a new type of weapon?"

Kalnikova knew it would be best to save that information until the very end, and even then, the less she revealed, the better. She saw that the man understood it would be useless to ask for more from her. The details of their partnership had to be established first. But he couldn't resist another question. "Do you know where he is? Where he's going?"

Kalnikova moved her queen to check. "I have way to track him." She closed her eyes, ready to drift off to sleep. "Partner."

19

"What happens now?" Matt asked.

Sam Arlo flipped through the stack of documents Matt had signed, confirming there was a signature at each red flag. "It all goes away." The documents were in order. He held them upright, tapped them into a neat pile on the desktop. He could see Matt didn't understand.

"We all go back to our own work, our own lives," Arlo said.

Matt had no more reserves to draw on—physical, mental, or emotional. His state had nothing to do with lack of sleep, though he hadn't slept for more than twenty-four hours. It had everything to do with Laura Hart, whatever it was she was. He couldn't stop thinking about her.

"As if what?" Matt asked. "None of this ever happened?"

Arlo looked down at the documents. "Pretty much. That's what these agreements say. I know it's hard, maybe doesn't seem fair, but you had a glimpse into something pretty awesome. Something we need to keep secret from . . . well, from people who don't have our best interests in mind. What we do here at CROSSWIND is important. For the country. And for science."

Intellectually, Matt knew all that. He had signed the nondisclosure forms and secrecy oath without hesitation. But it was one thing to agree never to talk with anyone on the outside about what he had learned, something completely different to never talk with anyone on the inside. There was still so much he didn't understand about what he had experienced. And there was no way he was forgetting . . .

"Look," he said to Arlo, "I just need some . . . closure." At once, Matt regretted the pleading tone of his statement. But in no way was he ready to let go. Not yet.

Arlo checked his watch, looked to the closed door of the small office they were in as if expecting someone to burst through at any moment. Then, as if he felt equal regret for the decision he was about to make, said, "Okay. But fast. Anyone comes in, I'm in big trouble. What do you want to know?"

Matt pulled up a chair. "Everything you can tell me."

"We don't know everything. Ask me something specific."

"Why'd Laura come to me in my apartment? You said she was going to go to hers. You set up your equipment there."

"Your guess is as good as mine," Arlo said. "It's not something we can measure in the lab. We do know there's got to be what we call an emotional resonance between a remote viewer and their subject—usually that's a person, sometimes it's a place. So, I guess it makes sense, sort of, that the same type of resonance plays a part in the 'ghost' phenomenon.

"If you think of it, Laura died outside that diner you were in, and that's where she manifested, so everything pointed to her resonance being keyed to a particular place. Since the last encounter she had in the diner somehow upset her, we anticipated she'd return to another place she had a deep emotional connection to, like her apartment. Instead, she turned up at yours. So what can I say? We were wrong."

"You mean, she didn't establish emotional resonance with a place. She established it with me."

Arlo nodded. "We knew you were connected. Just didn't know how strongly. Caparelli made the call to prepare her apartment, and I agreed with him."

Matt had to confirm the other detail that no one would discuss. "Caparelli . . . he's the 'Daniel' Laura was calling for, when she was dying."

Arlo looked uncomfortable. "Yeah. He's her uncle. More like a father. His sister died when she was a kid, and he took her in. Definitely against policy for him to have recruited a family member, but she had the talent, so he went through channels and . . ."

"He was the boss."

Matt could see Arlo needed to defend the man he worked for. "Completely off the record, he and Laura were a good team. They knew each other so well; they clicked. Whatever you want to call it, it didn't interfere with the project or with any missions. It's not like . . . well, there's usually no risk involved to remote viewing. Headaches, a bit of disorientation at the end of a session, that's about it. Far as I know, nobody in the project ever died in the line of duty, as it were. Until now, that is."

Matt reflected on that, realized it was the answer to the sense he had of Caparelli withholding information from him: He had felt responsible for Laura, and blamed himself for her death. And then, Matt, a stranger, had appeared from nowhere and erased their family bond with something deeper, more personal.

"Caparelli must've been pissed Laura connected with me, not him."

Arlo leaned forward, hands resting on the desk. "Look, our best guess is that you connected with Laura because you were there, holding her hand as she was dying. I mean, it's not like you'd ever met before, right?"

Matt nodded. He'd interacted with thousands of people as a police officer. But Laura was someone he would have definitely remembered.

Arlo continued. "But what came back, that wasn't her. It was an echo, an imprint. Some bizarre standing-wave phenomenon with information encoded in it. A lot of information. We tried to extract it. It didn't work. The wave dissipated. The echo faded. End of story."

"I don't believe that."

Arlo spoke more forcefully. "When I said 'echo' I mean that whatever you connected to—whatever you felt you connected to—was only an *illusion* of life. The memory of it. That's why Caparelli isn't 'pissed.' You experienced an image of Laura Hart, and that's all you lost. The director, he lost the child he had raised." Arlo looked at his watch again, picked up the documents. "Trust me. Once I file these, you'll be the last thing on his mind. So, move on."

Matt understood, accepting that the briefing was over. But he wasn't about to accept that the story was. He wasn't ready for it to end.

Matt walked through his day in a fog of distraction. Out of habit more than necessity, he went to the grocer at the corner of his street. He bought cans of soup, though he knew it was too hot to consider eating them. Bread. Eggs. A pound of bacon. A six-pack of beer. Breakfast.

He walked back to the apartment building knowing that every person he saw, everyone who drove past him on the street, in cars and trucks, buses and bicycles, all had a quantum field—could he say it? A soul? Some ghostly essence that might persist after death.

What if he had it, too? Everything was different now because of that. But according to Arlo, everything had to remain the same.

Matt collected his mail in the anteroom off the lobby. He still checked the hallway before getting off the elevator, still looking for any signs that the Mauricios were ready to tie up loose ends. He examined his apartment door, saw the paper was still in place.

He put the groceries away, left the mail on the kitchen counter unopened. He plugged his phone in to recharge, saw Helena had called again. He felt like a robot, going through the motions, knowing he had to call the station to arrange a return to desk duty, knowing he had to check in with Internal Affairs to find out how much longer this charade would continue, how much longer Downey's family would have to bear the burden of the false stain on Jack's integrity. How long he'd have to endure the same. Matt felt weighed down by daily life, overwhelmed by the knowledge there could be so much more to existence.

Faced with all he had to do, he felt incapable of doing anything.

He sat on the beige couch in the beige living room, stared out at the patch of cloud and sky visible through the window over the balcony. Drank three beers. Tried and failed to find peace in sleep.

And woke as a noise roused him in the dim light of dusk, knowing he wasn't alone.

20

The first punch was to his gut, and even as Matt reflexively crumpled forward, strong hands clamped down on his shoulders and dragged him back against the couch. The second punch glanced off his jaw, badly aimed, but the impact drove a tooth into his cheek. He tasted blood.

A gruff voice cursed him. Whoever had struck him hid behind a ski mask, but Matt knew him anyway. It was a cop from his own division.

"Bailey?! What the—" The man behind wrenched open his mouth and jammed a dishcloth down it. Matt gagged as bile burned in the back of his throat.

Bailey forced his head up. "We got a good thing going, Caidin. No way you're doing to us what you did to Jack."

With the sudden awareness brought by adrenaline, Matt got the message loud and clear. The Mauricio brothers weren't going to take care of him on their own. The Arlington cops who'd been arrested the day after Lowney's suicide attempt weren't the only ones on the Mauricios' payroll.

Bailey's next punch knocked Matt backward to the couch, and then a second man, behind him, lifted him by his shoulders and pushed him to his feet. *Hickman*. Bailey's partner. Of course they were on the take together: They never worked alone.

Acting on instinct, not thought, Matt rammed his body forward, still in the grip of the man who held him, and head-butted Bailey in the face, spilling the three of them to the floor.

Matt rolled away, one hand pulling the cloth from his mouth, the other flailing at Bailey, then Hickman, to ward them both off.

He was grabbed from behind again but wrenched himself away. Hickman aimed a kick at him, but Matt caught his leg and flipped him, made him fall, even as Bailey took his place.

Matt rolled away, pulling the coffee table in as a shield to give him the second he needed to jump up.

"This is a mistake," he shouted, even though he knew they hadn't picked the lock and come to listen. "You can get out of this. Come clean. Go into protection!" *They won't kill me here*, he thought. Too much forensic evidence. It was to his advantage to make the crime scene as messy as he could.

Bailey and Hickman moved apart, obviously preparing to rush him from both sides.

Matt leapt up and sprinted for the hallway. His gun was in his bedroom, in the side table.

Hickman tackled him and knocked him to the floor before he reached the bedroom door, and both men kicked him savagely again. Matt's vision clouded and his ears rang. He was vaguely aware of being hauled into a chair. Felt his feet and hands being tightly bound with duct tape. Saw the two men rip open a large cardboard box. Pull out black plastic garbage bags. Lawn and leaf. He was right. They were preparing to take him somewhere else. Somewhere no one would ever find him.

Matt shivered. The air was colder. The two men had stopped their preparations. Had they changed their minds? Had they opened the sliding door so they could throw him out and claim his death a suicide?

The two men were speaking to each other, but he wasn't listening. He was looking at their ski masks. In the half-light of dusk, he could make out a dusting of white beneath their hidden nostrils. A rim of frost. Eddies of vapor from their breath swirled in the ever-cooler air. The temperature was continuing to drop. As if a storm was gathering.

Matt thought of Arlo and his tales of apparitions and energy extraction. He heard what sounded like the sound of wind rustling leaves. He looked beyond Bailey and Hickman. He laughed.

Hickman yanked off his ski mask, outraged. "What's so funny, asshole?" For just a moment, he seemed distracted by the cloud his breath formed. He held his hand up to his mouth, exhaled, puzzled.

"Look behind you," Matt said.

Bailey pushed Hickman aside to loom over Matt. "You think we're stupid? Nothing's going to save you."

But the rustling sound was louder, and both men turned to see—

Something darkly billowing in midair.

One of the black plastic bags hung at eye level, pulsing like a living thing, or like a living thing was inside it, breathing heavily, impatient.

Hickman reached out to the black form, hesitant at first, then suddenly pulled it aside as if ripping open a curtain and—

Nothing. The empty bag drifted to the floor.

Hickman stamped on it with his boot. Turned to Bailey. Opened his mouth to speak, and—

A second sheet of plastic snapped tight over Bailey's face. He was lifted back into the shadows with a muffled yelp.

Hickman froze. *"Who is it? Who's there?!"*

Matt saw Bailey's form in silhouette, leaning back at an impossible angle as if supported by something unseen, both hands clawing at the suffocating plastic wrapping his head, both feet helplessly kicking out.

Giving one quick glance at Matt, Hickman rushed for his partner, pulling him upright, shredding the plastic until Bailey gasped and coughed and sank to his knees, chest heaving.

Hickman's look at Matt told him he'd pay for this. "Who else is here?!"

Matt gave the only answer he could. "Get out while you can."

Bailey rose up with a roar and charged Matt, fist held high. Then stopped, squealing like a frightened child, because Laura suddenly stood before Matt, blocking Bailey's path. Her short jacket was brown leather, her jeans well-worn, old. Different clothes again.

Bailey's fist was still raised high; his mouth had gone slack. "Where'd you come from?"

Hickman was by his partner's side. "Forget that, man! We gotta take her, too!"

Matt didn't see what Laura did next; her back was to him. But as both men suddenly stumbled back, astonished, Matt heard the wet sound of wheezing congested lungs and liquid dripping on the carpet.

While Hickman kept backing toward the door, Bailey halted, muttered something almost inaudible, then snarled and lunged at Laura.

Still bound in the chair, Matt could only watch as Laura abruptly *shifted* to the side. It was if he were watching an old film that had broken, and frames were lost in the repair.

Bailey missed her, recapturing his balance directly in front of Matt. But before Bailey could do more than look enraged, dark, blood-slicked hands reached up from behind him and clawed at his face, gouging flesh, his unprotected eyes, and he howled as his own blood flowed.

Laura *shifted* once again, and vanished.

Hickman turned and ran, and Bailey stumbled after him, hands covering his ruined face. The door slammed after them. Matt was alone again. Alive.

He took a deep and calming breath. When he exhaled, no cloud of vapor floated into the moonlight shining through the sliding glass doors.

Warm fingers sought his bound wrists, tightly taped behind him. Ripped the duct tape from them. His hands were free and Laura knelt before him, peeling off the tape that had secured his ankles. The moonlight haloed her, or was it reflected streetlights? Or did she herself glow? Matt wasn't sure.

He was trembling. Shock from the assault, masked until now by the adrenaline of his panicked struggle to survive. Knowing he was going to die.

"You saved my life," he said to her.

She lifted her head and he stared into her gold-flecked green eyes. Almost imperceptibly, her lips parted and her warm breath touched him with a whisper. "You saved me."

Her touch was electric. A memory stirred. Matt didn't understand, didn't care. All he knew was that, like him, in this one precious moment, she was alive.

One precious moment. This moment. No past. No future.

He moved without volition. Was this something he had done before? Something he had wanted to do? Something *she* wanted?

But the questions meant nothing without the concept of time, of past, of future.

"When?" he asked. "When did I save you?"

She smiled at him as if they were kids and he was being silly.

"You know," she said.

"But I don't."

She shifted, and for an instant, Matt saw her not as she had been when she had manifested to face Bailey and Hickman, but as she had been the night she died: a bloodied, mangled corpse.

His eyes widened in surprise, but he betrayed no shock, no fear. And in that moment of acceptance, she shifted back and was in her jeans and hooded pullover, just as she had worn when she had first appeared in the café.

"That night?" Matt asked. Was that what she meant?

She looked away, troubled. "No. It was daytime. We only saw the dog in the daytime."

Matt didn't understand. He wanted to question her, but was afraid the wrong words might send her away.

She blurred, as if whatever mechanism was responsible for manifesting her as a living being was caught between settings, didn't know what she was supposed to be. She was the woman in the café, the woman in the suit on her way to her interview, the woman dying in her crushed car, then a child, no more than five, gazing up at him with eyes full of fear. . . .

"The dog," she whispered.

He reached down for her, and she shifted and looked out at him from the shadows of her hood, her face so beautiful, so sad, so full of yearning.

She was both light and heavy as he swept her up into his arms.

As he passed the mirror in the hall, Matt saw but didn't see her battered body, fresh from the crash, scalp ripped, blood streaming, her sightless, staring face glazed dark red. *That's not what she is.* He bent down to kiss her perfect lips, and her blood smeared across his face, then vanished again in his acceptance of her.

In the shadows of his bedroom, Laura slipped off a different jacket, and Matt hesitated, remembering the woman in the crash—she'd worn one like it, drenched in blood.

Then broken, twisted fingers tugged on his shirt to hurry him, and Matt forgot the flash of discordant memory, stroking tender palms, caressing soft, unblemished skin. He held Laura close as he heard and felt but had no awareness of her shattered ribs grating against him. All that he registered was her intoxicating heat.

Without past or future, there was only now.

Matt closed his eyes as Laura Hart rose up to take him and—

His eyes opened and he screamed as a ravaged, rotting corpse pulled him down into the same dark realm in which she was trapped.

21

I am the ghost now.

It is the only explanation that makes sense to Matt.

He is a passenger, a passive observer. He is the one taking action. He is seeing through her eyes. Through his own eyes. All at the same time.

No. Not seeing. Perceiving.

Laura wakes in a rumpled bed. Not Matt's. He doesn't recognize it. She does, and in that moment, so does he. A woman's bedroom. He can smell the perfume. Laura stretches; Matt feels the stiffness in her shoulder relax. She gets up. It's familiar this place, to her, to him. He doesn't understand why; then he does. It's her bedroom. Her apartment. She's lived here for three years. Matt's lived here for three years.

A word comes to him.

Entanglement. His consciousness overlaid on hers. Hers on his.

She's showering now. He breathes in the vapor, cleansing, refreshing. The soap smells like peppermint. She's alive. He's alive.

A dark flash. The opposite of light. Death will come.

She eats breakfast. Dresses. A touch of makeup. Then driving. A silver car. The car. *Two-door. Midsize. Korean. Tonight, this car will crash. But Matt drives it now. Going to—*

He sits in a dark room. "What's happening?" *he asks. The room shrinks and turns white, and Matt's in the first briefing she had, in the conference room, her hair tied back, pen in hand, eagerly listening to her uncle, the director. Caparelli's younger.*

"As far as anyone else in the group knows, you're just another potential recruit," he tells her a week earlier at dinner. "It's called remote viewing," he tells the newcomers in the white room. "But it's not that simple."

Another word comes to Matt.

Superposition.

"You will be both the observer, and the observed. One can't exist without the other."

The white room expands, and Matt is on the phone to Laura's aunt, Caparelli's second, younger sister. Your cousin's coming home this weekend. Dinner Sunday, yes. What can I bring? Matt asks.

Then Norma Chu is laughing. Matt feels a wave of the love for the slight, white-haired woman. She's his personal interface technician, assigned to him from the beginning. Not a coworker, but family.

Norma shows Laura a video on her phone. Two kittens wrestling. A single ball of fur.

Matt's allergic, Laura isn't, and the conflicted memory of that snaps him back across the lab. Disconnected.

"Each of you has been selected because you have the ability," Caparelli tells him in the first briefing. "That's nothing we can teach you—you can do it or you can't. But we can train you in the techniques you'll need to process the experience. To wall off a part of yourself from the experience. Guided dream imagery. Separation. Otherwise, what you observe will become unintelligible, like double and triple exposures, a random assortment of sensations and memories from which it'll be impossible for us to extract useful information."

This is what's happening to me. This is what it's like to perceive.

This is what it's like to continue to exist, caught in the past, not in memories, but reliving entire experiences. As if—

As if an entire life was passing before her eyes. His eyes.

Matt stands quietly in the corner of the Projection Room, aware of his own breathing, of the metallic scent in the air, of the deep hum of powerful machinery from some hidden source.

This is what it's like to be a ghost.

Laura sits on an examination table. She wears loose white pants and top. Her feet are bare. Norma measures her blood pressure. One wall is dusted with frost in a pattern of grid lines, something cold behind them. In the center of the room, a long base clad in curved, white panels that makes Matt think of hospital equipment, an MRI scanner, except it's open on the sides. At one end, it rises up and arches over to form a matching canopy above the base. The space inside is open, waiting, like a giant's hand ready to cradle a baby.

Cradle.

That's the word that comes to him.

The sound of the machine grows and pulses. Matt feels the hair on his arms and scalp bristle. Laura is in the Cradle.

Floating in the empty space.

Total isolation.

The lights in the room dim. A strobe begins flashing over Laura's face, the pattern and colors subtly changing, fading in intensity, becoming almost subliminal. The temperature is perfect. Her hair has fanned out with a static charge. Her loose clothing ripples, then holds its shape as if inflated, at no point touching her. Darkness then, and Matt falls again into that deep connection, that—

Superposition. Entanglement.

He's in a desert, in a van, outside it, driving along a dirt road. Ahead, a house, but nothing else around it. It's night. The air is dry. Laura's tired. The general is tired—

The general.

Matt feels himself spin with the conflict. He's Matt. He's Laura. He's Borodin, and his mind fills with thoughts in Russian that he understands yet doesn't. Images form. A lab? Cold? Someone screaming, dirt falling, each cry a knife through the general's heart. The mission. The lies. The target.

I am perceiving.

The van has stopped. Metal boxes on the gravel. Footlockers? No, the words come to him in Russian, but he understands them: containment units. His mind fills with images of blueprints, wiring diagrams, einstone resonator, battery strength, operational ranges and temperatures . . . A cloud of facts and figures that mean nothing to Matt, nothing to Laura, everything to Borodin.

Small status lights shine on the containment units' number pads. Matt understands what each signifies. The general doesn't want to open them. The general has to open them.

To call them forth.

Matt stands in the courtyard, observing. Something happening—

What is it?

He and Laura are swept by a wave of black smoke into the house—

The hacienda.

—and now Matt no longer understands what he sees as people scream and soldiers in black hack them into pieces.

But they have no weapons.

Then how are they doing it? Bullets fly and pass through Laura, pass through Matt, pass through the soldiers in black. But the people in the house—

Screaming.

—are shredded, torn, ripped—

Blood everywhere.

How?

Laura's never seen this before. The shock, the fear, the pain, the screaming, of all the fields—

The souls.

—dying around her, shock her, disconnect her from the experience.

Matt stands in the courtyard. He sees a man from inside the house run out. Sees him wheel, sees him fire his automatic weapon at the soldier in black who pursues him.

The soldier is untouched, unstoppable.

The soldier's hands pass into the man's chest—

Impossible.

—then rip him apart.

Laura watches from the window. Matt doesn't understand what he sees. The general does. Three viewpoints in superposition. Three thoughts entangled. One thought above them all.

My son.

Laura stands in the window, and the general knows she's there. Observed and observing.

A soldier's unleashed, and the dark wave sweeps Matt into its wake, into the house, into—

Laura wakes in her rumpled bed. Matt fumbles for the phone. It's tangled in the charging cord. She drops it; he catches it. Speed dials Uncle Daniel. Matt looks all around the room.

Where is this?

Voice mail.

"*Daniel! Pick up! I had a spontaneous link! Borodin's got something new. It was tearing people apart. Don't know where, a desert maybe, stucco walls, tile roof, but . . . it was so bloody. Five others with him? Six? I don't know. In a truck, I think. Somewhere hot and dry. Those poor people . . .*

"*Look, I think he connected with me on his end. Maybe even saw me. There was something going on I need to process. I'm coming in. Call Norma. We really need to sift through this. I really need—*"

Matt feels something in the bedroom. A shadow shifting? The sound of darkness?

He's already running from the apartment, car keys in hand, shrugging on a leather jacket.

Her car is in her building's underground garage. He gets in. She starts it, speeds out. He drives. She drives. Entangled, they race to escape the coming shadow.

It's there. In the rearview mirror. The dark wave. Rushing forward. A wind. A wave.

A presence within range.

She drives faster. Matt drives faster.

I have been back-traced.

The wave reaches the shore of the car, sweeps inside, coldness reaching with dark talons—

Fear drives the car, a sudden twist of the wheel, a lurch, and flying.

Matt stares ahead in that still moment, tracking the headlights as they paint the buildings ahead, spike across the road, into the window of the diner.

Matt stares ahead from the car and sees himself staring back from the diner. Observer and observed.

Then all the waves collapse and there is only the cacophony of death.

Life bleeds from her, and she reaches out to take his hand.

Not Daniel.

The medics. The firefighters. The pain. The ebbing.

On the gurney. Peace descending.

"You can help me," she says.

"Like you did before," she thinks, he thinks.

A memory stirs. The ghost dog is barking.

Then—

Eyes looking up, seeing what waits.

Then—

Eyes looking down. Seeing her body on the gurney, lifeless. Seeing himself beside her, useless.

Peace ascending.

The dark wave gone.

Only the need to come in. To report. To continue. To—

Finish.

DAY SIX

22

The most secure section of the VEKTOR facility was in the lowest level of the old mine, protected not only by electromagnetic shielding, but by a half mile of rock.

Chief Administrator Gorokhov rode the facility's main wire-cage lift to that level, accompanied only by the lift operator. He needed the latest inventory figures, but he didn't need his deputy administrator to know that he did.

The antique lift creaked and rattled. The air, growing warmer as Gorokhov descended, reeked of diesel fumes despite the gigantic air blowers up top. The stench of stale cigarette smoke clinging to the operator's oil-stained coveralls was even stronger. It was a familiar smell. It made him remember.

It was raining that April morning when Evgeny Gorokhov hurried across Lubyanka Square, rushing for the entrance to the headquarters of the Komitet Gosudarstvennoy Bezopasnosti—the Committee for State Security of the Soviet Union—known, and feared, as the KGB.

Gorokhov, then twenty-five, a *serzhant*—sergeant—in the Soviet Army, knew very well the history of this building, the notorious prison it housed, the thousands tortured and killed here during Stalin's reign. He knew what occurred within it now in defense of the Motherland. But perhaps alone among the millions of his comrades, he wasn't troubled by that knowledge, or by the enigmatic orders he had received earlier this morning to report here, smartly.

The USSR, despite the uncertainty of last October when Krushschev had stepped down, remained secure under the leadership of the new premier, Kosygin. That unwavering strength and security arose from the KGB, so how could young Gorokhov think of criticizing its procedures? He was a loyal servant of the State, so why should he be at all concerned about stepping through the narrow door beneath its ornate crest of hammer and sickle that so many never returned from?

As a child, he had felt the searing pain of his burning flesh when his drunken beast of a father had thrown him into the blazing fireplace before killing Gorokhov's mother. As a child, he had made his father pay for what he had done. That event had shaped Gorokhov as surely as the Revolution had shaped modern Russia, and all for the good. He had no regrets, no remorse, and no fear.

And that, he learned later, is why he had been summoned this day. After what he had already endured, there was nothing left in this world for him to fear.

The hot and smoky conference room was already dark before its overhead lights were switched off. Heavy curtains had been pulled across narrow windows along one wall, isolating the room from the weak sunlight threatening to break through the clouds outside. When Gorokhov saw the equipment set up at the back of the room, he understood at least part of the immediate reason for his presence. He wore the black shoulder boards of a technician specialist, communications. The equipment was a motion picture film projector, an old model, but one Gorokhov had no doubt he could operate. It would be a simple task, more suited to a lowly *ryadovoy*—a private—but the thought of questioning his orders never crossed the young *serzhant*'s mind.

As Gorokhov entered the room, a general he had never met and didn't recognize gave him a curt nod, then glanced at the projector. Gorokhov immediately made his way to it, quickly taking off his drenched overcoat. At the same time, he noted the other individuals in the room, seated around the large conference table. All were smoking, filling the room with slow eddies of thin blue haze.

Among those present, Gorokhov counted two other army generals and seven civilians, all men. All looked stern and dour, and all but one, the eldest, ignored him. That man watched him closely. He was frail, with thin white hair. His hand, holding a black cigarette, trembled.

Gorokhov looked down at the film canister beside the projector. It was dented, scraped, and the largest of several labels on it carried a swastika and writing in what Gorokhov recognized as German, though he couldn't read it.

The newest, least-worn label was more easily understood: OSOAVIAKHIM. Like KGB, it was an acronym: Society of Assistance to Defense, Aviation and Chemical Industry. In the aftermath of the Great Patriotic War, the tireless volunteer workers of Operation OSOAVIAKHIM had rescued Nazi Germany's most brilliant scientists, engineers, and storerooms full of scientific marvels. To a man, and a few women, they had all been spared capture by the so-called Allies' Operation PAPERCLIP, saved from performing forced labor in support of capitalist oppression.

Knowing that proud history, Gorokhov had a sudden realization. The film in the canister had to be one of the OSOAVIAKHIM's heroic trophies. If he was right, would the generals make him leave the room once the film began to play? He looked up, wondering, but only the old man met his gaze. He inhaled deeply from his black cigarette, smiled as if he knew a joke known to no one else, and nodded at Gorokhov to proceed.

Gorokhov reacted promptly. He took out the film spool, 35 mm, threaded it onto the old machine. When all was ready, he waited a moment for the generals to order him from the room. No one did. Instead, one of them switched off the overhead lights.

Gorokhov started the projector.

A solid cone of light formed in the smoke-filled room.

On the screen at the room's opposite end, the unreadable handwritten scrawl on the film leader flashed by as the projector clicked and whirred. Then a title card. More words in German, AHNENERBE INSTITUT, beneath an elaborate insignia, again with a swastika.

Next, the actual filmed footage began, black and white, badly scratched, but steady, definitely shot on a tripod.

The first harshly lit images were of an old chest.

In close up, a hammer and chisel broke the chest's badly corroded clasp.

A pair of hands opened the chest.

Then the shadows changed as a light source from above moved to reveal what was inside—but just for an instant because the light quickly moved away.

Gorokhov had glimpsed three objects in that instant, but hadn't been able to register just what they were. Jewels?

The film jumped, no longer in close-up.

Four men now stood around the open chest. Clearly pleased with themselves, they were speaking animatedly, and silently, to others off-screen.

Gorokhov couldn't be sure where the images had been filmed. In a cave? But two of the men were wearing German naval uniforms.

On-screen, the junior officer moved to reach into the open chest, but the senior officer waved him away, reaching in himself.

Whatever he took out, he held it for the camera, and in the shadow of his hand the disk-like object appeared to glow. The officer waved to the others off-screen, and six men closed in around the cask—by all appearances men who had done hard work and were pleased their efforts had paid off.

And just as Gorokhov was pondering what the point of this exercise was, and how it could possibly be important to the Motherland, everything happened at once.

A hand—an impossible hand—erupted from the chest of one of the civilians, twisted, and tore the man apart!

No one around the table said a word or reacted in any way, except the old man. He laughed. Softly, almost silently, as if amused.

The camera was off its tripod now, its movements jerky, unfocused. Gorokhov could only imagine the panicked photographer trying to escape the carnage he was filming: human limbs ripped off by invisible forces, trailing streamers of blood in strobing flashes of gunfire.

Then nothing but black.

The flapping of the tail end of the film spun around the take-up reel, and a final blast of pure light shot from the projector for just a moment before Gorokhov switched off the lamp.

The general who had summoned him turned the overhead lights back on.

All others in the room turned to the old man.

A death's head. Grinning.

The old man took a silver object from his jacket pocket. At first glance, it looked to Gorokhov like a flask, or an ornate cigarette case engraved with yet another swastika. *No, not a swastika,* Gorokhov realized. The symbol on the object was made from three interlocked triangles.

He had no idea what the symbol meant.

The old man spoke then, in halting, German-accented Russian, explaining what they'd just seen, telling them why the work that his institute, the Ahnenerbe, had begun, and the work that Almaznyy Ogon—DIAMOND FIRE—had done since, must continue.

Gorokhov remained motionless and silent throughout, determined to be invisible to the men in the room, to hear every astounding word, to imagine the possibilities.

The old man concluded his performance by placing the silver case on the table. He called what was in it the "einstone."

He stood then, bowed his head, clicked his heels, laughed softly again, and made his way to the door, where two soldiers waited to escort him somewhere else in Lubyanka.

A young woman wheeled in a cart with a samovar of tea and plates of cakes, and the smoke in the room swirled out in the rush of fresh air from the open door.

One of the generals approached Gorokhov then, saying DIAMOND FIRE needed technicians. Then he added a single word, a question. *Zainteresovany?*

Interested?

Gorokhov couldn't believe the general even bothered to ask.

A half mile underground, the lift clanked to a halt and the operator unlatched the safety door so it split in the center and opened up and down. Gorokhov stepped out onto the damp rock floor, turned to the right where a string of overhead utility lights stretched along a rock corridor to a metal door, painted bright red.

Beyond that was what would save the Motherland, and VEKTOR, and his own career. Because he was beginning to realize that Popovich—his slight, nervous, and traitorous deputy administrator—was correct. With Major Kalnikova's disappearance and presumed loss, there was nothing more VEKTOR could do to stop Stasik Borodin, whatever it was he was planning. And if Stasik Borodin truly was unstoppable, and in the next hours or days he unleashed the full fury of his shadow warriors in some manner to outrage America and the world, Gorokhov had only one option available.

Operation Scythe.

He thought it a brilliant plan. In terms of destruction, it would have minimal effect. Buildings and monuments would still stand. Hospitals would remain operational. But ten thousand Americans would be killed on the first and only day of the operation, including politicians in their chambers and missile firing teams in their deep, protected bunkers and generals in their Pentagon offices. All torn to pieces with no possible rational explanation.

In a world of billions, a nation of hundreds of millions, ten thousand deaths were a negligible statistical blip. But when the American people woke to realize that those ten thousand lost had left them with no leaders in government, no commanders in their military, no heads of their civil services or judges on their Supreme Court . . . the country would be paralyzed, the citizens in frenzied shock, because there would be no explanation, no weapon system to point to, and most important, no enemy to identify and unite against in rage.

It would be as if the scythe of God had passed over America and punished it for its wickedness and arrogance.

The Kremlin's analysts predicted that a civil war would begin within twelve months of the attack, as groups of American states fled their broken union. Even if actual regional fighting didn't break out, America's spirit would be crushed and its economy flattened. No more would that sanctimonious nation look beyond its borders and seek to impose itself on the world. Like a beaten dog, it would stay in its kennel, cowering in fear of the unknown as Mother Russia reshaped the century and the world, fulfilling her interrupted destiny.

Gorokhov approached the red door, checked his watch. In three hours, just as the communications staff changed shift, Popovich would hear a knock on the door of his quarters. He would answer, puzzled why Gorokhov's security guards were troubling him at such an early hour. How they'd subdue him, Gorokhov didn't know and didn't care. Their only orders were to leave no marks.

The shock of the quarry lake's icy water would undoubtedly revive him, but not for long. Twenty minutes should do it, Gorokhov had estimated. If the guards could keep the deputy administrator from climbing out of the lake at least that long, then they'd be able to leave, and the blue corpse could be safely found in the morning—a victim of trying to be like his beloved chief administrator, and the first unheralded victim of Scythe.

Gorokhov allowed himself a smile, appreciating the elegance of his ma-
neuver like a well-played gambit in chess. By moving ahead so boldly, he would
not allow Scythe to be taken over and squandered by the army. It would remain
in VEKTOR's hands. He reached for the handle of the red door. Behind it was
the storeroom holding the heart of Operation Scythe, the long-sought breakthrough achieved through the brilliant work of the Fond Perspektivnykh
Issledovaniy—Russia's answer to America's DARPA, the Defense Advanced
Research Projects Agency.

No longer did the shadow warriors have to be limited in number by the
handful of pure einstone wafers painstakingly sliced from the only known
natural sample discovered so long ago in the ruins of Berlin. Now the crystal-
line mineral had been synthesized, so that thousands of shadow warriors could
be created to—

"Chief Administrator."

Gorokhov froze. What was that voice doing *here*? He turned to look back
over his broad shoulder.

Popovich stood at the end of the corridor. Gorokhov's own trusted security guards flanked him, weapons drawn, directed not at the deputy, but at
Gorokhov.

"It's not a smart place to fire guns," Gorokhov said evenly. "The risk of
ricochet . . ."

"I have contacted the Kremlin." Popovich was both nervous, and smug.
Gorokhov bemoaned the realization that he had let this worm outmaneuver
him.

"I have been authorized to take charge of VEKTOR until a new administrator can be selected."

"You are willing to destroy all we've worked for?"

Popovich motioned for the guards to approach Gorokhov. "I'm placing
it in better hands. Wiser hands. The generals will control the future of
VEKTOR."

Gorokhov glared at the guards, but accompanied them back to the main
lift, head high, bested for now perhaps, but unbowed. "You still don't understand, you little man," he said. "Only one general controls the future of our work
now—and when Borodin unleashes his shadow warriors in America, the Kremlin will have no choice but to do what I'm prepared to do now."

Gorokhov was gratified when Popovich stepped back from his path, clearly
still afraid of his former superior, even with armed guards to protect him.

"Unleashing Operation Scythe would be the end of everything," Popovich said.

"Quite the contrary," Gorokhov replied. He looked at the guards, the lift, thought of the lake, and began to plan the new moves that would allow him to be vindicated, and see Popovich shot.

23

"That's what I saw." Matt Caidin looked up from the tablet displaying photos of the carnage in the Sonoran desert. "I mean . . . what she saw."

Across the white table from Caidin, Caparelli leaned back in his chair. He looked at Dr. Norma Chu, on his left, but saw no reaction other than the strain of the past few days already evident in her shadowed eyes. To the psychologist, the death of her most gifted operative was as devastating as it was to Caparelli: the loss of a child. Beside Caidin, Sam Arlo raised his eyebrows, signaling he saw no reason to doubt the disgraced police officer's claims.

But for Caparelli, something was missing.

The previous time Laura had manifested in Caidin's apartment should have been the last. She had realized what had happened to her. The folktales apparently had been proven true: When a ghost knew it was dead, it vanished. Forever.

But Laura had come back.

According to Caidin's story, he had returned home, fallen asleep on his couch, and when he awoke, Laura had been standing before him. The next thing he knew, he had been swept up in a surreal experience in which he seemed to relive her last day, and other events, from her perspective and his own. At the same time.

That part, Caparelli could believe. He had heard similar stories of shared sensations from his perceivers.

But the detective was definitely holding back on how Laura had appeared, and what prompted the shared experience.

Caparelli resumed pushing. "Then put it together for us."

"A spontaneous link." Caidin said. "That what you call it?"

Caparelli sensed Caidin was trying to steer the discussion in a particular direction, decided to go with it. "Where'd you hear that term?"

"The phone call. She made it after she . . . I don't know . . . 'jumped' back to her apartment. The call was to you, right?"

Caparelli nodded, willing himself to remain focused on the here and now, and not on what had happened the night he hadn't answered Laura's call. He'd seen the number come up on his phone and had tapped "decline." It had been late, and he'd known he'd be seeing her in just a few hours at work. The week ahead was going to be hectic, but there'd be time to talk then. They had lots of time to talk.

Except they hadn't.

"So, is that what happened to me and her?" Caidin asked.

The psychologist shook her head. "It takes years of imprinting for that kind of entanglement to occur between a perceiver and a target. Or a profound event involving strong, shared emotions—more than your appearance beside her at her death. It can't possibly have—"

Caparelli interrupted her. "But it did. Go on."

The detective pushed the tablet away, stared down at the gleaming table-top. The overhead lights of the conference room were unforgiving so late at night, so early in the morning. "I was . . . with her. In, uh, the Projection Room. The . . . uh, Cradle—I think you call it."

Caparelli caught Arlo's expression of surprise. "You saw that? You heard those terms?"

"I saw it. I didn't exactly hear anyone speaking. But . . . I just knew those were the words."

"What else?" Caparelli prompted.

"She . . . she floated in the Cradle and . . . something happened. It was like I was in a river and a current picked me up and carried me along with her and then . . . then there were three of us in my head, or . . . I was in all their heads. Laura, me, and the general. Stasik Sergeyevich Borodin." Caidin stumbled over the pronunciation.

"What was his mission?"

"It was important, I know that much."

Caparelli was unused to questioning a perceiver at this basic a level. But somewhere Laura's information was there, in this civilian's memory. They had to extract it before it became hopelessly compromised by his untrained, instinctive attempts to make sense of his experience. That would lead to reordering, reimagining, and total information loss. "Let's break it down together. You said you saw metal boxes."

"Containment units."

"Okay. What did they contain?"

Caidin thought for a moment. "Equipment? Batteries? Some kind of crystal? They had status lights, number pads. . . . Um . . . A pen. Anyone have a pen and paper?"

Caparelli gestured to Chu, who flipped to a blank page in her notebook and slid it across to Caidin. Arlo offered him his pen.

"Don't think about what you're writing," the psychologist cautioned. "Don't stop to understand it. Just get it down, as quickly as you can."

Caidin's pen began to move across the page of Chu's notebook.

None of the three watching him was surprised. In the lore, it was called automatic writing or, as CROSSWIND classified it, subliminal memory recovery. It occurred most often when perceivers encountered objects and information completely unfamiliar to them—especially those documents and signs written in languages they didn't know. Although they weren't able to read them, for a few minutes to hours afterward, the perceivers could replicate what they'd seen. That's what Caidin did now, drawing diagrams, writing words in the Cyrillic alphabet, strings of numbers and equations—things he'd observed, but not comprehended.

He wrote for almost five minutes, filled three pages, drew a final image—a symbol made of three interlocked triangles—then stopped, looked at what he had done. "I don't know what any of this is or means."

Arlo scooped up the notebook. "That's all right."

Caparelli resumed the process. "You also saw soldiers."

Caidin opened and closed his writing hand reflexively, as if to dispel cramps.

"You said they attacked the building. That was the immediate objective?"

Caidin frowned. "The soldiers . . ."

Caparelli tapped the table, impatient. "The first thing you told me was that you had seen the general and his soldiers. Don't overthink it, Caidin—close your eyes, visualize, then describe what you see right now."

Caidin did as told, began speaking slowly. "There were two groups with him. Yeah . . ." He opened his eyes as if struck by a new memory. "The soldiers in the truck. They were . . . they were . . . real, in civilian clothes. But the others . . . the ones in all-black uniforms . . ." He hesitated. "They ran *through* walls and put their hands *into* flesh-and-blood people, and then they shredded them. I mean, how is that . . . ?"

He looked at Caparelli. "What were they?" He stopped, startled. "I know the word. Russian, English, it's almost the same. Berserker."

The debriefing took less than an hour, but it was far more than that. The details Caidin had revealed amounted to a profound reordering of all CROSS-WIND researchers had come to understand about remote viewing and its related phenomena.

By the third time through the detective's account of his link to Laura Hart, some of those details were already dropping out, the impossible "corrected" by the logic of the human mind: Bullets hadn't really passed through the soldiers in black; the soldiers had reacted to the impact of the shots, though they remained unhurt. Why? Because of the ballistic armor they must have been wearing. Whatever Caidin remembered past this point, Caparelli knew, it would have no value. There'd be no way to distinguish between what he'd actually perceived and what he now believed he *should* have, including the missing details about how Laura had appeared and how the shared experience had begun.

"So what are we left with?" Caparelli asked his team. They had left Caidin in the conference room and taken his handwritten pages to Burton Hirst, CROSSWIND's chief science analyst, for a preliminary breakdown. Now Chu and Arlo were in Caparelli's TEMPEST-secure office. No windows, of course. Nothing in the way of decoration. A desk, a couch, a small round table with four chairs. A gray wastebasket for ordinary trash. A red one for classified material destined to be incinerated.

Chu and Arlo were on the couch. Caparelli was on his feet, leaning back against his desk. Arlo spoke first. "No question the guy linked with Laura. The things he knew, those were things only she knew."

"But it's just not possible," Chu countered. "Not with strangers. A true resonant connection can't be forged in so short a time." She looked at Caparelli with silent apology. "If the link had been with you, Daniel, then I could accept it. Instead, I have to question what kind of emotional bond this man could possibly have with Laura based on so short an encounter."

Caparelli allowed no hint of weakness, or regret, to shade his words. "She was dying, Norma. He was present when she was . . . suffering, confused . . . driven to fulfill her mission."

"To report here," Arlo jumped in. "To you, to us. She definitely had unfinished business. And we all know she was absolutely dedicated. I'd say that was powerful motivation."

Chu shook her head. "But not enough. The heightened emotion of death, I'd accept that as a trigger that could explain Laura's manifestations in a stranger's presence. But to go that one step further—to actually entangle minds, to share thoughts and memories in such detail—there must be something more intense between them."

Caparelli could guess what Chu was driving at. He thought back to Caidin's extraordinary arrest record, and reassessed the reasons for it. "You're thinking it's likely that Caidin might have some innate talent for this."

Chu nodded.

Arlo looked thoughtful, reconsidering. "We ran him through a standard Vogel-Tathwell psychic sensitivity inventory, and there were a few hits that stood out. His arrest record is remarkably strong—seems to have good instincts for ferreting out guilty parties. That could indicate a latent ability for perceiving others' thoughts that's persisted into adulthood. He also talked a bit about childhood experiences indicative of sensitivity, had a few more than the statistical norm."

"Imaginary friends?" Chu asked. "Monsters watching him from the closet, that sort of thing?"

"Yeah. He did say he saw a lot of monsters when he was a kid. But reported that he was never particularly scared by them. Always saw himself as a superhero fighting the bad guys. It carried over to his choice of occupation. Righting wrongs."

Chu didn't seem convinced. "Cop or no cop, that all sounds fairly typical for a young boy. Nothing more?"

"He also saw his grandfather two nights after the old guy's funeral."

Chu looked surprised by that. "An actual manifestation?"

"According to his Vogel-Tathwell score," Arlo said, "I'd say yes. It certainly fit the profile. Granddad appeared younger. Dressed appropriately. Gave assurance. Caidin wasn't troubled."

"Okay," Caparelli interrupted. "So maybe Caidin is borderline perceiver material. But everything you're describing is at such a low level, it still doesn't fully account for their bond."

Chu gave him a curious look. "The more I think about it, the more I think it's obvious. Caidin's in love with Laura."

Arlo frowned. "But she's dead. That's not even rational."

Chu sighed. "Does love require reason? They have a connection, however it came about." She looked back to Caparelli. "Daniel, I know how close you were to Laura. I can't know what you're feeling. But I think Laura's surviving personality is what we should be concentrating on. That's what's driving her manifestations and her connection to this man. He's only a placeholder in this equation. We can forget him."

Caparelli disagreed. "No. He's not leaving the facility until I'm certain he's told us everything. If he's withholding other details that Laura wanted us to know, she died for them. We owe that to her. I owe her."

"How will you explain that to him?" Chu asked. "That he's not free to go."

"He won't be a prisoner. It's for his protection. By his own account, we know there were three entities entangled in the link at the hacienda. Caidin, Laura, *and* General Borodin. The fact that Borodin sent something after Laura confirms that the general was aware of her presence. And if he was aware of her presence, then because of his entanglement with her . . ."

Arlo gave a low whistle. "He could share enough of it now to become aware of *Caidin?*"

Caparelli nodded. They had more than enough evidence to know that once two minds connected, the effects persisted, even if only at a subliminal level. There was no reason to think the effect couldn't spread to three entangled minds, or more. "In any case," he added, "we have to assume that now Caidin himself could be a target for VEKTOR perceivers. So until we sort all of this out, he stays here, protected by our countermeasures. He stays safe. So do our secrets."

"But safe from what?" Chu asked. "Whatever Borodin used to kill those people, those 'berserkers,' they weren't VEKTOR perceivers. We don't know what the general sent after Laura."

Before Caparelli could even form a guess, his desk phone buzzed. It was Burton Hirst.

The analyst insisted Caparelli meet with him at once. Caidin's pages were more than legitimate.

They changed everything.

"VEKTOR has weaponized ghosts," Hirst said. "That's what berserkers are." He waited for Caparelli to object.

But all Caparelli said was, "Go on." At CROSSWIND, the unthinkable was business as usual.

Hirst fanned out copies of the pages Caidin had filled in during his debriefing. They were annotated with red notes now, each in the science analyst's small and precise printing. "I'm inferring a few things here." He tapped three equations on two of the pages. "Some of these equations are meaningless, so I have to assume Caidin garbled them. But these . . ." He indicated another block of equations scrawled beside a rough sketch of what Caidin had called a containment unit. "They're significant. In fact, they're more advanced than what we're working with in our field-enhancement and stabilization programs."

"How so?"

"The short answer is the Russians have achieved what we're still struggling to even conceptualize: giving mass to a field entity."

Caparelli looked at him, stunned by the implications. To date, the best theories attempting to describe the scientific underpinnings of remote viewing assumed the perceiver's projected field had no mass. That assumption relegated the perceiver to the role of passive observer only. They could see remote events and, on occasion, enter an inexplicable entanglement of thoughts with their target individual, but they could not take action at a distance. Physical interaction by a perceiver at the remote location was impossible.

However, since perceivers *could* register light and sound phenomena, some form of weak interaction had to be taking place. That implied their quantum fields had, at the very least, if not mass, then mass-like attributes. The challenge to CROSSWIND researchers was to determine the strength of that interaction, then stabilize and ultimately strengthen it.

It was a staggering idea to think CROSSWIND could someday send a perceiver to any location in the world and have that perceiver physically disable equipment in an enemy facility, or enter code into an otherwise secure computer system, or kill a single terrorist protected by a group of innocent hostages. No enemy would be beyond reach.

But Caparelli saw a flaw in Hirst's reasoning. "If VEKTOR has that capability, why did the Russians need to send the general here? Why not run the operation from their compound?"

Hirst's confidence was unshaken. He pointed to a sketch on another page: what appeared to be a wiring diagram for a fractal antenna array. "It's the energy requirements. As far as we can ascertain, our personal awareness exists in an entangled state with our physical nervous system. Perceivers have the ability to separate their awareness from their nervous system and project it anywhere, and because their awareness is essentially massless, and in an entangled state, and who knows what else, there's no measurable energy cost to the operation.

"However, projecting *mass* is something else again. It's a much more energy-intensive operation. And while we don't know how to approach the problem, according to what's on Caidin's pages, VEKTOR does and they've solved it. They're stabilizing the quantum field with what looks to be a metallic mineral rectifier circuit, then transmitting energy to it through this antenna array. I'd love to know what mineral they're using. . . ."

"What's the energy source?"

"Batteries, fuel cell, it's not important. But it has to be portable."

"Because . . ."

"Limited range."

"How limited?"

Hirst considered the pages again and muttered softly to himself, a string of numbers. He looked up. "For these containment units, the power source they're using, and the size of the antennas, say fifteen hundred meters. Little less than a mile."

"Why not use a nuclear reactor and increase the range to twelve thousand miles? They wouldn't have to leave home."

Hirst shook his head. "The issue's stabilization. There's a limit to how much energy the quantum field can absorb. Too much, and it dissipates. Same as a five-volt flashlight bulb. It'd vaporize if you ran a hundred and twenty volts through it."

Caparelli felt he was looking at a whirlwind of jigsaw puzzle pieces. There was an image hidden in it, and parts of it flashed into view. But he still couldn't see the pattern overall.

"Okay," he began, "let's say this is the information Laura wanted to report to us. Let's say Caidin hasn't garbled it too badly and that your analysis is correct—"

"In general terms. I still need to test the—"

"Fine, fine—in general terms." *Scientists,* Caparelli thought. "But overall, you're saying VEKTOR has the technology to create a quantum field capable of acquiring mass, and project that field about a mile."

Hirst nodded, no objections.

"Then what the hell came after Laura the night she died, when she was two thousand miles from Borodin's operation?"

"Can't say. Not enough data for a theory. Not even for a hypothesis."

"How about a guess?"

Hirst looked uncomfortable, reluctant to be imprecise. "I'd have to say Laura's own quantum field somehow became a power source. First, the VEKTOR field entity—the berserker—was being powered by a containment unit at the scene of the hacienda murders in Mexico. Then, when Laura's awareness snapped back to her body, the VEKTOR field was drawn along the back-trace with it, and Laura, in effect, powered it until.... Well, until she lost consciousness. That effectively pulled the plug on the thing and it would've dissipated."

For Caparelli, another piece of the puzzle fell into place, but it still was not enough.

"I want you to pull everyone in," he said. "Set up a Tiger Team. Go at these pages with everything. I want confirmation. Ungarble those other equations. We need to know how real this is. I mean, projected mass capable of taking action at a distance..."

"It explains what Caidin described," Hirst agreed. "The soldiers in black passing through walls, not affected by bullets, capable of penetrating a human body in a massless state, then becoming solid to...well, to do what the photos show." The analyst paused, as if there was something more he wanted to say, but hadn't yet.

"What is it?"

"Well, we've all seen the same capacity for interaction in Laura's manifestations. And we know Laura was physically present in the diner, reflected light, created sound. Even more, Caidin reported actually *holding* her hand."

"That's a false memory," Caparelli said. "He *wanted* to hold her hand, so—"

Hirst interrupted. "I know the angle was partially blocked, but you can see his arm move as if he's reaching across the table, then remain still. I'd say the video confirms some form of actual contact."

Caparelli stiffened. "Your point?"

"The concept that a disembodied consciousness could not only be capable of manifesting itself with a physical appearance, as well as with actual physicality, well . . . It could explain the entire ghost phenomenon that's at the heart of our research, and our capabilities. It's worth considering."

"Ghosts . . ." Caparelli's thoughts reluctantly went back to the first words of the analyst's report, ones he'd neglected to question at the time.

"Why say that VEKTOR's weaponized ghosts?" he asked now. "Why not say they weaponized remote viewers?"

Hirst pushed one of Caidin's pages closer to Caparelli. "It's these containment units. They're not large enough for a person, and inside . . . These are complex induction coils and nanoscale mesh designed to maintain a quantum field in a highly stable magnetic environment."

"So?"

"So I don't think the Russians are using remote viewers for this, because they don't need living bodies. With these containment units and that metallic crystal, a disembodied consciousness could persist well past the six-day limit we've identified, maybe indefinitely.

"Daniel, I think each one of those berserkers is a real ghost. And the people they've come from, they're already dead."

24

Caparelli had no desire to invite Lomax into CROSSWIND's main facility, so he'd chosen Lafayette Square. The constant stream of bicyclists and joggers, and tourists snapping pictures of the White House across Pennsylvania Avenue, and especially the many trees still in full leaf would make any third-party observation of their meeting more difficult. The Department of Homeland Security wasn't the only one interested in obtaining CROSSWIND's secrets, and Caparelli was on guard against them all.

It was 10:00 a.m., but the day was already unseasonably humid and hot in DC. The sky's uniform gray haze didn't even offer the promise of a rainstorm to bring relief. Caparelli had been up since 3:00, when Caidin called CROSSWIND to report the results of his link experience with Laura. Only adrenaline was keeping Caparelli's exhaustion at bay.

Yesterday, when he'd first met with Lomax, Caparelli had believed Laura was irretrievable, along with the information that had cost her her life. That was the only reason he had stepped into the lion's den that was the Department of Homeland Security. He needed to have them working for him, without jeopardizing CROSSWIND's independence.

But by linking to Caidin last night, Laura had succeeded in her final mission: to report. The next move was Caparelli's: Act on her report and create a new plan. Conceiving that plan had consumed the rest of his morning. Now all he had to do was continue his manipulation of Lomax and the DHS.

For his part, Lomax seemed to embrace the heat, as if invigorated by it. He carried a bottle of water, barely glancing at Caparelli as they fell into step with each other along a pedestrian path. The big man's eyes moved constantly over the shifting scene in the park, a soldier on patrol, looking for snipers and IEDs in every shadow, and enjoying the rush of it.

"I thought CROSSWIND's source had dried up," Lomax said.

"We have more than one."

Lomax smiled, and didn't ask him who the new source was. To do so would be, both knew, a waste of time. But the tone of his next question was a shade condescending. "So, do we know exactly how many Russian terrorists we're looking for today?"

"If you don't think this is important, why agree to meet?"

Lomax took a quick swallow from his water bottle, wiped at his thick mustache. "I gather data points. Finer minds than mine determine their worth. I'm assuming your new source brought you new intel."

"The target."

Lomax didn't break stride, but Caparelli was gratified to see his expression change. Now he was serious. "Go ahead."

"The UN next Thursday. When the president speaks."

"Your source told you this? Definitively?"

"Given other information we have, it's the only target that fits."

"Why not the Greenbrier's Anti-terrorism Conference or the joint session with the Brit prime minister at the Capitol?"

Caparelli knew this was where he'd have to tread delicately. "The security perimeters at the Greenbrier and around the Capitol are more than adequate to prevent an attack."

"Adequate. For an attack by whatever mysterious weapon you say the Russians have."

"We have a handle on its capabilities. It has a limited range."

"Which is?"

"Fifteen hundred meters."

Lomax slowed his pace. "Unless you're talking about a tactical nuke with a blast radius of a mile, no one's going to get close enough to launch any kind of missile. Or have any kind of sight line to any of the three venues, UN included."

"It's not a missile, and they don't need line of sight. They just have to be within a mile."

Lomax halted. "It's back to sounding like an explosive."

"You saw the photographs. Victims are subjected to severe trauma, but not from blast effects."

"If it's not explosive, that leaves chemical, biological, or radiation." Lomax held Caparelli's gaze for long moments. "You're not going to tell me, are you?"

"No."

"Unbelievable." The big man's jaw tightened. "You have the balls to say CROSSWIND is aware of a threat to the president, and you won't share the information."

"I understand your frustration. All I can tell you is that we now know the technology is something we're also developing. I can't say more."

"CROSSWIND is an intelligence-gathering operation. And now you're saying you're also developing weapons?" Lomax leaned closer, not for privacy this time, for intimidation. "I can get clearance."

It didn't work. "You can try," Caparelli said. "But it's need-to-know. And all you need to know is that the Russians plan to get within a mile of the president when he's in New York. Your job is to stop them."

Lomax shook his head in disbelief. "Look. This isn't a pissing contest. It isn't personal. You have to give me something. The second source."

"CROSSWIND. That's the source."

Lomax snorted. "Goddamn magic intel."

Caparelli was inured to this reaction. "Our track record speaks for itself."

Lomax scanned the passing crowds, as if running each individual through a personal facial recognition routine. "The Russians, then. Has your source provided more intel about them? We still got ten of them in the wind?"

Caparelli chose his words carefully, hiding his relief. "We understand there are two groups." He was puzzled to see a flash of quickly suppressed heightened interest in Lomax. "The first are military, combat experienced, six or seven."

"And the second?"

"They're the ones who'll deploy the technology. If you stop the first group, the second won't be a threat."

"How many needed to deploy their weapon?"

"Unknown."

Lomax frowned, thoughtful. "The UN's security perimeter is larger than the ones around the Greenbrier and the Capitol."

Caparelli continued with what his plan required. "Size may not be the most important factor. The Greenbrier's a resort set in open countryside—there's no way to sneak up on it. And DC's always tightly controlled. But Manhattan . . . the boundary's porous."

Lomax gave him a sharp look. "Porous? With what we have in place, it might as well be a wall of iron."

"On the surface, sure. But that city's a warren of underground passages, storm sewers, subways . . . All it takes is one forgotten bootlegger's tunnel, one old unmapped sewer line that passes under the perimeter."

"Not a problem," Lomax said. "Even if the Ruskies can pass under, they can't come up."

"They won't have to," Caparelli said. "As long as they get within a mile. The photographs are the evidence of the weapon's capability."

"So, in a perfect world, I do what?" Lomax asked. "Cancel the president's speech?"

Mission accomplished, Caparelli thought with relief. The DHS continued its unacknowledged partnership with CROSSWIND. "That's a last resort. In a perfect world, you stop the Russians."

Five minutes later, drenched in sweat from his stroll with Caparelli, Lomax was on his way back to St. Elizabeth's in the back seat of a departmental limousine. Not a dot of perspiration shone through the close-cropped military haircut on Ames, the Secret Service agent and friend who sat beside him. The limo's air-conditioning was set to frigid.

A privacy screen sealed them both from the driver. Armor plating, Kevlar, and thick, blast-proof glass sealed them from world. Ames had his earpiece in, and had heard every word Lomax and Caparelli had said to each other in Lafayette Square. The mike had been in the cap of Lomax's water bottle.

"The big takeaway," Ames concluded, "was Caparelli's statement that there're two groups of Russians working together—one for action and one for deployment. He doesn't have the whole story."

Lomax drained his water bottle and wiped his forehead with his sleeve. "And we do?"

"We have my new girlfriend, Major Kalnikova. Her team was in pursuit of the first team—it has the superweapon. They're *not* working together."

"That's what she told us," Lomax cautioned. "Whether it's true . . ."

"She's on morphine and hypnotics. I doubt she has the capacity to lie."

"My friend, the woman's on drugs, has only one hand, and yet we've still got her tied down to her hospital bed. She's Russian special forces. Don't underestimate her."

"Hell, I want to marry her. But all right. Let's play it out. Scenario one: She's telling the truth. What's the outcome?"

Lomax checked his watch. "In that case, within the hour we'll have the laptop she stashed in her motel room in Colorado Springs. It has the GPS tracking specs for the van stolen from the warehouse in New Mexico, and we'll grab the Russians with the weapon by end of day."

"Scenario two: She's lying."

Lomax shrugged. "So there's no laptop."

"Or," Ames said, "there is a laptop, and it points us in the wrong direction, or gets us following a Greyhound bus or a big rig heading in the wrong direction. Or the Russians it does point us to are in the stolen van, all right, but *they're* a decoy team. And then, even if we take them out, we still won't know if our Russian major told us the truth or lied. Not until the president is, or is not, attacked."

Lomax looked out through the heavily tinted windows. Faceless crowds passed, oblivious to the fragility of their peace and well-being. "Combat's so clean. Good guys and bad guys. Just kill all the bad guys and that's that."

"If only," Ames said.

Lomax sighed. "I do miss it. The simplicity."

"Our next step is about as simple as it gets," Ames said. "We act on the major's intelligence, but don't trust her."

"That's your definition of simple?"

"What's the alternative?"

"The major's not the only game in town."

His fellow Marine didn't understand.

"Caparelli's got his own second source," Lomax said, setting in motion his next mission. "Turns out, we've already been tracking him. And now we're going to make him ours."

25

"Everything's magnetic," Arlo said blithely. "Even water."

He let go of a plastic bag of saline solution and it remained in midair, floating between the top and bottom surfaces of the MRI-like machine that CROSSWIND had dubbed the Cradle.

Inside the antiseptic Projection Room with Arlo, Matt Caidin stared at the bag without surprise or wonder or even curiosity. Of course these people could make a bag of water float. After getting caught up in whatever it was they were doing every day, he himself had linked minds with a ghost, suffered flashbacks of other people's past events, and read the thoughts of a Russian general. The word "impossible" would never mean the same to him.

"Of course," Arlo continued, "there's magnetism and there's magnetism. What most people know is 'ferromagnetism.' You know: bar magnets, iron filings, that sort of thing. It's specialized and fairly strong. Now, the magnetic property of water—which is what our bodies mostly are—is called 'diamagnetism.' That's not as strong, but just as real." He gave the saline bag a push and it slid through the air, stopping abruptly the moment he took his fingers away. "Basically, what we've got here is a superpowerful magnetic field being generated between these two surfaces. It's what we call 'hellacious' strong." He grinned. "That's our highly technical scientific term for a classified superconducting solenoid more efficient than anything in the commercial world. By a factor of about ten." He looked at Matt for his reaction, found none. "Not a math guy, huh?"

"Will this fry me?"

"Nah. It's a steady field. Doesn't oscillate. That's why it doesn't interfere with the perceivers, either. Neat, huh?"

Matt's face told him he needed to say more. "Think of it this way: It's like all your water molecules are going to line up to repel the field top and bottom. That's the beauty of it. Each individual molecule in your body will be responding to the field. I promise you, you won't feel strain anywhere. No pressure. No sensation. No distractions. Just don't move your head, 'cause the liquid in your ear is also floating. You make any sudden moves and you'll regret it."

Matt nodded. He didn't know what else was expected of him.

Arlo pointed to a glass panel on the inner surface of the Cradle's overhead canopy. "These are the lights that were flashing on Laura when you saw her in your entangled state. Whole time you're in here, we'll be monitoring your brain-wave patterns, and these strobe lights will help guide you into a deep theta state. Anything else you want to know?"

Matt felt he couldn't be more out of place if he were on the moon. "When do I step through the looking glass?"

"Soon as the sun sets."

"So I've heard. And after that?"

"Launch time. The general's in the same hemisphere we are, probably close to our time zone, so that's slightly different from what we're used to. But once you're projected, given the way Laura linked you to him, it should be simple for you to reestablish contact." Arlo patted the side of the Cradle. "Especially with all the support we can give you. This procedure's come a long way in twenty years."

Not as far as I have in a week, Matt thought.

The door to the Projection Room slid open and a young tech entered, holding up a phone. "Wasn't sure what to do about this." She handed it to Arlo.

It was Matt's phone.

Arlo read its screen. "Helena?"

"My wife," Matt said.

Arlo passed the phone to him. "Five messages this morning. Something we should know about?"

"We've got some financial things to sort out. We're, uh, separating."

"Can it keep?"

"For me, sure. But for her . . . ?" Matt suddenly saw his situation with more clarity than he had for months. He had been living in suspended time, putting off decisions, not wanting to acknowledge the constraints of his failed marriage, his stalled career—all constraints of his own making. It was time to move on, take control. "I'm going to see her."

Matt could see that Arlo wasn't in favor of his decision, but the young researcher also sensed Matt's resolve, understood this wasn't negotiable. "You need to be back before sunset."

What he meant, Matt understood, was that until then his life could continue as normal.

Another word that no longer worked for him.

An hour later, Matt was at a Starbucks breathing in the scent of coffee, hearing the hiss of the espresso machine, the rattle-rumble-whine of ice being crushed, and a dozen conversations a world away from his new reality.

He sat at a corner table with the small coffee he'd ordered from habit. He watched Helena enter, look around, see him, no smile, just a glimmer of recognition.

"You look wiped," she said as she pulled out the chair opposite him, sat down. Her face, so familiar for ten years, that of a stranger now. She was the one who looked exhausted.

"Thanks."

"You haven't been at work the last few days." She wasn't even looking at him. She was digging through her large black-and-white tote. It looked expensive, and bore the logo of her new employer, one of DC's luxury boutiques.

"What are you up to?" She dropped a thick stack of mail, bound by an elastic, on the table. Placed her tote beside it.

"Got a new assignment."

She made a noise of acknowledgment, signifying neither interest nor belief. "We need to work out something."

She met his eyes, then quickly looked away, and it struck him that wasn't right. She had every reason to be upset with him, disappointed. She wanted to be free of him and their past and his connection to his damaged partner. But in all the time he'd known her, Helena had never seemed nervous, never been furtive.

Like an old bear rising from hibernation, Matt's police instincts stirred. *What's the suspect hiding?*

He pushed the stack of mail aside. "Bills we can deal with. Is there something else we should be talking about?" He needed to know what had unsettled her.

Helena seemed to prepare herself for an enormous effort, took a nervous breath, then, "They've been to see me, Matt."

Matt decided there was only one thing she could mean by that: the ongoing investigation into Jack Lowney and his connection to the Mauricio brothers, complications that seemed years and another life ago. In time she'd know the truth, but not yet. "It's standard procedure for Internal Affairs."

She shook her head. "Not them. This isn't about your partner, it's you."

"What?

"Homeland Security. Two agents showed up. At the *store*."

He rocked back in his chair. *Homeland?* "What about?"

"They didn't tell me a lot, but . . . there was a young woman, who worked for, well, I don't know. Some government agency. And she was killed, Matt. Last week. They said you were at the scene."

Matt felt his mind accelerate to put everything Helena said into context, but it still made no sense. "The young woman—Laura Hart?"

"They didn't tell me her name."

"She was in a car crash. Outside Molly's." He wanted to say it was an accident, but he knew that wasn't true, and he knew Helena would recognize the lie.

"I'm just trying to warn you. This time you might need someone other than a union lawyer."

Matt read between the lines.

"Did they say I had something to do with her death?"

Helena went cold, unreadable. "Did you?"

"Helena!"

"They have a phone call, Matt. They told me the woman had information, something important about national security. And that she was deliberately killed before she could pass it on."

Matt was startled that someone other than CROSSWIND personnel knew that much of the story. Helena, who knew him so well, read his expression and knew.

"Oh my God. It's true."

"Even if it is," Matt said, "how could it have anything to do with me?"

Matt, who knew her so well, read her expression, and saw she had an answer.

"They said . . . they said you're working for someone called Caparelli."

Matt's eyes widened.

"They said . . . they said he stepped in and saved you. Used government influence to protect you from being linked to what Jack was doing. That's why you helped this Caparelli . . . helped him kill the girl."

Helena looked down at the table, as if her purse was more interesting than anything they spoke about. "I need to hear the truth, Matt. I need you to tell me what your connection to Caparelli is. Your connection to that girl."

In that moment, Matt wasn't an estranged husband. He wasn't a falsely accused suspect. He was a cop. A detective. He knew exactly what was happening. He knew why Helena's words and her questions sounded so rehearsed. She didn't care about the truth, wouldn't believe him in any case. She just wanted him on the record.

"Helena," he said quietly.

She looked up at him, and he saw how nervous she was, how unsure. He couldn't blame her.

"I'm sorry they came after you. Involved you in this. I really am."

He reached out and took her purse, then pulled out the microphone and transmitter that were inside, much more sophisticated than the ones the Arlington County Police Department used.

Helena opened her mouth to say something, but had no words.

"It's all right," Matt said. But in the same moment he spoke, two men with stern expressions got up from a table near the front door, eyes locked on him.

Matt ran.

"Who the hell is Matthew Michael Caidin?" Ames asked.

Owen Lomax kept his eyes on the main screen in the DHS command center for domestic operations. A satellite image showing two square miles of DC, centered on the Starbucks at Pennsylvania and 3rd. It was overlaid by street names and the GPS indicators of his two agents converging on a third indicator.

"He's Caparelli's weak spot. Came up on our standard phone sweeps three days ago. He's got something to do with CROSSWIND, but damned if I know what."

Ames flipped through the four sheets of paper that made up their quarry's slim dossier. "An Arlington cop."

"Supposedly under investigation, but turns out he's a Boy Scout. He's working undercover for his department's Internal Affairs. Going after corrupt cops."

"CROSSWIND involved in any of that?"

"No connection yet." Lomax held his fingers to his earpiece. "What are they doing?"

On the main screen, the GPS indicators had split up. His two agents had exited behind the Starbucks, moving quickly. But Caidin's indicator was now traveling away from the front of the building.

Lomax tapped SEND on his earpiece. "Bird Dog, Big Chief. The suspect's out front. Why aren't you following?"

A moment later, Caidin's moving GPS indicator winked out.

Lomax immediately figured it out and grinned. This was going to be entertaining.

Matt moved quickly away from the Starbucks, but not so fast to draw attention. He popped the SIM card from his phone, dropped it in a trash can. The phone followed half a block later.

He risked stopping at a store window, looked in at a selection of shoes, glanced back, no sign of pursuit. But he knew they'd still be coming. He had no reason to doubt Helena's story that it was the DHS that had sent her to meet him with a wire. Since DC was webbed with surveillance cameras, he knew he had only minutes before facial-recognition subroutines began looking for him.

The inexperience of the two men who had chased him out of Starbucks was further confirmation of a DHS pursuit. They'd clearly been trained as soldiers before becoming domestic agents. Their military instincts had clicked in when he bolted and they'd charged after him in full gung-ho combat mode.

But he'd had different training, provided by street-smart thugs and addicts who never played by rules. The DHS agents had seen the back door to the Starbucks swinging shut, heard the alarm triggered by the door's opening blaring in the small backroom, and they hadn't stopped to consider the possibility that their prey had set them up.

As they'd barreled through the door, drawing weapons from inside their jackets, Matt had simply waited for the door to close, then stepped out from behind a storage rack and, after jamming the door closed with a metal shelf, he went back the way he had come to exit from the front.

There was a pharmacy up ahead. Matt made straight for it, face angled down, away from the cameras that blossomed on every building, at every intersection.

He'd buy a new phone, call Arlo. He knew Homeland had no reason to be coming after him.

Which could only mean they were after CROSSWIND.

In the DHS command center, six technicians worked individual screens to monitor the progress of SPARROW as the system checked all video feeds from DC's more than 18,000 surveillance cameras installed on ATM machines, traffic lights, tunnel security installations, Metro stations, building lobbies, store security systems, parking lots, cabs, and car-mounts in police and security vehicles. With each second, billions of bits of data were sifted in the search for a match to the specific polygonal pattern of Detective Caidin's facial geometry.

"He's there," Lomax said to Ames. "And he has to look up sometime."

Ames checked his watch. "He's fifteen minutes gone. Maybe he's not just a cop."

Ames held up the dossier. He had read the whole thing now. "Then why'd he reach out to Caparelli with so many unsecured calls?"

"Maybe it goes the other way. Caparelli reached out to him first."

"To a supposedly dirty cop under active investigation? What's he got to offer an outfit like CROSSWIND?"

"Something brought them together," Lomax said. "Could be the accident. The woman had something to report. She made her call on an unsecured personal line so she didn't give details, but you can hear the urgency. Caidin was at the scene. Maybe she said something to him before she died."

Ames frowned. "If that's all it was, Caparelli would only have questioned him once. 'Hey there, what'd she say to you? Okay then, thanks.' End of interaction." He tapped the dossier. "But this has them in constant contact. What's up with that?"

A technician suddenly raised a hand. "Sir! We have him!"

"Big screen," Lomax said.

A moment later, color video from what appeared to be a pharmacy's security camera appeared. It was mounted low, to capture everyone who approached the cashier. Caidin was there. A mesh of polygons flashed over his face, locked on.

"Where is that?"

"CVS drugstore. A couple blocks from the Starbucks."

Lomax checked the time code. "We're five minutes behind him. What's he buying?"

"Got to be a phone," Ames said.

It was.

"Identify the make. Start vacuuming every call made from every phone like it until we can track a specific ID."

"I know a faster way," Ames said.

"Don't waste my time," Lomax warned.

"Who's he going to call?" But even as he asked that question he knew the answer. Was he really that tired?

He gave the order to his team. "I want every phone connected to CROSS-WIND and CROSSWIND personnel on real-time monitoring. Use our own assets. Do not reach out to the NSA.

"I don't care if all the calls are encrypted, I just want to see the connections. But start with Caparelli's lines. I want to know where and when he sets the meet with Caidin." He nodded his thanks at Ames; the hunt was on. "Wherever it is, we'll be there first."

26

At the small table in a corner of the ridiculous restaurant, Borodin tore open a sugar packet with his teeth, shook it into his coffee, and stirred with a plastic stick. It was an awkward procedure with his left hand. His right arm was still compromised. The bullet fired by one of Kalnikova's officers had passed through his biceps, the track no deeper than a centimeter. When he had been younger, he would have laughed off so minor a wound. But the swelling had stiffened the arm to near immobility, so he kept it in a sling, taking care not to further inflame it. His plan for Monday didn't require he have the use of both hands, but it was always better to enter combat prepared for the unexpected, because the unexpected was combat's one great constant.

Monday. That thought stopped his reflection on his physical condition, turned his attention to the future. More than two years of planning, and in less than eighty hours it would be over. *Vengeance.*

The insipid coffee had cooled enough for him to drain the cup, treating the sugar and caffeine as fuel. Though his squad was still on schedule, it wasn't time to rest. That would come later. There were still preparations to make and now tests to run. The general would never send an untrained soldier into battle. It was time to see what TYR's replacement could do.

Borodin settled back, tensing his right shoulder as his wooden chair creaked against the flimsy wood paneling of the wall behind him. He didn't understand how this rundown establishment, little more than a shack off some dismal side road, could remain in business. Ten tables, a short counter with eight stools, the awful stench of years of burnt meat, old oil, something rancid. How could anyone entering this place have an appetite? The gaudy movie posters, mounted deer heads, steer horns, and framed and badly faded photographs of nameless grinning fools added to the miasma of neglect. But all that made this a perfect proving ground.

This restaurant would not be missed, and neither would the seven customers and three workers currently in it at the supper hour, none of them knowing they were eating their last meals.

Borodin checked his watch, set it to stopwatch mode. Then he slipped a pack of cigarettes from his jacket pocket, placed it by his empty coffee cup, put a lighter on top.

"Yo, man!" It was the chef of this establishment. Portly, unshaven, in a stained white apron, calling out from behind the counter.

Borodin gazed at him, an insect beneath notice.

"No smoking!"

Amerikantsy, the general thought. *So many rules, so little discipline.*

He couldn't resist.

Keeping his eyes on the chef, he shook out a cigarette from the pack. Picked it up from the table, held it between his lips.

"Hey, man! You could get fined!"

Borodin laughed. Operated the lighter with his left hand.

"I'm warning ya!"

The chef balled up a rag, slapped it down on the counter like an aggrieved nobleman in the time of the czars, throwing down a glove in anticipation of a duel.

Borodin lit his cigarette, inhaled deeply, well aware that now everyone in the restaurant was staring at him, the man who broke the rules!

The chef stormed out from behind his counter, marched officiously toward Borodin at his table.

Stopped in shock as the others in the restaurant gasped.

One old woman gave a short scream. A plate crashed to the floor.

Borodin was no longer alone at his table.

Across from him sat what remained of the late Colonel Yuri Vasilyev, now TYR, attired in the black uniform of a shadow warrior.

The colonel's containment unit, fully charged, was in the Winnebago in the dusty parking lot outside, watched over by Korolev and the others.

Borodin's squad had released TYR, given him the first stage of his mission: Find his commanding officer, General Borodin.

Borodin was pleased at TYR's prompt appearance as scheduled. It meant Vasilyev had properly imprinted on him during the drawn-out process of his physical death.

"What the shit . . . ?" the chef wheezed, standing still, frozen by growing fear. "Where'd he come from?"

Borodin stared at the chef without compassion, without contempt. He just didn't care about the man or about any of the others. They weren't even the enemy. Only targets.

"TYR, to me," Borodin said.

He looked into the face of the dead man, the echo, the berserker. Its eyes were lost in impossible shadows, unseen and unknown. For a moment, Borodin wondered if Vasilyev comprehended his transformation, or if, as the experts maintained, he was simply an automatic system who would operate as programmed. In the end, it didn't matter. Whatever else he might be, first and foremost, he was a weapon.

It was time to test him. Borodin started the timer on his watch.

"Kill them all," he said.

Afterward, when TYR had been recalled and slept in the safety of his containment unit, Korolev and Janyk joined the general to assess the newest warrior's effectiveness.

They wore painter's shoe covers to avoid tracking blood.

"Interesting," Korolev said. "Almost all are head kills."

Borodin had noticed the same thing. "Trained as an assassin," he said. "Not as a soldier."

The other shadow warriors almost always struck their victims in the chest, the center of mass where soldiers were trained to fire their weapons. Ideally, the first bullet would hit the enemy's heart, but even if the aim was off by a few centimeters, it would still strike something. Aiming for the head was a different matter. A much smaller target, increased opportunity to miss, though favored by snipers who had more time to be certain of their aim.

The chef had been the first to fall. TYR had stretched his hand so that it passed through the screaming man's face, then solidified so that the face erupted in an explosion of gore.

A few of the doomed customers had tried to escape then, rushing for the main door.

Borodin had been pleased to see his newest shadow warrior effortlessly disappear from beside the chef's body and instantly reappear in front of that door. There, TYR had dispatched his targets two at a time.

Then he had swept the room, first obliterating those who cowered and begged, then searching for the two who had sense enough to attempt to hide and remain silent. One behind the counter, the other in the restroom.

In all, it took one minute, thirty-seven seconds. Exactly.

Janyk cocked his head as he studied one of the headless corpses. A baseball cap sat atop a blood-glazed mound of shattered bone and lumps of glistening brain matter. "Might this not cause a problem?"

Borodin and Korolev joined him. "How so?" the general asked.

"Identification of the dead," Janyk said. "What's the sense of killing so many notable people if the authorities can't confirm who has been killed?"

Borodin treated the question seriously, though he knew it didn't matter. His men still believed they were on the mission he had described for them—one to make them proud.

"There will still be fingerprints," he said. "DNA. Even the contents of their wallets. If there is confusion, even better, yes? If photos are released showing injuries like these . . ." He gestured to all the mangled corpses. "So much outrage."

Borodin's soldiers agreed with their general: The more confusion, and the more outrage directed at America, the better. They didn't know that America wasn't the target. Certainly some notable people would die in three days when his shadow warriors were unleashed at the target site, but to the general, those victims would be inconsequential.

His squad didn't know it, but this mission had only one target.

Korolev started the fire in the kitchen. Janyk opened the valve on the 200-pound propane tank outside the back wall. By the time the authorities sifted through the charred rubble and connected the shattered bodies to those at the hacienda in Sonora and the warehouse outside Albuquerque, it would be too late.

Borodin heard the explosion as they drove away: thunder from the approaching storm.

27

After Matt left the pharmacy, he walked south on 2nd, head down, eyes on his new phone, his relaxed body language deliberately incompatible with that of a fugitive who'd be anxious to avoid observation.

On his first call to Arlo, it took Matt less than a minute to relay the basics of the situation: A government agency that might or might not be the Department of Homeland Security had tied him to Caparelli via the death of Laura Hart. They considered that death a possible homicide committed by Matt as payment for Caparelli's help in clearing Matt's name in the investigation of his partner.

He had Arlo's full attention as he went on to quickly relate how two agents, probably from the same agency, had just tried and failed to capture him. That there'd be more coming soon, likely within minutes, and that he couldn't evade the cameras for long.

"Where are you now?"

"You understand that if they're not listening to this call in real time, they will within ten minutes."

"Shit."

"Can you get me out of this? Or do I run?"

"Call me back in five minutes."

"They'll be listening then."

"They won't be the only ones." With that cryptic remark, Arlo cut the call.

Caidin scanned the buildings on the street, chose the tallest one, and stepped into its glossy lobby, bright with glass and pristine marble. Instead of heading for the bulky guard in a navy blazer who sat behind a vast, bleached-wood counter, he strode confidently to the building directory, locating a law office with five partners in its name. Reception was on the eighteenth floor. Odds were it would be huge, meaning his pursuers would have to question a lot of people.

He turned and walked back to the guard, keeping his head down as he pulled out his wallet. He gave his real name, handed over his driver's license, said he had an appointment with his lawyer at the five-name firm.

The guard didn't ask which one, signed him in, then turned back to watching the row of security monitors on his side of the counter. A quick glance told Matt he would have been recorded entering the lobby. It would only take minutes before Fort Meade's massive computer system identified him. By now, it'd be processing video from every camera in DC.

He pressed the UP button on the wall of elevators, anticipating that the first reaction to his identification would be a phone call to the security desk. The guard would remember him, check the register, read out his name, and say what he was doing in the building—going up to see his lawyer.

That should get a good response, Matt thought.

A melodic chime announced the arrival of an elevator. Matt stepped aside to let a half dozen passengers get out, then joined them as they headed across the lobby, all the while keeping his head down as if checking messages on his phone. Just as he reached the glass door that led into the building's coffee shop, he heard the guard's phone ring.

Matt checked his watch, called Arlo.

Arlo handed the phone to Caparelli. "You're on."

Caparelli spoke fast. "No names, don't make it easy for the machines. You know who this is. Let me hear your voice."

"They're hearing it, too."

"Our favorite restaurant. You remember, right?" It was a long shot, Caparelli knew, but how else could he speak in code to someone he barely knew?

"Amazing. I do remember. That's—"

"Stop," Caparelli interrupted. "Can you get there from where you are?"

"Won't be a problem."

"An independent's going to meet you. He's heavily armed. Do you recall the challenge and response?"

"I do."

"I'll see you when you get here."

Caparelli handed the phone back to Arlo.

"You think he understood?" Arlo asked.

"She would have."

In the DHS command center, two minutes after the call had been captured and decrypted, Lomax had heard the whole conversation, rapidly issued a string of commands, beginning with Caparelli's credit card records. "Run them against Caidin's. Pull up the names of any restaurants those two visited in common."

"Their favorite restaurant?" Ames asked. "Far as we know, as of last week, they'd never been in contact."

"There's a world of hurt in 'far as we know.' Then again, it could also be a code."

"Well, wherever Caidin is now, we sure as hell know where he plans to go."

"If I've learned anything in this business," Lomax said, "it's there ain't anything that's sure."

It wasn't a restaurant, of course.

Caparelli had raised Laura since she was seven, and her relationship with her Uncle Dan was as close as any child and parent. Even when she had graduated and moved from his home, they stayed close, and had made a point of having lunch together almost every Sunday afternoon. But when she had joined CROSSWIND, the nature of those meals had changed. No discussion of any work-related topics could take place in public. Instead of the small deli in Georgetown where they had met so regularly, lunch was now something that Caparelli ordered in to serve in his own kitchen, where they could talk without being concerned about others overhearing. Laura had made a joke of it: Uncle Dan's Kitchen was their favorite restaurant.

Caidin didn't know how he knew that; knew exactly how he knew that.

He had shared Laura's mind and memories of her last day of life. *But not her last day of existence.* That word again: impossible. His conscious mind wanted to reject his knowledge because there was no rational way he could possess it. But in the same way, he knew where Caparelli lived, the townhouse in Georgetown, ten miles away, past hundreds, if not thousands of cameras. There was no way to evade them, so that left only one strategy: He'd have to swamp them.

Matt walked onto the street and hailed a cab.

A minute later, he slipped into the back of a Yellow Taxi whose security shield and reinforced front seat gave scant room for his legs. He leaned close to the payment slot, well within range of the camera installed above the front windshield. "I need to pick up my motorcycle," he told the driver, and said he'd direct him to the parking lot where he'd left it.

Matt estimated it would be three minutes before DHS knew which cab he was in. Seconds counted, but it might be long enough.

Ames drove while Lomax tracked the progress of the search on his encrypted phone. No common restaurant had turned up in the credit card records of the two men. But Caidin had been picked up on a security camera in an office building, and had signed in to visit his lawyer. Not good. Agents were already on their way to the law firm, even though Caidin's bank records revealed no payments to it.

Two minutes later, another alert came from SPARROW. The target was in a cab, miles away from the law firm. As Ames battled traffic, Lomax redeployed the agents at the law firm to their next best lead. The cab driver had dropped his fare at the entrance to an underground lot where Caidin said he had a motorcycle.

Though another data search found no record of his ever owning one, it did confirm he'd completed the police motorcycle course as a condition of employment, so Lomax set his first set of agents to tracking every bike that left the underground lot. It would have to be a manual task, since facial recognition was blocked by helmet visors. At the same time, he dispatched another team to check the license plates of any other motorcycle parked in the garage.

Then the target was spotted in another cab. Two minutes after that, in a Metro station.

Lomax had had enough. Caidin was playing the system in an attempt to strain the capability of DHS to stay on top of him. "Forget all the individual sightings," he ordered his technicians in the command center. "What's his overall direction? Where's he heading?"

The answer came back quickly: Georgetown. Too general, but at least it provided focus. "Put Georgetown cameras in the SPARROW priority queue,"

Lomax ordered. Then he redirected half his scattered teams to converge on Georgetown, while, with a nod to Ames, he sent the other half to 610 E Street, southwest: CROSSWIND.

One hour later, twenty-four agents covered every vehicle and pedestrian entry point to the office block that included CROSSWIND's main facility.

Lomax and Ames remained in their vehicle across from the parking garage entrance as chase cars reported a black Chevy Suburban, retrofitted with armor and blackened windows, speeding toward their location. The driver was not identifiable, the passenger in the back seat a silhouette.

Lomax readied his forces to intercept, reminding them that Caparelli had informed Caidin that the driver was heavily armed.

When the Suburban was two minutes out, Lomax and Ames exited their vehicle, crossed to the parking garage entrance. Other agents had already arranged to have the metal garage door closed.

Across the street, two snipers hunched in position.

The Suburban rounded the corner, obeying traffic lights, and Lomax stepped forward, motioning its driver toward the curb near the blocked entrance.

The Suburban stopped. Its motor running.

Lomax radioed his team. "Give him time to assess the situation and do the right thing. Any phone calls coming from inside the vehicle?"

A technician at the DHS command center responded there was no indication of any communication by phone, radio, or Wi-Fi.

Two minutes passed.

Lomax sighed, told the others to be ready, then walked toward the Suburban. He approached to the driver's window, tapped on the tinted glass with his badge.

Too many seconds later, the window slid down.

The driver was young, lean. Black T-shirt, no shoulder holster. "Yessir?"

"Hands on the wheel," Lomax said. He waved his hand to signal his people to be ready to surround the vehicle in case Caidin bolted. "I'm going to need your passenger to step outside."

"Whatever." The driver turned to the back seat. "Door's unlocked."

The back passenger door opened and Lomax stepped back, hand sliding inside his jacket.

An older woman with a briefcase got out. "What's this about?" she asked.

Lomax swore, pushed her aside, checked inside, but she was the only passenger.

"Ames, the back."

The Secret Service agent swung open the Suburban's tailgate. "Nada."

It was then that Lomax saw Caparelli step out from a lobby entrance. "Lomax," he said. "You lost?"

"Where is he?"

To his credit, Caparelli dropped the game. "Already inside."

"I have a warrant for his arrest."

"And I have a restraining order. National security."

"I am national security."

"You're Homeland. CROSSWIND is NSA. You really want to get into that shooting war?"

Lomax ranked his options. They ranged from strangling Caparelli to outright gunplay to get his man. He had twenty-four agents on the street. His target was behind a few doors, up a few flights of stairs.

Caparelli seemed to read his mind. "Remember where you are. Civilian streets. And the nation's most effective intelligence agency isn't so poorly defended that your thugs can just shoot their way inside."

Lomax took the word "thugs" as the insult it was. But he didn't respond in kind.

"There's no need for this."

"I know."

"We should be cooperating."

Caparelli gave a tired smile. "I'm afraid we have different definitions for that word. I cooperate by sharing intelligence. You try to control it."

Lomax bristled, but kept his tone calm. "If you make me force the issue, I will get whatever warrant it takes to set yours aside and get me through that door."

Caparelli responded just as evenly. "Your choice. But when they hold the congressional hearings, I'll remind them that when CROSSWIND obtained intel that was so time sensitive we had to share it with you without going through channels, you were so concerned with coming after us that you did nothing to save the president."

Caparelli turned away to reenter the CROSSWIND building.

Beside Lomax, Ames spoke quietly. "If we're going to take him, this is the moment."

Lomax felt his finger twitch, as if it were on a trigger. "No. We do this by the book. CROSSWIND has to run by the same rules we all do. And Caparelli just gave me the excuse to make sure it does."

28

"One thirty-two over ninety. Borderline high. Is that normal for you?"

In the Projection Room, on an examination table, Matt looked down at the loose white hospital top and pants he wore. "Apparently, it is now."

Chu ripped the Velcro band from Matt's arm, looked back at Caparelli. "He's good to go."

"A minute," Caparelli said.

Chu nodded and joined Arlo at the Cradle's control panel.

"Nervous?" Caparelli asked Matt.

"More like numb."

"Good. This works best without distractions."

"Like the DHS trying to arrest me?"

"Blowing smoke. They're after us, not you. Homeland's been trying to assume operational authority over CROSSWIND for years. They'll never get it."

Matt wasn't so sure. "That might explain their having a recording of Laura's last call, but not why they wired my wife and sent her to tell me Laura's death was a homicide."

"I can deal with Homeland. I need you to focus on one thing only: linking with General Borodin. He's not trying to hide his trail. That means whatever he's planning to do with his berserkers, it's going to be soon. To stop him, we need to find him. Tonight. And now that you've been linked to him through Laura, you're the only one who has a chance of finding him that fast."

A deep, low hum resonated through the Projection Room. The Cradle was up and running.

Caparelli handed Matt two small red earbuds. "These'll block the background noise of the machinery, but we'll be able to talk to you. Just speak normally. There're mikes in the Cradle."

"Where will you be?"

"In the next room."

"Next room? Your man Arlo said there'd be no radiation."

Caparelli hesitated for a split second before answering. "To project your consciousness to another location, we have to open this room's section of protective shielding."

"Shielding . . . ," Matt said. "From what?"

"Intrusion. By other remote perceivers."

"Russian?"

Caparelli looked at his watch and frowned. "Mostly. But China has a program. Israel. India either has one or is very close. And there are always independents turning up. People who can do this on their own. If we detect them, and they're American, we recruit them."

"What happens if they're not American?"

"Not your concern. Again, don't distract yourself. Stay focused on 'right now.' And the target."

"Stasik Sergeyevich Borodin." This time, Matt's pronunciation was flawless.

Matt tried not to think how foolish he would look to his former colleagues. He was lying flat on the inner surface of the Cradle, and Chu positioned his arms at his side as if he were a puppet. Speaking over the earbud receivers, the psychologist told him to keep his eyes fixed on the pale blue light centered in the glass above him in the canopy and again cautioned him not to move his head. He felt her hand touch his shoulder and heard her whispered voice, *"You'll be fine."*

Then there was silence. The light in the room began to fade until the only radiance he was aware of was the blue light, now brighter, now larger.

There was a faint hiss of static in his ears, a channel opening. Caparelli spoke. *"How are you doing?"*

"Fine. When do we start?"

"You're halfway there. Already suspended."

Surprised, Matt reflexively tried to raise his head, then gasped as he felt himself spinning head over heels, over and over.

"Don't move!" Caparelli ordered. *"Hold on. . . . Arlo's adjusting. . . ."*

The spinning stopped and Matt realized he'd never moved. It was the weightless fluid in his ears that he had set in motion.

"Better?"

"Yeah. Sorry. Won't happen again."

"Good. We're bringing you back up to equilibrium."

This time, by concentrating on the slowly changing detail of the blue light's housing, Matt was aware he was rising, even though there was no matching sensation of movement. Or of weight or weightlessness.

"That's it," Caparelli said. *"Everything's set on our end. Dr. Chu will take over now. Do what she says, report what you experience. Any questions?"*

"Have you turned off the shielding?"

"Don't worry. When we do, we can turn it back on instantly if we have to. And we have other safeguards, as well. Here's Dr. Chu."

Chu's voice was calm and reassuring over the tiny speakers.

"Are you looking at the light overhead?"

"Yes."

"What color is it?"

"Blue."

"I'm going to fire the first strobe flash now. Tell me if it's too bright."

It wasn't.

"Good. Now we're going to start a calibration sequence. We can stop any time you feel uncomfortable."

Lights above Matt began to flash. Faster, slower, sometimes with a rhythm, one sequence more chaotic like flashlights sparkling off shattered glass, another more like the play of sunlight on waves, its pattern regular, but always moving.

The blue light became blue sky, and Matt was driving along a road, sunlight flashing through trees, the rays rising and setting, off and on, stuttering, jarring, soothing, and then—

"What do you see?" Chu asked.

Such an odd question, Matt thought. "You tell me. I'm sitting right beside you."

Matt saw Chu look ahead, past her console, through the window into the Projection Room. He followed her gaze, saw himself suspended in the Cradle—

"Whoa." He was back in his body, floating without sensation, staring up at blue light, the soft flashes of the strobe lights.

"Where are you now?" Chu asked.

"Back in the Cradle," Matt said. "But I was just beside you."

"You're doing well. Say the general's name again, please."

"Stasik Sergeyevich Borodin."

"Very good. Again."

Matt repeated the general's name. Each time Chu asked, he said it, again and again until the words were sounds without meaning. Then—

"Where is he, Detective Caidin?"

Matt felt bathed in sudden heat . . . as if the door to a blast furnace had just opened. The smell of . . . acetone? Gasoline? Mixed with the pungent scent of cedar. His right arm hurt. He tasted Coca-Cola then—

He was floating in the Cradle. "I . . . I don't know."

"Let's try again. Say his name . . ."

This time Matt felt cold. Very cold. *It's winter. It's always winter here,* he thought. He saw metal shelving stretched before him. Empty, waiting. Heard screams, but they were distant, then—

Back in the Cradle.

Chu's voice was soothing. *"We're going deeper now. Close your eyes. The lights are going to be very very bright."*

Matt closed his eyes. Red flashes strobed his eyelids. Heat pulsed from them. Like summer sunshine. Like—

The lake. The sun high in a perfect blue sky. The sparkle of waves moving in perfect formation, swells glinting silver as they ebbed onto the beach, and off, the pattern repeating but never the same. The smell of water, the keening cry of wheeling gulls chased by the barking dog. The grit of sand beneath his feet.

"I like it here," Laura said.

Matt turned and there she was. No sense of illusion or hallucination. "Where are we?"

"How should I know? The question is, Where are you?"

"I'm in . . . I was in the Cradle." Matt's heart raced. None of this was real, but there was no escape from it.

"Why not?" Laura said.

They stood together in the Projection Room, wild strobes creating blinding light, deep shadow, light, then shadow, as the machine's deep hum pulsed loudly.

Through the observation window, Matt saw Caparelli, Chu, and Arlo at the console, looking intently at—

His body in midair in the Cradle, his features striped by light and shadow, light and shadow, again and again, the pattern repeating but never the same.

Matt fought down panic. "This isn't right."

Laura frowned. "Well, where are you supposed to be?"

He said the name.

In the Winnebago, Borodin checked the status lights on the five operational containment units stacked at the back. All lights steady green, his shadow warriors at rest. He placed his hand on ODIN's unit. Then realized what a meaningless gesture that was, and turned away. He hooked a six-pack of Coke from the cooler and stepped down with a grunt through the narrow doorway, into the cool fall air of the West Virginia night. Janyk and Korolev were sitting at a picnic table, smoking by the pale light of a fluorescent lantern, monitoring the progress the others made on the van.

Originally, Borodin's schedule had called for the vehicle to be painted three nights ago, in Colorado. But the unexpected encounter with Major Kalnikova had prompted him to make a change, deciding to cover more ground toward the target before pausing for the day it would take to complete the van's refitting. Its camouflage.

The day after the encounter, Janyk had read from the Internet a few local news reports citing an attempted carjacking outside the Walmart in Colorado Springs. The brief stories described a car fire, but reported no deaths, no injuries, and no description of suspects.

It was one thing for there to have been no mention of the restaurant they had burned down. That would remain a local story until someone got around to asking why all the victims had crushed skulls. But the lack of detail of what had happened in Colorado Springs had put Borodin on alert. The gun battle had cost the lives of at least two police officers, one of Kalnikova's squad, and possibly the major herself. The fact that none of that was reported, or even hinted at, told him that the news was being suppressed. Janyk had expressed mock horror to think such a thing could be possible in a country where the government could never interfere in the workings of such a free and noble press!

To Borodin, the cover-up meant either the authorities knew everything, or nothing. In the absence of a confrontation with American police, the second was more likely: Lacking an explanation for what had happened, the authorities preferred to keep their ignorance to themselves. He only needed to count on that state of ignorance lasting for seventy-two hours more. He and his men would spend one more day at this camp, drive into position by Sunday. And on Monday night, shortly after sunset, the authorities would be ignorant no longer.

He walked around to the other side of the Winnebago, where the video-news van was parked, out of sight of the narrow roadway that snaked through the isolated campsites. He could smell the fresh paint, but doubted the telltale odor would travel far. The rich cedar scent of the campground's trees and bushes would overpower it.

"Be careful how much of that you inhale," he told Yegor and Gulin. The Dronov brothers were the youngest of the team, and the ones requiring more direction. But, he noted approvingly, they had done a commendable job of masking the van's windows and brightwork with tape, and were now diligently attending to spray-painting with an equal attention to detail. Working by night, which Borodin had thought would be more difficult, actually made the quality of the painting easier to judge, because of the directionality of the halogen flashlights the brothers used. The new blue finish on the vehicle was commendably smooth and glossy, and gave no indication of a rushed and temporary job. Tomorrow, Amir Mazurenko would paint on the logo—he had the steadiest hand.

The Dronov brothers put down their spray guns, careful to balance them on the gravel so they wouldn't tip over. They thanked him properly for the soda he had brought them, gulped down a can each, laughing as they burped. Borodin took another can for himself, to join them.

Footsteps crunched on the gravel, and Borodin turned to see Janyk walking toward them, offering a packet of cigarettes.

"Perhaps away from the paint fumes," Borodin said, and the four of them stepped back to admire the van from a few meters' distance.

The paint gleamed in the light from the flashlights.

"Very nice," Janyk said.

Borodin lit the cigarettes of his men with a butane lighter. As he lit his own, he saw Captain Korolev approach, and so held out that cigarette. "Konstantin, take this one."

"General?" Janyk said.

Borodin saw Janyk giving him a questioning look. "What?" He turned to the brothers. They shared Janyk's expression. He turned to Korolev. "Is there . . ."

It wasn't Korolev he had seen approaching. It was a presence.

Borodin felt the hair on his neck bristle, felt a chill that was not any part of the night air.

He had felt this before. VEKTOR was sending perceivers to track him, so many and so often that he could sense their presence.

He looked back at the Winnebago.

In the window, a figure.

"You see it?" he whispered.

"See what, sir?"

Borodin sensed his men's confusion. *Korolev was the one who saw her first in Mexico. The others never did. He must be a sensitive, as well, also capable of seeing these—*

"In the window ..."

The spectral face of a young woman.

The young woman from the hacienda. Not from VEKTOR at all.

"It's her ...," Borodin said in amazement, though he knew the men with him would see nothing. He turned slowly to the figure he had assumed was Korolev, and wasn't.

"And she's not alone ..."

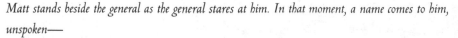

Matt stands beside the general as the general stares at him. In that moment, a name comes to him, unspoken—

Misha.

"He sees you." Laura's voice whispers in his ear.

Where is she? Matt looks away—

—and she's beside him, someplace else. . . .

Through a window, blurred with grime, they watch the general gather his five men, whose names surface one by one: Korolev, Janyk, Mazurenko, Dronov, and again Dronov. The general points at the window and they rush toward it, toward the—

VEKTOR containment units.

Matt turns away from the window and Laura turns away from the window and they see the VEKTOR containment units stacked at the back of the camper van where the bed should be. Again the names come to him. HOD, LOKI, BALDUR, TYR, and then, another name, confused and fluctuating . . . ODIN/Misha/Misha/ODIN.

Matt hears, feels, the floor beneath him shift and creak as the general and his men burst into the camper van. Three men charge him and—

—pass through his body.

General Borodin and Korolev stop—

Aware.

Do they see me? Sense me? Matt can't hear the commands the general shouts, though he catches their intent: Not ODIN . . . not my son . . . not Misha. *The general is insistent. Send another.*

"It isn't safe," Laura says.

"How do you know?" Matt asks.

"It's that dog again. It's barking. Do you hear it?"

Matt can't be certain.

One of the general's men, Janyk, approaches a containment unit, punches in a code. Lights change from green to red. The unit opens on hydraulic hinges. Blue light glows from within and—

BALDUR wakes.

Matt feels Laura's hand take his hand—

"Come with me," she says.

They stand by the picnic table. Old wood rough and scarred with initials. The dim light of a fluorescent lantern.

Laura's eyes shine. Matt touches her face. Her skin is smooth and warm.

"How is this possible?" he asks.

"How is it not?" she answers.

A cold wind blows. The wind is dark. The light fades, or is it swallowed? Matt's unsure.

"I can help you," Laura says.

"Do what?"

The dark wind becomes a wave of water.

BALDUR. Closing.

Matt's vision fragments with the rhythm of the light on waves. Now a dozen Lauras are before him in superposition, every form she ever was all at once. Young and beautiful, mangled and bloody, naked and alluring, torn and whole . . . And all with hands and talons, bones, outstretched . . . pleading, urging, clawing, ripping flesh from—

"Stop!" *Matt covers his eyes to block the vision . . . dream . . . nightmare as—*

Sunlight glinting off the waves on the beach . . .

Strobe lights blinding . . .

"Laura?"

The barking dog. The hiss of static in his ear and—

"It's coming!"

Caidin's voice over the control room speakers was panicked, hoarse. His suspended form struggled against the magnetic fields that adjusted automatically, attempting to keep him stable.

Caparelli yanked the microphone from Chu. They had no time to process who—or what—Caidin might have seen. "What's coming, Caidin?"

"Get us out of here!"

Us! Caparelli turned to Arlo, who'd already flipped open a safety cover, revealing a red rocker switch.

"No!" Caparelli said. "Not yet. Ease him down." Into the mike, he said, "Caidin! Did you see her? Did you see Laura?"

"Yes! She's here with me! Get us out!"

The confirmation of his wildest hopes froze Caparelli for just an instant.

Arlo was insistent. "Sir, we need to reestablish the shield!"

"Do it," Caparelli shouted. He ran for the door.

Matt jerked upright in the Cradle, chest heaving as he gasped for air. The strobes had shut off. The room lights were on.

Caparelli rushed to his side. "Where is she?"

Matt felt nauseous, dizzy. His head pulsed with pain as if the strobe lights still continued. But what he'd just experienced . . . seen . . . felt . . . had seemed just as real.

He grabbed at Caparelli. "Why can't I tell the difference?"

Another hand gently pushed him back, wrapped a Velcro sleeve around his arm. "Soon. Soon. I can teach you," Chu said. "Right now, you need to tell us where the general is. Describe the location for us."

"Laura," Caparelli said. "Describe Laura."

Matt opened his mouth to speak, then froze. Past Caparelli, past Chu and Arlo, now working at the Cradle's controls, he saw the window into the control room. In the window, a reflection—

"She's there . . ."

All turned to the window where Laura stood. Such sadness in her, Matt felt tears rise in him as if the sorrow were his.

"Where?" Caparelli pleaded. "Laura . . . ?"

Laura pointed back into the room.

"She's pointing . . . ," Matt said.

Caparelli was stricken, Arlo fascinated. Chu quietly inflated the blood pressure cuff.

"Where?" Caparelli said, almost a gasp.

Chu activated the cuff. "Keep describing what you see."

"Pointing in here . . . pointing at—" Matt turned to look in the direction Laura indicated. Arlo and Chu and Caparelli turned with him.

This time, they *all* saw it.

A young man in a black soldier's uniform. Eyes so deeply shadowed they were lost in black. He stood in silence, chest and shoulders moving with slow, deep breaths.

"Berserker . . . ," Matt whispered.

Caparelli's voice was tight, controlled. "Everyone out. Now."

Arlo rapidly tapped keys on the Cradle's control panel. "Pulse is armed!"

Caparelli was emphatic. "Not yet. Caidin—where is she now? Where's Laura?"

And suddenly Laura was there, in front of the berserker.

"She's blocking him . . ."

Caparelli gasped. "I see her!"

"Shall I fire the pulse?" Arlo asked. His voice cracked. Matt felt the pressure, didn't know the reason why.

"No!" Caparelli ordered. *"You'll kill her!"*

Arlo wheeled to his superior, his hand still on the controls. "Sir! She's already dead!"

"No!" Caparelli pulled Arlo away.

And with that the berserker sprang for Matt.

Like an image distorted in antique glass, the silent soldier stretched up and dissolved into a coil of black smoke. It blew past Laura's form, coalesced behind her.

She spun around, incapable of stopping it as it rushed toward Matt. Its mouth expanded in a cry of soundless fury, arms blurring as they reached out for him, dark fingers spiraling into obsidian shards to—

"Run!" Chu shouted at Matt as she threw herself in front of the berserker. Instantly it shrank back into the form of a soldier, then leapt *into* her like a diver plunging into a waterfall. And in that one moment of passing through her—

—the berserker became solid and thrust his arms apart to—

Tear her body in two.

Hot blood and flesh rained down on all of them.

Blurring into focus once again, the berserker seemed to shiver, and more blood and gore dropped from him to the once-white floor.

He turned to Matt again.

From the corner of his eye, Matt saw a hand swing out toward the control panel of the Cradle—Caparelli's hand—and heard the loud thump of a capacitor discharging.

The berserker lost form, billowed out, a storm cloud dissipating into—

Nothing.

Across the room, Arlo stood motionless, streaked with blood.

In the center of the room, Caparelli knelt by what was left of Dr. Norma Chu.

Matt fell back against the Cradle, stared into the empty space where the berserker had been, and was no more. Looked over to where Laura had been.

Nothing.

DAY SEVEN

29

Like a prehistoric monster bellowing on the attack, the dull green Ka-226 helicopter descended from the cloud-darkened night into the floodlit glow of the
landing pad.

The violent wash from its spinning rotors sent streamers of snow spiraling
down like falling comets. At the edge of the cracked concrete pad, Gorokhov,
swaddled in his heavy coat, saw Popovich turn away from the growing gusts of
cold wind, ice, and fine grit.

Gorokhov did nothing. He would not turn away from his executioner. He
had no doubt that was who was arriving: Lieutenant-General Iosif Gavrilevich
Solomon, dispatched from Moscow less than a day ago. Despite his situation,
Gorokhov was impressed that the cumbersome bureaucracy of the Russian
Army had been able to react so quickly. The general's jet had set down at Sokol
Airport only forty minutes ago, and the helicopter journey to the VEKTOR facility took at least thirty. The efficiency on display was not only astonishing to
the former chief administrator, it gave him hope. Perhaps the faceless generals
in Moscow had some glimmer of what was at stake here.

The small transport helicopter touched down, the rotors slowed, and as the
cabin door opened, a new shaft of light stabbed out from the craft to catch the
swirls of snow.

Soldiers poured out first, five of them armed with AKMS assault rifles and
wearing urban Gorod camo parkas; the black, gray, and white pattern as effective
in this mountainous and barren cold-weather region as it was in the steel and
concrete of cities.

Four swiftly took up positions around the helicopter. A fifth ran to the waiting security detail that stood apart from Gorokhov, Popovich, and the two VEKTOR guards. There was a brief conversation; then the soldier signaled to the helo, and a sixth passenger emerged, same camo uniform, but only a holstered pistol on his belt, no rifle.

He walked to Popovich, and as he came closer, Gorokhov wondered if this general was even old enough to shave.

The general handed Popovich a thick envelope, no doubt containing his documents of authority. Popovich didn't open it, tried to say something, but the general ignored him, looked to Gorokhov.

"Chief Administrator?"

Gorokhov enjoyed the dark expression that clouded Popovich's face. "Former chief administrator."

The general didn't react, looked back and forth between the two men, then told the two VEKTOR guards to join the security detail.

"Your failure here is not acceptable," the general said, making sure Popovich and Gorokhov understood he was addressing them both.

Whatever Popovich was about to sputter in response, Gorokhov interrupted. "General Solomon, it's not a failure yet."

Popovich found his voice. "But it is! A total disaster!"

"I see it as an opportunity," Gorokhov said. He could see how the general planned to play this out, with the two VEKTOR administrators pitted against each other to each make his case for why he shouldn't be dismissed, imprisoned, or shot.

Even Popovich seemed to grasp their situation. "General, we should move inside, to be protected by our shielding, so the American perceivers can't overhear us." He gestured to the Defenders parked by the pad, exhaust clouds billowing around them. "We can continue our discussion there."

Though this general looked youthful, Gorokhov recognized the coldness of his gaze, the mask of his expression. This man knew war. He knew adversity.

"Discussion?" the general said. "There's no discussion." He looked again from one to the other. "I understand there's a lake nearby."

Gorokhov sighed as if he were already submerged in it. He saw Popovich's mouth open soundlessly. But if there really was nothing more to be said or done, Gorokhov was determined to be remembered as a Russian.

"The quarry lake," he said. "I know it well." He pointed beyond the pad. "A short walk in that direction."

The general remained impassive.

"But it's so cold," Popovich said faintly.

Gorokhov inhaled deeply, feeling the icy air sting his lungs, fill him with life. "We should go." He met the general's eyes. "Whoever has to deal with Borodin, he will need to start at once."

Popovich finally seemed to understand that whatever the general's decision would be, he hadn't made it yet. "The lake's this way," he said. In an evident effort to regain his composure, he began to march across the pad, through the floodlit glow, into darkness.

For a few moments, Gorokhov watched him go, then said quietly to the general, "If I were to deal with Borodin, I would capitalize on what he's doing, not stop him."

Solomon stared at the chief administrator with dead eyes.

"He could be the first strike of Operation Scythe," Gorokhov said.

"A year ahead of schedule?" The general didn't sound impressed.

"Our perceivers have been tracking him, listening in, as it were. I'm certain I know where he's going, and if the proper steps are taken, it will serve our purpose."

At the edge of the floodlights across the pad, Gorokhov saw Popovich stop, look back. The general watched the small man, and the chief administrator could see he was still holding both men in the balance.

"Assuming so, how soon could we follow with a second strike?"

"We're no longer limited by the one small sample of natural einstone. We have produced enough of the synthetic variant, manufactured enough of the resonators. If we begin the processing of the shadow warriors now, we could strike again in thirty days. The Americans won't have recovered by then. The world will not have recovered."

"The world?"

Gorokhov could see the general was at least intrigued by the possibility he suggested.

"Are you confident General Borodin will succeed in his plan?" Solomon asked.

"I have no confidence at all. He is a traitor to the Motherland who stole our greatest weapon for personal vengeance."

Solomon finally gave a reaction, one of surprise. "Personal vengeance? Then how . . . ?" he began.

"Fortunately, there is a great patriot in position to take over Borodin's squad at the target location." Gorokhov smiled. "Major Kalnikova."

The general gave a snort of disapproval. "She's a prisoner of the Americans."

"We have many friends among them who can pass on orders and aid. We can be in contact with her within a day."

The general narrowed his eyes.

"If I were to deal with Borodin," Gorokhov said, "I would have the major deal with him. Take command of his team. And complete our mission, not his."

"What is his mission?"

"Everything he has done, the crimes he has committed, are all in the service of killing one man, and one man only."

"Who?"

The chief administrator shrugged, a movement that barely registered through his heavy fur coat. "No one you know. Someone I do. What's important is, the man Borodin is after will be surrounded by many of those already targeted by Scythe. It is a perfect opportunity." He smiled. "If I were to deal with Borodin."

With the fate of the world, his country, and his life in the balance, Gorokhov breathed deeply the frigid air of his homeland, his nurturing fire.

Mother Russia gave him life, and only she could take it away.

He could wait for the general's decision. He didn't think it would take long.

30

"The general has four more of them," Matt said.

In CROSSWIND's stark white conference room, Burton Hirst, Caparelli, and Arlo stayed silent, their faces shuttered, guarded. Norma Chu's empty chair was an accusing absence. Someone was to blame, and Matt could feel who they had chosen.

"And one of them . . ." He grimaced. It was so difficult recalling the experience, catching only glimpses like a half-remembered dream. "One of them, I think, is the general's son."

Hirst looked up in surprise but said nothing.

"A berserker?" Arlo asked. "You sure?"

"Yeah. Real name, Misha. Code name, ODIN."

"Makes sense," Caparelli said quietly. "Emotional connection. It's what drives the phenomenon." He sounded exhausted. "I imagine we'll discover he was one of the first. Could explain why everything the NSA has on Borodin has no mention of family connections." He turned to Arlo. "Get records to run a new search, this time for a Misha. See if there's any connection the Russians forgot to expunge."

"I know I'm the outsider," Matt said. "But aren't there other priorities to look into first?"

"There are," Caparelli said. "And we will. And you're not an outsider. Not anymore. Burton?"

Hirst picked up a red pen, smoothed the pad of paper before him. "You were in a campground, Mr. Caidin?"

"Yes. But I don't know where."

"Look, this isn't some drive-by murder investigation after the fact. We're trying to prevent any more deaths that could happen at any time. So . . ." Hirst cleared his throat, as if embarrassed he had revealed his emotions. "So just give me whatever impressions you recall. Don't try to make them make sense. The kind of vegetation. Bodies of water. In any order."

Matt thought back to Chu's instructions, to go blank and let impressions come to him, rather than struggle to recall step by step what he'd seen. "Cedar . . . a strong scent of cedar. . . . That's the first thing. And cigarette smoke. Paint. They were painting something. . . ."

Matt was surprised by how easily the next words slipped from him. "He was . . . the general . . . was pleased with the progress, but worried they were breathing fumes."

"Emotional connection," Caparelli murmured again.

"What else?" Hirst asked.

"Laura knew what to do." Matt was aware of Caparelli's gaze, but spoke to Hirst. "I saw her first, and . . . I don't know where we were. A beach, I think. She said she liked it there. But . . . I needed to get to the general so, that's where we were. She took me there."

"You spoke to Laura?" Caparelli asked.

"Yeah. She was very real. She took my hand. It all felt real." Another flash of memory came to him. "Borodin could see her."

"Mutual awareness," Arlo said. "Wow. It sometimes develops between perceivers and their targets. But usually takes years."

"Laura has been tracking him for years," Caparelli said. "Mutual awareness was inevitable after all that time."

"But he could see me, too," Matt added. "And one of his men saw both of us. A man with a scar. Korolev. Captain Korolev."

"I know that name," Caparelli said. "Arlo?"

"Got to be Konstantin Korolev. Army captain. Heads up VEKTOR's security unit." He looked at Caparelli. "Could Korolev be sensitive?"

Caparelli didn't care. There was no time for side trips. "Did you get any other names?" he asked Matt.

Matt recited the names he remembered for the general's men, and the berserkers.

"Okay," Arlo said. "*All* of those are from VEKTOR's security unit. We'll have full dossiers on all of them."

"So this *is* a sanctioned operation?" Caparelli asked.

Hirst disagreed. "No. It can't be. No reason for it. This berserker technology is like nothing else we've seen. Why bring it here where one tactical error means we get our hands on it? What could the Russians possibly hope to gain from committing an act of terrorism on American soil that can so easily be linked back to them? It's beyond senseless. It's . . . insane."

"Insane," Caparelli repeated. "Cold War days, we always used to fear the one mad Soviet general with access to launch codes. The Russians probably feared the same about us. Both sides installing all kinds of fail-safes to be certain the authority to launch went through a chain of command. Checks and counterbalances. But VEKTOR . . . it's one small research unit. Borodin *is* its chain of command. . . ." Caparelli's face blanched.

"What is it?" Arlo asked.

"What if *Borodin* is insane? What if there is no objective? There are three potential high-value targets of opportunity in this country in the next seven days. The Capitol. The UN. The Anti-terrorism Conference. What if he's going after all of them?"

"He has to get within a mile of anything he targets," Hirst said.

"Run the scenario," Caparelli countered. "He's got those containment units in a Winnebago. He could send the berserkers ahead as a ground force, and drive behind them as they tear open any perimeter we have. If we take rationality out of the equation, eliminate any need to hide identity or desire to escape, we have no defense."

"But in the Projection Room," Matt said, "you stopped a berserker."

"Not exactly," Arlo said. "Quantum fields being sensitive to electromagnetic disturbance, we have electromagnetic-pulse generators in all of our Projection Rooms—in case any rogue perceivers gain access to our facility when we've shut down shields for an operation. A one-megawatt micropulse in a contained space destabilizes the perceiver's projected quantum field, and forces its awareness back to its body."

Matt read between the lines. "What if it's just a quantum field like Laura? No perceiver to return to?"

"Then there's no place to go back to," Caparelli said. "They're just gone."

An hour later, the formal debriefing had ended, and Arlo and Hirst had new orders. Arlo would direct research teams to cross-correlate CROSSWIND's files on the VEKTOR operatives now known to be with Borodin. The researchers would be looking for hidden connections, anything to suggest Borodin's mission was something other than a madman's random act. Hirst's Tiger Team would redouble its efforts to define the scientific and engineering details of the new berserker technology. They'd be probing for any and all weaknesses that could be exploited. Specifically, was there a defensive system similar to the facility's EM-pulse generators that could be made portable, and ready within days?

Then it was just Matt and Caparelli, in the facility's small canteen, each with an untouched cup of coffee.

"How're you holding up?" Caparelli asked. To Matt, he almost sounded as if he meant it.

"Compared to what?" Matt said. "I have nothing to compare this to."

"I understand. Every perceiver before you has said the same."

So I'm a perceiver now? Matt thought.

"But there's a lot more to it than just *seeing*, right?"

Matt knew what he meant. "I can still smell the cedars."

"Ever wonder how you perceived the scent without having a physical nose?"

Matt hadn't even thought of that.

"It's a different way of knowing," Caparelli said. "You can't hear sounds, yet you understand what people are saying. Not because you hear the words they say, but because you share their thoughts about what they *intend* to say.

"The truth is, you're not really there as an independent perceiver. You're piggybacking on the minds of the people who *are* physically present. Your awareness somehow flickers along the edges of theirs, picks up their perceptions. But it's too disorienting to try to make sense of thoughts and sensations coming from so many different sources. Fortunately, your mind already has a mechanism that can bring all that together into a logical context. It's that sense of proprioception. The one that tells you the shape and position of your body. You understand? You're picking up sensations and signals from one or two or more people at the remote site, and then creating the illusion that all those sensations are arising in you.

"That's explains why you seemed to jump back and forth between being inside the camper and then outside by the picnic table. All those people in that area had created an overlapping world of perception, a map of that particular site, and to maintain sanity, you unconsciously choose to see it from one specific vantage point."

"Like being in virtual reality?"

"Good analogy. Someone creates a complete environment in a computer: castles, caves, endless forests. Yet you, as the user, can select the one part of it you want to see on the screen, or in your 3-D glasses. It's the same reason why manifestations of people appear with clothes. The form they take is a projection of a person's own perception of themselves. Sometimes young, sometimes old. In a wedding dress or a uniform or whatever it was they were wearing on the day they died."

"Okay," Matt said. He remembered how his grandfather had appeared at the foot of his bed, wearing his treasured flight jacket that had looked brand new. Maybe it hadn't been a dream. Maybe he was what Arlo called a "sensitive" and—

And then Matt had it.

"I'm the one in control because I have the whole map," he said. "I can look anywhere."

"And there you go," Caparelli said. "It's all in your mind. You just have to pick out the parts that you think are important."

"Like Laura," Matt said, and then wished he hadn't.

They sat in silence for long moments, both staring into their coffee cups, until, "What did she look like?" Caparelli's voice was so low, Matt wondered if CROSSWIND's director had meant to ask the question aloud.

"Same as the first time." Matt didn't add that Laura had grotesquely flashed back and forth from the way she'd looked before her accident, and after.

"Was she . . . happy? Or . . ."

"She was . . . restless. Like she needed to get things done. Frustrated. Maybe, even angry."

Caparelli flushed.

"Sorry," Matt said.

"Don't be."

They had chosen to sit at a small table against a wall. The opposite wall held a sink, cupboards, the coffee machine and supplies, along with signs asking people to clean their mugs after use. *An ordinary room for anything but an ordinary situation,* Matt thought, wishing he was not having this conversation.

"And . . . I appreciate the honesty." Caparelli's hands gripped his coffee cup tightly. "Norma said you and Laura . . . There was a particularly intense emotional . . . something beyond what she expected."

Matt chose to paraphrase the words that Arlo had given him. "My feelings don't count here. What you told me about the observed and the observing becoming the same thing . . . It's why there's no way I can separate Laura's feelings from mine, from yours. Even the general's. I *feel* love for his son, too. I share his loss, whatever happened to him. I know you and Laura were close, that you raised her as if she was your own. I experienced an echo of it."

But Arlo's words weren't Matt's truth, and he could see that somehow Caparelli knew it. Even though it had been the right thing to say to him, the right thing for him to hear.

"It was wrong of me to bring her to CROSSWIND," Caparelli said. "She could have had a better, safer life."

"That's not what she felt," Matt said.

It was as if Caparelli hadn't heard him. "I told myself I'd never get caught in a conflict, where I'd have to choose her safety over a mission." He looked off into a distance only he could see. "Because our missions aren't dangerous, y'see. No risk." Then he looked at Matt, hiding nothing. "And because I hesitated, because I didn't want to lose just her echo, I told Arlo not to fire the pulse and Norma died. As surely as if I had killed her myself."

Matt said nothing.

"I know you understand," Caparelli said. "I obtained the Internal Affairs report from Arlington. I know how you're involved in the investigation into corruption. And what happened to your partner because of that. It's clear it's not your fault. But that's not how you feel."

Of all the things Matt wanted to talk about with Caparelli, this wasn't one of them. He didn't reply.

Caparelli continued. "You feel you basically put the gun in his hand. That by not telling him the truth about why the charges were laid against him—to protect your undercover role—you committed the sin of inaction."

Matt didn't know what raced through him at the moment. Relief? Guilt? Anger? Some of each.

Caparelli seemed to understand.

"So what if you had done it differently? What if you had had that conversation with him, and saved his life, but exposed the investigation and ended up endangering a dozen others?"

Matt's confusion of emotions came into focus as anger, born of frustration.

"None of that's important. Jack Lowney was my partner."

Caparelli held up his coffee cup. "To loyalty."

Matt couldn't be certain if he was being mocked.

"I mean it," Caparelli said. "You faced a hard choice. You set a good example." He put his cup down. "And I should follow it." He stood up.

"I don't understand," Matt said.

But Caparelli wasn't ready to explain.

"Too little, too late," Lomax said.

Caparelli had anticipated several possible responses the DHS director might make to his offer. This wasn't one of them.

"You do understand what I just said?" Caparelli looked past the speakerphone on his desk to see that Arlo and Hirst were as puzzled as he was.

"You want a joint operation? I agree. But my director's made the case that you belong under the jurisdiction of Homeland, not the NSA, and the National Security Council's ready to make that call.

"You want to turn over the keys to me now, fine. But no half measures. I want full access to your whole organization. No conditions. No restrictions."

Caparelli couldn't believe the man's arrogance. "Bringing you into our operation has to be a process. That'll take time we don't have. After we've dealt with the immediate threat, I'll need to bring you up to speed on almost forty years of operations."

"Say again?" Lomax's surprise sounded genuine.

Caparelli pressed his argument. "We've been at this a long time. Operated under many names. And you'll get them all. But right now, our joint priority has to be stopping the Russian terrorists intent on harming the president."

"So you say."

Caparelli momentarily visualized hurling the speakerphone across the room. "You saw the photographs. You know what their weapon can do."

Lomax's next words left him speechless. *"Right—the magic weapon that you won't tell us a thing about. Other than you're building one of your own. Gotta tell you, Caparelli, you don't have a track record of telling the truth. I've done the digging. I know you've used the CIA, FBI, even the DIA same as you used us last year in Dallas.*

"So, bottom line for all the so-called 'evidence' you've shared so far—photographs can be faked and so can intel. To be blunt, that is what I believe you're doing now. You probably have your reasons. From what you've just said, I'm guessing they're leftovers from forty years ago when the world was different. One way or another, it's time you joined the rest of us in the twenty-first century."

Caparelli stared at his staff, stunned. Arlo indicated he wanted to join the conversation, and Caparelli motioned for him to go for it.

"Mr. Lomax, Sam Arlo here. I'm manager of research at—"

"I know who you are, Mr. Arlo. I'm looking forward to meeting with you when I review your division."

Arlo lost his rhythm, started again. "Well, here's the thing. CROSS-WIND's not the most prolific source of intelligence this country has, but what we do produce is exceptional. We've saved thousands of lives, not just American. We've stopped wars. We've—"

Lomax cut him off. *"Here's my problem, Mr. Arlo: There's no record of any of your accomplishments."*

"They're classified."

"Not to me. And that's your problem. You guys are all smoke and mirrors. If Homeland can't pull up any deep background on your operations, there's only one conclusion I can reach."

Caparelli cut him off. "That we're very good at keeping our secrets."

"That you're a fraud."

As much as Caparelli wanted to end this call, he knew he had a higher duty, a higher loyalty. He prepared to go all in. With the president's life in the balance, the stakes for failure were that high.

"Lomax, for the sake of the country, it's imperative we work together, starting now. So what do I have to do to get you to accept my offer?"

The silence that followed made Caparelli think that Lomax had his own colleagues clustered around his speakerphone. Then, *"The first step's mighty simple. What is the source of CROSSWIND intel? The line is encrypted and secure. You may speak freely."*

Caparelli couldn't see how Borodin and five berserkers left him any choice. He looked over at Arlo and Hirst. Their expressions said it all.

If there was no more time to play this game by the rules, then the rules had to change.

Caparelli took a breath. "All right. How do we do it? In layman's terms? 'Remote viewing.'"

From the speakerphone, there was a sound like a quickly cutoff laugh from someone sitting just out of range.

"Go on."

"We have several individuals working with us who have the ability to project their consciousness to a location independent of their physical body."

"You have proof of this, do you?" It was impossible to tell what Lomax's reaction to the revelation was.

"We do."

"You could arrange a demonstration?"

"Of course."

More seconds of silence, and then, *"What color is my tie?"*

Before Caparelli could protest, more laughter came from the speaker-phone. "It doesn't work like that," he said.

"Director Caparelli, I think you're half right. We'll be in touch."

The line went dead.

"That ignorant—"

Caparelli cut off Arlo, though he shared the sentiment.

"It's all right. We know what has to be done. It's just that this time, we're going to have to do it all ourselves."

31

Lomax studied his prisoner on the security monitor. She was sitting up in her hospital bed, still in the secure medical wing of St. Elizabeth's. Each compartment in her dinner tray had been cleaned out. He understood. She was replenishing supplies, a soldier preparing for battle.

Beside Kalnikova's bed, Dr. Mars stood with a tablet, apparently asking her questions, tapping in her replies. Lomax decided not to intrude, to give her a few moments of respite.

Finally, the doctor's questions came to an end and he closed the cover of his tablet, held it at his side. But he didn't leave. Instead, he seemed to ask her another question, and she seemed puzzled by it. But Mars must have cleared up any confusion, because after he spoke again, she gave a quick nod, and the doctor had left.

Lomax met him in the corridor outside the major's room. "Patient recovering?"

Dr. Mars appeared to misread his intent. "You don't have to be concerned. In her condition, she can't get out of her restraints."

"The only reason she's not out of her restraints is because it doesn't suit her purposes. Yet."

"Are you getting what you need from her?"

Lomax held up a laptop, two years old, basic. "I got what she promised. But it's no good to me."

"The sedation might be interfering with her ability to pass on useful information," the doctor said.

Lomax wondered how someone so naïve had ever come to work here. "The drugs may slow her reflexes so she can't fight her way out of here effectively. But that mind of hers is sharp. Now I have to find out if she's playing me, or just negotiating for a better deal." He was looking forward to the challenge.

Mars told Lomax to contact him if he had any other questions about the major's prognosis, headed down the corridor.

Lomax entered the prisoner's room on his own. His prisoner wasn't surprised to see him, but she seemed puzzled by the laptop.

"That is not computer I told you about."

Lomax cleared her dishes, put the laptop on the bed tray, switched it on. "We thought we'd keep the original to ourselves. So we cloned the hard drive. Everything you told us about should be here."

"Should be?"

She's suspicious. Good, Lomax thought. *We're even.*

A password screen appeared.

"Famous NSA was stopped by this?"

Lomax gestured to the keyboard. "In the interests of time."

Kalnikova raised her left hand, making a point of tugging against her restraint. It was just loose enough to allow her to use a plastic spoon for meals. She'd need the laptop moved so she could reach all the keys.

He slid the computer closer, and Kalnikova pecked out a long string of letters and numbers. She smiled at him. "Fully random. Fortunate I remember."

Lomax put a slip of paper beside the computer. The passcode she had just entered was printed on it, courtesy of the NSA. It had taken less than three minutes to crack. "In case you hadn't," he said.

The desktop appeared on-screen, and Kalnikova called up a directory of applications. "There." She opened a program, sat back. "Just as I told you. What is problem?"

"Wait," Lomax said.

A few seconds later, a window opened to a map of Missouri. A red line stretched across the middle of the state, following Highway 70, then ended outside St. Louis.

"So there he is. My half of deal."

"Look at the date."

Kalnikova looked annoyed, but she maneuvered a cursor arrow over the red line, clicked at the end point, read the tag that opened. "Two days ago."

"Borodin's turned off the GPS tracker."

"I took laptop from garage after he stole van. He couldn't know tracker was there. Obviously, he found it." She moved her fingers like scissors. "Disconnect. Bad luck."

It was time to push. "That leaves you with no deal," Lomax said.

The Russian major's face became a mask, no sign whatsoever of sedation diminishing her capabilities. "I told you what I know. I gave you . . ." She hesitated, searching for a word. "Actionable intelligence. Your response was too slow."

"The date, Major. The tracker was already off when we made our deal. Maybe it's bad luck. Or maybe you already knew that because you're working with the general, and you made the deal with us to retrieve the laptop from Colorado just to slow us down."

Kalnikova's eyes were cold. "Major Lomax, you have lost men in battle?"

Lomax didn't know why she asked the question, but accepted it at face value: the respect of one soldier to another despite their different uniforms. "I have."

"General Borodin killed two of my men. You understand?"

Lomax knew of one dead Russian national recovered from the firefight in Colorado Springs. That there might be a second somewhere was a revelation.

"I can't be sure of that," he said.

Kalnikova lay back against her angled mattress and stacked pillows with an exaggerated air of fatalistic acceptance, which Lomax did not believe for a second. Though he did admire her performance.

"You know how general entered your country. I have told you he stole white van with GPS tracker. So he turned it off. You have satellites and traffic cameras. How far can a white van have traveled in two days?"

"Well, that's the thing, now, isn't it?"

Kalnikova gave him a long-suffering look. Lomax got the sense that she was enjoying her side of the challenge as much as he was. "As I have said, I do not know why he is here."

"Why'd you come after him?"

"I was told he stole new weapon technology he planned to sell to you. My orders: to stop him, return with weapon. But . . . he's not here to sell after all. Otherwise, you would have it and him already and I would be going home."

"And you don't know what the weapon is?"

She held up the bandaged stump of her right wrist. "Obviously yes, and no. They shot something at me. My gun exploded. And . . . was very painful."

Lomax didn't believe that the Russian major had told him all she knew, but what he didn't doubt was her frustration, and her determination to complete her mission.

"One more chance," he said. "You help us stop the general *before* he uses his weapon, we send you home. We don't stop him, and the weapon gets used, it's—"

"Supermax," Kalnikova said. "What do you want me to do?"

They began with photographs. Kalnikova was correct. The DHS was monitoring thousands of traffic cameras in the northeastern quadrant of the country, responding in real time to sightings of any white Ford E-Series van. But the Russian general wasn't careless, and Lomax took it as a given that the stolen van was now hidden inside a truck, or otherwise disguised. Thus, the department's priority was to confirm facial data for the general and his men, so the cameras could begin looking for individuals.

But the first revelation Kalnikova provided Lomax was that none of the photographs the NSA had of General Borodin were actually of him.

"He is very important asset," she said, almost proudly. "We don't, what would you say, advertise him."

The identity of the general's senior officer—Captain Konstantin Korolev—was also shrouded. But for two others in the general's team, Yegor and Gulin Dronov, the NSA's photographs were accurate. It was a start.

"What next?" Kalnikova asked.

"Battle space," Lomax said. He placed three files on her bed tray. "There's a chance he's going to attack a soft target, almost at random, just to cause civilian casualties. Though, if that were his intention, he would have done it by now. So, we also have to consider the possibility that Borodin has a specific agenda. One that might point him to a higher-value target." He touched the files for emphasis. "Is there anything in these files that would appeal to him, connects to him, to his politics?"

Kalnikova leaned forward to check the top sheet of each file, seemingly intrigued by the challenge. "United Nations? With Russian ambassador and ambassadors of friendly states in attendance?" She gave a short laugh. "Anti-terrorism Conference? Maybe he do world a favor. Russia was not invited, but all countries the west is reaching out to there, a lot of Russian allies. No sense to attack friends. And US Capitol? *All* your politicians? How could that not trigger nuclear holocaust?"

"Could that be his plan?"

"A war that can't be won? That's no soldier's plan."

"Then read the full files," Lomax said. "What *are* his politics? Is there a topic of discussion with significance for him? Is a rival due to achieve something he feels should be his? Anything that might justify an attack."

Kalnikova's remaining hand assessed the thickness of each file. "I suppose vodka is out of the question."

"I'll get coffee," Lomax said.

The major rolled her eyes. "Land of the free. Ha."

"I think I've got something," Arlo said.

Caparelli looked up from his desk, guessed his distraction was evident because Arlo then asked if he should come back another time.

"No, no." Caparelli closed his laptop. "I was, uh, writing a letter to Norma's grandson . . . her only family. . . ." *And what exactly do I say when I'm the one responsible?* "What is it?" he asked.

Arlo closed the office door, held a tablet close. "I got a hit on the general's son."

"Misha."

"Right. It's the diminutive for Mikhail. And, well, there's this." He handed over the tablet.

Caparelli studied the web page on-screen. "The *Moscow Times?*"

"English-language newspaper in Russia."

Half the page was taken up by an advertising photograph of a luxury SUV. The caption below it read: *The model of the vehicle involved.* "So?"

"Sorry." Arlo leaned over, scrolled the page down to reveal the headline. "Just over three years ago."

No Prosecution in Hit-and-Run Killing.

"Check the victim's name."

Caparelli read it aloud. "Mikhail Borodin. Is it a common name?"

"It's not uncommon. But here's the thing. There's almost no other mention of the accident. Nothing in the Russian-language press, and no follow-up story on this site."

"So?"

"Reminds me of how we handled Laura's accident. Blocked the traffic cam records. Kept it out of the news."

Caparelli thought it over. The news blackout over Laura's death was a standard procedure when active agents died. Their deaths would be reported eventually, though with altered details. The idea was to keep potential enemies off guard, never sure that if they had had a hand in the death, that it had taken place as planned.

"You're thinking the general's son was in the business? FSB agent? Something like that?"

"Anything's possible. But Russians play by different rules. If the general was involved in some domestic conflict, say a turf war in their intelligence community, well, they're not shy about going after family members."

"The sins of the father . . ." For Caparelli, the whirlwind of puzzle pieces began to collapse into a single image, no longer fractured. There was no evidence to prove the connection, but it *felt* right. "You're thinking Borodin might not have a political agenda. That he might just be after the person who killed his son?"

"Like I said. Right now, anything's possible."

Caparelli could understand the general having a personal motive for revenge. But the scale of his undertaking, the number of deaths he'd already caused—it all seemed too big, too complex.

"Did the police ever find out who was responsible?"

"Fortunately, they didn't wipe the official files. The driver's name was Josiah Oliver. An American. And they had to release him."

Caparelli knew the reason before Arlo could state it. "Diplomatic immunity."

"Exactly. He was in charge of security at the US embassy. Recalled."

"So maybe it's not just a father's sorrow, a father's rage." *But still . . . it has to be something else than just wanting to kill one man for revenge. Something more.*

"For now, we've got nothing else."

"Do we know where this man is today?"

"We're looking."

It took the major two hours. Lomax looked up from a text message on his phone when she swore in Russian.

"What is it?" he asked.

She held up a file. "Is not politics. Is not mass terror."

Lomax got up from his chair, went to her side. "He's got a smaller target?"

"In here." She held out the file.

The Joint Anti-terrorism Conference. Lomax took the file from her, a pulse of anticipation heightening the moment. He flipped through to the list of participants, arranged by country, so many names and faces familiar, the leaders of the most powerful countries on the planet, with the exception of Russia. If only a quarter of the people on that list were killed in some terrible attack, the repercussions could devastate governments around the world, destroy the global economy. Even Russia would not escape that kind of collapse.

"Is it one particular country he's targeted?"

"*Nyet*—no," Kalnikova said. She tried to take the file back, but her tethered arm couldn't reach it. "Not *country*. Back to beginning."

Lomax put the file back on the tray so she could see it. "Who?"

She paged back to the second sheet in the file, and for a moment, Lomax was confused. The page she turned to wasn't a list. It was a general note of introduction, broadly describing the approach to security undertaken by the DHS.

"A man." Kalnikova put a finger on the bottom of the page, on the name of the man who had signed the introduction as Operations Chief, National Protection and Programs Section, Department of Homeland Security. "This man."

Lomax read the name. "I don't know him. . . ."

"Twenty-four hours," Kalnikova said, "whole world will know his name. And the people who died because of him."

The freshly painted Ford van was in the motel's parking lot where it attracted no attention because it was such a common sight, especially with all the news crews arriving to cover the anti-terrorism conference. The van's microwave transmitter mast had been reinstalled and was folded flat along the roof, though it was no longer connected to anything. All the electronics and video equipment that had once been inside had been removed and left in the Winnebago, replaced by the five VEKTOR containment units.

Borodin's men were in their motel rooms, sleeping through the day, the general hoped. They were excited. Proud to think they were patriots, doing battle in service to their country. Borodin envied them that. He felt no pride in what he would do tomorrow. Only righteousness. Because what he would do was what he understood he *must* do.

Tonight, his squad would make their final preparations—Korolev had told him it would take almost seven hours to make everything ready. But after that, the containment units would be in place, and all that would be left would be the waiting for tomorrow's sunset.

And vengeance.

Borodin, though, didn't sleep. It was the price of command. His plan had brought him this far, almost perfectly, and certainly on schedule, but he felt compelled to run through the remaining stages again and again, searching for weakness, for any opportunity in which the unexpected might arise.

So he sat in the van, on the operator's chair that was bolted to the floor, smoking American cigarettes that weren't as tasteless as the others complained, staring at the steady status lights of the units, thinking.

They were a two-hour drive from the staging area. This far from the small town of White Sulphur Springs, West Virginia, there was no indication of increased security measures. Local news presented nonstop updates detailing the arrival of delegations from more than twenty nations. The reports also emphasized the unprecedented security arrangements in place. But security wasn't a concern. His squad and the containment units wouldn't have to penetrate any form of security perimeter—the shadow warriors would do that.

Borodin blew out a slow, perfect smoke ring that floated in the van's still air. It seemed to glow in the status lights on the units' control pads. All green, at peace.

He looked at Unit One. Not the first by any means. But the first to be successful.

"Misha," he said, and the name hung like smoke in the stillness.

It had rained that night. Summer rain, relief from the heavy heat of a Moscow summer. He had been at dinner with Sergei and Ivana, old friends with little to do with his new assignment, a rare chance to escape for an hour or two.

There was tension at the project—when was there not? Always the pressure to perform. The theory was solid, but where were the results? Borodin felt he had pushed his scientists and technicians as hard as he could. He'd begun to suspect the theory was not as complete as the director believed. He'd read the equations, and his intuition told him there was an element missing, perhaps one that hadn't yet been quantified. So he was preparing to request the work be stepped back, to rethink, reconsider, choose another angle of attack. He knew the stakes: Succeed in his request or be reassigned. He was ready to accept either outcome.

He was Russian. He could only do what he could do, and that would be the end of it.

So he drank and he laughed with his old friends, and the call had come just after ten, as the setting sun stained the summer rain clouds bloodred.

He'd rushed to the street, ready to drive, but a car was already there to meet him, the driver grim, a member of the project. They didn't go to Burdenko, or any hospital. Instead, they went to the clinic, a private one, where Misha had been taken. For one brief elated moment, he'd thought it was because his son's injuries were not severe, that hospital facilities weren't required.

But as he'd passed through the old wooden doors, into the marble-lined reception area that reeked of disinfectant, he'd seen Evgeny Gorokhov—the ancient, scarred and hulking bear who ran the project—waiting for him. A dour-looking doctor with blood on her white smock, a surgical mask dangling from her neck, was with him.

"The project is providing all possible assistance to the police to track down the criminal responsible," Chief Administrator Gorokhov said. "But for your son, there's no time. It's a tragedy, no doubt."

Borodin only heard half the description of the injuries: the broken spine, shattered pelvis, internal bleeding from dozens of lacerations, and even if he could be stabilized, to never walk, to never use his hands, his arms . . . There was more, but the room was already spinning too quickly.

Gorokhov's powerful hand gripped his arm to steady him, draw him close. "You know there is another way," he whispered. "The project has facilities here. If you love your son, he does not have to die. You just have to answer one question."

If you love your son . . .

So he'd answered the question that three years on was keeping him from ever sleeping peacefully again, that had brought him to an American motel, sixty miles from the leaders of great nations who knew nothing of that night in Moscow.

There'd been no paperwork, no authorization. The chief administrator was there. The technicians. Even doctors from the project. He hadn't questioned that level of coordination.

When the preparations were almost complete, they'd brought him to an operating chamber. No sheet had covered Misha's mangled body, only thin bandages bright orange with antiseptic. Half his face was scraped raw; his scalp had been shaved; one eye lost in swollen tissue, the other staring, horribly aware.

Misha . . .

Twenty years old, and his son's life was over.

Through shattered teeth, from a mouth trickling blood and spittle, his son had spoken to him. "The pain . . . Papa . . . stop it . . ."

Misha's IV drips were saline only. The project's researchers had long ago determined that the chemical cascade of neurotransmitters fueled by pain was a necessary element—as necessary as a father's love.

"Soon," Borodin had promised.

His son's breathing was ragged, labored. He flinched at the noises the technicians made with their machines as they finished winding their coils of copper, attached them to his son's limbs and started up the generator in the next room so there'd be no interruption of power. Gorokhov himself had brought the copper-lined lockbox that held a shard of the remarkable mineral that somehow made the process possible, every time. The einstone.

Then the gurneys rolled in with the bags of dirt. Potting soil, they were labeled. So mundane.

Borodin looked at the director. The preparations were complete. They both knew what he had to do.

Borodin leaned in close to his son, placed his hand on one bare shoulder, perhaps the only part of him undamaged. "Look at me, Misha. . . . Look at me, my son."

The one good eye trapped in the ruins of a dying body looked up at him. Trusting in a father's love.

"The pain will end, you'll see. Right now, because I love you. You know that, don't you?"

A twitch, perhaps a nod, a desperate sign that he would agree to anything, say anything, if only his father would make this end.

"I love you, Misha. Keep looking at me. Let me be all that you see, all that you know."

He heard the bags ripped open, the struggle of the technicians. Saw the fear in his son's eyes. Had only love for him.

Misha gasped as the dirt poured down on him.

Borodin felt love, and thought only of the director's one question.

What does your son fear most?

Misha realized what was happening. His lips parted, but he had no strength to scream, only to whimper as the soil spilled up over his face, into his mouth, and covered, finally his one staring eye.

The mud of the battlefield filling his lungs, Borodin had answered. *Being buried alive.*

And so that was what they had done to his son.

Because fear was a necessary element. As necessary as a father's love.

No one spoke then. There was the growl of the generator, the hum of capacitors. The smell of blood and fresh dirt and disinfectant.

And then it was done, and the director clapped a hand on his back. "Now he will always be with you. We have him."

Borodin broke down then, sobbing, and they all thought it was in relief.

"Fools," Borodin said to the still air and the smoke in the van.

He lit another cigarette, staring at the steady green lights on his son's containment unit. He went over his plan, again and again.

It was perfect.

32

"So you're as nutbar as your boss."

It was understandable why Agent Ames might be hostile to him. Yesterday, Matt Caidin had led Ames and dozens of other agents from Homeland Security on a wild chase through DC and embarrassed them by evading them, a few hundred cameras, and the world's most sophisticated artificial-intelligence video-monitoring computer network. Today, less than twenty-four hours later, in broad daylight in front of the Lincoln Memorial, he was giving himself up.

"Technically, I work with Caparelli, not for him."

Ames slipped off his sunglasses, eyeing Matt like a prizefighter trying to decide which part he'd hit first. "You know you're not safe here. The crowds, the tourists, they're no protection for you."

Matt knew that was true: Ames would have other agents at this unofficial rendezvous, hidden amongst the civilian throngs. But he also knew why they hadn't arrested him yet.

"The fact we're having this conversation instead of me being hauled off tells me you're here for the same reason I am. Caparelli and Lomax, they're alpha dogs. World could go to hell and they'd still be growling over a bone. You and me, we're cogs. We don't run the machine, but we make it work."

Ames snorted. "Gimme a break. You're a civilian detective cleaning up two-bit dope dealers, which puts you about as far from the machine as you can get." He stepped close. "And my friend Owen ain't the only alpha dog in town."

"And yet you took my call," Matt said. "You're here, and you want to know what I'm going to say."

Ames stepped back. Waiting.

Matt let him have it. "I can give you the names of the Russians."

"Don't care about their names."

Matt took it up a level. "I can tell you where they're planning to hit."

"We can guess, too." Ames betrayed no particular urgency, but Matt interpreted that as an exercise in self-control, certain the agent was eager for him to continue.

So he did. "And I can tell you who they're after."

"Impress me."

"The target's not the president," Matt said. "In fact, it's one of yours." He saw Ames's flicker of interest, then said the name. "Josiah Oliver."

Ames looked toward the wide white steps leading up to the statue of Lincoln, brushed two fingers past his temple, an innocuous gesture, but clearly a signal to the unseen watchers. He turned back to Matt. "All right. I'm impressed. How did you get that name?"

"The leader of the Russian team is General Stasik Borodin. Three years ago in Moscow, Oliver killed his son in a hit-and-run. He was never prosecuted. Diplomatic immunity."

Ames locked eyes with Matt, as if looking at him through a rifle sight. "Am I going to regret asking how you obtained that information?"

"Probably."

Ames frowned. "Don't say remote viewing."

Matt shrugged. "Everything Caparelli said, it's true."

Ames looked to the heavens. "Oh, for . . . It *can't* be true. Anyone claims they can do that crap could just as well be making it up, no way to confirm one way or another."

Matt took his biggest step yet, didn't know if it would move this meeting forward, or end it.

"I've done it. I saw Borodin. I saw his men."

"Cut the crap, Detective. We already know it's Borodin. We know Oliver's his target, and we know why. All your bullshit's telling me is that CROSSWIND has a mole in the DHS and you're feeding our own information back to us!" Ames was angry.

But Matt wasn't deterred. "I saw the weapon Borodin's going to use. The one that rips people to shreds."

"You have superpowers like that, then why the hell are you still a cop?! Shit! Why aren't you a goddam millionaire in Vegas?!"

"Good point, except this just started happening, this week. Because of Laura Hart."

Again Matt caught the flicker in Ames's eyes. He was right. Laura, and what she'd been able to do, was of interest to Homeland. At least she was beyond their grasp, now. He suppressed a shudder at the thought of what they would have put her through, if—

"All right," Ames said, "keep going."

So Matt told him his story, hiding nothing. The accident, Laura's death, the visit from Caparelli, the manifestations, and how it all worked.

Ames paid close attention throughout, and when Matt was finished, the question he asked was, "So what's the weapon?"

"They're called berserkers." And Matt described those, too.

"You know how totally screwed up that all sounds," Ames said.

Matt nodded.

Ames made another gesture, saw that Matt noticed. "Just letting my friends know that all is well."

"Is it?"

"Here's the situation. The solid intel you just gave me—people, places, target—we already know, and Lomax is going to say you got it from someone in Homeland. The wild shit—remote viewing, manifestations, *berserkers*—that's nothing we can confirm. What I need, if you're serious, is for you to give me something else solid. Something we don't already know, that we can check out for ourselves."

"I understand," Matt said. Impressively, this conversation had played out almost exactly how Caparelli had predicted it would. He'd identified Ames as someone who could be approached to open a back channel and had coached Matt on how to tell his story. Now Ames had asked the question that would clinch the deal, because Caparelli had given Matt the answer, and told him to keep it until the end.

"We know how the general's going to get through the perimeter."

THE LAST DAY

33

The Gulfstream V descended from the storm clouds, and Matt stared out the narrow window of the small jet, watching as the green swells of the Allegheny foothills surfaced in the mist. Here and there, the first rust tinge of fall leaves dotted the landscape. DC sweltered, but below, almost three hundred miles away in West Virginia, early autumn had taken hold.

Still, green remained the dominant color. It was the cedars, he knew. The scent seemed to reach up to Matt, but it was just a memory of what he had seen with Laura.

No, not seen with her—perceived. . . .

Matt had a moment of vertigo as he once again relived his appearance at Borodin's campsite. The same stuttering avalanche of images and sensations, as disjointed as the strobe lights of the Cradle, had engulfed him after Caparelli was turned down by Lomax. All in the same moment he had smoked cigarettes, drunk Coke, dozed on the picnic table, smelled the cedars, told jokes, carried containment units, painted the van—

The van.

Out of the confusion and chaos of experiencing *everything*, he'd pulled out the information that Caparelli so desperately needed.

The freshly painted van with the antenna mast. With the logo for VIDEO SUPPORT PARTNERS LLC. With five containment units stacked inside.

That was when Matt knew how the general was planning to do it, and that was what Caparelli had told him to tell Ames.

The Gulfstream was courtesy of the DHS, and cut four hours from the travel time between DC and White Sulphur Springs, West Virginia. It had begun its descent almost as soon as it reached altitude, and one of the fighter escorts that had accompanied it for the half-hour flight from Andrews Air Force Base to the Greenbrier Valley Airport now peeled away. The trees loomed closer, and that's all Matt could see through the rain-streaked window. No roads, no clearings. The middle of nowhere. Then the last low-rise was cleared and replaced by the tan-and-green checkerboard of farmed fields, and the plane was down.

Humvees were spaced out on the single runway's service road, along with two yellow fire trucks. The largest collection of vehicles, however, formed a barricade around a section of the tarmac where the instantly recognizable blue-and-white Air Force One 747 was parked. Beyond it, on another, equally protected apron of the tarmac, three distinctive green Sikorsky helicopters were at rest, each with the presidential seal.

Seeing the official aircraft and helos broke Matt out of his reverie. He was in the last hours of an operation with incalculably high stakes. Ghosts, remote viewings, his impending divorce—nothing in his life was as important as what might happen after sunset today. The world could be changed forever.

There was still, however, the chance that by now everything was over. A Department of Homeland Security Special Response Team, led by Owen Lomax, was already on-site, armed with all the information CROSSWIND could provide. Matt might be about to learn that the Russian general and his squad were already in custody, the berserkers safely contained. As if there was such a thing as luck.

Lomax and Ames were waiting for Matt and the others as they stepped down from the Gulfstream's folded stairs. Despite a runway long enough to handle 747s, the Greenbrier Valley Airport was a small regional facility with no jetways. The DHS director and Secret Service agent looked grim, the hoods of their blue nylon jackets pulled over their ball caps giving only marginal protection from the light rain. Ames pointed to the Chevy Suburban parked off the apron, billowing exhaust twisting up into the wet wind. Matt, Caparelli, and Arlo got in. Ames drove. Lomax gave the report.

"We've vetted every news van and trailer on the grounds. They're all legit. We have biometrics for each member of the media, from every country. We expanded procedures to recheck all supply vans, every trailer. We have Kates Mountain Road and Main Street blocked off for the duration. And we've set up checkpoints to stop and search every vehicle passing by the Greenbrier on Highway 64. And we got nothing." Lomax turned around in the front passenger seat to look at Matt with cold eyes. "Have we missed anything?"

Matt focused, refused to open the door to panic. "Still a couple of hours before sunset."

"Five hours, twenty-three minutes," Ames said. "You're certain he won't attack till then?"

"Sun has to set," Matt said. "But the moment it does . . ." He didn't have to finish. They all knew the timetable. They all knew when hell would break loose.

Ames drove slowly past other government vehicles on the airport access road. There was a security checkpoint staffed by armed Marines at the T-intersection of the two-lane road it connected with. In one direction, the road led directly to the Lewisburg Readiness Center, a National Guard installation that was serving as a security staging area. In the other direction, a police checkpoint was set up a few hundred feet away at another T-intersection. Ames was known to the personnel he passed, but he still stopped at both places to show his ID.

"Makes sense Borodin doesn't want to play his hand too soon," Caparelli suggested. "He could be waiting until dark before making his approach."

"Then it would make more sense if he'd stolen a tank. A news van doesn't have a hope in hell of running any of the checkpoints."

Arlo spoke hesitantly. "He does have berserkers."

Lomax leaned back against his headrest. "Well, then, I stand corrected. The general could definitely get past the first checkpoint he encounters. But by the time he reached the second one . . . Gentlemen, the leaders of twenty-two world powers are in the Greenbrier tonight. We have assets with shoulder-launched missiles in the woods. We have helicopter gunships two minutes out. We have two F-35s loitering at all times. Thirty seconds after one of our checkpoints is breached, whoever did it—whatever did it—will be a smoking pile of ash. I am not worried."

Matt understood that kind of bravado, knew the unadmitted uncertainty that prompted it. "But you still asked us here."

Lomax gave a short laugh, but said nothing else. Matt understood that reaction, as well.

Lomax wasn't just uncertain. He was scared.

The Greenbrier Resort spanned more than 6,500 acres of nature trails and golf courses, real estate developments, hunting grounds, a falconry range, even a casino, but the heart of it was its century-old hotel, a gleaming white jewel set within West Virginia's Blue Ridge Mountains.

Matt recognized the classic lines of the imposing main building, a seven-story, columned, whitewashed pastiche of Washington formalism and Southern Colonialism. The design seemed fitting, considering the resort had been used in the Civil War by both the North and South. In a different life, he and Helena had come here on their first anniversary, a wild extravagance at the time, and little seemed to have changed for the fabled establishment in the decade since.

Given that the resort had existed here as a hot springs spa since 1778, maintaining the illusion of timelessness was one of its selling points. That it was an illusion in line with the deceptive modernization of the hotel was revealed by a more recent chapter in its past. From 1959 to 1992, the hotel had sat atop a continuity of government installation that had been code-named the Greek Island Project. Construction of the 112,000 square foot underground fallout bunker had taken place during an extensive remodeling and expansion of the hotel. In the event of nuclear war, the entire legislative branch of the federal government would supposedly have been relocated here and sealed in with its own air, food, water, and electrical generators. "Supposedly" because as large as the bunker was, no allowances had been made for legislators to bring their spouses and children, and even in Washington DC, there were very few who could contemplate leaving their loved ones to fend for themselves while the bombs fell.

To those families' good fortune, though, by the late 1960s Soviet intelligence pierced the secrecy of the Greek Island Project. Had war broken out, the bunker would have been targeted with a direct hit by a four-megaton nuclear warhead it could not survive. However, US intelligence was aware of the Soviets' discovery, and used it to their own advantage by not giving any indication that they knew that the Soviets knew.

Instead, the bunker was maintained war-ready for years. Food supplies were routinely swapped out and replaced with new shipments. Training exercises were held. Emergency communications equipment was tested and serviced by on-site personnel disguised as the resort's own television repair team. As the Soviets tracked all this activity over the years, confident that in the event of war the survival of the US government could be measured in hours, a new, larger, deeper, and much more secret bunker complex was built in a completely different location, and it had room for families. After the dissolution of the Soviet Union in 1991, the charade that was the Greek Island Project lasted only a few months more. A national newspaper broke the story of the thirty-year secret history of the bunker and it was quickly decommissioned, a relic of the Cold War.

Still, the existence of the bunker was why the nearby small regional airport had a runway that could handle the presidential plane. And though the bunker doubled as a tourist attraction and a highly secure computer data backup storage facility today, the resort's remote location and bunker-related high-security infrastructure made it a secure choice to host the Anti-terrorism Conference.

Normally, it was a ten-minute trip from the local airport to the resort, but with the newly added security checkpoints and barricades, getting there took almost forty. Even then, Matt, Arlo, and Caparelli were further delayed as they exited the Suburban and were escorted into a security tent on the main entrance's courtyard. From there, they went through a pat-down, walked through a metal detector, stood in a chemical sniffer that blasted them with air, and only then were they given laminated photo IDs on lanyards to be worn at all times. Matt noticed his last name was now "Brown," and that Caparelli and Arlo had also been subject to a name change.

As they left the security tent to walk through the rain to the main lobby, Matt saw that the rest of the courtyard, usually a lush expanse of green grass, was packed with other tents, most of them for news crews. Lomax had said more than three hundred media personnel were accredited, and none of them, so far, had been matched to any of the members of Borodin's squad whose identities were known.

That was part of the problem the security detail faced. There still were no photos of General Borodin, and only two people on-site could recognize him. One was Matt. The other was waiting in what now functioned as the DHS security office: the Greenbrier's conference services offices off the main lobby with the boldly patterned, highly colored carpet and equally striking wall prints that were unique to the hotel.

The DHS security office was a crowded warren of temporary cubicles and open areas. Whiteboards with intricate schedules and maps were everywhere, as were large video screens and unsmiling men and women, some in suits, some armed in battle-dress camouflage, even two or three in evening wear, and all with lanyards and plastic ID tags.

Lomax led the others to a corner cubicle, where a young woman with short white-blond hair, obviously new jeans, and an oversize DHS sweatshirt sat in front of a bank of video displays. Lomax introduced the woman as Sofia, didn't add a last name. Matt was simply "Matt," and Caparelli and Arlo were Lomax's "colleagues." Ames wasn't introduced. It seemed he and the woman had already met. Sofia's photo ID, which Matt assumed had also been altered, bore the last name "Green."

The next thing Matt noticed about her, other than her pallid face and fatigue-shadowed eyes, was the padded bandage covering her right wrist—her hand was missing. She saw where he was looking, held up her stump, and said, "You should see other guy."

From her accent, Sofia Green was Russian, but Lomax offered no further information. He invited Matt to take an office chair beside her, in front of eight screens, each with six video windows. Each window displayed a succession of views from the hundreds of security cameras deployed throughout the hotel and around the resort. Matt soon noted that almost every individual who appeared on-screen was accompanied by a small green marker—square in shape—that tracked above their heads. Occasionally, a red marker appeared, larger and flashing, but when the person moved or stepped into better light, the red square turned to green.

"We're running a SPARROW subsystem," Lomax explained. "Everyone who has authorized access to this site for the summit has had a new photo ID recorded. We've made a database of those biometrics, and the system indicates everyone it can positively identify with a green marker. You and Sofia will look for red markers, see if any of them are Borodin." He showed Matt the controls he could use to freeze images, expand them, and tag individuals. Sofia had a similar control taped to the arm of her chair so she could use it with her left hand.

"Any questions?"

"Where's Josiah Oliver?" Matt asked.

His detective's instinct caught the blond woman's almost imperceptible reaction. She knew the name.

"On-site." Lomax had put on his best poker face.

"Here? Why?" Matt didn't bother to hide his surprise.

"Because here he's in the same protective envelope as the president."

There was more to it than that, Matt knew. "He's also bait."

Caparelli put a hand on his shoulder—apparently he'd known this part of Lomax's plan. "VEKTOR has its own perceivers, so there's a good chance they'd locate Oliver no matter where we put him."

"I thought Borodin was rogue," Matt said. "Why would VEKTOR pass him information?"

"I'm still not convinced Oliver is Borodin's target. It might just be a smoke-screen."

"What?"

"Think about it. If all Borodin wanted to do was get revenge on one ordi-nary man, why do it here? And why bring berserkers? Why not just go to the man's house and shoot him? Misleading us like that, it could be part of VEKTOR's plan all along."

Matt couldn't argue strategy, but he was intrigued that Caparelli had men-tioned VEKTOR, perceivers, and berserkers in front of the woman. Obviously, she was deeply connected. Then he amended his conclusion: Given she was Russian, she was probably from VEKTOR herself.

Sofia caught him looking at her. She smiled, much as he imagined a wolf might before ripping out the throat of her prey. He smiled back.

"Now all is needed is popcorn," she said, and together they watched the screens in silence.

Two hours and three false alarms later, Matt gave in to his headache. He put the controller on the table holding the displays.

"I need a break," he said.

"No you don't." Sofia kept scanning the screens, methodical, almost ro-botic.

"My head hurts and my eyes are tired."

"You know what berserkers can do?"

Matt hesitated, so Sofia held up her bandaged wrist. "And you complain about headache?"

Matt reassessed her. "Is that what happened to your hand?"

"What happened to my hand was worse. Is why I had doctor cut it off."

Matt thought of what he and Laura had seen done to living bodies at the hacienda in Mexico. "You survived a berserker attack."

"*Da.* This I did."

"I've seen them."

Sofia glanced at him, doing some reassessing of her own.

"Not in person," he added.

Sofia gestured to the screens with her left hand. "Like this? Video."

"No." Matt paused, unsure how much more he should say.

But he didn't have to say anything. Sofia raised her eyebrows, impressed. "You are, what would you say, a perceiver."

Matt wondered if that were true. All the experiences he had had so far involved Laura Hart. She was the true perceiver. He was just . . . "Yeah, I suppose I am."

Sofia leaned closer, conspiratorially. "You have power to change world."

Matt hadn't thought beyond the moment, but he realized she was right.

"Which is why," she whispered, "I must kill you."

Matt rocked back in his chair as if she had hit him, and she laughed. "Americans. All so serious."

Matt sat forward again, acknowledged that she had got him.

"So how's head now, cowboy?"

"Still hurts, but I'm not complaining."

"Good. Hope for you yet. We keep watching. Maybe save some lives."

Matt picked up his controller, started scanning the screens again, checking the color of the marker above each person. He even saw the president walk along a hallway for a few seconds. The square marker above his head was green.

The power to change the world, he thought. The president had it, without a doubt. *Do I?*

During the next hour, the SPARROW subsystem experienced a slowdown when two briefing sessions finished at the same time and the Greenbrier's colorful hallways and lobbies filled with hundreds of people at once. Suddenly, dozens of individuals appeared with flashing red markers—not that they hadn't been recognized, but because the local system didn't have the resources to match them to their biometrics profile in a timely manner.

Matt and Sofia had alerted security staff to the high number of false alerts, and two technicians had arrived to reset the system. When the screens had all gone dark, Sofia stretched and said, "Now you take break."

Since they weren't permitted to leave without an escort, they were taken separately to washrooms, then to a table with sandwiches and coffee, then brought back, a guard remaining outside their cubicle. The screens were still dark. Matt had heard thunder rumbling from outside, but one of the technicians assured him there was no danger to the power supply. The resort had its own generators, courtesy of the bunker and its need to have uninterruptible power for its enormous data storage servers.

So they waited, eating their sandwiches. Matt saw Sofia ate as mechanically as she had watched the screens: a small bite, ten chews, swallow. Then repeat.

She caught him looking, again, didn't seem to mind. "Are you soldier?" she asked.

"Detective."

That seemed almost as acceptable as being a soldier. "Like *CSI*?"

"You get that show in Russia?"

"I've seen it."

It struck Matt that she was being evasive, keeping up a conversation while adding no information about herself. Cop's instincts kicked in. "Are you a soldier?" he asked.

"Father, brother, two uncles, yes. But me, no."

He kept going. "What do you do?"

She gave a half smile, as if recognizing the game they had started to play. "Research."

"For VEKTOR?"

"No, no. Could not get clearance."

"But you know about them?"

"Of course. And perceivers and berserkers. Is what I research."

"How do you know General Borodin?"

"Interviewed him. Once."

"What do you know about his son?"

She sipped her coffee, seemed to be trying not to smile. "You must be good cop."

"Misha, right?"

"Is tragedy. Father loses son. Not right what he tries to do now, but . . . I understand."

"So you're here to stop him."

The smile again, giving away nothing. "I am here to help your people stop him."

"No," Matt said. It was as if he could read every word she wasn't saying. "You tried to stop him." He looked at her bandaged wrist. "He sent a berserker after you. You know how to fight them. Which makes you a soldier. For VEKTOR."

Sofia laughed. "You have good, what would you call it, imagination. Very wild."

Matt ignored her denial. "How do you fight berserkers?"

She seemed to decide the game had ended in a draw. "Hope you never find out."

The screens came back to life, and after a moment's delay, every person on them had a green marker.

Sofia turned back to begin watching. "Good show. Even better than *CSI*."

Another hour passed, and Matt dutifully scanned the video windows in each screen, falling into the pattern of Sofia's methodical movements. But he didn't believe there was any point to their efforts. As good as the security envelope was, Borodin would never have undertaken his mission without knowing a way around it.

"How would you do it?" he asked Sofia. "Come after Borodin's target through all this security?"

"I wouldn't. If point is to kill, then like other guy said: Better to get target at home, on way to work, someplace else."

"Then why's the general coming after him here?"

"Because he can." Sofia kept her eyes moving over the screens. "Is called, sending a message, yes?"

"Who's the message for?"

"You are perceiver. You tell me."

Before Matt could ask another question, Caparelli returned to the cubicle. His blue jacket was soaked, his hair plastered to his forehead. He wanted Matt to come with him. It was half an hour until sunset. Matt knew what that meant; so did Sofia. She wished him luck as he left, but never took her eyes from the screens.

"Nothing?" Matt asked as they made their way through the security office.

"I'm wondering if the general played us. He knew our perceivers would be tracking him, so he set up a false plan to distract us. The stolen news van is a decoy to get us looking in the wrong place."

Matt wasn't so sure. "But if the target is still this Josiah Oliver, that means the general still plans to hit him here."

"Then where is he?"

They crossed the exuberantly decorated red-and-green lobby and headed up a sweeping staircase flanked by a green-toned wallpaper with extravagantly oversized tropical fronds. Matt could guess where they were going. "I think you're about to ask me to find out."

"Good call, Detective." They came to one of the hotel's guest rooms on the third floor. Caparelli used a keycard, and the door clicked open.

Arlo was waiting inside. Three black equipment cases, opened to reveal complex electronics, were jarringly out of place in the quaint room. Its bold primary colors and strong contrasting patterns made Matt think of children's birthday decorations. "What's that?" he asked.

Arlo looked nervous. He held up what looked to be ski goggles with blackened lenses, trailing a twisted set of wires. "Projection Mask. Not much of a substitute for a Projection Room and Cradle, but best we can manage in the field."

Matt looked at him, then at Caparelli. He knew what they expected him to do, and the risk it meant. But now that Laura had ceased to exist, destroyed with the berserker by the EM pulse from the Cradle, he realized he no longer cared about risk. They needed his help, and he would give it. "If it works," he said, "and I make contact with Borodin, what happens if he sends another berserker?"

Arlo looked away, and that told Matt what the stakes really were: If another berserker came after them here, without an EM pulse defense, they were helpless.

But Caparelli wasn't ready to give up. "Don't give Borodin the chance." He had peeled off his jacket, was using a towel from the bathroom to dry his hair. "You see him, you let us know, we pull you out five seconds later. He won't be able to respond in time, but you should get an impression of where he is."

"Should?"

"At this point, you're all we've got."

"Sunset in five minutes," Arlo said. Then he coughed, his throat dry. It was already dark outside. Between the storm clouds and the foothills, the sun was long gone from the sky. But its electromagnetic effects in the upper atmosphere would continue until it had dropped below the horizon.

There was another flash of lightning. Thunder followed a few seconds later, the storm moving closer.

Matt settled back in the brightly striped armchair Arlo had indicated. He tried to relax, but his headache had returned. "Is lightning anything I need to worry about?"

Arlo made some adjustments to the goggles. "Only if it hits you. Just a few frequencies are problematic." He placed the goggles over Matt's eyes, adjusted a strap to hold them in place until not a trace of light got through. Matt could feel the young man's hands tremble. More and more he was realizing what he was about to do could quickly become a suicide mission.

"This'll be just like the Cradle," Arlo said. "You see the blue light?"

Like a single star rising, a point of blue radiance appeared in the darkness, and Matt understood each of his eyes was receiving a slightly different placement of the light, because he had to focus on it as if it were several feet away, the illusion very convincing.

As soon as he confirmed he could, indeed, see the light, Arlo had him say the general's name, then repeat it just as he had before, for Norma Chu.

To either side of the blue dot, white lights began to strobe, the sequence alternating between chaotic and controlled. The general's name became nothing but sound without meaning. The light washed out Matt's vision and—

—Laura took his hand.

34

It was the beach again.

The sun glinting on the water, gulls dipping, diving, avoiding the big black dog that chased after them barking wildly, as if on the hunt. The soft sand beneath his feet felt comforting, reminding Matt of the beaches he had visited as a child. There was a familiar feel to this place.

"I like it here," she said. She was in the short leather jacket she had worn the night she died.

For an instant, her hand against his felt cold and skeletal. She seemed to shift out of focus, eyes dark pits, then back to bright, light green.

He stared at her in wonder. "Do you know what's happened to you?"

"More than you know." She stared at him sadly, and now her face was torn and soaked with blood.

He saw past it, though, and gently touched her face, and she was whole again. "Then how can you be here?"

"That's the question, isn't it?"

He had a sudden terrible thought. "Are you just an echo?"

She looked away. "We need to go."

He turned to see what she saw, and the light was suddenly artificial and the air thick with heat and wonderful smells from sauces and ovens, and he realized they were in an enormous kitchen.

He turned in a circle to take it all in, seeing dozens of men and women hurrying, all in white jackets, carrying trays and plates and bowls. At the side of the busy room, near two sets of swinging doors, he recognized the unsmiling men who stood guard in blue jackets, earpieces in place. He was in the hotel's kitchen, probably no more than a few hundred yards from where he sat in—

He was back in the chair, the pale strobe lights of the Projection Mask flashing in a regular rhythm. "How long has it been?" he asked.

He heard Caparelli's voice. "Did you see him?"

"No. How long?"

Arlo answered. "No more than two minutes."

"I saw Laura. We were in the kitchen. In the hotel. I saw two of Lomax's people."

"Why there?" Caparelli asked.

"I'll let you know. Arlo, get the lights going." Matt began saying the general's name, again, and again, and—

He spun around in the kitchen just as a young chef rushed through him with a platter of roasted potatoes. The smell and the taste of them exploded in his nose and mouth, and he laughed at the sensation and the impossibility of it all.

He kept turning, in tune with the tempo of the place, the action, activity, the life of it, until—

In the corner, by a gleaming stainless steel preparation table, one person in the room stood still. Not a guard, but a kitchen worker in white. He was staring at something in front of him. Matt tried to see what it was, but another worker stepped through him, distracting him enough that—

—he was across the kitchen and beside the still man.

Now he saw what the man was staring at, something hovering near: a gray cloud, a visual disturbance, like mist over cedars in the foothills.

Then he knew: The cloud was Laura, insubstantial, but a presence.

Matt thought of a green marker.

He looked at the man, standing motionless, staring at what he shouldn't be able to see, and then the man turned to *him*, and he saw an enormous birthmark, a port wine stain, wrapped round the man's nose and under his left eye, taking up most of the left side of his face. The same mark was on the face in the photograph on the ID card hanging from the lanyard around his neck.

The man looked directly at Matt, then quietly said, "*Boo.*"

Matt leapt out of the armchair in the guest room, tugging at the mask.

"Borodin's in the kitchen! He's—"

Lomax was in the room now. He held out his hand for the mask, and Arlo passed it over.

"We've identified and cleared all kitchen staff." He studied the mask, his face impassive.

Matt persisted. "He's the tall man at the food prep table in the corner. He's got a dark red birthmark on the left side of his face."

"Yeah, I've seen him. Stands out in a crowd."

"That's Borodin."

"Calling attention to himself with something noticeable?"

"What's a birthmark like that do to facial-recognition systems?"

Lomax's skeptical attitude faded. "Screws them up big-time." He touched his earpiece. "Blue Team, Big Chief. Guy in the kitchen with the birthmark left side of his face, put him in restraints, bring him to holding. Consider him armed."

Caparelli spoke before Lomax signed off. "What about the berserkers? Did you see the containment units? Any of Borodin's men?"

"No. But Borodin saw me. And . . . Laura . . . She was there again, with me. . . . The general saw her too."

"What's going on here?" Caparelli asked Arlo. He looked at Lomax, as if suddenly realizing he was about to give away more of CROSSWIND's secrets to the DHS, but then decided something else was more important. "Why is Laura . . . ? I mean how can she . . . still be here? She's completed her unfinished business. She knows she's dead. It's been more than six days. And the pulse from the Cradle, she couldn't have survived that."

"What the hell are you two talking about?" Lomax demanded.

"Nothing." Caparelli sounded as if he regretted having said anything at all, and Matt understood how much that reply cost him. Laura had been so important to Caparelli, and still was.

Lomax looked away, pressed his earpiece again, listening. Then he swore. "Lost him by a minute. Couple of workers saw him rush out."

Matt reached for the mask. "I need to find him."

Lomax held it back from him. "Can anyone use this?"

Caparelli took the mask, gave it to Matt. "Fortunately, no. It's just a concentration aid for those with the ability."

Lomax turned away again, hand to earpiece. "Where?" he asked. He turned around. "They found the van. Three miles away." Lomax looked to Caparelli for confirmation. "Out of range, right?

"Are the containment units inside—like metal footlockers with control panels?"

Lomax listened to his earpiece, then looked up. "There's a team heading to check it now. It's parked by an old radio tower in the middle of the woods. Picked it up on video taken from the helicopters. Feed's downstairs."

A minute later in the DHS security office, Matt, Caparelli, Arlo, and Lomax joined a half-dozen other personnel by a large video screen. On it, the view from an orbiting helicopter, its powerful spotlight spiking down through the dark rain to illuminate the van, just as Matt had seen it. Now, though, its antenna mast was deployed.

The van was parked in a circular gravel clearing, maybe fifty feet across. A radio tower rose up from the center and, intriguingly, two other vehicles were parked there: cube vans also with antenna masts.

"What are the other trucks doing there?"

Someone from the back called out, "They're microwave repeaters for some of the local news teams broadcasting from the resort. That's the highest hill in direct line of sight to commercial towers. Every truck's cleared to be there."

On the screen, a second spotlight swept across the clearing. A few moments later, a small helicopter descended into view. Four dark figures dropped from it on belaying ropes.

"There's my team," Lomax said.

"Are you sure about how far away the van is?" Caparelli asked.

A technician answered. "GPS checks out—just over three miles outside the security perimeter."

On the screen, the four figures were on the ground, automatic weapons drawn, surrounding the van.

"They won't have a chance," Matt said.

Caparelli's eyes were locked on the screen. "If the berserkers were there, those agents would be dead by now."

"Switching to ground," the voice from the back of the room called out.

The screen flashed, then four video windows took the place of the view from the helicopter. Each feed was from a camera mounted on the black battle helmet of one of the four agents on the ground, starkly lit by a small light mounted above each. The window labeled AMES approached the side of the van. Rain smeared the scene, a flash of lightning washed it out for a moment, and thunder rattled from a speaker by the screen.

A gloved hand reached out to the van's side door, grasped the handle, then yanked the door open and—

There was only a chair bolted to the floor inside. No video equipment, no containment units.

"Send me back to the room," Matt said. "I can make contact again. Find out where those things are."

Caparelli kept his attention on the screen, held up his hand. "We know they're not here, but there's got to be a reason why the van is there. Let's see if Ames finds anything."

On the screen, the video window marked AMES showed a search of the van, the glove box, a trash bag with fast-food wrappings—nothing of importance. The other video windows showed the cube vans being checked. Technicians ran the license plates shown on the screen, and all were confirmed. Ames and Lomax carried on a conversation about the van, its condition, any sign of other vehicles having been parked beside it in order to transfer the metal lockers it was supposed to contain.

Then someone said, "Wait, what was that?"

Lomax had noticed it, too. "Ames, swing your camera around to the other side of the clearing, opposite the van."

The image in the AMES window panned left, its spotlight made solid by the now-torrential rain. It played over the trees that surrounded the clearing, then found an opening, and something shadowed within it.

The image in the window jogged across the clearing; lightning washed the screen along with instant thunder. The storm was right on top of the team. The other spotlights joined the first, all driving forward, swinging in to find—

A door.

"The hell . . . ," Lomax said.

It was metal, paint flaking, inset into a small concrete structure covered over with grass and leaves, disguised. A sign on the door read WEST VIRGINIA DIVISION OF FORESTRY.

"What's that doing there, and where does it go?" Lomax thundered.

Two agents flipped through topographical maps on a large table. "Here!" a young woman called out. Matt joined Caparelli, Arlo, and Lomax to see what she'd found.

"You are?" Lomax said.

"Agent Zaglada, sir."

"Tell me what that is."

"It's part of the bunker complex, sir."

"Three miles from the bunker?"

Zaglada wasn't fazed by Lomax's brusque manner. She traced the structure on the map, a more or less straight line leading from the hotel to the old radio tower. "It's not the main entrance or supply tunnel. It was an escape route of the last resort, to take survivors outside the blast zone if the hotel got hit, turned to rubble over them."

"Tell me it doesn't lead inside the hotel," Lomax said.

"No, no, here," Zaglada said. She pointed to a length of the tunnel marked in red. "The tunnel was sealed in 1998, when this section of the bunker was turned into a secure data-storage facility. Basically, they plugged this stretch of it here with fifty feet of concrete, top to bottom, for insurance purposes. Visual inspection of the barricade is part of the daily sweep, sir. Inside the bunker, we have guards stationed twenty-four/seven with acoustic monitors to detect any indication of drilling or blasting."

"How far away is the concrete 'plug'?" Caparelli asked Zaglada. His voice sounded tight, and Matt knew why. Her answer would define how the rest of the night might play out.

"Far away from what, sir?"

"Us, here, the hotel."

Zaglada checked the map. "About five hundred feet out from the foundation. Why?"

"Then that's where they are," Matt said. "Just on the other side of the concrete."

Lomax didn't understand. "Fifty feet of concrete. Nothing gets through that."

"They can," Matt said.

Ames's voice crackled from the speaker. *"Big Chief, charge is in place and we're good to go out here. What's the word?"*

In the four video windows, four different angles on the door, all from safe vantage points by the cube vans. A long cord ran from the shadowed door.

Before Caparelli could object, Lomax told Ames to open it.

Seconds later, a bright flash filled all four windows along with the pop of an explosion as a small demolition charge detonated.

The camera views approached the camouflaged concrete structure. Ten feet away from it, the metal door lay on the gravel, badly twisted, steaming in the downpour.

Four lights converged on the opening.

"This is so not a good idea," Arlo said.

Four lights converged on a single figure standing inside the opening.

Matt's chest constricted. "Tell them to get out of there!"

Lomax looked back at him, dismissive. "It's one guy." He touched his hand to his earpiece. "Ground Team, Big Chief: Approach with caution. We could use him alive."

"No!" Matt grabbed at Lomax's earpiece. "Run! Get outta there!"

From the speaker, *"Say again, Big Chief. Didn't copy."*

Lomax pulled back his earpiece, shoved Caidin aside, said to Caparelli, "Keep your boy in line!"

"Holy shit . . . Do you see that?"

It was one of the other agents on the ground.

In the four windows, the lone figure was moving forward, and though four spotlights shone on it, it remained a silhouette, no details other than a black shape, a lightless void in the rain.

Then the berserker attacked.

35

The display screen was a chaotic mosaic of light and shadow, glaring spotlights, flashing lightning, the ghastly image of a severed head splashing through the gravel in one window, while a second window showed the spinning video captured by the dead man's rolling helmet camera.

In another window, the berserker whirled to face an agent who bravely stood his ground, emptied his weapon into its chest on full automatic.

In the security room, a stunned voice in the group watching asked, "What kinda armor is that guy wearing?"

Then the berserker drove his fist through the agent's chest, and as the man looked down bewildered by the phantom arm that pierced him, it visibly *solidified* and twisted, and the agent sagged without a sound, sliding lifeless to the rain-soaked ground as the solid arm changed back to smoke.

The group watched in horrified fascination. By now, all knew they were watching something beyond rational understanding.

Then the berserker turned to the final camera, to Ames. Started forward.

Matt heard a sharp intake of breath from Lomax, who pressed his ear-piece. "Get outta there, Ricky! Go! Go! Go!"

But in the foreground of the AMES window, all saw the barrel of the agent's weapon swing up and flash with fire as the berserker rushed closer, taking on form and substance. Several watching cried out, startled by the pale face that now emerged from darkness, glistening in the threads of rain made silver by the spotlight; by the staring eyes receding into hollows deeper than the death's head holding them; by the inhuman mouth stretching open, impossibly wide, that lunged at the camera, which blinked to static, and then went blank.

The video screen abruptly jumped back to the feed from the first circling helicopter. The voice of the pilot crackled over the speaker. *"What is that thing?! What is it?!"*

The image shook, buffeted, as the second smaller helicopter dove into view, its side-mounted .50 caliber machine gun sending down a stream of fire. The fusillade passed through the lone dark figure standing in the midst of the four dead agents. Untouched, it looked up to track the helo's passage, then—

Vanished.

"Where'd it go?" Lomax asked. He spun to Caparelli, to Matt. "Where the hell did it go?!"

Then the pilot cried out as the image from the first helicopter flared with orange light and the second helicopter fell past it, trailing flames.

"I didn't see ground fire!" the pilot shouted. *"There were no weapons fired! What are they—"* Then he just screamed. The image pitched forward, and the ground rushed up and lightning flashed, and when the screen cleared, the video link was gone.

Cutting through the sudden babble of reaction in the room, Caparelli's voice rang out. "Lomax. You have no choice. Evacuate. Get everyone out of range."

"Range of what?!"

"The end of that tunnel, five hundred feet out from the foundation. That's where those things will have their containment units."

The DHS director was still struggling to process what had no business happening. Matt knew what that felt like.

"No," Lomax said. "That thing in the clearing, that was more than three miles away!"

"They must've left one unit there to be a sentry. I would've. But I guarantee there're four more right up against the concrete barricade in that tunnel, only five hundred feet from here."

Matt saw the gleam of battle in the big man's eyes. "Tell me how I can kill them."

"You can't," Arlo said, from beside Caparelli. "What you need to do is destroy their power source. The containment units."

Now they were talking Lomax's language. "Down there, in the tunnel— rifle-launched grenades. That should do it."

Caparelli put a hand on the DHS director's arm. "No, you still don't get what these things are. I do."

Matt knew what Caparelli was going to do next, and how dangerous that decision was. But it was the right one.

"Give me a team," Caparelli said. "I'll go to the clearing, take out the sentry, then get to the end of the tunnel and take out the rest of them. Your responsibility is to evacuate the people on-site and protect this man." Caparelli pointed to Matt. "Arlo will stay to assist him."

Lomax still looked unwilling to surrender lead position. "What can he do for us?"

"He can find Borodin, and Borodin controls those things. He's got to have some way of communicating with them, tracking them, and if he does, we need it."

Lomax was on-board. He began to bark orders. Matt and Arlo ran out, heading for the room on the third floor. Caparelli remained behind as Lomax had a team of hulking agents form around him. Matt looked back in time to catch Caparelli's eye, just for a moment, and then he was gone.

Borodin welcomed the certainty of battle. Nothing else mattered now. Even if he himself died, he would still be the victor because of what he'd done.

Josiah Oliver sat on the eccentric patterned carpet before him, hands behind his back and tied to the king-size bed's heavy, wooden frame. His captive.

He was, in the end, an ordinary man in a crumpled business suit, with a face more lined than it had been three years ago in Moscow. For now, he leaned back, breathing heavily through his mouth, blood trickling from his broken nose. Borodin had clubbed him before the man realized what was happening.

"Can you hear that siren?" The American's voice shook with defiant rebellion, outrage. "That's a fire. We need to leave the building."

The clanging of the alarm in the hallway outside was bearable. In the small room, its shrill squeal was not. Its source was a small round device mounted high on one wall. Borodin shot it once. It sparked and fell silent.

"It's not a fire. They've found your bodyguards."

It had been so easy to approach them with a room-service cart bearing a silver tray, carafe of coffee, and plate of sweets. Borodin hadn't bothered to risk smuggling a gun into the resort. But the Greenbrier's kitchen had an excellent supply of knives, and Oliver's guards an even better selection of weapons.

He'd left their bodies where they fell, then quickly shoved the stunned Oliver through a connecting door, gun to his head. There were hundreds of rooms in this hotel, and the general knew there was only one way he could be found before his mission was completed.

But this time he was ready for her. The spectral woman.

"How much do you want?" Oliver asked, his American sense of entitlement undamaged by his capture.

Borodin leaned in close to the mirror above the hotel room's narrow desk. "That's not why I'm here."

"Then I can protect you. Make sure you get out." Oliver's prideful voice told the general that his captive still did not understand his true position in this hierarchy of retribution and death.

Borodin started pulling at the thin layer of silicon skin that had so effectively created his distinctive port wine stain. The technology of facial recognition was based on computers mapping each individual's unique geometry. But distort that geometry with blocks of contrasting color around the eyes and cheeks, and the technology failed, every time. In a country whose people had such faith in their machines, it had been a simple matter to take the place of a resort worker who was recognized only by a pattern on his skin. After all, if a machine found nothing suspicious about him, why should anyone doubt his identity? Borodin ripped off the birthmark, rubbed away the adhesive. Turned back to his prisoner.

"Now do you understand?" he asked.

Oliver's face paled.

"I thought you would," Borodin said.

"What . . . what are you going to do?"

"To you? Nothing. But for all these people whose safety is in your hands. Your president. The British prime minister. All the great leaders, their ministers, their families . . . I'll do to them what you did to my son. And the world will know all the blood and horror and despair is because of you!"

"What happened to your son was an accident!"

"So the police report said."

"I didn't mean it."

"So you say."

"You can't do this!"

Borodin just stared at the man.

Oliver's face reddened. He spat out blood in defiance. "Then what are you waiting for?!"

"Company. Or should I call them witnesses?"

Matt sat back in the guest room's striped chintz armchair. He forced himself to breathe slowly, wondered what Norma Chu would say about his blood pressure now.

Arlo gave him the Projection Mask. Matt hesitated before slipping it on. "Look, if one of those things gets in here, you run."

"I have a better idea. Let's not let one of those things get in here."

There was no time to argue. The fire alarm began to sound, an effective way to get everyone out of their rooms. Arlo handed him earplugs. Matt put on the mask.

He stared at the lights, fell into the rhythm, said the general's name, pictured him as if he could see him.

And like that, he could.

Borodin felt the garish room grow colder. It was a subtle sensation, but one he had come to recognize.

He turned, spread his arms in greeting. "Welcome. Don't be shy."

"Who're you talking to?" his captive said.

Borodin ignored him, looked all around until he saw a pale shadow where none should be. "Which one are you?" he asked.

The shadow blurred, a presence more than anything real.

"It doesn't matter," Borodin said. He pulled out his phone. The number was already programmed. He waited for the call to go through, heard the click, then gave the order.

"Now."

The presence had moved to Oliver's side, but Borodin's captive wasn't sensitive to it, couldn't see it.

"What have you done?" Oliver said.

Borodin slipped the phone back into a pocket on his white jacket. Oliver would have his answer soon enough.

The muffled thud of the first explosion rumbled through the room. The lights flickered. Outside in the hallway, the fire alarm stuttered. Then the second explosion followed, then the third. That's when the lights went out and the alarm fell silent.

The orange glow of a battery-powered emergency light spilled out from the bathroom. Borodin went to the hallway door, stood close, held up a hand to silence Oliver's questions and demands.

He felt the chill of the presence beside him.

"Listen," Borodin said.

It only took a few seconds longer.

Then the screams began.

The dull thump of the first explosion shook the DHS security office.

"Give me an answer!" Lomax shouted. He was tracking developments on a large map showing the resort's color-coded evacuation zones. Agents connected by radios to colleagues directing the crowds scrawled rapid updates on the map showing locations where buses and other vehicles were being deployed to relocate the summit attendees—all according to established contingency procedures. Video screens displayed security-camera views of groups forming outside the white-columned main hotel. So far, all was orderly.

"Whatever that was, it cut the power lines," a technician called out. "The switchover to on-site generators is—" His words disappeared in the rumble of the second explosion, louder than the first.

The lights failed, outside and in.

Now the security office was awash in the glow of dozens of computer screens and video monitors, all running on backup battery sources. Emergency lights shone from wall-mounted fixtures.

Several of the security-cam screens switched to display exterior views of a fire raging in a small building a quarter mile away from the main hotel.

Lomax swore. The backup generators had just been destroyed. "How'd anyone get explosives on site?"

"They can't have," an agent close to Lomax said. "We've been using dogs to check every building for weeks. Nothing could've been pre-positioned."

Agent Zaglada spoke quietly. "Maybe that wasn't explosives. We all saw what that thing did to the helicopters."

Lomax touched his earpiece. "Caparelli, Big Chief. What's your position?"

Next to a blank screen, Caparelli's voice came on speaker. *"Starting our descent. On the ground in one."*

Lomax gave him a quick update on the loss of power. "Rest of those things could be here already, so move smartly."

"Copy that," Caparelli confirmed.

Talk ceased in the security room as over the speaker came the sound of a helicopter's roar, fast breathing, running, then shouts and two quick explosions.

"We're on the ground, doorway cleared with grenades, heading in. No sign of intruder."

"Can we get video?" Lomax called to a technician.

Before she could answer, the crack of gunshots rang out—not from the speaker, but from the back of the security office.

In a swift reflexive action, Lomax had his weapon out as he and three other armed agents ran in the direction of the shots, but even before they could reach the corner cubicle with the full suite of security-camera monitors, he knew what he'd find.

A guard bleeding out on the floor, and Major Kalnikova missing.

Matt was a presence in a hotel guest room with Borodin, saw the general staring at him and pulling out a phone.

Matt didn't hear what the general said, but understood it was an order, calling for destruction. The lights flickered and Matt saw a man on the floor, tied to the bed frame. Matt had never seen him before, but knew his name just as he had known the general's intent. Josiah Oliver. The lights went out, leaving only a weak orange glow from an emergency light in the bathroom.

"You want to see this," Laura said. She was by the bed, looking down at the nightstand. She, too, was a presence, and Matt felt no surprise that she was here with him again.

He didn't move, but then was beside her. He followed her gaze, looked down.

The number of the room was on the phone: 525.

"Now you know," she said.

Matt reached out to her, almost a compulsion, but she pulled away.

Matt was aware of the general approaching, eyes going from Laura to him, aware of both.

"Laura—can you keep him here? The way you stopped the men in my apartment."

"Do you want me to?"

Matt was puzzled by the question. "Yes! I'll come back with Lomax!"

She blurred, fell back into nothingness, and then the floral-patterned bedspread rose up as if something moved beneath it.

Matt saw the general back away from the bed, and then—

—Matt jumped up from the chair, tugging off the Projection Mask to find the third-floor room almost blacked out, lit only by the glow of Arlo's equipment and the emergency light in the bathroom.

"Borodin's in Room 525! We have to tell Lomax!"

But Arlo looked uncertain, and it only took an instant to realize why.

Out in the hall, a man was shouting, pounding on the door because—*"It's coming for me! It's*—*"* The shout became a rising wail of pain, abruptly cut off.

Matt and Arlo stared at the door.

A shadow grew from it, like a spreading stain.

Borodin backed away as the bedspread rose up. His first reaction was to laugh because it was so like a children's story: the ghost revealed as nothing more than a prankster in a sheet. But then the bedspread snapped out like a whip and wrapped around him, pinning his arms and knocking him over.

He struggled on the carpeted floor but couldn't do anything except squirm. He felt a sharp blow to his side—*a kick.* Then another. Then his breath exploded from him as he felt someone jump on his back, landing knees first. He lay gasping, barely able to draw in enough air through the heavy fabric pressed against his face. He thought of Misha. Saw his terrified eye looking up as the last of the dirt flowed over him. Borodin cried out as he reexperienced what his son had felt. He tensed for another kick, another crushing blow.

But nothing came.

He began to roll, untwisting from the bedspread, freed one arm, then his head, saw only Oliver staring at him in shock.

The room's temperature was back to normal. The presences he had sensed, both of them, were gone.

He didn't waste time wondering why.

In the third-floor room, the shadow took shape in front of the closed door, became a young soldier in black, standing silently, eyes set on Matt and Arlo.

Matt edged away from the researcher, putting distance between them. "Whichever one of us makes it," he said, "it's Room 525. Lomax has to know."

From the corner of his vision he saw Arlo nod nervously.

The dark soldier stepped forward, began to raise his hands, eyes receding into black pools as it—

Stepped back again because Laura was in front of it.

For a moment, they faced each other, unmoving. Then, the soldier stretched up and coiled into a dark tendril that lanced down and into her.

She exploded into mist and the soldier re-formed, came for Matt, and then froze as Laura, whole again, grabbed it from behind, and this time her hands became skeletal talons that tore inside the soldier's chest.

The soldier twisted, spun, and vanished, leaving Laura as she had been in her car, broken and bloody. "Go," she said. "While there's time."

Matt grabbed Arlo, pulled him ahead, past Laura as she seemed to pulse from corpse to living being and back again.

Matt opened the door to the hallway, froze as he saw the gory remains of the man who had tried to escape the berserker. But there was no time for the luxury of disgust. He stepped carefully over the glistening shreds of bloody flesh, guiding Arlo, who was still too stunned to speak.

Matt took one last look into the room. Two shadowed figures spun in the half-light as the raging silent fight began again. He caught one glimpse of Laura as she had been, whole and alive, and then she was a blood-smeared skeletal creature that matched the soldier's frenzy.

He fought the sudden drive he felt to return to her, to fight at her side. But the berserker was Laura's fight. To end it, Matt knew he would have to face an enemy of his own: Borodin.

He ran for the security office to join the raging battle.

36

Smoke from the first round of rifle grenades hung in the close, damp air of the tunnel. Caparelli moved through it cautiously, the flashlight mounted to his M16 probing ahead, a sword of light.

Five DHS agents in black Nomex followed, keeping the sides of the tunnel illuminated with their own rifle-mounted lights, alert for any movement from behind.

The floor of the tunnel was covered in three inches of water, and Caparelli could hear more dripping ahead. The structure was at least fifty years old. West Virginian winter thaws and summer storms had taken their toll.

He caught the glimmer of a different type of light ahead.

He raised his right hand, made a fist, pointed his flashlight to the tunnel floor, switched it off. The five agents did the same.

Caparelli squinted, peering forward. A few dozen yards along the tunnel, a grouping of small lights was laid out in the pattern sketched by Caidin. Some of the lights were red, some green, but all shone steadily. It was a containment unit.

Caparelli flicked his light on again, looked back, pointed to Williams, indicated the lights ahead. The tall, narrow-shouldered agent came forward, a grenade already loaded in the launcher beneath the barrel of her M16.

Williams held her rifle at her hip, judged the distance, and then the tunnel roared and flashed with automatic gunfire from behind.

Caparelli turned to see the other four agents empty their rifles into the black cloud sweeping toward them through the crisscross web of light beams.

"Fall back! Fall back!" he shouted.

Two agents did as ordered. A third kept firing as a fourth was lifted screaming into the air by the cloud that had become a berserker.

Caparelli wheeled to Williams. "Forget that thing—hit those lights!"

Williams turned, took aim, and fired the grenade. The flash of the explosion and the sudden blast of air were immediate, and Caparelli twisted around in time to see the shadowed shape behind him flutter like a flag in high wind, then expand into . . . nothing.

The four agents, shaken, focused their lights on what was left of the unlucky fifth.

"We'll come back for him," Caparelli said. "But now we know how to stop the others."

Grim, they moved on, deeper into the darkness, no longer ignorant of what awaited them.

Directing the now-terrified conference attendees in the main lobby, Lomax tried not to think beyond the mission at hand. Ames was dead, Borodin was loose, Kalnikova had escaped, and things that could only be called supernatural apparitions were attacking an international summit. It was madness. Such things couldn't be. They were no more possible than . . . than remote viewing or the ghost of a young woman bringing messages from beyond. Start believing in those things, start accepting that the world is not as it seems, and reality begins to crumble, taking rationality with it.

So Lomax refused to believe. There would be another explanation for everything he *thought* he had seen, and it would all make sense. But he wouldn't look for that explanation until the mission was complete. It was, for him, the only way forward.

Then he saw Matt Caidin and Sam Arlo racing through the crowds for him, and he knew ignoring the madness wouldn't be that simple.

"Borodin's in Room 525," Caidin said. "He's got Oliver."

"I'll handle it. Now will you leave?"

"Not till I know you've got him."

Thinking just of the mission, only of the mission, Lomax didn't argue, tried not to think past the next five minutes. "Then let's get him." With that, he pushed through the hurrying crowd, back into the security office, running for the stairs at the far end of the hotel's main wing. He didn't have to look back to know that Caidin was following.

They charged up the wide stairs, meeting few people coming down. The evacuation plan was working smoothly, likely because most of those in attendance came from government service and at least once in their careers had received a briefing on what to do if under terrorist attack.

By the time they reached the fifth floor, Lomax was breathing hard but still had reserves. He was impressed that Caidin had kept up, not surprised that Arlo, panting, was a flight behind.

A sign showing room number directions indicated Borodin was to the right. Lomax and Caidin charged around the turn in the corridor, then abruptly stopped. Two men in dark suits blocked the way, sidearms drawn and aimed.

Lomax was furious. "What the hell are you still doing here?!"

"Protecting our primary." Lomax instantly placed both gunmen as members of the German contingent's security team. The door they stood by held the German flag in a polished brass frame. Their primary was their country's defense minister.

"Then get him out of here!" Caidin said.

"Where he can be picked off in the crowd? I think not. We have a private helicopter on its way. We'll go by the roof."

"Two helos have already been brought down tonight," Lomax said. "We're under attack, but the target isn't your man. It's not any of the politicians. So get your primary the hell out of here, and let us pass!"

The men exchanged a look, then stepped back to flank their minister's door. Lomax charged past, heard Caidin say, "Really. You need to leave." Then he heard gunfire, wheeled.

The German guards were firing at a dark silhouette that stood across the corridor from them. It wasn't moving, and it wasn't harmed.

Lomax drew his own gun, but Caidin waved him back. "No, keep going. Get the general to stop the attack. I can help these guys. Go!"

Lomax had seen what happened to Ames and his team. He knew Caidin wouldn't have a chance. But stopping Borodin might make a difference.

"Good luck," Lomax said. He charged for Room 525.

"Stop shooting!" Matt shouted. "You can't stop it that way!"

The German guards paid no attention, emptied the magazines of their automatic handguns, stopping only when they needed to reload.

In that lull, the berserker moved for the guard nearest it. The guard slapped a new magazine into his gun, began to fire with both hands on the grip.

The apparition clasped its own hands around the guard's, then squeezed *through* the guard's hands and gun. The dark cloud of the insubstantial joined hands suddenly flared with internal light as the cartridges in the crushed gun exploded. The berserker released his grip and the man dropped to his knees, moaning, his hands fused into a bloody ball of scorched meat and bone. The second guard stared at the apparition in shocked horror.

It started for him.

Matt was incapable of seeing an innocent face harm. Some part of him knew it was hopeless, even senseless, but he charged the berserker, shouting for the guard to run.

The apparition lashed out at Matt as he closed, its arm turning solid as it swung into Matt's chest and threw him across the corridor to slam against the wall.

Matt jumped to his feet, leapt on the back of the berserker, and at the instant of that contact, knew the name of the thing he battled: HEIMDAL. Matt's momentum carried both of them past the two guards to sprawl on the floor.

Matt scrambled to get off the thing, knew it would become insubstantial any second, try to reach into him and rip him apart. But as soon as he was back on his feet, the berserker took hold of Matt's arm, wrenched him close, punched him hard. Matt returned the punch, kept hammering at the thing. Blow after blow landed, forcing the berserker back and back until it coiled into smoke and dropped through the floor and . . .

Matt stopped, realized the impossibility of what he had done. He looked at his fists. No broken skin, no blood, just pain.

He looked back along the corridor in time to see the two German guards slip back inside their minister's suite, and to see—

—*his own body, slumped against the wall where the first blow from the berserker had thrown him, a thin thread of blood trailing from his nose.*

Matt stared, aware of his breathing, his heartbeat . . . all illusions.

He felt a gentle hand on his shoulder, turned to Laura.

"Am I dead now, too?" he asked.

Without moving, they were farther along the corridor, standing over Matt's body. "What do you see?" she said.

Matt looked down, saw his chest move up, move down, relief, wonder. "I'm . . . unconscious?"

"You're in your projected form," Laura told him. "A spontaneous projected state. I did the same with Borodin, while I slept, unconscious." She closed her eyes, seemed to flicker out of focus, became solid again. "I know that now."

"And now I'm linked with you?" Matt asked. "Because you're always here. My guide."

She shook her head, couldn't meet his eyes. "Not me. It's you. My link to you is all that keeps me here."

Matt could almost make sense of that. Perceivers linked with their targets, and somehow that connection anchored one to the other. The same mechanism must be at work here. The same impossible mechanism.

Laura knelt by his physical body, touched that cheek, speaking to that Matt. "And when you go, we both do."

"Go where?" Matt asked.

She stood again. "You need to stop them, Matthew."

"How?"

She gave him a puzzled look, held out her hand. "You already know."

He took her hand, and they were—

Lomax didn't slow down. He came to Room 525, fired two shots into the lock, then kicked the door open and charged inside.

The room was empty.

Caparelli picked up the pace. The tunnel was angling up now; the floor was mostly dry. There had been no more incidents. He estimated they'd reach the concrete barricade in the next ten minutes. Then he'd put an end to everything. Because without Laura in his life, he had nothing.

Above the Greenbrier's row of shops, in a small operations room unmarked on any public map, Borodin finished tightening the plastic restraints around his prisoner's hands. He'd positioned Josiah Oliver's chair in front of a video console used by the hotel's own security staff to monitor public areas of the hotel, including the entrance to the casino, the parking lots, the lobbies, and the main exhibit hall above the bunker. Since the system wasn't as extensive or as computerized as the specialized equipment installed for the summit, it hadn't been used by his captive's security team. But it would be used now, and without inter-ference.

Borodin had been able to obtain the technical specifications for the room months ago, checked them carefully. With the metal fire door closed, the small room's almost primitive installation of coaxial cables and hardwired electronics functioned as a crude Faraday cage. Neither CROSSWIND's per-ceivers nor VEKTOR's remote viewers would ever find him here.

"Time to contemplate your future," Borodin told Oliver. "What's left of it."

He switched on the console, and ten small color monitors came to life, displaying ten different scenes of ten different areas in the hotel.

Borodin's berserkers were in four of them, and the carnage was under way on schedule.

Schedule was everything.

37

—elsewhere. The sun shone brightly, sparkling off the gentle waves moving in their perfect patterns.

"No," Matt said. "We can't be here."

"We're always here," Laura said. She held her hand to shade her eyes, looked out at the blue horizon. "Ever since the first time."

"We need to be at the Greenbrier. We need to help Lomax and Caparelli."

She looked up at the clear blue sky, forehead creased in thought, as if trying to remember something just out of reach.

"We need to help Daniel," Matt said.

That seemed to register. She looked back at him. Her fair skin was freckled from the sun, her hair lighter, glinting strands of golden brown floating in the onshore breeze.

"You can help him," she said. Then she surprised him by stretching up on her toes and kissing him lightly on the cheek. She smiled at his reaction, and when she dropped back to her feet again—

—they were in the hotel's casino.

Through the center of the main room, flanked by thick white pillars, the floor was awash in bodies, the blood from their savage wounds lost in the red carpet and dim emergency lights.

Dozens of terrified people still alive, most in evening dress, huddled behind a row of video slot machines whose screens now were dark. In front of the machines, what might have been a barricade of high-backed green-and-gold chairs smoldered. Jet sprays of water hissed down from ceiling sprinklers, soaking everything and everyone. Thick mist filled the air.

Except where a shadow left a void.

The berserker stalked along the row of machines, like a gleaming-eyed panther that paced behind cage bars. But unlike a living creature of blood and flesh, no barrier could hold this predator.

Before Matt or Laura could intervene, the apparition suddenly moved toward a machine, blurred into it, then vanished. A heartbeat later, screams erupted on the other side and a panicked wave of guests surged toward the wall as a severed arm landed in the center of the room. Another blur of shadow brought the berserker back to his original position, with the shoulder of his latest victim, to which was still attached a head and arm and nothing else.

As if feasting on fear was as important to it as dealing death, the berserker brandished its bloody trophy at the guests who cowered against the wall and then threw it over the machines, prompting more screams. But before it could strike again, Matt was on it.

How it happened, he didn't know. He thought of attacking, and then he was, with no sense of how he'd crossed the distance between where he had been, and where the apparition stood.

He locked his arm around its head and in that moment of contact felt what he now recognized as a flash of entanglement. Instantly, he knew the berserker's designation: BALDUR. Tight together, they spun forward into the video machines, effortlessly passing through them to roll into the gaping crowd on the other side.

Matt felt the strain and growing exhaustion of battle, but in his projected form he had become, incredibly, the berserker's equal, as if every police academy lesson in unarmed combat was now permanently burned into his mind and reflexes. Whatever twisted laws of physics ruled this realm, he was as solid to his adversary as it was to him, and neither he nor it could become insubstantial and pass into the other. This realm's battleground, however, was anything but solid, and BALDUR, as if sensing his thoughts, wrapped its arms around him and together they fell *through* the casino floor, as if it had no more substance than the mist in the air.

In the operations room, Borodin watched in concern as on one of the surveillance video screens he saw BALDUR and a mysterious attacker melt into the floor and disappear. Was it possible CROSSWIND had also learned to create induced specters, and had managed to keep that secret from VEKTOR's operatives? Or had the new TYR, induced from Colonel Vasilyev under rough conditions in the field, become unstable, and it was he who attacked BALDUR?

Borodin frowned, disturbed. There'd been no time to thoroughly condition Vasilyev, and it was possible that TYR retained the colonel's drive to stop the general's mission. It was why Borodin had placed his new, replacement shadow warrior as a sentry at the entrance to the tunnel through which the other containment units had been carried to within range of the hotel. Defending the tunnel was a simpler assignment than slaughtering the hundreds attending the summit: less chance of a conflict with whatever beliefs Vasilyev held about duty and honor.

Borodin studied the other screens to determine if BALDUR reappeared on any of them. LOKI was playing a game of picking off civilians as they tried to run from the North Lobby, letting one or two escape to give courage to those who watched from hiding, then striking when a group of them attempted to follow. HEIMDAL, who had been tasked with destroying the resort's backup diesel generators, was now moving efficiently from room to room on the main building's top floor, killing all who had decided against evacuation. There were no cameras that allowed Borodin to follow HEIMDAL's progress, but he knew it must be effective because other cameras showed that no one had entered the stairwells from the fifth floor for at least ten minutes. And ODIN prowled the many function rooms on the second floor, hunting even more civilians who'd sought sanctuary there. That part of the hotel had many cameras, and Borodin made sure the screens arrayed before his prisoner displayed his son's work.

"Look," Borodin said. He forced Oliver's head up to watch ODIN reach into the back of a fallen guest, become solid, and gut him.

Oliver was hyperventilating. "Why are you doing this? You have me!"

"So you'll understand." Borodin kept a grip of iron on the man's neck. "You need to understand that if you had behaved honorably three years ago, if you had driven safely . . ." He squeezed hard and felt the man shudder. *Good.* "If you had not killed my son that night and left him to die in the rain, then all these people you see would still be alive, as well." He leaned down close to Oliver, looking ahead to see what Oliver saw. "Their deaths are your fault. You evaded responsibility for Misha's death. The world will not allow you to evade it for theirs. *Look.*"

On the screen, a security team charged into the North Lobby. They wore helmets and armor, carried rifles, formed a skirmish line, and motioned for those in hiding to come out.

Borodin could guess every unheard word they said, promising safety and the protection of an armed escort.

Three men emerged from a door at the side of the lobby. Two women followed. Then more. When at least fifteen were in full flight through the lobby, LOKI attacked.

He sliced open two of the soldiers to begin, then stood still, arms wide and taunting while the others emptied their weapons into him. When the gunfire lessened as the security force reloaded, LOKI moved on the civilians and swept through them like a Cossack galloping into battle with a sword, cutting down all who dared stand in his way.

Oliver gagged as if swallowing bile. "What are those . . . things?"

Borodin smiled. "Someday I might tell—"

The small room echoed with the crack of a bullet that shattered the door latch, sending it clattering to the floor. With battle-trained instincts, Borodin wheeled to face the door, but made the mistake of attempting to draw his gun with his right hand. His right arm was still stiff, still compromised from its wound. His gun slipped from his grasp, and as he looked up—

—Major Sofia Kalnikova aimed her gun at him.

According to the map, Caparelli and his team were within five hundred feet of where the tunnel ended at the concrete barricade, and now they began the final approach with their flashlights off and their thermal-imaging eyepieces folded down from their helmets.

As a unit, they moved slowly, keeping all noise to a minimum. Caparelli knew the containment units would be at the tunnel's end—open, and empty of berserkers. But since Borodin had five other flesh-and-blood members in his squad, it was common sense to expect they'd be on guard beside the units. That would be the real fight.

The claustrophobic tunnel's ceiling curved up eight feet at most, its crumbling walls a scant ten feet apart, its concrete floor cracked, uneven. There'd be no cover, and the close quarters meant any explosives would have equally deadly effects on both target and attacker. To Caparelli, that left only one option for his plan of attack: Go in waves and win by attrition.

He'd be up first. Between his combat experience and a few gun battles in the Army's CID, he felt confident he could make an effective assault. Williams bravely volunteered to join him. After the first engagement was over—a euphemism for what would likely be his and Williams's certain death, a second pair of agents would carry the fight forward. When their engagement ended, the third and final pair would reach the containment units and destroy them. It was a brute-force plan and Caparelli knew the cost would be high. But the cost of failure would be higher.

The rest of his team took up defensive positions as best they could, flattening behind irregularities in the cracked blocks and tiles where sections of the tunnel's failing walls had heaved out. Then, he and Williams advanced warily. Their imagers detected no heat signatures ahead, and that indicated to Caparelli they were still in the curved section of the tunnel, about eighty feet from the concrete barrier.

He'd selected the end of the curve as the spot from which Williams would fire a last explosive grenade. After that, he anticipated, they'd be close enough to the general's five-man squad that only flash-bang grenades could be used. Those grenades would provide distraction only, not stopping power.

He held his hand in front of Williams so she could see it in her imager, then signaled this was the point from which to fire her grenade.

Williams knelt on one knee to be better prepared to duck and cover, and Caparelli started the countdown. He held up three fingers . . . then two . . .

Then bullets sparked and whined through the tunnel as Borodin's squad attacked from the rear.

38

Matt tumbled as he fell, arms locked around BALDUR, entanglement connecting him to everything the berserker was in life. *No . . . not BALDUR . . . His name is Ivan . . . Ivan Andreovich Tereshkov . . . a soldier . . . no, a prisoner . . . no,* tenevyye voiny *. . . shadow warrior . . .*

Matt saw the main floor of the hotel beneath the Casino Club as if he hovered above it, and at the same time through Ivan's eyes saw the gulag, the other prisoners, soldiers, everything confused and merged, flashing from the humid thunderstorm of West Virginia to the agonizing cold of—

It's always cold here. . . .

Matt and BALDUR hit unyielding concrete in an underground room, rolled apart, leapt up, faced each other.

BALDUR shimmered with frost, shook off a layer of ice, became a shadow warrior . . . berserker. . . .

Matt understood. He had seen Ivan's death. Felt the fear that fueled the ferocity of the creature before him. "They froze you to death. . . ."

BALDUR charged, hit him head down, shoulder out, driving him back against a wall of pipes and electrical conduits.

Matt felt his breath explode from him, and even as the shock of the impact flashed pain through his chest, he knew it couldn't be real.

Proprioception. His mind possessed a map of his body, and that map knew where everything was, how everything moved. So when BALDUR had struck his projected form, his mind had created the illusion of how the blow *must* feel.

His mind's reaction might be logical, but Matt knew logic had no place here.

Even so, it hurt.

BALDUR sprang at him, and Matt took the impact and cried out in pain. But he didn't let it take him from the fight. He punched BALDUR in the face, the chest, trading pain for fury, knocked him back into—

—Laura.

She locked BALDUR's arms behind him. The shadow warrior struggled, kicked, mouth open in soundless screams of rage, but she wouldn't let go, and Matt attacked again.

But as devastating as Matt's assault was, it did nothing to BALDUR. If Ivan felt pain, he gave no indication.

"How do we stop them?" Matt asked Laura, a conversation outside of time.

"Find whatever gives them the energy to be here, then shut it down."

"The containment units?"

"For berserkers, yes."

BALDUR was still in Laura's grip, its dead eyes locked on Matt, its shoulders heaving with deep and silent breaths. Meaningless. Illogical.

Matt looked past him to Laura. "What gives you the energy to be here?"

She didn't look away. "Laura—what gives you the energy?"

A sudden image flashed within Matt. As if floating, he was looking down at his physical body. Alone. In the fifth-floor corridor. Unconscious. More blood pouring from his nose, his face bruised, *his body showing all the damage BALDUR had inflicted on his projected form.*

And just as Matt realized the danger his physical body was in, BALDUR lunged forward, broke from Laura's hold, and flew up in a billow of coiled smoke that disappeared before reaching the ceiling.

Matt knew exactly what had happened, where BALDUR was going.

To the fifth-floor corridor.

To kill him, Laura's only link to life.

Major Sofia Kalnikova stepped inside the operations room and closed the door behind her, her eyes and her weapon trained on General Borodin.

Borodin shifted, to keep his prisoner between him and the major, then glanced down at his fallen gun.

"General," Kalnikova warned, "Don't make me shoot you again. Just . . . step away, against the wall."

"And then what?"

"Call back your berserkers. Your mission is accomplished."

"I can't."

"You're their commander. You induced them. They're imprinted on you."

"Let me clarify. I *won't* call them back."

Borodin was surprised by the flush that colored Kalnikova's face. *Anger?* If so, it was unusual such a hardened soldier would take this mission so personally.

"Why are *you* doing *this*?" she asked. "You've given so much to VEKTOR, your career . . . your son. And yet now, in this moment of our victory, you—"

"Our victory?" Borodin wasn't sure he had heard her correctly. "You've come here to stop me."

"I was sent to stop you, and when I couldn't, I was ordered to help."

"You're lying."

"I'm here to help you withdraw from the field. With your shadow warriors."

"I don't understand. . . ."

Kalnikova didn't look as if she cared. "You are no longer a traitor to the Motherland; you are a hero of the first strike of Operation Scythe." She nodded toward the carnage on the silent screens. "The humbling of America. It begins here. You've done what all the generals and bureaucrats in Moscow have been unable to do—accelerate the schedule." She laughed.

"The generals and bureaucrats are insane."

Again, the major didn't seem to care. "Probably. But for now, we need to keep our secrets. We can't allow even one prototype to be captured. Recall your creations."

"No."

Kalnikova narrowed her eyes. "General, we can't let the Americans obtain a containment unit. The main strike is still thirty days away. We can't give the enemy any chance to develop countermeasures."

"I don't care."

Kalnikova regarded him with what he could only see as pity, without understanding. "I understand your loss. But don't mourn your son's death. Honor him. Preserve the project. Call them back."

Borodin pointed to the screens. "*This* gives meaning to my son's death." He pointed at Oliver. "It ruins this man's life."

"How does one equal the other?"

"This is the man who struck my Misha with his car and left him to die and never paid the price!"

"No!" This time, the protest was from Josiah Oliver. The American had said nothing during the confrontation, kept his head bowed, not even looking at the screens. But now, he glared at the general, and it was clear that though he spoke English, he had understood every word they had said in Russian. "You're wrong! The accident wasn't my fault! It wasn't even an accident!" Oliver turned to Kalnikova. "Tell him!"

Borodin saw the odd reaction Kalnikova gave to the man: A shake of her head? A cautioning look?

"Tell me what?" Borodin asked in English.

"Call back berserkers," Kalnikova said, also in English.

"It was VEKTOR," Oliver said. "VEKTOR was behind it all."

Borodin looked at Kalnikova, who merely shrugged. "If this is what you need to hear, then hear it."

"I did things in Moscow. . . ." Oliver sighed. "I mean, I paid the girls. I always paid. And I had diplomatic immunity. But . . . the FSB knew what would happen to my career. They had pictures . . . the medical reports . . ."

"You were blackmailed . . . ?" Borodin said as his world reversed itself. "To kill my son?"

"No . . . no . . . not to kill him. They told me he owed the mob . . . that they needed to send a message. . . . Just break his legs, they said. . . . Use an embassy car so the police would know who did it and they'd stop looking any deeper. . . . Then I'd be sent home. . . . I'd be out of it. . . . They'd handle everything. . . ."

Borodin felt his hands ball into fists as if they belonged to another body. Every word of the American's rambling apologia unraveled all that had propelled him here, made him—

"The boy . . . your son, he was drunk or drugged or something. . . . He had no idea what was going on. . . . They put him on the road, and he . . . he just stayed there and . . . They made me do it. . . . It wasn't my idea. . . ." Oliver's voice trailed off. He sighed, fell silent.

Borodin's eyes locked onto the weak and useless coward. "Then whose was it? Why do you say VEKTOR was responsible?"

The man looked furtively at Kalnikova, then just as quickly turned away.

"Who told you to . . . break my son?"

"Major Kalnikova."

Caparelli and Williams hit the broken floor and stayed low. The hail of bullets was thunderous in the narrow, hard-surfaced tunnel. But over it, Caparelli heard enraged cries of pain, his people hit.

He pointed back down the tunnel, his movements visible in the strobing sparks of bullets ricocheting off concrete and tiles. "Williams! Fire that way!"

"I'll hit our guys!"

"They're already hit! Aim high! Go long!"

Williams wrenched herself up, aimed her rifle, and fired the grenade on a low angle. It flew for two seconds; then a wall of air blasted through the tunnel and Caparelli's ears rang.

But no more shots were fired.

Williams turned to Caparelli. "We need to check our guys."

Caparelli shook his head. "We go forward." He scrambled to his feet, stayed crouched and moved ahead, M16 held ready. After a few feet, he heard Williams following. He glanced back, saw her loading another projectile into the launcher attached to her rifle. He looked forward again, saw the first pale smear of a heat signature, then scrambled back as more shots were fired from directly ahead.

As bullets struck and rebounded from the opposite wall, Caparelli and Williams hunched against the last few feet of curved wall. But there was still no activity from behind them.

"Just shoot it straight down the middle," Caparelli said. "We're fifty feet from the end. If we're lucky, you'll get them all."

"Fifty feet," Williams repeated. She was psyching herself for rolling out into the line of fire.

In his imager, Caparelli saw a blotchy blue-and-yellow version of her face as she gave herself a silent countdown—*Three . . . two . . . one*—then threw herself out to the center of the tunnel, rolled once, braced her rifle, fired, and rolled back, halfway.

A burst of automatic weapons fire sprayed over the concrete floor and across her head and shoulders a second before a deafening blast whumped and the shooting abruptly stopped.

Caparelli pulled Williams back into cover.

There was no need to check for a pulse. She was gone.

He unwrapped the sling of her rifle from her arm, loaded another grenade into the launcher. He didn't care about being in the blast zone. If that grenade had taken out the last of Borodin's squad, then he could walk up to the containment units and use one more grenade to destroy them all. And if he went with them? What would be the loss? For him, there would be no more unfinished business.

He didn't bother with a countdown. He rolled out into the tunnel and rose to his feet, jogging forward, finger on the trigger of the launcher.

No one fired at him.

Ahead, he saw the red and green lights on the panels of two containment units. The last grenade had started a fire in some debris piled against one wall, and flames lit the tunnel's end.

He saw two bodies sprawled on the tunnel floor and didn't hesitate, shot them both, three-round bursts to the head. No room for error.

He slowed, looked carefully for any sign of other enemies, living or dead. The only reason he didn't fire the grenade right away was because he wanted to be certain the other two containment units were here.

They were.

The section of the tunnel where the concrete barricade had been poured had been slightly widened to create an alcove in the wall. The two additional units were tucked inside.

Caparelli estimated the distance between the two pairs of metal lockers. They were too far apart for one grenade to guarantee all four would be destroyed. He'd have to do it one at a time with his M16. Maybe he would live through this, after all.

He swung Williams's rifle with its grenade launcher to his back, raised his own M16, turned back to the two containment units side by side in the tunnel alcove, then stumbled backward in shock as a shadow formed from nothing.

The units were guarded by a berserker, and it lunged for him.

39

In a basement utility room of the Greenbrier resort hotel, Laura took Matt's hand and said—

—"I like it here. Ever since you helped me."

Gentle waves on the lake rippled molten silver in warm rays of sunshine in a cloudless sky of blue. She was on the beach, bare feet, waves lapping, almost at her toes. But—

Matt resisted, fought it off. "No! The hotel—we have to get back before—"

They were beside the door with its German flag in a polished brass frame. But it was already too late.

BALDUR had arrived first.

He was standing at the end of the corridor, motionless, except for the heaving of his chest as he breathed deeply in, and slowly out.

"What's he done?" Matt asked. *"What's he done?"*

Across the hall from the German minister's suite, there was nothing.

Matt's physical body was gone.

"Is it true?" Borodin asked.

Kalnikova looked mildly indignant. "Of course not. I've never seen this man."

Oliver laughed in derision. "I got her into the country." He looked up at Borodin. "The FSB, they never let me go. They still have me do 'little things' for them." He glared at Kalnikova. "False visas for her, Colonel Yuri Vasilyev, Captain Gregor Malkov. Contact codes for her and her contact at the DHS. Her doctor." Back to Borodin. "How else would I know that?"

"CROSSWIND perceivers," Kalnikova said.

Borodin continued with his exploration of this man's guilt or innocence as if she hadn't spoken. "Did you also prepare supplemental documents for the major and her team to leave the United States?"

"You mean, for different identities, in case the authorities were after them?"

"Yes."

Kalnikova betrayed her growing impatience. "We're running out of time, General. You have to call them back."

"In a moment, Major." He turned back to Oliver. "For whom did you prepare the supplemental documents?"

The American blinked, puzzled. "Kalnikova, Vasilyev, and Malkov."

Borodin weighed the truth in the man as he studied Kalnikova.

"You said you wanted me to go back with you. No reprisals. Even now you called me a hero. And yet you had no plans for me to leave with you. Alive."

She shrugged. A hard look in her eyes. "What else would you expect me to say?"

"I expect you to apologize. For deliberately manipulating me into sacrificing Misha to become the first of the shadow warriors."

"You were slowing down the project. Creating obstacles. You needed to be . . . encouraged. But by all means then, I apologize."

"No, not to me. To my son." With his left hand, Borodin gestured to the door behind Kalnikova. "I called him to me while we talked. He's waiting outside that door."

Kalnikova's eyes widened. She turned to the door, sweeping her gun around to cover it, as if the weapon could possibly save her.

With his right hand, Borodin swiftly drew and threw one of the exceptional knives he had taken from the kitchen, and this time he did not permit the weakness of his arm to interfere.

But Kalnikova was a different breed of soldier. Younger. Faster. Perhaps not as strong. But even more ruthless.

The knife lodged in the side of the thickly bandaged stump of her wrist.

She slowly lowered her right arm. Shook the knife loose to clatter on the floor. She held her gun steady with her left hand. Didn't take her eyes off Borodin and his startled expression.

"Recall your berserkers," she said evenly.

Borodin felt numb. All the planning, the sacrifice, the horror to get to this moment, and now to find that nothing was as he believed it to be. He looked at the savagery on the screens. It had to mean something. It had to.

"General?"

Borodin shook his head at her. "No." Little more than a whisper.

Kalnikova stared into his eyes. He felt her judgment.

"Then we go to the next contingency," she said.

Borodin didn't know what she meant.

"We let the brave Americans kill you, let them recover your body while we express our deep regret that in your madness, you were able to defeat our safeguards and carry out such an atrocity by means that have no official status in our country. A rogue operation that we will help the Americans investigate."

"Their perceivers will know the truth."

Kalnikova disagreed. "Not all of it. And by the time they do, it will be too late."

Borodin was confused. "You said if they recover a containment unit, they could develop countermeasures."

"Americans love their secrets even more than the Kremlin. Their agencies don't share what they know. Yes, maybe CROSSWIND could develop countermeasures, but not if we destroy them first, make them the first target of Scythe. Then there will be no one else who would even begin to understand the concepts and technology in so short a time."

Borodin saw the logic in that strategy, but doubted the Kremlin would dare take such drastic steps until Scythe was fully operational. "Taking out CROSSWIND would be too provocative. An act of war."

"But that's what's coming, General. The war you've started. The war you will take the blame for." She smiled. "And this time, it won't be a cold one."

Borodin lowered his head as he contemplated how everything was spinning out of control. He heard a metallic click.

When he looked up, he saw the door closing.

Kalnikova was gone.

Borodin looked over at Oliver.

The American was ashen with fear. "I am sorry."

"So you said."

Borodin went to him with the knife clutched in his hand trembling with restrained anger. Oliver tensed, eyes closed. The general cut off the restraints.

Long moments later, Oliver opened his eyes.

"Leave now," Borodin said.

Oliver stood up, unsteady, uncertain.

"My mission," Borodin said, "was to make the person responsible for Misha's death atone for that crime." He looked at the screens, felt rage building. "And now, I find . . . that I am that person."

Oliver hesitated, suspicious. "What about me?"

Borodin didn't care. Struggled to control himself. To keep the knife from slashing through this worthless man's throat in an explosion of blood. "What about you? You were a pawn, just as I was. Our game is over."

Oliver rubbed at his wrists, looked again at the security monitors, the bodies. "What about those things? They're still killing anyone they can find."

Borodin shrugged. "Let them kill everyone. I don't care." He looked at the savagery playing out on the monitors, wanted to be in the middle of it, to lose himself in the fire of battle. To become a berserker himself. "All I want is to find what remains of my son. All I want . . ."

Without thought, he drove the knife into Oliver's neck, slashed again and again as blood sprayed and covered him with its dying heat.

There was no reason for it. No reason for anything anymore.

And he feared there never had been.

The odds were fifty-fifty.

The berserker advancing on Caparelli either drew its power from one of the two containment units twenty feet away at the concrete barricade, or from one of the two units in the alcove directly across the tunnel. The grenade he'd loaded into the launcher barrel could destroy one pair or the other, but not both. Not that it mattered which target he chose. The explosion in this tightly confined space would kill him as well.

The berserker paused, its dark eyes fixed on him intently, as if it understood his dilemma, and its own.

Caparelli whipped his rifle to the side as if to fire into the units by the barricade.

The berserker didn't react.

Caparelli whipped the rifle back as if he were to fire at the closer units.

The berserker blurred sideways to position itself between the units and the rifle launcher.

That gave Caparelli the answer he needed.

"Go to hell," he said, and fired the grenade directly at the berserker, surprised by how at peace he felt, knowing he had less than a second to live.

The grenade streaked into the berserker and—

—didn't come out.

A heartbeat later, spikes of fiery light burst from the apparition, like lightning from deep inside a storm cloud. But nothing else.

For a fleeting moment, Caparelli thought how excited Arlo would be to see what had just happened, but then realized his own death was still imminent, though now he would have nothing to show for his sacrifice.

The berserker seemed to grin at him, its features distorting into a travesty of the humanity it used to have.

Caparelli didn't care. He had a new plan.

He lunged at *it.*

40

Matt remained in the hallway, watching BALDUR.

"If I'm still here," he said, "in my projected form, it means my physical body is still alive, right?"

Laura was beside him, attention also on the berserker at the end of the corridor. "I'm not the one to ask."

Matt understood what she meant, but she was wrong. "You are. You understand this. The fact that we're *both* here is good, right? You take your energy from me; I take my energy from my physical body. Everything's entangled."

"Until everything decoheres," Laura said. "And all the waves collapse and we become separate again, and alone."

Matt wouldn't be distracted. "I'm still alive . . . but I can't go back . . . so, I'm still unconscious." He had it. "Someone moved my body."

"Who would do that?"

"Lomax!" In his excitement, Matt grabbed her by her shoulders. "I know who helped and where I am!"

Laura's face and body suddenly decayed into the blood-covered corpse of the night of her death. Her voice was a liquid rasp. "But if you know that . . ." She pointed a skeletal talon down the corridor in time for Matt to see BALDUR twist into coiled smoke and drop through the floor.

Matt understood. Entanglement. If he knew something, so did BALDUR.

He took Laura's hand and—

Lomax eased Caidin's unconscious, battered body off his shoulder and onto the chair. "Now what?" he asked.

Sam Arlo rooted determinedly through the mess of electronics spread out across the bed, searching for something that Lomax half expected could be a crystal ball or magic wand. That was how incredibly off-the-map this week and this night had become.

Lomax was unsettled being away from his post. He kept telling himself the evacuation plan was working, that Caparelli was going after the damned containment units, that whatever was going on here that was on the wrong side of the rational divide, it was something he had to understand and Matt Caidin was the key.

"Here!" Arlo said. It wasn't a magic wand. Lomax recognized it from battlefield medic kits. An auto-injector hypodermic.

"Adrenalin?"

"No. Ritalin." Arlo looked at Lomax. "It's like adrenaline for the brain. Increases dopamine, wakes up the cortex."

Lomax supposed that sounded like a good idea. "Go for it."

Arlo placed the tip of the auto-injector against Caidin's neck. Hesitated. "How'd he get so beat up?"

The room suddenly felt cooler.

Arlo stopped, held out his hand as if checking the temperature. "That's not good."

Lomax didn't understand. "If the air-conditioning's back on, that means power's being restored."

"It's not air-conditioning." Arlo was transfixed by something behind Lomax.

Lomax turned.

It was the same thing Ames had faced in the clearing. Now it was here.

Lomax drew his gun.

"That's not going to do it," Arlo said.

Then there were two more figures in the room. Apparitions.

Lomax felt his mouth open in surprise. One of them was . . . Caidin? He looked back at the chair. Caidin was there, unconscious. He looked at the thing that had appeared just inside the door. Caidin was flanking it on one side. On the other side was a woman. He recognized her from photographs. It was Laura Hart.

The dead woman.

The berserker moved to meet Caparelli, and Caparelli pivoted like a linebacker, dove to the side, and emptied Williams's M16 on full automatic into the containment units directly across from him.

He felt a sudden burst of pain in his left foot and twisted to see the berserker had stomped on it with a booted foot, and that booted foot had *entered* his.

The berserker sneered, rotated his boot, and ground the flesh and bones and nerves and tendons of Caparelli's foot until they were compressed, combined.

Caparelli released his agony with a battle cry and turned away from the berserker to fire his own M16 with a fresh clip and—

—a gout of flame shot up from the containment unit to the left of him, and sparks crackled across its surface.

The berserker vanished.

Caparelli's pain was indescribable. But his new plan was working. Destroy the units, destroy the berserkers. With gritted teeth, he fumbled through his equipment harness, searching for new clips for the rifles.

Three more units to go.

Matt gripped BALDUR by one arm; Laura held him by the other. Matt knew they couldn't defeat the berserker in their projected state, but they could keep it from harming Matt's physical body.

As they dragged the berserker back, trying to pull it from the room, Matt had a moment of surreal disconnection as he saw his own body in the chair, face bruised and swollen from the damage done to his projected form. Arlo was beside him, holding some new device to his neck. He saw Lomax, standing, speechless, gun at his side.

Matt nodded at Lomax, mouthed the word "Thanks."

Lomax held up his hand as if to wave, but then seemed to think better of it. He continued to look overwhelmed.

Then BALDUR changed in some way. Felt heavier? Lighter?

"Hold on," Laura said. And then they fell with him and—

Borodin stood in the North Lobby, surrounded by death. Two dozen bodies, none intact, civilians and soldiers, all the same, in pieces.

LOKI appeared before him.

"Well done, soldier. Call the others."

ODIN appeared.

"Well done."

As expected, TYR did not answer the call. But neither did HEIMDAL.

Then BALDUR appeared, and he wasn't alone.

Borodin was shocked to see the shadow warrior being held by what could only be two CROSSWIND wraiths. One was the entity he had seen fighting BALDUR in the casino. Had that fight been going on all this time? And the second wraith . . . a woman? There was something familiar about her. Something . . .

And then he knew.

He clapped his hands in recognition.

"My perceiver!" he said. "The woman in the window! At the campground! In the kitchen!"

BALDUR stopped struggling. He was waiting for orders, as were LOKI and ODIN.

Borodin knew his three shadow warriors could deal with the wraiths. Unlike VEKTOR, CROSSWIND didn't have the einstone technology to support projected forms. That meant the two wraiths holding BALDUR must have living bodies somewhere, bodies that a berserker could easily find through backtracing.

His plan made, Borodin chose the warrior who would be freed. "LOKI, the man and woman holding your brother. Follow them home. Kill them."

LOKI snapped his head around to stare at the wraiths.

Borodin could tell they had no understanding of what he had ordered, and what was to happen to them.

LOKI began to change, to become the frenzied champion of legend. He moved toward BALDUR's captors, began to smear, and then abruptly stopped, doubled over, began to flutter back and forth like fabric blown by the wind and—

He was gone.

Borodin instantly knew what had happened. Shouted new orders.

"Return to the tunnel—your units are in danger!"

ODIN began to twist into a coil of dark mist. BALDUR struggled to do the same. Then the female wraith suddenly released BALDUR, and he and ODIN and the wraiths vanished at once, together.

Caparelli used the stock of his rifle to batter the interior of the second containment unit in the alcove because he had no more ammunition. He had to do it from a kneeling position. It was impossible to stand. His foot felt as if he had stepped in lava. Each impact of the rifle butt sent a new shudder of pain through his swollen leg. He could barely think. But the containment units had to be destroyed.

There was a gout of flame and a spray of sparks and Caparelli fell back, knowing another berserker had been . . . what? How could something already dead be killed? *Deactivated*, he decided. They were weaponized ghosts, Burton Hirst had said. The word fit.

Now he only had to crawl twenty feet to the end of the tunnel to batter the last two units. Then it would be over.

That's when two other berserkers appeared before him.

He tried and failed to stand to face them. He didn't want to die helpless on his knees. But his crushed foot wouldn't support him and he fell, racked with pain, burning with frustrated rage, waiting to feel the berserkers tear into him again.

They didn't.

He looked up.

One berserker was fighting the other.

Then he realized, only one of the spectral forms was dressed as a soldier in black battle dress. The other was—

Laura.

Caparelli froze, pain forgotten in the shock of recognition. Laura and the berserker battled in silence, but in his mind he heard her voice on his phone, her final message. *Daniel, pick up!*

And he hadn't.

A single, split-second decision that could never be taken back. A decision that had changed everything—except his need to make up for abandoning her.

At the sight of Laura, that one pure thought flooded through him, freed him from his paralysis. Caparelli knew he could still have a chance to help her, to undo what he had done, and there was only one way he could. As the two entities battled, he began to crawl the final twenty feet to the tunnel's end.

Flames from the burning debris sent the shadows of Laura and the berserker flickering against the tunnel walls and ceiling. Smoke filled the enclosed space with acrid haze. Caparelli coughed, eyes stinging, kept crawling forward, wincing each time he had to drag his crushed foot along the broken concrete of the tunnel floor.

He looked back once to see Laura slam the berserker against the wall, then rush at it swinging, connecting again and again. Yet eerily, there was still no sound from the impacts, no sound from either fighter, as if their combat took place only in a dream.

He reached the containment units. Each had only one green status light remaining. All the rest were red.

He pushed himself up on his knees, glanced back one more time to see—

The berserker rushing directly for him, Laura sprawled in the alcove, too far away.

Caparelli twisted to swing his rifle like a club, knew how useless that would be. And then the berserker was blocked by Laura!

In an instant, she had vanished from the alcove and appeared between Caparelli and his attacker.

Laura shouldered the berserker away, turned to Caparelli, pointed urgently to the containment unit on the right. The berserker hit her from behind, and the fight was on again.

Caparelli struggled to edge closer to the unit Laura had indicated. He lifted his rifle, brought it down on the control panel, ignored the pain that lanced through his leg, through his body.

The berserker was on the offensive, knocking Laura back farther and farther. Caparelli could see what it was planning: to delay Laura just for the few seconds it would take to rip Caparelli in half.

Laura fell back. Caparelli lifted his rifle, brought it down again and again.

The berserker broke off his attack. Streaked for Caparelli—

—as the rifle came down a final time and the containment unit sparked and the berserker reached out to Caparelli and—

—stopped. Held back by Laura gripping it from behind.

The berserker's arm blurred out of focus, stretching into a tendril of smoke.

Then the battery in the containment unit finally shorted out and exploded in a flash of sparks, and the berserker fluttered and was—

—gone.

Caparelli sank back against the concrete barricade.

In the smoky haze, he saw Laura, or whatever Laura had become, look down at him, her expression one of puzzlement and concern.

Caparelli reached out his hand to her.

She hesitated, seemed to blur, then snapped into sharp focus. She reached out.

Their hands met.

In that moment, Laura was real again. Alive. He had answered the phone on Sunday night, taken her call, heard her report. All was as it had been, as it should have been—

No, Uncle Dan . . .

He heard her voice. Didn't know how. Her lips hadn't moved. Her impossible hand squeezed his harder.

The berserker that back-traced me would have killed us both.

Caparelli shook his head, didn't want to believe that because it was true.

Then no one would have known about the general.

"No," Caparelli whispered.

This is the only way it could be.

"Please no . . ."

Laura smiled.

It's okay.

Laura abruptly turned to scan the tunnel, turned back, then—

She was gone, and his hand was empty.

Caparelli reached deep within himself, past the pain, past the sorrow and regret and exhaustion, to find the strength for what had to be done. What Laura needed him to do.

There was one more containment unit.

His arms trembled as he struggled to lift his rifle.

He didn't know if he could do it.

41

Matt looked up and down the beach in growing panic. She wasn't here. But she was always here. Always with him. He had followed her from the North Lobby. Knew that this was where she had intended to go. Why this place, he didn't know. But she liked it here.

"Laura!" he shouted, and the gulls answered. He could hear them. He could hear the waves. As if this place were real. As if he were actually here. Or had been. "Where are you?"

In desperation, he held out his hand as if to take hers. As if she were standing right—

Lomax and Arlo knew they had to get Caidin out of the hotel before Borodin's berserkers visited a third time.

They'd carried the detective's still-unconscious body from the fifth-floor corridor to a third-floor guest room, and now they carried him all the way down to the main level.

Once at the bottom of the stairs, they were able to move more rapidly through the back corridors to the security office, with Arlo scouting ahead and Lomax slinging Caidin in a fireman's carry over his shoulder. Lomax was feeling better for taking action, even if it involved retreat. Today, he acknowledged, he'd finally seen the impossible for himself and, tomorrow, his life would change because of it. But they still had to make it through the night.

Once in the DHS security office, he and Arlo mutually decided to leave the hotel through the North Lobby. That would put them farther away from the estimated location of the containment units, five hundred feet out from the hotel's foundations. If there were still evacuation vehicles operating, fine. If not, they would only have to carry Caidin another few hundred yards to be out of range of the berserkers.

Together, they moved quickly though a corridor lined with closed shops, windows filled with clothing and shoes and jewelry. Inside, the battery lights were dimming. Outside, lightning flashed nonstop, like the strobe lights in the Projection Room.

At the doors leading to the hotel's North Lobby, Arlo stumbled to a halt. The area beyond was a sea of blood and body parts, glistening darkly in each flash of lightning from the continuing storm.

"There's someone there," Lomax said.

Ahead, silhouetted against the glass wall of the lobby, a lone man stood as if in contemplation.

Arlo's voice was low, hushed. "Is it a person . . . or . . . ?"

The man turned, and lightning lit his face. A stranger.

"Person," Lomax said, relieved. They walked carefully forward on the blood-slicked carpet. "Are there any more buses?" Lomax called out to the man.

The man looked away. They were close enough now that Lomax could tell he was looking at something under one of the grand sweeping stairways that curved up at the side of the lobby entrance.

"Someone else there?" Lomax asked. He shifted Caidin on his shoulder. "Go check it out," he told Arlo.

Arlo jogged over to the man, grimacing as each of his footsteps across the sodden carpet gave a liquid squelch. He stopped abruptly when he saw what was hidden under the stairway. "Lomax!"

It was a berserker. It wasn't alone.

Lomax approached slowly, trying to comprehend what he saw. The apparition had the ghost of Laura Hart in a stranglehold. She struggled, but the arm locked around her neck was as unmoving as stone.

Laura blurred for a moment, became a spectral corpse, then snapped back into focus.

"What's he doing to her?" Lomax said.

Arlo stared in helpless fascination. "Draining her."

Lomax turned to the silent man. He was older, in a stained white jacket. "Who are you?"

"I'm not important," the man said. He nodded toward the berserker. "My son is."

Arlo put it together. "Borodin!"

Lomax knew what he had to do. Eased Caidin off his shoulder, ready to grab the general.

Borodin saw what he was doing, and in a flash of lightning, a look of recognition appeared. "That's the other wraith's body," he said. "Let me help you."

Unexpectedly, he strode toward Lomax, one hand out as if to steady the unconscious Caidin.

"That's all right," Lomax said. "Stay where—"

Another flash of lightning. Another detail revealed: The knife in the general's other hand, an instant before Lomax felt the fire of its bite as it slashed into his gut.

—in front of Matt, Laura fought in the grip of a berserker, pulsing from one form of herself in life to another of herself in death.

For a moment, Matt was disoriented by the darkness punctuated by lightning. He looked around to get his bearings, recognized the North Lobby. Arlo was staring at him. Lomax was on his knees for some reason.

And his own battered body was slumped on the floor with Borodin standing over it.

The general seemed to sense Matt's presence, turned to him, grinned in a flash of lightning.

"You can help me," Laura said.

Matt looked away from the general, saw Laura blur in the berserker's grip, starting to fade. But the general—

He pulled a knife from Lomax as the big man clutched at the blood pulsing from the wound. Borodin held the knife up over Matt's body.

Laura was almost gone.

She and Matt were about to die.

Arlo ran screaming for the general and leapt at him and knocked him over and—

—Matt tore Laura from the berserker's grasp, and in that entangled contact knew his name *was ODIN, knew his name was Mikhail Stasikovich Borodin, knew that he was Misha and that his father had buried him alive—*

Matt pulled Laura to him as a corpse and embraced her and felt her restored as she drew her energy, her life, from him.

She smiled at him then and seemed so familiar, skin freckled, sunlightened hair caught in the—

Matt was snapped back from her, dragged down a long tunnel of darkness as he helplessly watched ODIN rise up behind her and coil his tendril arms around her to drag her away forever.

Matt's eyes opened in shock. Pain coursed through him. He was back in his body. He gasped for air. Couldn't breathe. Looked up to see Borodin looming over him, his hands tightening around Matt's throat.

Lomax writhed with spasms on the blood-soaked carpet.

Arlo clutched at the knife driven into his shoulder.

ODIN and Laura merged in each other's grip, their bodies blurring, then coiling together to form a single tendril of dark mist that drew in ever tighter, spinning ever faster.

Matt's vision shrank until all he saw was the implacable face of the general above him. All he felt were his lungs burning for air. All he heard was the thundering rush of blood in his ears.

Lightning flashed, and he began to rise into the welcoming light.

In the tunnel, Caparelli drew on his last resources to drive the rifle stock down one last time and—

—it was the stock that shattered.

Caparelli looked around in disbelieving desperation, but there were no loose objects at hand, no chunks of concrete, no other weapons.

The flames were dying, the light falling, the smoke thick.

He wheezed, throat raw. There had to be something down here he could use. Something other than just his two hands. . . .

His hands. Caparelli stared into the open containment unit, into its web of copper wires and circuitry, a slender sliver of a translucent crystal glowing blue. Could it be that simple?

He reached in, found thick cables and bare wires, took deliberate hold.

He thought of Laura.

He pulled and wires tore and the world turned white and he wondered what would happen ne—

The light faded, and Matt gulped in a flood of air. The general was still above him, but his hands had lost their strength.

He looked to the side, eyes wide. Matt followed his gaze to see—

—a single pillar of writhing mist.

Lightning flashed, and Matt struggled to see what lay within the darkness. He thought he saw Laura, but Misha was there, too, a dark soldier, a disbelieving son, Laura dead in the crash, alive on the beach, all combined in madness, until only one impression stood out from all the rest.

Hate.

The pillar collapsed into a single entity, moved forward, tendrils shooting out to embrace Borodin, who screamed as he was wrenched into the air and the darkness moved inside him and became solid and the general flew apart like an uncontrolled machine tearing itself to pieces.

Matt tried to sit up, but couldn't. He was flat on his back; the room spun.

The pillar was above him.

He looked up at it. Into it. Couldn't see what lay within. And then, he could see nothing at all as the darkness claimed him, and this time there was no welcoming light in it to carry him away.

42

VEKTOR's new deputy administrator marched along the wooden flooring of the facility's main corridor on the administration level. He brought with him the major's latest, most complete report from West Virginia. It was surprising, to say the least.

He knocked on the door of the chief administrator's office—polished oak and not the raw pine that made up most of the other wooden constructions here. He had selected it himself, in another time.

Lieutenant-General Iosif Solomon's measured voice answered, "Come," and Evgeny Gorokhov entered the den of his new master.

He put the report on the general's ornate desk, worthy of the Hermitage. Again, another of Gorokhov's own personal choices. But the new chief administrator didn't touch the file. Instead, he leaned back in the enormous leather chair that Gorokhov had selected because it seemed more like a throne.

"Summarize," the young general said. "How bad?"

"Remarkably, not as bad as we'd feared."

"Explain." General Solomon didn't believe in wasting words.

"The Americans have called it an act of *domestic* terrorism, so . . . they have no need of sending drones to strike against a third-world country in order to maintain a cover story."

"But the bodies . . . How do they explain what happened to the bodies?"

"Quite clever, actually. They claim the attack was carried out by a handful of fanatics who released a biological warfare agent. Specifically, a weaponized Ebola virus."

The chief administrator nodded in appreciation.

Gorokhov continued his brief. "So, the structures have been declared contaminated. No one is allowed in, and truly, no one wants in. As far as the public knows, special units from the Centers for Disease Control will be decontaminating the site for the next year. And all of the fanatics responsible perished in the attack." He was careful to convey no hint of resentment at his demotion. How could there be, given that he still served Mother Russia? More importantly, it was not his body at the bottom of the quarry lake, waiting to be discovered in what passed for spring in Magadan.

Solomon tapped a thoughtful finger against the arm of what had once been Gorokhov's chair. "That is the one area in which the Americans always surpass us: the imaginative tales they weave to hide the truth from their own people."

Gorokhov felt compelled to qualify the general's statement. "Not all the people, sir."

Solomon's keen eyes stared at him, waiting.

"There were survivors, including CROSSWIND personnel. We have confirmation that forty-eight hours after the event, CROSSWIND was separated from the NSA and now reports directly to the president and the Security Council. No other interference."

"Which implies they know what we've achieved, and wish to keep their knowledge hidden from our operatives in the DHS and NSA."

"I believe it would be wise to proceed as if they do."

"Undoubtedly, now that they know what's possible, they'll embark on their own program."

Gorokhov suppressed his smile, certain of what the general was considering. Perhaps he wouldn't lead the coming effort as he had hoped, but he would still be part of it, a loyal soldier, a willing worker for the State. "I believe that likely, too."

The general looked down at Major Kalnikova's unopened report on his desk. Gorokhov had already read it. The major had executed her final contingency orders and had ensured that there would be no path for the Americans to trace concerning how Borodin had entered their country. For now, she was in a safe house in the heart of enemy territory, recuperating, not only ready to be activated at any time, but eager.

"Then the question is," Solomon said, "will the Americans conclude that Stasik was acting on his own, that it was not a sanctioned mission?"

Gorokhov thought it interesting that Solomon referred to Borodin by his first name. How well had they known each other? How much had Solomon actually known about VEKTOR before being ordered here in response to Popovich's attempt to take control himself? But the former chief administrator knew better than to betray his curiosity, or concern. "Who's to say, sir."

The general rested his chin in his delicate hand, closed his eyes, sucked on his teeth. Gorokhov understood. He imagined the general was looking at the equivalent of a chessboard, plotting moves and countermoves far into the future, just as he had, and still did.

Solomon put both hands on his desk, a decision made.

"Operation Scythe will continue. On the new schedule."

Gorokhov was pleased beyond measure, but knew he couldn't appear too eager. "Then the testing protocols . . . ?"

The general didn't appear concerned. "As you suggested, we'll consider Stasik's rogue operation a successful proof-of-concept experiment. He's done our testing for us." His mouth twitched up in what might have been a smile. "How many units on hand?"

Gorokhov was prepared. He had checked the inventory of synthetic einstone just before arriving with the report. "As of end of shift yesterday, four hundred and forty units. In a week, running all three shifts, we can ramp up production to twenty containment units per day."

The general nodded approvingly. "And how many prisoners?"

"Just over eleven hundred."

"Prepare them for processing."

Gorokhov understood the need for the euphemism. The prisoners would be killed in the most horrific way each could imagine for himself. But their sacrifice was a necessary one.

"And then inform Operations," the general concluded. "We have moved to Phase Two."

Gorokhov politely bowed his head to the new chief administrator. He had made his sacrifice as well, chosen adversity for the present in order to remain here, knowing the strength that choice would eventually bring him.

VEKTOR had been his, and it would be again. Sooner than the general could possibly imagine.

43

On the second day after, Matt Caidin regained consciousness. He knew he was in a hospital room, but he didn't know where, and none of the staff would speak to him about anything other than medical matters.

On the third day after, Owen Lomax came to visit him. The big man moved stiffly, and used a cane. "They tell me you'll be okay," he said.

Matt brushed such irrelevance aside. Nothing would ever be okay. "What about Caparelli?"

Lomax sat down on a chrome-and-plastic visitor's chair, shook his head. "But he's the reason the rest of us made it."

"Arlo?"

"Recuperating. I don't think he'll ever leave the office again."

Matt saw there was something more Lomax seemed hesitant to say. "Whose office would that be? CROSSWIND, or DHS?"

"Mine. I'm acting director of CROSSWIND, now. It's out of the NSA, and I'm out of Homeland. We're on our own."

Someone got what he wanted, Matt thought. *Just not the way he wanted it.*

Lomax finally got to what had really brought him here. "I want you to stay with the project."

Matt had already considered that, knew he didn't have a choice. How could he turn his back on the new reality he had glimpsed? How could anyone? "So do I."

Lomax looked pleased. "Good. According to Hirst and Kushner, you're something more than the other perceivers. You were able to manifest, project mass, take action . . . I'm still catching up, but . . . the people who know this stuff, they're impressed. So, I guess I'm impressed, too."

Matt didn't care.

Lomax shifted in the flimsy chair, winced as he put a hand on his side. "First thing to get our heads around: We can't risk assuming Borodin was just a lone madman out for revenge. What if it was a sanctioned test of our defenses? What if there're more coming?"

"I'm not the guy to ask," Matt said. "I didn't open the door to Borodin. Laura did. She's the one who tracked him and . . ." Matt stopped, surprised at how much this conversation hurt.

"You opened it, too."

"Not on my own. Anything I did, I did through her. Always through her."

Lomax didn't argue. He explained the theory Arlo was developing: how it appeared that over time the EM fields of consciousness in two individuals could begin to resonate in sync with each other. It explained how, after years of building and reinforcing that link, perceivers could lock onto their targets almost instantly from half a world away. It might even explain how the link established between Matt and Laura had been so strong that Laura's wraith hadn't vanished after six days, no longer dependent on its own diminishing energy, but able to draw it from Matt. Arlo was still looking for a reason why that link between them had become so strong in so short a time, when all other factors suggested it could only have been strengthened over years of contact. But that was a problem for another day.

"Maybe you can do it through her again?" Lomax asked.

Matt shook his head, decisive. "I've been in this room three days. Three sunsets. That's when she could come to me. And she hasn't. And that's all there is to it." The terrible finality of those words struck Matt anew, and he looked away so Lomax wouldn't see how devastated he actually felt.

"Caidin, do you know where you are?"

"A hospital. Somewhere. No one will tell me."

"This is CROSSWIND. In DC. We have a medical wing. You've been in a Faraday cage for the past three days. To protect you from VEKTOR."

Matt pulled his covers off, sat up. Outraged. Heartsick. "You knew that I was Laura's only link to life, and you deliberately cut me off from her? Even if she had wanted to come to me she . . ." He broke off. "I need to get out of here."

"Done."

Thirty minutes before sunset, Matt was in a wheelchair, in the Projection Room. Waiting for a miracle.

The facility's shielding could be dropped here, to permit CROSSWIND perceivers to project their awareness to other locations. Even more important to Matt now, if anything else . . . someone else . . . was out there, then the lines of communication worked both ways.

Lomax was waiting with him. Though Matt didn't encourage him, they talked of Laura, and how nothing made sense but had felt so right.

Lomax told him there was a name for that. Matt was relieved when he didn't go on to state the obvious.

His eyes were on the clock, watching as it marked the time until sunset.

Ten minutes more.

Lomax began talking to him about the conference, and the evacuation. About how more than one hundred people had been killed, but that the president had managed to escape. Though Matt didn't ask, Lomax also summarized the Ebola cover story. Apparently it was holding up.

He spoke about other work-related details. The Russian woman with the missing hand Matt had sat with at the Greenbrier was Major Sofia Kalnikova, a special forces soldier assigned to VEKTOR. Matt wasn't surprised. Lomax said she had disappeared from the site, no body found, no record of being evacuated. He added that the physician who had treated her at the DHS medical facility had been found murdered in his Logan Circle apartment. Cause of death was the same as for the physician Kalnikova had murdered in Colorado. Lomax was certain it wasn't a coincidence.

Then he changed gears, asked Matt about what it was like, to be in that other realm, a projected presence, and because his interest now seemed genuine Matt did his best to tell him what he'd experienced, what he'd thought, what he'd done.

It was difficult to find the right words, but he tried to describe the sensation he'd felt of being pulled back into his body when Laura had fought Borodin's son, and of coming to consciousness with Borodin strangling him. And how he had tried to see which of . . . of . . .

"Which of what?" Lomax asked.

Matt blinked. "There were two of them," he said, replaying the events as he had witnessed them. "Laura and the berserker, fighting. Merging into . . ."

He felt his heart start to race. "What was there at the end . . . I think it was only one of them."

"Laura, right? Because she attacked Borodin and killed him to save you."

Matt shook his head, somehow knowing that wasn't the only explanation. "Borodin's son hated his father. He could have killed him just the same as Laura."

Matt looked at the clock.

The sun had set.

"Then which one was it?" Lomax asked. "Which one made last contact? Which one's drawing strength from you now? Laura Hart? Or the berserker?"

"I don't know."

On the wall behind Lomax, a subtle distortion gained substance—a gray shadow . . . growing. . . .

He was about to find out.

THE BEACH

Matt liked it here. He was five, and the warm days stretched endlessly as he built his towering forts of sand and splashed in gentle waves and dreamed each summer night of even greater adventure in the green cottage by the lake.

He had pails and a shovel and a plastic Jeep and soldiers, and they explored the landscapes he created and destroyed. He was a tiny god who made sure everything always came out right and the good guys won, because that's the way it should be, and someday it would be his job to see it always was.

Others came and strolled on the beach that summer and the boy ignored them, caught up in the world he made. The pattern repeating, but never the same.

But that one day, he couldn't ignore the barking.

It was the big black dog again. The shadow he saw sometimes from the corner of his eye but that seemed to worry no one else, as if they couldn't see it, as if it was a ghost. As long as it kept its distance, the boy had decided he didn't have to worry either.

That day the dog was barking and snarling and sounding dangerous, and there was someone else on the beach who saw and heard it, too.

A girl, not as old as five, crying and frightened, and the boy knew that wasn't right and ran at the barking dog with his shovel and his pail and the dog went away, and no one else on the beach acted like it was ever there at all.

The girl sat in the puddle of a pond she'd dug in the sand and sniffed, then looked up and smiled at him. The boy stood transfixed. She had golden freckles in her eyes of green. Her sun-streaked hair was as brilliant as her smile. Then her parents came and said, Laura, we have to go, and she went off with them, but she looked back once, at the boy who'd helped her, the connection made.

The pattern repeating, but never the same.

Entangled from the beginning.

ACKNOWLEDGMENTS

While writing is a solitary undertaking, *preparing* to write and then *publishing* that work requires a large and dedicated team. We are fortunate to have had such a team at our sides during *Wraith*'s transformation from a one-sentence idea in our heads to the book now in your hands—or on your screen.

Mel Berger, our agent at WME, was the first to hear this story, then ask the insightful questions that guided us through the original outline—or, more precisely, outlines.

At Thomas Dunne Books, Pete Wolverton, our editor—aka the reader's vital first line of defense—guided us once more on the inspiring journey of writing, rewriting, adding, and subtracting, which made *Wraith* a much richer experience for us, and, we hope, for you.

Erin Gray, also at WME, deserves our thanks and appreciation for taking this story to a wider audience, which in turn prompted our thoughts to turn to Operation Scythe and the much larger canvas that this book is now part of.

Also at Thomas Dunne Books, we are deeply appreciative of the exceptional contributions made by so many others at the company, among them: David Rotstein, Loren Jaggers, Paul Hochman, Omar Chapa, Joseph Brosnan, Joy Gannon, and Justin Velella. Special thanks go to our meticulous copy editor, Deanna Hoak, our diligent proofreader, Anna Chang, and to Emma Stein, who kept all lines of communication open and moving smartly. We look forward to working with all again on new books to come.

As for our preparations for writing this story, we must acknowledge the kindness and enthusiasm of every member of the staff of The Greenbrier Resort during our visit, especially Robert Conte, its Resident Historian. Note, though, that not all details of the Greek Island Project came from official sources. The Greenbrier is utterly unique, a completely charming blend of the old and new, and we invite everyone to consider a visit. (We understand that any damage sustained during the recent Joint Anti-Terrorism Conference has been completely dealt with, considering it was entirely imaginary to begin with.)

And now we come to ghosts, if not a proven phenomenon, then certainly a subject of great and continuing interest to every culture throughout history. Even today, we have no doubt that everyone who reads these words—in fact, anyone who might be questioned at random on the street—will have heard at least one "true" ghost story involving a family member or friend. We certainly have.

This universality of the concept of ghosts is one of the subject's most compelling attributes. Why do stories of ghostly encounters exist in all cultures and in all time periods? Is it because humans, as a species, refuse to accept the apparent finality of death and make up stories to support the idea that existence continues beyond the grave? Or is it because the phenomenon does, in some yet-to-be-defined form, truly exist?

Holding to the tenet that there is no such thing as the supernatural, only those things which have not yet been studied by science, any definitive answer to those questions will have to wait until there is unfalsifiable scientific evidence. To date, outside the pages of this story, such evidence does not exist. Then again, that's exactly the situation we'd expect if a CROSSWIND-type organization is successfully withholding it.

Stay tuned . . .

J&G Reeves-Stevens
Los Angeles – White Sulphur Springs – Victoria
February 2016